'Cella

The Cedar Cove Chronicles, Book Three

By Cynthia Ulmer

To Eileen
Hope you enjoy the book.
Love,
Cindy

Mimosa Swan Books

This is a work of fiction. Any resemblance to any person, living or dead is purely coincidental.

100 Enterprise Way, Suite A200 Scotts Valley, CA 95066
CREATESPACE.COM

Chapter One

I been trying and trying all morning long to sneak outta here. I been trying but it ain't working. I thought I was gonna be all by myself, but no, once Papa left for the bait and tackle shop and Mama left to go sew with Aunt Callie, who shows up but Gran. I told her I was fine all by myself but she says I might not be. Then she sits about making me do all sorts of chores. Right now she's got me dusting off the tops of all the canned vegetables we keep stacked up on the back screened porch. I keep waiting for a chance to get outta here and do what I know I gotta do, but every time I think I got a chance to run, here she comes again, pulling her big old self along, calling out, "'Cella, girl, I think we oughta...." Only there ain't no we's in her oughta's—it's just me doing the real work and her coming up with the idea.

I hear her coming again. Gran don't move too quiet. She can't. She's too big. My cousins Mart and Trent say they always watch to see what she might knock over when she passes through. "'Cella, 'Cella," she calls before she reaches the kitchen door, "come here, girl."

Holding my dusting rag, I go back into the kitchen. She's there, her hand on the counter. "I been thinking about taking a nap. You sure you alright, 'Cella? Thought for sure Madge would be home by now. Been gone all morning."

I smiled inside but not out. "Oh, Gran, I'm good by myself. I ain't a baby no more. I'm fourteen now. I can take care of myself."

Gran eyed me closely, "Fourteen, huh? I was just fourteen when Gil and me got married. When did you turn fourteen?"

I fought the urge to roll my eyes and replied, "April eleven, same as always."

Gran nodded and rubbed her eyes, "Got so many gran-youngun's its hard to keep up with you all. I was sure you weren't but ten or so. You sure you fourteen, 'Cella? You sure it ain't Annie or Fran or Dot? Seems to me like one of them oughta be fourteen, not little bitty you."

Little bitty. I hate being called little. If one of my cousins called me that, or someone at school, I'd jump them quicker than anything. But it's Gran so I gotta hold my tongue and not jump on her back and swat her every which way I can. I shook my head instead, "No, Gran, Annie is almost twenty and so's Fran and Dot's just twelve—younger than me."

"She's bigger though....Well, think I'm gonna head home. Rest my tired body. Don't you go to using that stove or lighting any fires—hear?"

"I won't."

"Don't be using any knives or matches."

"I won't."

"Don't play in the icebox—you do that and you could suffocate to death. Ain't no air inside them things."

"Gran, I don't play no more. I'm fourteen."

She stares at me again, "I ain't sure you telling me the truth, 'Cella. I'm gonna talk to Madge about this you fourteen business. I think you might be pulling my leg."

"I'm telling the truth, Gran. I'm fourteen. I promise I'll be good and won't do nothing dangerous. You can go home and take your nap."

"Think I'm gonna do just that...You get that dusting done?"

"Just about."

"When you finish that, sweep that porch and make sure you get those steps. I came up those back steps the other day and they had so much dirt on them it was shameful."

"I'll take care of it. Promise."

She nodded and turned, causing me to think she might finally be leaving. She took a few slow steps; then said, "Walk me home, 'Cella."

I cringed. I did not want to walk Gran home. Walking Gran home most of the time meant she'd come up with work for me to do there too. But I didn't dare protest. One time I protested and Gran made me cut a switch. I thought she never would stop hitting me. So I followed her out of the kitchen, through the living room and out the front door, which took a whole lot longer than it sounds because Gran moves slower than a turtle. I'd never get around to doing what I had to do.

I followed Gran all the way to her house which is right next to ours. Gramp was sleeping in a chair in the yard. Gran looked at him, "Man can sleep anywhere. Not me. I gotta have a bed."

I went inside with her, followed her to the bedroom and watched as she laid across the bed. "Ah, yes," she yawned, "this is the way to sleep. Not in a chair like old Gil does." She closed her eyes and I waited, sure she'd come up with something for me to do. Instead she opened her eyes and said, "Go on home, Marcella Antoinette, I don't like to sleep with no one staring down on me."

"Yes'um," I answered politely and walked out of the house as quiet and polite as I could, walked past Gramp who was snoring in his chair, went home, looked through the house for Mama, and when I saw she wasn't there, took off running out of the yard and down the road.

I didn't run far. Just until I got around the curve, then I slowed up. But not too much. I wanted to get this over with. So even though I weren't running no more, I walked faster than normal. I kept thinking of what I might have to say and worried about how to say things without telling too much about the wrong thing I'd been doing.

Chapter Two

I was going to see a witch. Not just any old witch, but the best witch in this part of North Carolina. Some folks around here used to call Miz Essie Mae Sherman a witch. I barely remember Miz Essie. But she weren't no real witch. Papa says she was more like a spiritual healer. The person I'm headed to right now is a true honest witch. Now you'd think a witch would have a good witch name. Something like Zenobia or Twila or even Aquina, but no, those are all names of my cousins and ain't none of them witches. The witch's name is Sue. That's it. Just plain old Sue. But she can set spells and undo things and that's just what I need doing—some real big undoing. And if it takes a spell to undo it, then I'm just fine with that too. I been praying and praying and praying and I got the feeling the praying ain't working one bit. I think maybe once you get yourself into such big trouble, God is like Mama and Papa and Gran and Gramp—He tells you you gotta suffer the consequences. I don't want to suffer no consequences. I just want things back to normal.

Old witch Sue lives just about at the dividing part of Cedar Cove. There ain't no railroad track dividing Cedar Cove or no river—course we got railroad tracks and a river, but that's not what divides the white part of Cedar Cove from the colored—it's the old Beamer house. Used to be a rich colored man named Silas Beamer who lived in a big old house up past a clump of oak trees and his house starts the colored part of Cedar Cove. I ain't sure what caused old man Beamer to be rich. That's one thing you don't hear of often—a rich colored man. Ain't no white people live down here and no colored people live up past the Beamer house. Ain't no one in the old Beamer house now either. I think old man Beamer died in ancient times—like 1913 or something like that. And it's all the way up to 1952. House is still there. It's haunted—so they say. One time my cousins Mart, Randy and Twila made me come down here past dark. They all bigger than me and just drug me down here. They all the time doing stuff like that. Twila said if you stood out in the front yard long enough, you'd see old man Beamer's eyes staring out all the windows at once. Mart claims he saw them once and it was the spookiest thing ever. I wouldn't look. I kept my eyes closed tight. All them must not a been listening when Gran told us if a haint ever looked into your eyes they could steal your soul and you'd be no more, but the haint would exist again. Let me tell you, I want to exist.

I'm glad that I ain't got to pass the Beamer house on the way to Witch Sue's. Witch Sue lives close to the Beamer house but there's a big curve in the road between her place and the Beamer house so I ain't got to see it at all. Bad enough I gotta deal with a witch today, much less a haint.

Old witch Sue lived in a bright blue house in a yard full of statues and bird baths. Folks say she painted the house bright blue to ward off ghosts and other haints—they all dead and might think the blue is water so's she's safe inside. I think it was smart of her to paint her house blue like that since she's so close to the Beamer house. I wished Mama and Papa would paint our house blue but Papa says no.

I got to witch Sue's house and went up to the front door. I knocked three times and waited as I heard someone moving inside. The door opened just a little. Witch Sue stuck her head out. She wore a tight pink scarf around her slicked back hair. "And just who are you?" she enquired.

I swallowed, "I'm Marcella Lewis. I need some help real bad."

She opened the door all the way and motioned for me to come in. I stepped inside, greeted by a very strong spicy smell. There was stuff hanging from the ceiling and smoke coming out of bowls set up on little tables all over the room. Witch Sue stared at me, "Have a seat on the red couch."

I sat, feeling the velvet beneath my legs and hoped I wasn't dirty after all the dusting Gran had me do earlier. I was silent as the witch stood over me and stared at me some more. She was big and tall, wearing a long flowing flowered dress that drug the floor. She had bracelets up and down both arms. She had rings on every finger and great big silver hoops in each ear. As she stared down at me it crossed my mind that she could turn me into a mouse or something and no one would have a clue whatever became of me. At last she spoke, "You're Marcella Lewis—Madge and Sammy Lewis's girl?"

"Yes'um."

"Gil and Lana Ballard's grandgirl?"

"Yes'um."

"And just what kind of trouble are you in that brought you here to me?" She moved a little causing the many bracelets she wore to jangle on her arms.

I didn't know how to tell her. I didn't want to tell anyone what I'd been doing. I bit my lip and said, "I think I might have something growing in me that ought not be there."

"Really. Where do you think it's growing?"

I pointed to my stomach, "There."

She sat in a bright yellow chair in front of me, "How did it get there?"

I wrung my hands together and whispered, "I have a boyfriend...."

"Who?"

"Jesse. Jesse Jenkins."

"Hallie and Leroy's boy?"

"Yes'um." I kept wringing my hands.

"You been letting him do stuff to you he shouldn't be doing? Things that should only be going on between a husband and wife?"

I nodded my head very little and whispered, "I ain't done much to stop him."

Witch Sue stood and moved about the room, blowing into her little bowls of smoke, waving it in the air with her hands, her many bracelets jingling like mad. She came back to the yellow chair, "Madge and Sammy know about this?" I shook my head wordlessly. Witch Sue sat again, "What about Gil or Lana?" I shook my head again. "Hallie or Leroy?"

I wrung my hands tighter, "Jesse don't even know. I ain't even sure of it. I just think there might be a....something growing in me."

"How long you think it's been there?"

I shrugged, "A month, maybe two....I ain't really sure."

"Alright. If we're lucky, a spell and some maintenance done by you should take care of it...." She stood and put her hands on my head, then began to chant in a language I'd never heard before. I kept my eyes closed and prayed God wouldn't punish me too hard for turning to a witch. But I needed help bad.

Old witch Sue went on and on with her chanting. Then she blew smoke over my head and said, "Sit still with your eyes closed tight. I'll be back."

I kept my eyes closed tight and waited. I wanted to move; my legs were cramped but I was afraid to do anything to mess up the spell. I felt a fly or something land on my leg and I cringed as it walked up and down, making me want to jump off the couch. I was gritting my teeth and doing my best to not move and keep my eyes closed when Witch Sue came back. She rubbed my head, blowing over me again, chanting some more. Best of all, for the moment, the fly flew off my leg.

"Open your eyes, child." I did. Witch Sue handed me a cloth pouch. "Chew these leaves every night—chew them up real good and swallow them too—until they're all gone—just a few at a time, mind you. And it has to be done in the dark. Probably gonna make you sick, you gonna be throwing up like crazy, but that just means the leaves and spell are working. Let's see, today is July 23rd, come back here on August 23rd, and I'll check you over, make sure the leaves and spell worked. If not, I'll set you up with my sister down in Myrtle Beach. She can get rid of the unwanted thing growing in you if all I did don't work."

Myrtle Beach? Just how was I supposed to get to Myrtle Beach? I stared at the pouch, "What kinda leaves are these?"

"Special leaves, child. Don't let no one know you got them. Now, how do you plan on paying me?"

"Paying you?" I hadn't thought about paying her at all. I had nothing with me.

Witch Sue looked hard at me, "I'll let it go this time. When you come in August, bring me two payments..."

"What kind of payment? I ain't got no money."

"Don't need money, child. Bring me two valuable somethings. Don't matter what. Just gotta be worth something. Nothing useless, now, hear?"

"Yes'um, I hear."

"You can be going now, child. Remember—chew up and swallow a few of those leaves every night until they are gone. At night in the dark."

I nodded and rose from the couch. She followed me to the door. "Didn't Jesse finish up school last year?" she asked.

"Yes'um."

"Got a job?"

"He helps his Daddy and those white farmers, James Jansan and Simpson Duvall. Every now and then he does little jobs for that man in the white feed store up there. They pay him."

She said nothing, then opened the door for me, "Oh, by the way, you'll tell when those leaves start working—you gonna get terrible cramps and bleed really bad. Just tell your Mama it's your time and stay in the bed."

"Yes'um." I walked out of the house.

Witch Sue followed me into the yard, "Now, if you decide you want to keep what's growing in you, toss those leaves and beg for forgiveness. But don't come back to me in that case. Be gone with you, child," She waved her arm and I took off running.

Chapter Three

Me and Jesse have been going together for nearly two years. He's nearly six years older than me, but that don't matter to us. Don't matter to Mama and Papa either, cause Papa is eight years older than Mama and they get along just fine.

I've always known Jesse, just never paid him much mind until I got in the seventh grade. He was a senior then. Up in the white part of Cedar Cove, there is two schools—an elementary school and a high school. Here in the colored part we just have one school. The white people get to name their schools Cedar Cove Elementary and Cedar Cove High School. We got stuck with Francis Marvin School for the Colored. I used to think Francis Marvin was an important colored man. Then I learned he was a white man who donated the money to build the school.

Anyhow, right at the first of seventh grade, my teacher, old Miss Cole sent me up to the twelfth grade hall. Now although I'd been going to that crazy school since first grade, I'd never been in certain parts of it and the twelfth grade hall was one of them. I ain't one for finding my way easy and even though I listened to Miss Cole, I got lost. I somehow wound up going down a hall that had nothing but supplies like paint and cleaning junk in the two little rooms on it. I felt so stupid. Lost in the school I'd been going to since I was six years old. I was trying to find the room Miss Cole wanted me to go to when Jesse came up behind me. He asked what I was doing and I told him. He helped me find my way to where I was supposed to be going and back to Miss Cole's room. By the time he walked me back to Miss Cole's room, he'd asked me out. That was on a Wednesday. He came over the following Friday night and Papa took such a liking to him, it weren't long before Jesse was over just about every night.

I love Jesse. He's the best looking boy anywhere and he's real sweet to me. I love it when he holds me and kisses me. I just don't know how to make him stop with his loving of me and we nearly always wind up doing what we shouldn't be doing. First time it happened, I cried and cried. He said it would be okay. He says he loves me and I'm too young to get a baby yet. But I'm thinking my too young time has passed and that's why I had to go see Witch Sue. I don't know what Jesse would think of me going to Witch Sue. I just know I had to do something.

I was worried about Mama or Papa being home before I got there, but they were still gone when I returned from Witch Sue. I put the pouch of leaves in my dresser drawer, hid it under my underwear, swept the porch like Gran wanted, then set about getting ready for Jesse coming tonight. We gonna eat supper here with Mama and Papa; then we do something different. Jesse's gonna take me to a movie. I ain't ever been to a movie. I been trying to imagine what it will be like—seeing people that ain't really there moving around and talking. I'm all excited. Normally, we go riding up to Sandy Corners a lot. We just go up there and drive down in the woods and do things we shouldn't be doing. Maybe tonight there won't be no time for doing what we ought not be doing.

All my life things keep happening to me that I can't control. I'm little so my cousins have always been into picking on me. They sometimes just pick me right up and haul me to wherever they want. That's how I wound up down at the old haunted Beamer house one night. I try to fight them. I do. I hit and slap and pinch but they all laugh and say, "'Cella, you don't hurt no worse than a little bitty fly." I try hitting Jesse too, sometimes. Sometimes he laughs at me and I fly into one of my hitting rages. I jump right on him, hitting and hitting like mad. He just grabs my arms, holds me and says, "Stop it, 'Cella." I never stop right then because little things get me so worked up. Even though he's holding me, I kept struggling for a while until the worked up feeling leaves my nerves. It don't happen much with Jesse but it does happen sometimes.

My Mama and Papa don't seem to care about my hitting rages. They watch me with my cousins. Watch them pick on me and then watch me jump them, swatting for my life it seems. Papa just laughs and when it's all finally over, Mama nearly always says something like, "You gotta fend for yourself, 'Cella. You can't let them always get the best of you like that." I ain't sure what she means really. The fend for yourself part makes me think she's all for my hitting them and the don't let them get the best of you makes me think maybe she thinks it's all my fault in the first place. I just don't know.

I was busy squeezing lemons for lemonade when Papa came into the kitchen. "Where's your mama, 'Cella girl?"

"I think she's still sewing with Aunt Callie."

Papa nodded, wiping his forehead, "Jesse coming over tonight?"

"Yes," I kept squeezing the lemon I was working on.

Papa nods again, "Good. Maybe he'll go up to the bait and tackle shop with me and help me push that old truck back down here to the house."

"Why didn't you drive it home?" I asked, picking up another lemon.

Papa laughed, "I just think me and Jesse might have fun pushing it down here."

I knew he was teasing. I didn't say anything. I kept squeezing lemons. At last, Papa said, "Sorry old thing wouldn't start when I got off work. Left it right there and walked home. Garris offered to help me push it but I said no, I'd get it later. Think I might get Jesse to help me."

"Me and Jesse was going off tonight." I replied; squeezing the last lemon I'd laid out. "He says he's gonna take me to Brookville to a movie."

"They got a theater for colored people in Brookville?"

"It's the same old theater, Papa. Jesse says they put a balcony in there now. Says that Bob Duvall told him about it."

Papa went to the sink and got a glass of water, "That's the one thing bothers me about Jesse—he's way to close to them white folks. Hallie and Leroy are too. I was telling Leroy just the other day I'm sure his being colored does make a difference to those white men. But Leroy won't hear no sense when it comes to the Jansans and Duvalls. Even that white preacher, Joe Marley. Leroy goes on and on about how they eat right at the table with them—all friends no difference whatsoever and I tell him they probably fumigate the house once they're all gone."

I just listen as Papa goes on and on about how colored people can't trust white people. I know what he means about Jesse and those white people. I even went with Jesse to one of their weddings last summer. They all were very polite and nice, but I felt so strange. And that was a crazy wedding too. The white people getting married were already married. I kept thinking that don't make no sense. Then I got to thinking maybe getting married is something white people like to do a lot. So I asked Jesse if white people just get married a lot cause they like it. I figured he might know since he's such good friends with them. Jesse said it weren't because they just like getting married. He said they got married again cause they lost each other for over twenty seven years. I said they must be some dumb white people and he told me to hush.

It was a pretty wedding—everyone dressed so fancy and that little girl with her blonde curly hair and the little baby girl that one lady carried. Jesse introduced me to all of them. He knows all their names and everything. I smiled and nodded to them but I felt so nervous I could barely remember what he said any of them are called.

We went to another one of their white people weddings back in December—the Saturday after Christmas. This was a wedding where a preacher was getting married. I told Jesse I didn't think preachers got married. Old Reverend Burns weren't married and this new preacher we got—Reverend Wheeler ain't married either. Jesse says preachers do get married. He says that white preacher who runs that store—Preacher Joe—is married. The preacher we watched get married is the brother to one of Jesse's best friends—Bob Duvall. Yep, his best friends are white boys. Really, truly. He talks all the time about Bob Duvall and Todd Jansan. I try to overlook that flaw in Jesse—him having white boys as best friends. Because like I said, I love him and he's the best looking boy around.

Chapter Four

Jesse, of course, showed up and as soon as he got to the house, Papa had him walk down to the bait and tackle shop with him. I helped Mama finish with supper while they were gone. It took awhile but they pushed the old truck up into our yard at last and when Mama sent me to tell them supper was done, they were both staring under the hood of the truck like they are looking for something. Soon as I said "Supper is ready," they moved, closed the hood, wiped their hands on their pants and came inside.

Jesse sat beside me like he always does. We ate our food quietly, listening to Papa talk about his work at the bait and tackle shop and Mama go on about the dress she was making with Aunt Callie. I don't think Mama and Papa really listen to each other. They just talk and expect someone to care. Me and Jesse are basically quiet. I think that's one reason Papa likes Jesse. He thinks Jesse is listening to him. Soon as supper was over, Mama grinned at us and said, "Y'all go ahead with your date now. Know you don't want to stay around here with us old people."

We watched as Papa hugged Mama and kissed the side of her face, "Aw, Madge, we ain't old."

"We old to Jesse and 'Cella, Sammy," Mama said, but she was still grinning.

We left and I was all excited about the movie. I kept asking Jesse questions about it. What was it about? What was it like being in a theater? Did it really seem like the people were there but not there. Jesse told me slow down, he ain't ever seen a movie either. He said we gonna do this movie business together. But, as it turned out, we didn't go to a movie after all. We tried. When we got to the theater, we found out they ain't finished building that balcony yet and when they do get it finished, they only gonna let colored people in on Tuesdays and Thursdays. I was so upset; I was ready to go whop someone upside the head. But Jesse said settle down, 'Cella. Then we walked down to Robyn's Diner where he knocked on the door and waited and waited for someone to come. When a waitress finally came, Jesse ordered us two ice cream cones and then we had to wait some more for them to bring the ice cream to us. I told Jesse we ought to be able to go in there and sit at one of those tables and he just nodded without saying anything. When they finally brought the ice cream, Jesse paid them five cents extra and I asked why. He shrugged and said, "They expect it because of the extra trouble of having to bring them out to us."

I licked my ice cream and said, "They wouldn't have to go to any extra trouble if they'd let us inside like they oughta."

Jesse didn't say anything. He just led me to the car and we sat there, eating the rest of our ice creams. Then he started driving and I knew where we were going. I thought about telling him about my visit to witch Sue, but I didn't know how to bring it up. I mean how do you say, "Oh, by the way, Jesse, I went to see a witch today." It ain't something that is easy to bring up in conversation. Now if he asked me what I did today, I might be able to do it, but normally, Jesse don't ask me what I did. He might ask where I want to go or do, but asking what I've done evidently don't cross his mind.

We went to our normal spot in the woods at Sandy Corners and of course it weren't long before we were right smack in the middle of doing things we shouldn't be doing. I thought I really needed to tell Jesse what I thought might be going on with me, but I didn't. I kept quiet about it the whole time. I decided to just chew up and swallow those leaves Witch Sue gave me and maybe there won't be no need to tell him nothing at all.

Chapter Five

I am sick as a dog. I been trying to chew up and swallow those leaves just like Witch Sue wanted, but they are the nastiest things in the world. Talk about bitter. I ain't ever had anything in my mouth so bitter. Won't nothing take the taste away either and then I do nothing but vomit constantly. I been so sick Mama is threatening to call in Dr. Moore. There ain't no colored doctors close by. Dr. Moore is a white doctor, but the only one around that will come to colored people. And if we get so sick we need a hospital, we have to go all the way to Wilmington. I keep telling Mama I don't need Dr. Moore and I sure don't need no hospital. Papa is worried about me too; I can tell. He walks around frowning and wiping sweat from his forehead. Even Gran and Gramp have been over, watching me like they expect me to keel over dead at any moment. My cousins and aunts and uncles have been drifting in and out. My eight year old cousin Mollie Mae made me mad when she said, "I ain't never seen someone throw up so much 'Cella. When you die can I have your pink hair ribbons with the lace on them?" If I'd had the strength to slap her, I would have.

The one the most worried about me is Jesse. He's over nearly always, sitting by me, holding my hand, rubbing my head. I've thought over and over again about telling him the truth about what's going on, but so far I ain't been able to do it. At night, I still manage to drag myself out of bed and try to eat some of those nasty leaves. I don't think it's gonna work because I ain't managed to keep the first little bit of a leaf down. Lately, I ain't even got to put them in my mouth to start vomiting. It starts just by me thinking about the pouch being in my underwear drawer. I'll get up and start for the dresser, only to start vomiting all over the floor before I ever reach it and my dresser ain't that far from my bed.

Mama always hears me and comes to clean up my mess. Then she gets me back in bed. After three nights of this, while she's washing my face with a cold rag, she says, "'Cella, child, I know you don't want to hear this, but first thing in the morning, I'm getting Papa to go up to Dr. Moore. Ain't normal for no one to be this sick."

"No, Mama."

"Yes, 'Cella," she insists, still wiping my head.

I know right then I gotta do something. So I beg, "Please Mama, just give me one more day. Just one more. Please. I promise I won't throw up no more."

Mama laughs; then kisses my cheek, "Oh, 'Cella girl." She sighs, "I'll think on it." She adjusts the blanket over me and leaves the room. For the rest of the night, I think about how I just can't eat those leaves Witch Sue wanted me to and how I just have to tell Jesse what's really going on.

Somehow, just knowing I ain't gonna put those nasty leaves back in my mouth ever again helps me to feel better. Not all the way better, mind you, but better. I manage to fall asleep and sleep for the rest of the night without vomiting. When I wake up the next day, it is late. Morning is nearly over. I can tell because there is so much sunlight in the room. I can hear Mama talking. She's talking about me and how she agreed to give me one more day before getting Dr. Moore. I wonder who she's talking to. Then I hear, "I sure wish you'd do something, Mrs. Lewis." It's Jesse. I keep listening as he says, "I'll pay for Dr. Moore myself if you and Mr. Lewis ain't got the money right now. I been saving up the money I get from working."

"It's alright, Jesse," Mama says. "If there is a doctor bill, me and Sammy can take care of it. 'Cella is our responsibility."

I sit up a little, still feeling sick. I really need to talk to Jesse. Maybe if I tell the truth, God will have mercy on me and I'll get all better and there won't be nothing growing in me after all. Feeling weak, I call out for Mama.

She is soon at my door, "You're awake. How you feeling?"

I shrug and she comes to me. I see Jesse in the doorway. He looks worried. I don't like him looking worried. It ain't a good look on him. Mama sits on my bed and feels my forehead, "Don't seem to have a fever. But then you ain't had a fever during this whole sick time. Why don't you try to get down some weak tea and maybe some light bread?"

"I'll try."

While Mama is gone to get the tea and bread, Jesse comes into the room. He don't sit on the bed, but stands there, staring at me. I think about telling him the truth and then Mama is back.

She has a glass of tea and a slice of bread on a plate. She sits on the bed and tells me to sit up. I do and manage to sip some of the tea and eat a small bite of bread. Mama watches me the whole time and so does Jesse. They both look worried. At last, Mama says, "I think I shoulda told Sammy to go on up to Dr. Moore."

"I can go," Jesse volunteers.

"No!" I say, a little too loud. "I don't need no doctor."

Mama shakes her head and so does Jesse. They are both quiet for a long time and I eat more of the bread to prove I don't need Dr. Moore. Mama watches me and says, "I gotta go and help Callie with that dress."

"Go ahead, Mrs. Lewis," Jesse says. "I'll stay here with 'Cella. I'll take care of her."

Mama looks worried, but says, "Alright. If you need me, I'm over at Callie's. I wouldn't go, but we need the money from the dress I'm helping Callie make. We gotta get it done by this coming Friday for Mrs. Owens."

"Mrs. Owens?" Jesse asks. "The dentist's wife?"

Mama nods. "They got a great big party to go to Friday night and me and Callie are making her dress. That dress has more sequins on it than I've ever seen."

Jesse nods. Dr. Owens is a white people dentist in Brookville. He won't see colored people, but his wife sure don't mind two colored women making her clothes. Mama and Aunt Callie are all the time making dresses for that stuck up woman.

Mama gets Jesse to leave the room and stays with me while I get dressed for the day. She keeps asking if I feel better and I keep telling her yes. She keeps apologizing too for having to go help Aunt Callie. I tell her it's alright. Jesse will be with me.

And as soon as Mama leaves, Jesse comes into the room and lays in bed with me. He's quiet as he holds me and I'm quiet too. Then Jesse says, "'Cella, honey girl, I really think you need Dr. Moore."

I stare at the ceiling as I say, "No, Jesse, I don't need Dr. Moore. I needed to be able to eat those leaves Witch Sue gave me, but they are so nasty…."

Jesse sits up, "What leaves? What are you talking about?"

Suddenly, I'm crying. I wipe my eyes and whisper, "I think all our being together has a…has something growing in me. I went to Witch Sue… and…."

Jesse stands, "What are you trying to tell me, Marcella?"

I know right away Jesse is upset. He hardly ever calls me Marcella. I cry harder and say nothing. Jesse sighs loudly and walks around the room. I hear his feet slapping the floor hard. Then he sighs again and sits on the bed. I have my hands over my face. Jesse moves them, "You think there might be a baby? Is that what you're telling me?"

I nod slightly, still crying. Jesse pulls me up, holding me tight. "Don't worry 'Cella, honey girl. We'll take care of this. We gotta find out for sure, but we'll take care of it."

"How we gonna find out for sure?"

"Did old Witch Sue check you over? Did she tell you for sure you're gonna have a baby?"

"No. I just told her I thought there might be something growing in me and I didn't want it there. So she did a spell over me and sent me home with some leaves in a pouch. I was supposed to eat those leaves, but they make me so sick."

"Don't eat no more, 'Cella. I'll take you over to Mrs. Valerie Dale and get her to check you over."

"Jesse, Mrs. Valerie is a mid-wife."

"I know she is," Jesse says, "Ain't no telling what that old Witch Sue has done to you." He got quiet and I must have looked as scared as I felt because he said, "Look, 'Cella, I just want someone who knows what they're doing to look you over. I don't trust that witch woman. Them leaves she gave you might be poison. After we find out for certain about this baby business, we'll…well…let me think…I know what we can do. Carl is supposed to be home this weekend. We'll go talk to him. I'm sure he'll help us figure something."

"Carl? You mean the white preacher we watched get married?"

Jesse nods, "Yes. He's gonna be doing a revival at Hunter Baptist church this coming week. Bob's been telling me about it. Everyone is so excited about him and Libby coming home for a while. All the Jansan's and the Duvall's plan on going to that revival just because Carl will be preaching. We'll talk to Carl because I trust him. He won't lead us wrong."

Chapter Six

I thought we'd wait a few days on going to see Mrs. Valerie Dale or anyone else. But no, Jesse got up from the bed and wanted us to go right away. I said I didn't feel good and he said we gotta find out. So I got up and we went even though I felt awful.

Taking me to Mrs. Valerie Dale was a complete waste of time. The minute I mentioned that I'd been to see Witch Sue, she goes all crazy, shouting, "Oh, dear Lord Jesus, protect me from the evil that has come into my house! Cast out the demon! Oh keep me safe please!" She carried on like I was the devil himself sitting in her parlor. She shooed me out and of course, Jesse came with me. I was all ready to head back home, but Jesse said no. He knocked on the door and after convincing that crazy old woman he hadn't been touched by a witch, she let him back inside. They kept the door open and I tried to go in but she yelled, "Don't cross my threshold! You have consulted with Satan! I won't have evil in my home!"

I was ready to slap the mess outta her but I knew she wouldn't let me close enough to even try. So I stayed where I was. I weren't feeling none too good. I stood back listening as Jesse said, "Please, Mrs. Dale, 'Cella only went to Witch Sue because she was confused. She ain't ready to have no baby. But there might be one and we don't...."

I was getting sicker as I listened to her reply, "Well, boy if you think she ain't ready for a baby you shoulda kept off of her in the first place. Now take your little witch touched girl and leave my property!"

"But we're in trouble," Jesse begged and I looked for someplace to throw up because soon there'd be no holding it back.

I walked to the edge of the porch and vomited over the side and heard Mrs. Valerie Dale say, "Yeah, you in trouble alright. Doing things against the will of God, consulting with witches. Boy, all I can say for you is you need to get you and that witch touched child to a preacher. You need praying over you that I ain't equipped to do. Go on, leave! You ain't welcome here!"

Jesse came out and found me vomiting on Mrs. Valerie Dale's azalea bushes that were planted all around her porch. I couldn't help it. I had to throw up somewhere. But Jesse acted like I'd killed someone, "Oh, 'Cella! What are you doing? You got vomit all over that woman's azalea bushes!"

"I'm sick, Jesse Jenkins, in case you ain't recognized that fact!"

"I know you're sick, 'Cella, but....Oh Lord, let's go before she comes out and sees what you did."

On the way home, Jesse kept going on and on about how he wished his white preacher friend Carl was home now instead of coming in this Saturday. I told Jesse why don't we go see Reverend Wheeler and Jesse said, "I don't really trust that man. He's been to the house a few times and every time he's there all he wants to do is eat. All the time asking Mama what she's cooked and what she plans to cook. That man just wants to be a preacher for all the free food he gets. No, I want to talk with Carl. If anyone can help us, he can. We could go to Preacher Joe, but I feel better with Carl."

Jesse took me home and I went right back to bed. He came in with me and lay down too. After awhile, he started kissing on me and I told him I'm too sick for all he wants to do all the time. He just sighed real loud and I closed my eyes tight. Next thing I know, he's getting up and it ain't long I hear my bedroom door open and close. Then I went to sleep, thinking all I really wanted was to sleep and wake up feeling like my normal self again.

Later the sound of really loud music wakes me up. It's so loud my bed is vibrating from the sound of it. I can hear people laughing and carrying on. I don't feel like no loud music. Lately, in addition to me being sick as a dog, I been feeling real spiteful. I put my head under the pillow to try to drown out the sound. While I'm under there, I try to figure who it is that is making so much racket. I don't think it's Jesse. It must be some of my cousins or aunts and uncles.

I come from a very large family. My Mama has six sisters—Eliza, Elmira, Nilla, Nesta, Zona Mae, Callie and Terby. And my Daddy has three brothers—Bonelle, Rayson, and Dave, and two sisters, Gert and Hannah. And all of them are married with three or four children each. They are in and out of here all the time.

Mama and Papa only have me. But that's alright. I don't think I could stand having brothers and sisters on top of all my cousins.

The pillow don't help none. Before long I figure out it's my Aunt Nesta and my cousins Zenobia and Twila. Poor Zenobia, thinks she can sing, is drowning out the good singer on the radio. I drag myself outta bed and go to stand in the doorway of my bedroom which leads right to the living room. "What y'all doing?" I yell. But they so loud they don't hear me. I yell some more and at last Aunt Nesta looks my way, "Oh, 'Cella, how you feeling, child? Madge told me to come by here and check in on you."

I just nod and go to sit in Papa's old brown chair. The radio is so loud it 's making me sicker. Twila laughs, "Come on, 'Cella, dance with me." She pulls on my hands to make me get up.

"I don't feel like dancing," I say, pulling my hands back.

"But it's fun!" Twila exclaims.

"Leave her be," Aunt Nesta says. "Our poor 'Cella has been one more sick girl."

The song on the radio goes off and I'm glad. Then another one starts up, causing Zenobia to start her pitiful singing again. She's holding the curtain cord like it's a microphone and bellowing out the words like she thinks she's the greatest thing around. Twila is twirling and shaking in time to the music and Aunt Nesta is crocheting something. Aunt Nesta is always crocheting something. "Where's Jesse?" I ask.

Aunt Nesta waves her arm, "Oh, I run him outta here. Told him go on and do something useful besides sitting in this house. I'm sure he's got some work to do somewhere."

I sit back in the chair and close my eyes. I don't think I'll ever feel better. Aunt Nesta stands, "Think I'll go fix us all a nice hot bowl of cabbage soup. I brought some from home. Won't take long to heat it on the stove. Would you like some cabbage soup, 'Cella?"

Just the thought of cabbage soup makes me sick. "No," I shake my head and run out of the house to throw up some more.

Aunt Nesta comes after me, "Poor baby," she croons over me, "Poor little 'Cella girl. Honey, you just go lie right back down in that bed. I'll fix you up some toast and ginger tea. Of course you don't want no cabbage soup sick like you are. Don't know what I was thinking. Come on now, let's get you back in bed."

Aunt Nesta helped me back to my room and before I got into bed, she sprinkled talcum powder on the sheets. Then she let me get in and covered me lightly with the sheet, waving it up over me to cause a little breeze as it settled down. She put a cold rag over my forehead and told me to just rest while she got my toast and ginger tea ready. I fell asleep before she came back and dreamed about being a little girl. A little girl looking for roly-polys under the porch with no worries about something growing in me, witches, crazy old mid-wives and visits to white preachers.

Chapter Seven

Me and Jesse quarrel and quarrel over going to see his white preacher friend. I tell him just let me go back to Witch Sue. Maybe she can give me something besides those nasty leaves. I say maybe if she can't do nothing he can somehow get me to Witch Sue's sister in Myrtle Beach. But Jesse won't hear none of it. We gotta go talk with this Carl. In the end, I said, okay, let's just make sure we talk to him with no one else around. Jesse says we'll do our best.

This Carl is supposed to be back in Cedar Cove sometime Saturday. Then he's gonna be around until the next Saturday. I'm feeling a little better when Jesse comes over Saturday morning and I tell him I just want to go walk around Brookville. Mama and Papa tell us don't be long. We're supposed to have a cookout with Jesse's people sometime this evening. I keep on about going to Brookville. Jesse don't answer me but when we leave together and he starts to drive, he don't head toward Brookville. "Where we going?" I ask.

"We gotta talk to someone who's got some sense, 'Cella. We're gonna just go up to the Duvalls and see when Carl is coming. Then I'll take you up to Preacher Joe's and buy you a Pepsi and candy bar."

I don't say nothing. I look at my hands and hope these Duvall people have maybe decided to go to Brookville themselves and won't be home.

Turns out though we didn't have to go all the way to the Duvall's farm to find that white preacher Carl. On the way there, we passed by Hunter Baptist Church and Jesse suddenly stops right in the middle of the road. "Well, look at that!" he exclaims.

"We broke down?" I ask; thinking of Papa's truck that is still broke down in our yard.

"No, we ain't broke down. But look—that's Carl's car in the driveway there at the Hunter Parsonage."

I look. There are two cars in that driveway. But I don't recognize either one of them. Jesse pulls up behind the second car, making it three all in a row. Ain't no room for any more cars now. Then he gets out. "Come on, 'Cella," he says.

"Jesse, I don't wanta talk to him here. He's probably talking with the other preacher about that revival he's doing."

"Yeah, but I can tell him we need to talk with him and then we can wait until he's finished."

I stay where I am. "Jesse...."

I am interrupted by that Carl calling, "Hey, Jesse!" as he walks out of the parsonage. An older white man is following him.

I watch as Jesse walks toward them. I listen to them saying hey to each other and see Jesse hug that Carl like he's a long lost brother or something. They come to the car and Jesse says, "Come on, 'Cella, you've met Carl."

I get out of the car then. That Carl is grinning. "Hello, 'Cella, nice to see you again." He's holding out his hand to me.

I shake his hand, "Hi," I mumble. Jesse, Carl, and the other man start talking about the revival. I am quiet. The older man talks for awhile and then goes back into the house. Jesse and Carl keep talking about nothing important at all. I look around for Carl's wife; thinking of how those other white people we watched get married lost each other for over twenty-seven years. Maybe she ain't here cause he's lost her someplace. Right in the middle of all their church talk, I blurt out, "Where's your wife?"

Carl looks at me, "Libby's with her Mama and Daddy. We got in last night. She wanted to spend some time with them, so she went over there while I came here to talk about the revival services."

"Oh," I say, thinking so far they ain't lost each other.

Carl nods his head, and says, "So, Jesse, how are you and 'Cella?"

"We're fine...." Jesse says in a very unsure voice. I can tell this Carl don't really believe him. Jesse hesitates before telling the truth, "We're in trouble, Carl. We really need to talk with you in private someplace."

Carl gives him a strange look. "Alright. Let me go check with Rev. King. I'm sure he won't mind if we go over to the church to talk."

He leaves and I say, "Jesse, this ain't necessary. I probably ain't gonna have no baby. All the other people I know that have babies are bigger than me."

Carl comes back, "We're gonna go talk in the pastor's study in the church. Rev. King just wants us to move our cars because one of his deacons is coming by soon."

"Sure, Carl," Jesse says and we get back into the car, drive just a little distance to the church, park and get out again. As we follow Carl into the church, Jesse talks like there ain't no tomorrow. He's talking about the tobacco on the Jansan farm, the Duvall's cattle, pecan trees, hot weather—nonstop.

White preacher Carl leads us to a little room in the back. The room has a shelf with a lot of books on it, a big desk with a chair behind it and another chair. The extra chair in the room is a hard, straight back chair. Real polite, Jesse stops his rambling talk just long enough to say, "'Cella, have a seat," and I give him a strange look as I sit on that hard chair.

Carl moves behind the desk and rolls the other chair out as Jesse keeps on talking. I ain't never heard so much come outta Jesse's mouth in one sitting. "Here," Carl interrupts him, "you can sit in this chair, Jesse."

Jesse nods, "Sure, but where are you gonna sit, Carl?"

He props hisself up on the desk, "Right here," he grins. Jesse grins back and keeps right on his nonsense talk. Me and that Carl both listen knowing Jesse is just running off at the mouth. Then Carl says, "Jesse—did you want to talk with me about farming?"

Jesse swallows so hard I can see it. "No, not really. We....me and 'Cella...we....we didn't mean for it to happen...I didn't mean for it to happen I know....I'm sure 'Cella didn't either....but it did...or at least we think it did and now....." He got quiet. Not another word outta his mouth.

Carl moved on the desk, his face serious, "What happened, Jesse?"

Jesse swallowed hard again, "We think....maybe 'Cella might be gonna have a baby."

Carl stood from the desk and exclaimed loudly, "A BABY! How did that happen?"'

Jesse looked confused, "Carl, you're married. You mean you don't know?"

Carl sighed, shaking his head, "I ain't stupid, Jesse. Of course I know about all that. I just mean....Jesse, you and 'Cella aren't married, are you?"

"Course we ain't. 'Cella's too young to be married."

"She's too young for what you're talking about doing with her too." Carl sat back on the desk and stared at me and Jesse for a while. "How old are you, 'Cella?" he asked.

I twisted the cloth belt from my dress in my hand. "I turned fourteen back on April eleven."

"Fourteen!" he let out. "Jesse, this child is only fourteen years old. My goodness—she's just a month older than Lilly Jean. Do you realize what you've done, Jesse?"

"I realize we're in a mess of trouble. If my Daddy finds out, he's gonna kill me. I realize that. That's why we came to you. We gotta figure out a way to stop this."

"Stop it?" Carl repeated.....

"Yeah," Jesse interrupted. "We need to stop it. 'Cella went to Sue Jones and she gave her some leaves to chew up. They didn't stop anything—just made 'Cella sick is all.

"Sue Jones?" Carl remarked. "Isn't she a witch? Or so they say?"

Jesse nodded, "Supposed to be the best witch around. But she didn't do 'Cella no good."

Carl rubbed his face. "Oh, Jesse....Jesse...Jesse. What in the world have you done? Committing adultery....consulting with witches. Oh Jesse."

"Now you wait just a minute, Carl Duvall," Jesse sounded upset. "First of all, me and 'Cella ain't married to no one so we can't commit adultery and...."

Carl cut him off, "That's what you think? You think because you're not married it's not wrong? Let me tell you, Jesse, it's wrong. It's very wrong. Jesse, relations like you and 'Cella have been having are permitted only in marriage. Any other way is considered adultery, fornication. You've committed it and you've caused 'Cella to commit it too."

"Oh...I thought..." Jesse started.

Carl interrupted him again, "You need to read First Corinthians, chapters six and seven."

"I'll read it sometime...."

"You'll read it now," Carl said, picking up a Bible from the desk and quickly finding his place. As I watched him find what he wanted in the Bible so quick, I knew he had to be a real preacher. I could never find nothing in the Bible.

Carl handed the Bible to Jesse. "Read that," he pointed with his finger.

Jesse looked at Carl, "Before I do, I gotta say I didn't consult with no witch. 'Cella did and…."

"Just read, Jesse." Carl was firm.

Jesse began reading. It took some time and while he was quiet, I was quiet too. Carl walked around the room. He looked out the window that was on the side wall and came back to the desk. I saw him looking at me and wanted to tell him to stop. At last, Jesse put the Bible back on the desk beside Carl.

"Well?" Carl asked.

"Well, it's very confusing. I don't think I understand it," Jesse said.

"It means you're supposed to wait until you're married," Carl said. "And don't tell me you ain't heard that before. You've been raised right, Jesse. Hallie and Leroy are good Christian people. I know you've been brought up in church. You knew better, Jesse."

No one said a word for a long time, then Carl said, "How did you talk 'Cella into letting you do that to her?"

Jesse shrugged, "Didn't take much talking. 'Cella don't resist much…She's…"

"You just took advantage of her, Jesse. That's what you did. You should be ashamed of yourself."

"Oh I am. But can't you say a prayer or do something for us?"

"I can pray for you, sure. But as far as doing something for you…well…."

"We just want to stop it," Jesse said. "That's why 'Cella went to Witch Sue. Now old Witch Sue told 'Cella that she has a sister in Myrtle Beach who can help get rid of the baby—if there really is a baby. We ain't…."

"WHOA!" Carl cut him off again. "You're on a roll, ain't you, Jesse. You're just racking up sins left and right here. Now you want to add murder in addition to adultery and witch consulting."

"Look here, Carl Duvall, I done told you, I didn't consult with no witch. And we ain't talking about murder. We ain't got no real baby we're trying to kill. We just want to stop 'Cella from having a real baby if there is one trying to grow in her."

"It's a real baby now." Carl picked up that Bible again. "Look, here in Jeremiah 1:5, it's talking about how before God formed you in the womb he knew you and over here in Psalms 139:3, it's talking about God covering you in your Mother's womb…It's a real baby, Jesse. It won't suddenly turn into one. It's one being made right now."

"Can't we stop it from being made? I mean if there is one? I tried to take 'Cella to the midwife down where we live to find out if there really is a baby but once she heard about Witch Sue and 'Cella, she ran us off."

"If there is a baby, there is no way to get rid of it, Jesse," Carl spoke gently.

Right then, I got sick all over again. I stood from my chair. Trying to be polite in this white people church, I said, "Is there any place I can go to be sick? I been…." I couldn't say no more. The vomit was coming up in my mouth. I ran outta the church as fast as I could and threw up on the ground outside the door.

Jesse and Carl were right behind me. Jesse was saying, ""Oh, 'Cella, you gotta stop this throwing up all over the place."

"She can't help it, Jesse," Carl said. "We just found out back in May that Libby is going to have a baby. She was sick as everything at first." Then Carl shocked me by putting his hand on my back, "Come on back inside, 'Cella. I'll get you a cup of water."

We went back to that office and this time, Carl told Jesse to let me sit in that rolling desk chair. "It's padded," he said. "I think she deserves something more comfortable." He left and I stared at my hands the whole time he was gone.

When he came back he handed me a small paper cup full of cold water. It tasted wonderful. I drank it down and Carl asked gently, "Feel better?"

"I guess," I said, wishing I had more of that water, but I didn't say that.

Carl sat back on the desk, "So, Jesse, what are your plans?"

"Plans?"

"Yes, what are you going to do?"

"I ain't got no plans. I was just hoping you'd help us find a way to stop all this."

"Some things can't be stopped once they're started and this is one of them....So, 'Cella, you've been real quiet the whole time we've been here. What do you want?"

I hadn't expected this. Most of the time no one ever asked me what I wanted about anything. I was quiet some more as I considered what he asked, then I said, "If this really is a real true baby, I don't want to kill it and I don't want no witch woman making me kill it. I just chewed up those leaves thinking they'd make me not be having a baby—not that they'd be killing the baby."

Carl nodded, "Do your parents know what's going on?"

I shook my head, "Mama and Papa just think I've been bad sick."

Jesse spoke up, "Ain't no way I'm telling Leroy Jenkins what I've been doing. He'll flat out kill me. He's the one who'll commit murder. You don't know that man."

"Leroy ain't bad," Carl said.

"Ha!" Jesse exclaimed. "He is. Let me tell you, he is. Look, I've heard James and Clyde talk about how their Daddy, Mr. Robert used to be. Well, Robert Jansan couldn't a been worse than Leroy Jenkins. I've felt that belt of his far too many times. He ain't what you think...."

"I don't know about all that," Carl said. "But I do know that your only choice in this matter is to face up to what you've done. And that means facing your parents and Marcella's. You can't hide something like this forever."

"There has to be some other way," Jesse said.

"There ain't," Carl replied.

Jesse looked at the ceiling for a long time and finally said, "Will you come with us, Carl? I can't face my Daddy alone. I really can't. Come help me, please. Remind Daddy of forgiveness. Remind him that murdering your son is wrong. Please. Maybe if you're there, he'll listen and won't kill me."

"Sure, I'll go with you, Jesse. But Leroy ain't gonna kill you."

"That's what you think."

"Just let me call my Daddy so he can get a message to Libby for me and then we'll be on our way."

Chapter Eight

Jesse drove slow and gripped the steering wheel so hard I could see the bones in his knuckles. I kept quiet, trying to think of a way outta all this. I thought about jumping out a few times and probably could have without even getting hurt since we were moving so slow, but I didn't cause I knew Jesse and that Carl would stop and get me back in the car.

The closer we got to Jesse's house, the slower Jesse drove. White Preacher Carl crept along behind us. A couple of old trucks passed us and I finally said, "Jesse...."

But Jesse didn't say a word, just gripped the steering wheel even tighter and drove so slow we were almost stopped. When we finally at last reached the place in the road to turn up to Jesse's house, we came to a full stop right in the middle of the road and sat there. Jesse stared straight ahead, not looking at me. I called to him but he ignored me completely. "Jesse..." I said again. He still ignored me.

Then White Preacher Carl was at Jesse's window. "Hey, Jesse," he said, bending down to look in the window, "you've done something totally unheard of in Cedar Cove."

"What's that?" Jesse asked, his voice strained.

"Caused a traffic jam. Look behind you."

Jesse looked up in the rear view mirror then and I turned around. Behind Carl's car was old man Jake Ander's truck, behind him was a blue car and behind that was a delivery truck.

Jesse just swallowed hard and Carl reached through the window and patted his shoulder, "Come on, Jesse. It'll be rough but you'll get through it. Y'all sure ain't the first people in the world to go through something like this."

"Might not be the first in the world, but I'm the only one gotta go through it with Leroy Jenkins."

Carl just shook his head and patted Jesse some more. "Let's move on out of the way, Jesse. I'm sure all these people have someplace to go."

Jesse didn't say a word. Just sat. So I said, "We'd better move before Mr. Leroy sees us out here in the middle of the road like this."

Jesse glanced at me then looked back at Carl, "Alright," he mumbled and began to drive again. Carl walked back to his car and followed us slowly up Jesse's driveway; past Mr. Esau's old house. We parked by Jesse's house as usual and got out. Carl stopped behind us and got out too. You could smell fish frying. I started for the back yard but Jesse stood by the car. I stopped and watched as Carl said, "Let's get this over with, Jesse."

"Uhh....Carl, I think I'll do this some other time," Jesse said. "Let me think of how best to tell them about me and 'Cella. Sides, me and 'Cella might be worried over nothing."

"You need to tell them," Carl said.

Jesse ran his hand over his face, looking scared. Without a word, he walked up to me, held onto my arm and we walked into the backyard.

Hallie and Leroy were there but I didn't see any sign of Mama or Papa. There were two big pots with fires built underneath. In one pot was fish frying and I couldn't see what was in the other one. Leroy was stirring the fish and Hallie was sitting in a chair waving herself with a big fan. When we came into the backyard, Hallie got up from her chair, "CARL! What a great surprise! Come give me a hug!"

Carl walked past me and Jesse and hugged Hallie. She patted his back and kept talking, "Sure is good for you to come see us like this. How you been?"

"Oh, we're good. Libby's having a baby...."

"A BABY!" Hallie exclaimed. "Oh my goodness! The two of you having a baby!" She kept patting his back, "Sure glad you came. You can eat some fish and corn with us. Leroy and Sammy caught a whole mess of brim earlier and Sammy and Madge are bringing the corn soon. I got some cornbread ready to fry soon as the fish come up." She looked around, "Did Libby come with you?"

"No," Carl said. "She's with James and Vicky. Wanted to spend some time with them. Actually, my coming here today was kinda of unexpected...." He looked back at me and Jesse.

Leroy looked up from the fish and stared right at Jesse, "Boy, what's the matter with you? You look scared outta your gourd."

Jesse swallowed hard, "Well, I...we..."

Hallie interrupted by saying, "So, Carl, when are you and Libby gonna have this new little baby?"

"According to the doctor, sometime in January."

"January. I bet that makes James happy. Him being a January baby himself." Hallie laughed and waved her fan in the air some more. "A little Duvall and Jansan baby. My oh my."

Leroy was still staring at Jesse. "Well," he stared again, "are you gonna tell me what's got you so scared?"

"I ain't scared," Jesse lied.

"Ha! You're scared alright. I know you, boy, and you're scared. Now what is it? Did you bang up my car? Is that it? I've told you to make sure you're careful with it. I do my best to take care of that car. Never banged it up once."

"No, I ain't banged up the car," Jesse said, and looked not at me, but at white preacher Carl who just nodded his head in reply.

"Then what is it? I ain't gonna spend all afternoon trying to drag something outta you."

"Oh, Leroy," Hallie said, "let him be. Maybe he saw more of those space people that used to follow him around." She turned to us, "Is that what it is, Jesse? Did you see more of those lights? More space people?" Jesse started to answer but Hallie kept talking. "I know they say them space people ain't real. But those lights we had here a while back were something. Sure enough were. And the way I see it, if the good Lord could put us all here, which He surely did, then sure enough he could put people someplace else too. I mean it all stands to reason...."

"Hallie, I'd like to talk with Jesse," Leroy said.

"I ain't stopping you from talking with him, Leroy. I was just saying he might be scared because of those space people all over again. I've just now gotten where I ain't afraid to step out on the back porch at night. But if they coming out in the daytime..."

Leroy stirred the fish some more. "Well, Jesse, is that it? Did you see some space people?"

"No, I ain't seen no space people." He swallowed again.

"Then what is it?" Leroy asked.

"Well, I....we...me and 'Cella....well...'Cella has...might have a problem."

"If 'Cella's got the problem, then why are you the one acting like a scared rabbit?" Leroy asked.

"Well, Daddy, I…we…'Cella might be…she thinks she might be…but we ain't sure….but we think….'Cella thinks…."

"Boy, get to the point," Leroy demanded. "You're making me mad all this beating around the bush. Say what you got to say."

Jesse closed his eyes, "We think 'Cella might be gonna have a baby."

Leroy held the spoon he'd been stirring the fish with in midair. "Did you say what I think you said?"

Jesse opened his eyes, "We didn't mean for it to happen. I didn't mean for it. It just…."

What happened next nearly scared the life outta me. Leroy dropped the spoon he held to the ground and lunged for Jesse, knocking him to the ground. He had his hands around Jesse's throat. I began to scream as hard as I could. Hallie jumped up from her chair so fast she knocked it over. "LEROY! STOP!" she shouted. "LEROY! LEROY! YOU'RE CHOKING THE LIFE OUT OF OUR JESSE!"

Carl joined in by saying, "Come on Leroy; let him go."

Leroy didn't pay them no mind. He just kept choking Jesse so hard I thought Jesse's eyes were gonna pop outta his head. I kept screaming uncontrollably and Hallie kept shouting, "OH LEROY, PLEASE STOP! DEAR LORD JESUS MAKE HIM STOP! LEROY! DON'T KILL OUR JESSE!"

Jesse struggled to get Leroy off of him, pulled at Leroy's hands to stop the choking, but Leroy kept on.

Carl knelt down and began trying to pry Leroy's hands off Jesse. "Stop, Leroy. You're a better man than this. You don't want to kill your own son."

Leroy looked at Carl and loosened his grip on Jesse, but kept his hands on his throat. He lifted Jesse's head a little; shook him and as Carl said, "Leroy, come on," he finally let go of Jesse.

Leroy stood and said, "Ain't no son of mine."

Jesse sat up and began rubbing his swollen throat. I stood close to him and saw tears in his eyes. Then he got to his feet and I reached up and touched his throat gently. Leroy kept looking at us; the madness still shooting out from him. Carl just stood looking. Hallie said, "I don't know what to think of you, Leroy, you nearly killed our Jesse." Then she came to Jesse and held him close to her, pulling him away from me.

Leroy shook his head and picked up the spoon from the ground, "Oh, Hallie, quit babying him up so much. That's what's wrong with him now. You baby him all the time. Thinks he can do whatever he pleases and get away with it."

Hallie glared at him, "Leroy, this is our child and you nearly choked the life outta him."

"Are your ears working, Hallie?" Leroy asked. "He said 'Cella might be having a baby. That means he's been right down on her. Ever since he's been going out with her I've told him and told him about stuff like that. Told him not to even think about it, but do you think he listens to me? No way."

No one said anything for a while. Hallie still held Jesse, I still stood where I was and poor white preacher Carl looked lost. Leroy finally looked over to Hallie and said, "Let him go, Hallie. He's got to take his punishment like a man."

Hallie let Jesse go, but said, "That weren't punishment, Leroy. It came close to murder!"

"I should have murdered him. Shaming me like he did," Leroy seethed. Jesse walked to the back steps. I followed and sat next to him, rubbing his swollen throat. Leroy washed off the spoon with the water hose and Hallie sat her chair back up right. Carl just stood looking. Before anything else could happen, Mama and Papa walked into the back yard. Papa was carrying a basket of corn and Mama announced, "Here, we are, at last. Sammy insisted on trying to get that old truck going. We spent forever trying to get it started and finally had to walk."

"Brought the corn though," Papa said, holding up the basket. "Already shucked, silked and ready to cook. Hope we brought enough...." He stopped, "What's the matter around here. Y'all all look like somebody died."

"Not yet, but somebody's fixing to," Leroy said, glancing over towards me and Jesse and I wondered if he had plans for finishing Jesse off and then going for me.

Mama and Papa looked at us too and Papa said, "What's going on, Leroy?"

Leroy waved his spoon, "Sammy, that boy over there—my so called son has disgraced your daughter. He just told me 'Cella might be gonna have a baby."

Mama's face fell with disappointment and Papa grinned. "A baby! Well that sure explains her being sick so much! Madgy, we're gonna be Grandparents!" He sat the basket of corn down and came to us. Then he patted Jesse's shoulder, "Reckon this means I'm getting me a real fine son-in-law."

Hallie picked up the corn and began dropping the ears into the other pot. Mama said, "Sammy, you can't be happy about this. 'Cella's just a baby herself! And Jesse ain't got no real job! This is just awful!"

"It ain't so awful, Madgy," Papa said. "Your Mama got married at fourteen. My Mama was fifteen and you'd just turned sixteen."

"That may be, but none of us were already gonna have a baby!" Mama exclaimed. "A baby is hard work. She loses her temper every time Terby comes over with her babies! Them youngun's drive 'Cella crazy. And 'Cella burns everything she cooks. She can barely boil water!

"She's gonna have to learn," Papa said. "And those little boy's of Terby's are wild little monsters. They drive me crazy too. So I wouldn't pay no mind to that. Then he patted Jesse some more and held out his hand for Jesse to shake. As they shook hands, Papa asked, "So, when's the wedding?"

I couldn't believe this. Papa was all happy. Jesse swallowed, rubbing his throat, "Well, we ain't exactly got all that planned, but I'd like for Carl here to...."

Leroy cut in, "I ain't believing a word I'm hearing. Sammy, you mean to tell me that you ain't ready to kill him?"

"Kill him?" Papa looked at me and Jesse, and then back at Leroy. "Why would I want to kill him? I think the world of Jesse. I been praying and praying that he'd be the one 'Cella wound up with. I sure don't want to kill him."

"Do you realize what he's been doing with your daughter? Maybe you didn't hear me right. She might be having a baby."

"Oh I heard you. And yeah, they shouldn't a done that, but it is natural and they are together a lot. It ain't the end of the world. They'll get married, have this baby and start their own little family."

Jesse took this opportunity to be a little more brave. "I ain't talked it over with 'Cella yet, but Carl, I sure would like it if you could marry us."

Before Carl could say a word, Leroy said, "Boy, Carl ain't gonna marry y'all. You done shamed me and I ain't gonna stand for you to have a regular preacher wedding like y'all ain't sinned one bit. Take y'all down to the justice of the peace. That's what you gonna get."

Papa looked over at Carl; then said, "Leroy, I don't see why Rev. Wheeler can't marry them."

Leroy shook his head, "I'm gonna have some say so in this matter and I ain't gonna stand for them to get married by no regular preacher. They've done wrong and they gonna get married by the justice and that's it." Then to Carl he said, "Carl, I'm sorry you had to be a part of all this."

Carl nodded, "I understand. Well, I gotta be going. I'm sure Libby's getting worried about me."

Hallie turned to him, "Oh you ain't gotta go, Carl. Stay and have some supper."

"Some other time, Hallie," Carl said.

"At least get you some pecans. Get as many as you want."

Carl looked around at all of us, "Some other time, Hallie. Before Libby and me go home, I'll bring her by here to see you and we'll get some then. But I'm gonna be going." Then he hugged Hallie and Leroy, came over to us, patted Jesse and my shoulders and said softly, "Take care and love each other. Jesse, if you need to talk, just let me know."

Jesse nodded and held Carl's hand briefly, "Thanks." Then after waving to all of us, Carl left.

Everyone was quiet for the longest time, then Mama spoke up, "Well, I got a question. Where are 'Cella and Jesse gonna live?"

"They could live with us, Madge," Papa said.

"They could but remember how it was for us trying to live with my Mama and Daddy when we first got married Sammy? Married people need to be on their own."

Papa ran his hand over his face. "You're right about that, Madge."

Hallie spoke up, "I reckon we could let them live in Mr. Esau's place...."

Leroy began taking the fish up, "No, Hallie. They ain't living there. We fixed that place up for your Mr. Esau museum and it does bring in some extra money. They ain't having that. I know exactly where I plan on putting them."

"Where?" Mama asked.

"Down at Miz Essie's old place," Leroy said. "She left it to me when she died and I've planned all along to let Jesse have it. I was gonna help him fix it up and build a nice little house on it. But after what he's done, he's gonna have to put up with that shack until he can do better on his own."

Jesse spoke up again, "Daddy, that ain't nothing but a one room falling down nothing shack. We can't live there."

Leroy glared at him, "You can and you will. In fact you'll start cleaning it up tomorrow and soon as it's all ready; you and Miss Marcella here are getting married. And I'll tell you something else. Tonight, after we finish eating, she's walking home with her Mama and Daddy and the two of you won't see each other until you're standing in front of the judge to be married."

Chapter Nine

After Carl left, Leroy kept right on fussing about us. He wouldn't let up for nothing. For the longest time, it was Leroy fussing and Papa going on about how good Jesse was. Mama and Hallie just took care of the corn and the cornbread, all the while talking about gardens and sewing, like nothing was going on with me and Jesse at all. I just sat by Jesse on the porch steps, feeling sick and unhappy. Jesse finally got up and went in the house saying his throat hurt to bad to swallow. I got sick to the point of vomiting again, ran and threw up some in weeds at the very back of the yard. Mama watched me but this time instead of being so concerned, she said, "It's what happens when you're having a baby 'Cella."

Jesse didn't come back outside and when the food got done, I fixed my plate and sat back on the porch away from everyone else. I didn't eat much. I felt sick, mad and hurt. I didn't want to be here. I hated Leroy for choking Jesse like he did. For saying we had to get married and for saying he wanted to put us in that old shack in the woods. I didn't want to live in no shack in the woods.

When I finished eating, I sat my plate on the steps and waited for Mama and Papa. They talked and talked with Leroy and Hallie, making plans for me and Jesse. Planning out my life without so much as saying, "Hey, 'Cella, what do you want?"

It was after dark before we finally decided to leave. I didn't feel like walking home in the dark. I wanted Jesse to drive me home. But that was outta the question so I didn't even mention it. We began walking with Mama on one side of me and Papa on the outside, next to the road. We were all quiet for awhile as we walked along in the moonlight, slapping skeeters. I lagged behind just a little letting Mama and Papa get ahead.

Papa said, "Shouldn't take too long to fix up that little place Miz Essie had. Just the other day Bonelle was up at the bait and tackle shop. He was saying that he's getting a new bed for him and his new wife Varlene. I bet we could get his old bed for Jesse and 'Cella."

"Yeah, I would say let them take 'Cella's bed but it's only a single bed." Mama said. She paused. "Say, I could get that old rocking chair that Mama keeps on the back porch. Ain't nothing wrong with it. It's just old. But Mama keeps complaining about it being in the way. I'm sure she wouldn't mind 'Cella having it. She's gonna need a rocking chair once the baby comes."

Papa said. "Between all of us we can come up with dishes and pots and pans for them. This ain't gonna be no big problem. We'll get them all sit up and...."

"I'm fed up with this!" I shouted. Mama and Papa stopped walking and looked back at me.

"All this planning out my life," I kept yelling, "Everyone telling me what I'm gonna do. Jesse ain't even asked me to marry him!"

"Well he's just as good as asked," Papa said. "You're carrying his child. What more asking do you want?"

"I might not want to marry Jesse," I said. "I might want to marry someone else."

"Who else you gonna want to marry when you been sleeping with Jesse?" Mama asked.

I shrugged, "I don't know. I might want to marry Tom Matters or Josh Saunders"

"You been sleeping with them too?" Mama asked.

"No," I said, frustrated.

Papa laughed, "You ain't wanting to marry Tom or Josh."

"You don't know that," I mumbled. "Tom's real nice to me in school and Josh all the time tells me how to spell words I don't know."

Papa laughed some more. "I can't see any young girl wanting to tie up with Tom or Josh. Poor old Tom ain't got but one tooth in the front and if big old Josh fell down, no one could lift him up. We'd just have to roll him home."

"I ain't even sure I'm really having a baby...."

"Have you been sleeping with Jesse?" Mama asked.

I stared at her, "We ain't been asleep...."

"Marcella, you know what I'm saying. You've been physical with Jesse—right?"

"Yeah—but I still ain't sure about this baby business."

Mama shook her head, "Well I am. It explains everything about how you've been lately."

I rolled my eyes in the dark. "I ain't old enough to get married. I'm still in school...."

Papa laughed, "Your school days are over 'Cella. It's time to be a wife and mother."

I was so angry about everything, I just stomped my foot hard.

"Marcella Antoinette," Mama said strictly, "you are marrying Jesse Jenkins and that's that."

"But he ain't asked me. I ain't had no choice."

Papa laughed, "'Cella girl, you made your choice when you laid down in that bed with him. Now let's get on home."

Chapter Ten

I ain't had a say so in nothing. Absolutely nothing. It took Jesse a week to clean up Miz Essie's old place and for Mama, Papa, Leroy and Hallie to furnish it to their liking. I ain't even been taken out there to look at it or anything. Ain't had no say so in what furniture I'm getting, where it's gonna be sit up in that little one room shack or nothing at all. Even Gran and Gramp has had more say so than me. I'm like the forgotten person. Just little old pregnant 'Cella. Gotta keep my mouth shut and let everyone else run my life.

It is now Saturday, August the second and I'm sitting on the bench in the courthouse between Mama and Papa, waiting on Jesse to arrive with Leroy and Hallie so we can get married. Papa finally got his truck going. It needed a battery and some other parts. My Uncle Dave came over and helped Papa fix it.

Once we got here to the courthouse, Papa talked with the judge and he says he'll get around to marrying us soon as he can today. Says he has things to tend to and it might take awhile. Meanwhile, my Aunt Zona Mae, who works as a maid here at the courthouse keeps walking past us with her mop, pretending to mop, but I know she's really studying me. Zona Mae is the most religious of all our family. She's done run off three husbands because they didn't pray good enough to suit her. And all five of her sons left home soon as they were able cause Zona Mae drove them batty with all her religion.

Now, every time she walks past us, she shouts out, "Oh sweet Jesus, help this sinful child." Mama has told her to stop and Papa has too, but Zona Mae ain't one for stopping nothing once she's got started.

The door opens and I watch as Leroy, Hallie and Jesse finally come inside. Leroy and Hallie are wearing regular clothes, but Jesse is in a brown suit and he's carrying a bunch of flowers. I'm wearing my pink dress which I don't really like but Mama likes it and right now what I think don't matter at all. I start to get up to run to him cause it's been so long since we've seen each other, but Papa puts his hand on me and says, "Stay put 'Cella. He's gonna be your husband soon enough."

I sit back and watch as Leroy, Hallie and Jesse come to sit on the bench next to us. Leroy and Hallie sit on either side of Jesse, just like Mama and Papa are doing with me; preventing us from looking at each other unless we lean forward and they ain't letting us do that either.

We sit and sit. Zona Mae walks by with her wailing prayers to Jesus about mine and Jesse's sin. I close my eyes and try to ignore her. Try not to listen to her and try to pretend none of this is happening.

But it is happening and nothing will stop it. Nothing at all. The judge at last sticks his head out his door and says, "I'm ready to do that wedding now."

We get up and walk into his office with Hallie, Leroy and Jesse following. Then we all stand there in front of the judge's big desk cause none of us have a clue what to do. The judge leaves the door open, then settles hisself behind the desk and goes through some papers. "All righty," he says, "Who's getting married today?"

Leroy takes charge, "My sorry son here and this little girl he's been indecent with."

The judge looks up at us and nods like he don't really care at all. He goes through his papers some more and says, "Okay, what are your names?"

No one says anything for a moment, then Leroy shoves Jesse and says, "Time for you to speak up, boy. Be a man. Tell the judge who you are."

Jesse glares at Leroy and tells the judge, "I'm Jesse Leroy Jenkins."

The judge writes it down; then looks at me, "I assume you are the bride." I nod and softly tell him my name. He writes it down and says, "I want the two of you to step forward."

We do and I glance back to see Zona Mae standing in the door, holding her mop and staring at us. The judge stands, clears his throat and says, "Dearly beloved we are gathered here today to join this young man and woman in matrimony....."

Aunt Zona Mae wailed, "Oh Lord, they're not being joined in Holy Matrimony....OHHH...OHHH!"

Papa rolled his eyes and the Judge shook his head. He started over, "Dearly beloved, we are gathered here to join this couple in

Holy Matrimony. If there is anyone who objects to it, let him speak now or forever hold his peace….."

He was quiet for a long time; like he was waiting on a protest. Leroy finally said, "Get on with marrying them. I got protests about what they been doing. Marrying them is the only thing that can be done now."

The judge nodded and looked at Jesse, "Son, do you take this woman here to be your lawful wife? Do you promise to love, honor, provide for and forsake all others until death you do part?"

"I do," Jesse mumbled, handing me the flowers he held.

"Fine," the judge said and looked at me. "And you, young lady, do you promise to love honor, obey and forsake all others until death you do part?"

"Yeah," I nodded.

"Good….do you have rings?" the judge asked.

"No sir," Jesse mumbled.

"Alright," the judge sighed. "We'll skip that part." He cleared his throat again and Zona Mae let out one of her wails, causing everyone to look at her for a moment.

The judge stared at her too and said, "Mrs. Rivers, don't you have work to do?"

"Yes sir, I sure do," Zona Mae said. "But this little girl here is my niece and I would like to watch her get married. Sinful though she may be."

The judge looked back at us and Mama said softly, "She's my sister."

"Fine," the judge replied tiredly. He looked at Jesse, "Repeat after me. "Marcella Antoinette, I hereby marry you." Jesse repeated it. The judge nodded, "I promise to love, provide for and forsake all others in sickness and in health…." Jesse repeated it. The judge continued, "for richer, for poorer, for better or for worse, amen." Jesse repeated it all and the judge turned to me and had me say the same thing to Jesse, except he made me promise to obey and then he said, "By the power invested in me by the state of North Carolina, I hereby declare you husband and wife. You may kiss the bride."

Before Jesse could kiss me, Zona Mae hollered, "He's already done more than that! Oh sweet Jesus, take care of these sinful people! OHHHH!"

Papa turned around, "Zona Mae, please shut your mouth."

Zona Mae waved her hands in the air. "I pray for blessings. I pray for forgiveness for these two. I pray for the child 'Cella's gonna bear! I pray for their sinful ways! OHHH!"

The judge shook his head and said, "Go on, son. She's your wife now. You can kiss her."

Jesse gave me a small kiss and Zona Mae shouted, "They done gone past kissing! Done laid together in sin! OHHH!!!!"

Papa shouted, "Zona Mae! Hush your mouth now!"

I watched as Mama put her hand on Papa and said, "Don't pay her no mind, Sammy. Let's be going."

Papa sighed, shook his head and asked the judge how much he owed him. While Papa paid the judge, Jesse pulled me aside and whispered, "How have you been?"

I shrugged, "I don't know."

Jesse patted my arm and we followed Mama, Papa, Hallie and Leroy out of the courthouse. Once outside, we just stood there. Then Mama said, "We've got a surprise for you back at the house. Hallie, you and Leroy are invited, of course."

"What kind of surprise?" Leroy asked.

"Just a little get together in honor of Jesse and 'Cella," Mama said. "Not much. Just some cake and most of the family except Zona Mae is gonna be there."

"I don't know," Leroy said.

Hallie patted his arm, "Oh, let's go Leroy. Stop all this grudge holding you been doing. They married now."

"Might be married but the sin's been done. Can't undo it."

"That's right," Hallie said. "And all your anger ain't gonna undo it either. Let's go."

Leroy sighed, "I just want to go home, Hallie. Don't want to be no part of no celebration."

"Please, Leroy." Hallie spoke softly, "Please, for me."

Leroy sighed again, "Alright but they ain't riding in our car."

"They can ride in the back of my truck," Papa said.

"Fine," Leroy agreed.

And so, me and Jesse climbed into the back of Papa's truck. As we settled down, Leroy put a suitcase back there with us, "Here, this is the last of your clothes that was at the house, boy."

Jesse didn't say anything, just leaned his head against the cab of the truck and closed his eyes. I leaned against Jesse and closed my eyes too. Before long, we started to move. Jesse put his arm around me but still didn't talk. At last I said, "These are pretty flowers." I'd been looking at them more carefully.

"Glad you like them," Jesse said. "I picked them outta my Aunt Sybil's yard. Ain't sure what they are but I wanted you to have some kind of flowers."

I nodded, then looked at the suitcase and said, "They done moved all your clothes and stuff out to Miz Essie's?"

"All but this right here," Jesse pointed to the suitcase. "But it's our place now, 'Cella. Not Miz Essie's."

"Mama and Papa have taken most of my stuff out there too....Oh, Jesse, I ain't wanting to live in no one room shack."

"It'll be okay, 'Cella. I got it fixed up pretty good. My Aunt Sybil, Mama's sister, even gave us a stove so you ain't gotta cook on the fireplace and I got curtains hung to make us a bedroom so the bed ain't sitting right out in the open. It really ain't that bad."

"I ain't had a chance to even look at it. Ain't had a chance to do nothing at all that I wanted to do."

Jesse hugged me, "Honey girl, it's your house now and I promise you; you will have plenty to do with it." He squeezed my hand, "Oh, by the way, I really did want to marry you. I do love you, Marcella Jenkins."

I smiled, but it hurt. I wanted to be happy, but I felt miserable. I didn't tell Jesse though. I just leaned against him and closed my eyes.

Chapter Eleven

I kept my eyes closed for the rest of the ride. Then I kept them closed even after the truck stopped and I knew we were home at Mama and Papa's. I opened them only after Jesse moved and said, "Oh no, look at all this." I sat up, looking around. Gran and Gramp had a big table sit up between our houses. The table was covered with a white cloth and had a cake and lots of food on it. There were several other cars and trucks parked all over the place. Before me and Jesse had a chance to get out of the truck all the way, a whole pile of my cousins, aunts and uncles came running from both houses shouting, "CONGRATULATIONS!" like they was as happy as could be. Me and Jesse got out of the truck but didn't know what to do, where to go, or what to say. Then my cousins, aunts and uncles started throwing rice on us. They threw so much rice I could barely see. It was like it was snowing rice. Jesse and me ran to the porch, doing our best to get outta that rice snow storm. My cousins followed us but they ran outta rice. My cousin Zenobia was yelling, "We need more rice!"

"No you don't," Jesse said, shaking his head to get the rice off and brushing it off of me at the same time. "Y'all done threw enough rice to feed this whole bunch for a year!"

My cousin Aquina was saying, "Might be, Jesse, but it sure was fun throwing it! Come on, 'Nobi, let's go look and see if Gran has anymore rice in the kitchen!"

Aquina and Zenobia started for Gran's house, but Gramp stopped them, "You children threw more than enough rice already. Let's move out of the way so the newlyweds can come see the wedding cake Gran spent all last night making."

My cousins listened to Gramp and me and Jesse followed them to the table sat up in the yard. As we were walking over, I noticed Leroy and Hallie just standing in the middle of the yard. Hallie looked sad and Leroy looked ready to kill somebody. I stopped, staring over at Mr. Leroy with his grouchy face and Jesse whispered, "Don't pay Leroy no mind."

"You see him?" I asked.

"Yeah, he's been like that ever since he found out about me and you. That's his new permanent look—mad dog." Jesse whispered.

"Hey," Mama called, "Y'all come on over here and look at this pretty cake!"

We walked over and looked at it. It was pretty—all white icing with white flowers and a little bride and groom on the top that were colored just like us. Gran hugged me, "That's the same bride and groom that was on me and your Gramp's wedding cake, 'Cella. I was proud to put it on yours."

I touched the little bride and groom. That bride was colored, but she was wearing a real white wedding dress. Not a baby looking pink dress trimmed in lace like I was. "I never saw this," I remarked to Gran.

"That's cause I kept it up safe," Gran said. "And all the rest of the grand-youngun's that have got themselves married either haven't had a cake or they used something else on top. But I let you use mine, 'Cella."

"It's real pretty, Mrs. Ballard," Jesse spoke up. "Thank you for making the cake for us."

Me and Jesse cut the cake Gran made for us. Then we fed some of it to each other cause Mama said we had to. After that, Mama and Aunt Callie pushed us out of the way so they could cut and serve the cake to everyone else. In addition to the cake there was lots of fried chicken, tater salad, corn on the cob, sliced tomatoes, cucumbers, peppers, homemade cookies, lemonade and punch.

Before long, most everybody had a plate full of food. Jesse got him some food, but I didn't. Jesse asked did I want anything and I told him no. I weren't feeling too good at all. He wanted to know if I was gonna start vomiting on our wedding day and I said, no, I didn't think so. I just didn't want to eat.

Jesse led me to a chair under some dogwood trees and made me sit there while he sat on a tree root that was right by my chair. He balanced his plate on his lap. He tried to get me to eat, but I wouldn't. I just sit there, watching everyone. Hallie had walked away from Leroy; it seemed she was trying to act like everything was fine. But Leroy was still standing by his car, scowling at the world. My aunts, uncles and cousins were all laughing and carrying on like they'd planned on me and Jesse getting married for a long time. Uncle Bonelle came over to me and Jesse, "Well, well, hiding out under the dogwood trees! Y'all sure make a nice little couple. Want y'all to step out there so I can make a little speech for you two."

I stood and Jesse put his plate of half eaten food in the chair. We followed Uncle Bonelle out from underneath the tree and stood there while he said loudly, "Alright, everyone, we all know Jesse and our little Marcella got married this morning. Yep. Starting out life as man and wife. I think it's only fitting that someone should give them a few tips on how to have a happy married life! And so I have a few things I'd like to share with them..."

Papa pushed him out of the way, "Hold on! You ain't the one to be giving them advice, Bonelle—you're on what—number four in wives now?"

Uncle Bonelle slapped Papa's back, laughing hard, "Varlene is number six, Sammy. Six times I done been to the altar. This time it's gonna work cause I got it all figured out."

"Six! " Papa exclaimed. "You slipped some of them wives past me, Bonelle! I can't remember but four."

"Nah, Sammy, Varlene makes six. I'm pretty sure of it."

Papa shook his head, "Well, you sure ain't the one to be handing out advice on marriage!"

"Why not?" Uncle Bonelle chuckled. "I've done it enough!"

"Yeah and it ain't worked for you yet!" Papa laughed.

Me and Jesse were just standing, watching and listening to everyone. While Papa and Uncle Bonelle were still going to it, Jesse whispered, "Let's figure a way out of here, 'Cella. I want to show you our house. I want us to go home."

"I gotta get the rest of my clothes. I got them all packed."

"Let's get them."

We walked to my house with no one really noticing us—they were all too busy stuffing their faces, talking and laughing like crazy. We made our way to my bedroom without a soul asking what we was doing. My clothes were all packed up in a sack. Jesse picked them up, "This it, honey girl?"

"Yeah," I said, looking around the room. The dresser was empty, the closet empty. I used to have little collections of leaves, and dried flowers on the dresser but Mama made me throw them all away, saying that I was getting married and had to grow up. All that was gone. The old rag doll Gran made me when I was three and I named Rosieball was gone too. Mama thought I'd thrown it out like she told me, but I'd packed her at the bottom of my sack of clothes. Everything that made this room be mine was gone. The room looked sad. I felt like crying. Jesse put his arm around me, "It'll be okay, 'Cella. I love you."

I nodded. I couldn't talk. I wanted to close my eyes; open them and have my room look like my room again. I wanted my dresses hanging in the closet, my socks, underwear and nightgowns in the dresser drawers. I wanted my old doll, Rosieball, on the bed, my dried leaves and flowers on the dresser—I wanted things just like they used to be. But I didn't say a word about that to Jesse. I just squinched my eyes tight to keep from crying and followed him outta the room.

When we got to the front door to go back outside I said, "Jesse how we gonna get out to Miz Essie's place?"

"It's our place, 'Cella, and I reckon we gotta walk cause I sure ain't been able to get us a car or truck yet."

"I don't feel like walking all that long way."

"We'll take our time honey girl. We'll take as long as you need."

"But I don't want to walk at all. I don't feel good. And it's a long way out there."

"It ain't that long, 'Cella. Come on, we'll be fine. Maybe someone will come along and give us a ride."

I sighed and followed him outside. We were walking off the porch when Aunt Nesta called out, "There they are! Trying to escape!"

Jesse shook his head and stopped walking. "We're going home now," he said.

Mama came to us. She hugged me tight, kissing me. Papa came and hugged and kissed me too. Then he slipped his truck keys into Jesse's hand, "Here, you can take my old truck for a while."

Jesse stared at the keys, "Mr. Sammy, you need your truck."

Papa laughed, "Got along fine without it back when it was broke down. If I need it, I'll come get it." He laughed some more.

The whole time we'd been here, Leroy had been standing by his car mad at the world, not saying a thing. Now he shouted to us, "Sammy, don't you give that sorry boy your truck. Make them walk!"

Papa looked at Leroy, "You can be mad all you want, Leroy. I don't care one bit about that. But my little girl here is having a baby and I don't think she needs to be going on no long hard walks now. So I'm gonna let Jesse take the truck. It's my decision, Leroy. And that's final."

Leroy let out what sounded just like a growl; got in his car and revved up the engine. Then he yelled out the window, "Hallie, you'd better come on if you want to come with me. I've had enough of watching the circus they got going here."

"Oh, Leroy!" Hallie yelled back, walking to him all the same, "Why you gotta act up? Why can't you just let Jesse and 'Cella be?"

"I ain't bothering Jesse and 'Cella one bit! I'm just ready to get outta here is all!"

"Ain't you gonna tell them good bye? Give them your blessing?"

"No, Hallie, I ain't. Now come on."

Hallie shook her head; then came to me and Jesse. She held Jesse for a long long time; rocking back and forth with him. She held him until Leroy started blowing the horn. "OH STOP IT, LEROY!" she shouted to him. She let Jesse go and hugged me, "Be good to my Jesse," she said softly, giving me a little kiss on my cheek.

I nodded and Leroy blew the horn again. Hallie glanced back but didn't say no more to Leroy. Instead she looked at Jesse, "Just give him time, honey. He'll get over all this. You just wait and see. He'll get over it sooner or later. I promise you."

She kissed us both again and left; going and getting in the car with Leroy. They sped off and Jesse said, "Well, they're gone."

"Appears to be," Papa said.

Jesse nodded. "It's time for us to go too. I'll take real good care of 'Cella. Promise. I will."

We said goodbye some more, got in Papa's truck and drove outta the yard as all my aunts uncles, cousins, Mama, Papa and Gran and Gramp waved until we couldn't see them no more.

Chapter Twelve

It had been a long time since I'd been out to Miz Essie's place. I'd gone with Papa a few times when I was real little before she died and the very last time was back before my cousin Roscoe left for the Army. That was when I was around eleven. Roscoe claimed that he'd seen the ghost of Miz Essie walking in the woods around her old shack. He wanted a bunch of us to go find Miz Essie's ghost for ourselves. I didn't want to go, but he forced me by grinning at me and saying, "You gonna deny me my last wish before I leave for the Army, 'Cella? If I die you always gonna be thinking about how I wanted you to join us on the hunt for Miz Essie's ghost and you refused to come. That thought will haunt you forever."

And so I'd went, being drug along as usual, doing what I really didn't want to do, but doing it all the same. We never did see the ghost of Miz Essie. But we ran around her old place whooping and hollering and I fell through the porch. Right before I fell through the porch I felt someone push me. I was sure it was old Miz Essie and screamed like crazy. My cousins Mart and Randy came running to me. They said we was just having fun and another one of our cousins had to of been the one that pushed me. My cousin Mart got me out of the porch and Roscoe carried me home cause I was sure I'd broke my leg. Turned out it weren't broke at all. I was just scared. A few days later, Roscoe left for the Army. The rest of my cousins kept going back to Miz Essie's to play around but not me.

Jesse turned to drive up the long wooded path that led to Miz Essie's and I couldn't help but think about being pushed and falling through that rotten porch, I'd been thinking and thinking about having to live in that sorry old shack and it just made me sick. I closed my eyes while we was still going through the trees and briars. I wasn't ready to look at what had to be my house. At the shack home that had been forced on me. It wasn't long before I felt the truck stop. Then Jesse kissed me, "Open your eyes, honey girl, we're home."

I opened my eyes. The yard was no longer full of holes. It had been leveled out and all the holes filled in. The shack had lots of new wood in it where it had been patched. Jesse hugged me, "I been working on it all week, 'Cella, just for you. Come on, let me show you."

I started to get out of the truck, but Jesse hurried to me and picked me up. Then he carried me up to the shack. As we went up the steps, I noticed the porch was all new wood, all fixed now. There weren't any chairs on it like before, but the porch was solid now.

We went inside and Jesse put me down at last. He started kissing me like that was all he wanted to do but I wanted to see what he'd done to this place. I tried to pull away, but he wouldn't let me. So I just let him kiss me until he stopped. Then I was able to look around. The old wooden table Miz Essie had was still in the room but it was pushed to one side instead of being in the center. There was a new icebox and right beside it was a cabinet that I recognized coming from Aunt Nila's house. On the other side of the cabinet was a big sink with a hand pump for water. In the center of the room Gran's old orange rocking chair that used to sit on the back porch was next to another rocking chair and an armchair that used to be Miz Essie's. On the floor was the braided rug Aunt Terby had been working on for her own house but now it was here. Miz Essie's old oil lamps were on the table. They were all shiny and new looking. "I cleaned them special, just for us, honey girl" Jesse grinned.

I nodded, looking at the opposite wall, seeing the fireplace and the stove Jesse's Aunt Sybil gave us. In the middle of the room; behind the table and the little sitting area was a big thick gold colored curtain hung on a thick rod that was hung close to the ceiling. Jesse grabbed my hand and led me past that curtain. Behind it was a double bed, a small chest of drawers with an oval mirror over it and a little table by the bed. There was a new oil lamp on the table—one I'd never seen before. It was milky white with little blue flowers on it. "I bought that at Preacher Joe's store, honey girl Do you like it?" I nodded and Jesse started kissing me again, "This is our bedroom, honey girl. I even came up with the idea of hanging the curtain to make the bedroom separate from the rest of the house. I'm gonna make us a crib for the baby and we can sit it up right over there," he pointed.

"Who helped you do all this?" I asked.

"I did most of it all by myself. Your cousin Mart and Uncle Calvin helped some, but I did most of it."

I walked back around the curtain. The windows in the little shack were clean now and had blue flowered curtains hanging at them. "Where'd you get the curtains?" I asked, thinking the material looked familiar.

"Your Aunt Terby made them," Jesse said.

"Oh," I replied, now remembering her old blue flowered dress. I looked around some more, "We ain't got no electric, no running water or bathroom."

Jesse sighed, "Lots of folks still don't have electricity, 'Cella. We didn't get it until I was in the ninth grade at school and y'all just got it back in March. I know cause I was there when they hooked it up. And your Daddy just put in that little bathroom at the back of your house, so I know...."

I cut him off, "Yeah, I've lived without all that, but I like it better having it."

"I do too, Marcella, but we can't afford it now. We will in the future, but not now." He walked to Gran's old rocker and sat down. "Come here, honey girl."

I didn't go to him. Instead I walked to the cabinet and opened it up. There were several jars of canned vegetables, "Where did you get all this? Your Mama?"

"Vicky Jansan gave us all that. Old Leroy wouldn't let Mama do anything for us. He had a fit over Aunt Sybil giving us the stove and over me getting those flowers for you."

I closed the cabinet door and looked under the sink. There were a few old pots that I recognized as being old ones of Mama's, a small stack of plates, two cups and two glasses. In one of the glasses were some forks, spoons and knives. There was also two big bowls stacked together with some bigger serving spoons inside the top one. "Where'd you get all the dishes? I know the pots were Mama's."

"Alice and Simpson gave us the plates and cups; Clyde and Wanda gave us the forks, spoons, knives and glasses and Carl and Libby gave us the big bowls and serving spoons."

It seemed his white friends were doing everything for us. I closed the door and thought about my clothes and things that had been brought over here earlier. I asked Jesse about them and he said, "All that's in a cedar box under the bed, honey girl. I pushed it under there to save space. Now come here, I want to hold you."

I finally went to him and sat on his lap. I leaned against him and Jesse just looked at me for a moment then started kissing me. I let him kiss me, doing my best not to think of anything at all.

Chapter Thirteen

I am trying to make biscuits. Last night for supper I cooked me and Jesse some corn, field peas and rice. I burnt all of it. I ain't never been good at cooking and I was sure Jesse was gonna fuss at me but he didn't. He just helped me scoop the good parts outta the pots for us to eat and when we was finished, he took the pots outside to scrap the burned stuff outta the pots. Then after I'd washed the dishes we'd ate off of, Jesse helped me get some really hot boiling water going and we poured it and soap flakes all over the burned pots and let them soak overnight.

This morning when I got up, there was all kinds of burned mess floating up in the water but the pots were mostly clean. I scrubbed them out and hollered for Jesse that he needs to come dump the water outta this sink. I tried to lift it outta the cabinet but it's too heavy for me and I don't want water all over my floor.

But Jesse is still sleeping. Last night he said that since today was Sunday and he didn't have to go to work anywhere he was gonna be lazy. Said we weren't gonna worry with going to church or anything like that either. I woke up before he did and slipped outta the room real quiet cause I didn't feel like doing what Jesse was sure to want to do if he woke up and I had to go to the outhouse real bad.

As soon as I came back in, I got some eggs outta our ice box to scramble for our breakfast and decided to try to make biscuits. That Vicky gave Jesse a big bowl of eggs for us and Jesse bought some flour and lard for biscuits, some baking soda, salt, sugar and a small tin of pepper.

I'd never made biscuits before. I'd watched Mama and Gran but I'd never done it on my own. I'd mixed up the flour and lard in our only big bowl with some water because we didn't have any milk and then I started trying to pinch the dough off into little balls for biscuits like I'd seen Mama and Gran do. I was gonna cook them in our biggest frying pan and scramble the eggs in our other frying pan.

The dough was sticky and wouldn't get off my hands. So I put more flour on them and started again. I was working away when I heard Jesse, "Morning, honey girl."

I turned to see him standing by the curtain without a stitch on. "Jesse, go put on some clothes!"

He grinned, "Why? I'm in my own house with my very own pretty little wife. I can do as I please." He stretched and yawned, "Yep, I love this being married and being on my own. No one telling me what to do. No Leroy bossing me around. This is the way to live. Man, I'm loving this!"

"You gotta get some clothes on!" I demanded. "It ain't decent to walk around like you are!"

"Oh, 'Cella, honey girl, we're out here in the woods. Ain't no one around to see us. And 'sides, it's Sunday—everyone's in church and they all know we just got married yesterday......"

Right at that moment, our front door flung open and in walked my oldest cousin Shane, his wife Margaret and their twin boys Bill and Will.

Jesse screamed and did his best to wrap the curtain around him to hide hisself. Shane laughed hard, "Sure looks like you two are settling into married life right nice! Sure does!" He came to me and kissed the side of my face, "How you doing, 'Cella girl? Uncle Sammy wrote and told us you was getting hitched, but we couldn't make it here yesterday. Sorry we missed the festivities yesterday but I had to work and it was Margaret's turn to take care of her Mama. I reckon you've heard how her poor old Mama is so feeble. Poor old thing don't even know who Margaret and the other girls are. But they're good to her, taking turns taking care of her. We just couldn't help it. But we got up early this morning and headed right on down here. Stopped by Uncle Sammy's place and he told us how to get out here to where you live. Out in the woods, ain't you." Shane stopped talking long enough to look around the room, "Where's your husband? He was totally on display for the world when we came in. Where'd he disappear to?"

I was speechless. Shane mostly grew up in Myrtle Beach. I used to only see him every now and then. Then he and Margaret moved to Wilmington not long after they got married way back when I was only seven. I hadn't seen him since then. He'd sent Christmas cards and pictures of their twins but that had been it. But here he was, wearing a blue suit trimmed in white and a blue and white hat like he was some kinda preacher. Margaret was wearing a pretty yellow suit, a hat with yellow flowers on it and she was holding a square package wrapped all up like it was Christmas. I recognized the twins from pictures. I guessed they were about five years old now. They didn't look one bit alike so it was easy to tell them apart. I watched as Bill and Will began climbing all over our rocking chairs. Before I could speak, Jesse called, "Marcella!"

Trying to be polite, I wiped all the doughy goo from my hands and said, "Excuse me, I gotta go help Jesse."

"You go right ahead, honey," Shane said. "See if you can help him find some clothes while you're at it. I understand y'all ain't got much cause you're just getting started, but...."

I ignored him and walked to our curtain and then past it. Jesse was sitting on our bed, now wearing jeans and a brown plaid shirt. "Who are those people?" he demanded.

"My cousin Shane and his family."

"I ain't never seen him. What's he doing here?"

"You ain't never seen him because he lives in Wilmington. Before then he lived in Myrtle Beach. He's my Uncle Bonelle's oldest child—by his first wife Maelynn. When Maelynn left Bonelle she took Shane and his sister Clara with her. They grew up down in Myrtle Beach and used to only come up for family get togethers before my Grandpa Otis died. Grandpa Otis was my Papa's daddy. His Mama, my Grandma Alta died when Papa was twelve so I never knew her. But Grandpa Otis always liked Maelynn and wanted her to come to our get togethers."

Jesse held up his hand, "You ain't got to give me the entire family history right now. I just want to know what are they doing here and ain't nobody ever taught him how to knock on a door? Ain't nobody ever told him you ain't supposed to just go barging into someone else's home like that?"

I shrugged, "None of my people ever knock. They always just come right on in."

"Well they gotta knock when they come here!"

"I'll tell them. Come on; let's go out there so they can see you."

"They done seen more of me than they needed to, Marcella. I ain't going out there."

"Oh, Jesse, please. I don't know what to say to them. I ain't laid eyes on either one of them since I was seven."

"Well I sure don't know what to say to them either!" Jesse exclaimed. "You go on out there with them. They're your people."

I felt like crying, "I thought since we was married that my people are your people too now."

Jesse sighed and pulled me down on the bed beside him, "They are, honey girl. But I ain't going out there. I can't."

"I told you to put on some clothes."

"This is my house, Marcella. They should have knocked." He kissed me and stood. Then he opened the window that was on the back wall and started to climb out.

"Where are you going?" I cried

"I'm going to the outhouse and then I got some other business to tend to out here. Don't worry about me. Just go on and have a visit with your cousin."

I watched him climb out the window and went back around the curtain. Margaret was now sitting in the orange rocking chair, Shane was in the armchair and the boys were sitting in front of the fireplace. I walked to the table to try to finish my biscuits and Margaret said, "I see you're making biscuits."

"Trying to," I answered.

"I can make some good biscuits. Want me to help you?"

"Oh please. I never made biscuits."

Margaret stood, "You got an apron?"

"No, I've got to get one. We got some towels though."

"One of those will do."

I got Margaret a big towel from the cabinet and watched as she took over the cooking. She looked at the eggs I'd already cracked, "Were you planning on cooking eggs too?"

"Yeah, I was gonna scramble them for breakfast."

"Breakfast!" Shane exclaimed, "You just now cooking breakfast? 'Cella, it's time for dinner." I didn't reply and he said, "So where's your husband? Can't find any clothes?"

"He's got clothes," I said. "He had to take care of some things outside."

Shane stood, "Maybe I should go help him."

"I don't think he needs any help," I said. Then, thinking of something, I asked, "How did y'all get here? I didn't hear a car drive up."

Margaret was putting the biscuits in the oven, "That's because once I saw that path we were supposed to drive up here on, I told Shane to park the car on the side of the road and let's walk."

"Oh."

Margaret got busy with the eggs, "You sure ain't got many eggs cracked, 'Cella."

"Me and Jesse didn't want that many."

"Well we're here now. You got any more?"

I got the bowl from the ice box. Margaret cracked all but four of the eggs left in the bowl and began whipping them all up together. While she was working, she said, "Oh, I almost forgot. We bought you a present. It's right over there. Open it up."

She pointed to the package she'd brought in earlier. It was laying on the corner of the table. I picked it up and sat in one of our table chairs to open it. Inside was a clock to hang on the wall. It was all pretty with a silver and gold colored oval frame around it. "You like it?" Margaret asked.

"Yes, thank you."

"It chimes every hour," Shane said. "But you and Jesse have to keep it wound."

"I really like it. I'll get Jesse to hang it up," I said.

It was quiet in the room. The boys, Bill and Will seemed bored and finally Shane said, "So, tell me, how did you and Jesse meet?"

I started telling him, all the while thinking of Jesse outside, wondering just what he was doing. I wanted to go check on him, but I was stuck here. Shane and Margaret kept talking to me. The boys began chasing each other around the room. They started to go behind our curtain but Shane stopped them. Shane was asking me what Jesse did for work and while I was telling him, Margaret announced, "Food's ready, let's eat!"

I stood, still holding the clock, "I need to find Jesse." I took the clock to our room, left it on the bed and walked out to our front porch. I didn't see Jesse anywhere. I called him but he didn't answer. I walked off the porch to our outhouse but he wasn't there either. I called and called but he never answered. Worried outta my mind I went back inside. "Is he coming?" Shane asked.

I swallowed hard, not wanting to cry in front of them. Not wanting them to know that I hadn't been married two whole days and already had no clue where my husband was. "Later," I replied and sat down.

I ate very little, watching them eat like they ain't ate in ages. Margaret finally stopped Will from getting anymore eggs, "We gotta leave some for Jesse, honey. He ain't ate yet."

"Who's Jesse?" the little boy asked.

"He's 'Cella's new husband," Margaret said. "Remember we told you two all about 'Cella and her new husband we were coming to see."

The other little boy Bill piped up, "He the man with no clothes?"

I felt so shamed. Shane laughed, "Sure was, son."

"Why he not wear clothes?" Will asked.

I didn't answer. Margaret changed the subject by saying, "Madge says you're having a baby." I nodded, wanting Jesse to come in the front door.

"When's it coming?"

I shrugged, "The best me and Mama can figure February or March next year. I ain't really sure."

"I hear Jesse's daddy had one more fit over you two having this baby," Shane said.

"He sure weren't happy." I said, looking toward the door.

Margaret grinned, "Don't let it worry you, 'Cella. We got married in April and these two here came in July. I was already big by the time we said I do. You're alright."

I nodded again. Margaret began talking about the pain and horror of childbirth, scaring me half to death and Shane and the boys got up from the table and settled themselves into our sitting chairs once more. I was beginning to think they were never leaving. That I'd be stuck here with them and Jesse wandering around outside cause he was too embarrassed to show his face in front of them until the end of time.

But finally, at last Shane stood, "Margaret we need to be heading on. 'Cella, you and Jesse come to Wilmington sometime to visit us."

"Alright," I said, standing and following them to the door.

Margaret hugged me goodbye and when Shane hugged me, he whispered, "You tell that husband of yours I've seen plenty of naked men. He sure ain't the first. Tell him don't let it bother him."

"I'll tell him," I said and walked out on the porch with him. I watched them walk down the path until they passed the little curve in the road where I couldn't see them anymore unless I moved.

Then I sat on the steps and cried so hard my whole body hurt from it.

I'd been crying for awhile when I felt Jesse put his hand on my back, "Hey, what you crying for?"

I wiped my eyes and looked up at him. He was carrying a tool bag and was sitting some boards beside me. I didn't answer him and he asked, "Are they gone?"

"Yeah," I said, sniffling.

"Good," he sat beside me.

Suddenly I was so mad I couldn't see straight. I began hitting him and hitting him. Jesse grabbed my hands and pulled me on his lap, "WHOA! Settle down, 'Cella. Settle down! What are you hitting me for?"

"Why did you leave me? I looked all over for you! Why did you leave me!"

"Leave you? Marcella, I never left you. I got out of the house because of your whacky relatives, but I never left you."

"Well where was you?" I still cried.

Jesse wiped my eyes, "I went walking in the woods a little bit. That's all, 'Cella. I love you. I ain't gonna leave you. Okay."

I nodded some more still sniffling. Jesse kissed me. "But I gotta tell you something, 'Cella. I ain't putting up with you hitting me. I ain't gonna be hitting you and you ain't gonna be hitting me. Understand?"

"Yes," I said, wondering how I was gonna control myself.

He kissed me again, "Good. We ain't gonna have that kind of marriage. Now let's go inside. I'm starving and I have some work to do."

When we got in, Jesse looked at the little bit of scrambled eggs left and said, "Is this all we got?"

"We got some biscuits too," I said, thinking it was good I'd made up so much biscuit dough. We still had eight biscuits left.

He shook his head, but sat down and ate the rest of the eggs, three biscuits and washed it all down with a cup of water cause that's all we had to drink. Then he grinned, "Pretty good food, 'Cella."

"I didn't cook it. Margaret did. I just mixed up the dough and she took over."

"Well I bet it's the way you mixed up the biscuit dough that made them so good."

I didn't say anything. I knew I couldn't cook. I waited a little bit and then said, "Jesse, we only have four eggs left."

"FOUR!" He yelled, "Vicky gave me two dozen eggs. Why is there only four left?"

"Margaret cooked them."

"She cooked all those eggs and that little bit was all I had left to eat?"

"Yeah. I'm sorry. I didn't know how to handle them. I wanted you to be here to take care of things but you...."

Jesse scratched his head. "I gotta see about getting us our own chickens so we can have some eggs of our own around here." He stood. "And as for your barging in uninvited relatives, I'm gonna take care of that problem right now. We ain't gonna be having no one just come in on us. It ain't right. We could be taking a bath or whatever and have them come right on in on us being that they don't know how to knock."

"I need you to empty the water outta the sink for me."

"Sure," Jesse said. He got the sink and I opened the door for him. He went outside; dumped the water over the edge of the porch, brought the sink back, put it in place in its little cabinet and walked outside again. He soon came back with the boards and that tool bag he'd had on the porch. "Where'd you get all that?" I asked.

"I got the wood to fix our house with. Had the left over pieces piled up out back. Bought the tools from Simpson so I could fix the house. They're what I did this whole place with."

"You been keeping them tools outside too? They weren't in here."

Jesse smiled at me, "No, 'Cella, I ain't keeping them outside. We got a little shed attached to the back of the house. Ain't you seen it on your way to the outhouse?"

"Ain't paid it no mind."

He bent down and kissed the top of my head, "It's there. Got a shovel, hoe and rake in it. Broom's out there too and so is a big washtub for us to take baths in. You'd better start paying attention honey girl. Especially out here in the woods like we are. Don't want you getting snake bit."

I got to work getting water ready for the dishes and Jesse began making measurements at the door. I watched him and asked, "What are you doing?"

"Making a lock. Gonna fix this board up where it will barricade the door when we're inside so no one can come in on us in our private moments. Ain't ever gonna let that happen again."

Chapter Fourteen

For supper that night, I cooked up some more peas and corn and burnt them to the bottom of the pots again, but once again, we scrapped out the good parts and soaked the pots overnight. We had left-over biscuits too so the meal was more filling. The next morning, I scrambled the four eggs, burning them too, but Jesse didn't say a word, just ate like he was starving. Then he helped me with the pots in the sink, helped me get more water going so I could soak the burned frying pan where I'd cooked the eggs and kissed me goodbye, saying he had to go to work. He was going to help crop tobacco on the Jansan farm. I didn't want him to go but he said he had to. He asked if I wanted to go and I told him no, I didn't know those people and wouldn't feel comfortable.

Once he left, I went outside and walked around back to check out that shed he said we had. I got the broom and took it back in to sweep the floor. I swept the whole floor in no time and instead of taking the broom back out to that shed, I propped it up in the corner. Then I sit in Gran's old rocker and admired the clock Shane and Margaret gave us. Jesse hung it up on the wall opposite our chairs so we could look and see what time it was. It was pretty and made the whole place look better somehow.

I was just sitting there, looking at the clock and wondering what to do with myself when I heard a knock on the door. The knocking scared me cause like I told Jesse, none of my people ever knock. They just come right on in. I looked out the side window to try to see who was there but I couldn't see the porch from here. The knocking continued. I went back to the door and lowered Jesse's board barricade into place, then crouched down to where I could look through the crack under the door. What I saw scared me. There was the long flowered dress of Witch Sue. I backed up all the way to our divider curtain; trying to keep quiet so she wouldn't hear me.

Witch Sue finally stopped knocking and hollered, "Child, I know you're in there. If you want to keep that baby you got coming, it's fine with me. I just want payment for your visit and for the leaves I gave you to chew. That's all I'm here for—payment. I'm sure you got something of value."

Nervous I looked around. The only thing we had that even looked valuable was the clock and there was no way I wanted to part with that. I kept quiet and still, hoping she'd go away. Then I noticed her face trying to peak in our side window. I slipped behind the curtain, scooted across the floor and hid under the bed. I just lay there for the longest time listening to Witch Sue holler about how I owed her money. I wondered how she found out I was here at Miz Essie's old place, but then she was a witch and probably knew everything. I closed my eyes and prayed hard that she wouldn't cast a spell on me. I fell asleep and woke up hungry so I slowly crawled out from under the bed and cautiously peaked out our back window. There was no one there. I went back into our main room, looked out the side window and again saw no one. My mouth and throat dry with fear; I walked to the door; lifted the board and opened it just a little. Witch Sue must have gone home because she wasn't on the porch. I felt a little relief. Then I saw the paper tacked up on our door. I tore it down but couldn't get the tack outta the door. I didn't read the paper until after I brought it back inside. It said, "I will be back for my payment. You can count on it. Sue Jones."

I wadded up the paper and stuck it in my pocket. I'd never told Jesse I owed her anything. Just about me going to her and what she did, but I'd never said a word about her wanting me to pay her something. Scared she might come back, I put the board back in place. Then I ate our last left over biscuit for dinner and sat in the rocking chair, rocking away, wanting to go outside and collect me some leaves and flowers like I'd always done when I was bored, but I was too afraid to go outside. So I stayed inside. I dusted, scrubbed the table, swept the floor again, arranged everything in the cabinet the way I wanted it, and even cleaned the top of my stove. By the time I was finished I was bone tired and couldn't hold my eyes open. Forgetting all about the board across the door, I went to bed, falling asleep at once. I slept hard until I felt Jesse shaking me, calling my name. I opened my eyes to see him standing over me. "You okay, honey girl?" he sounded worried.

I nodded a little, sitting up. He sat beside me, "What you got the front door barricaded for? I had to climb in the window." He hugged me.

I pushed him away, "You're all sweaty and smelly, Jesse. Ugh!"

"I been working all day. Of course I'm all sweaty and smelly. I'll take a bath soon. Just tell me what you got the door barricaded for."

I looked down and told him about Witch Sue. I showed him the paper she'd tacked to the door too. "I was scared," I said. "I ain't got no money to pay her."

Jesse read it and balled it up again. "I'll pay her something as soon as I get paid some money. But she's just gonna have to wait until then. I want you to come with me tomorrow, 'Cella. I don't like the thought of you here all by yourself. I kept thinking about it today. While we was in the field, Simpson kept talking about how Alice is having to stay at the house with Grandma Cal because poor old Grandma Cal is just too old and feeble to even think about working tobacco anymore. We got so much work to do in those fields even missing one person is hurting us. So I talked with Simpson and he says he'll pay you to come stay with Grandma Cal while we work in the field."

I stood, "Jesse, I don't know the first thing about taking care of no old white woman."

"It won't be hard, honey girl. All you gotta do is make sure she don't fall or nothing. Alice will have food cooked so you won't have to worry about that. You just gotta sit with her and watch out for her. Simpson's gonna pay you and we could really use the money, honey girl."

"They got other people around there too, don't they? Like that man—what's his name who runs that store—what about his wife? I ain't ever heard you talk about her working in the fields. Why don't she take care of her."

"You mean Clyde and Wanda. She's done it some, but they've got those two little girls and the youngest one is now walking around and getting into everything. The last time she tried it, Grandma Cal nearly tripped over little Sharon. Simpson says he thinks it would be best if they had someone to watch her who didn't have small children."

"We gonna have our own baby sometime, Jesse."

"That's sometime, 'Cella. Right now, it's inside you so it won't be tripping up nobody." He paused for a long time. "Come on, honey girl. Please say you'll do this. I'll feel better having you close by and we'll make a little extra money too."

I looked at him and only because I loved him so much said, "Okay, I'll do it."

Chapter Fifteen

I didn't ask Jesse how his day had been until later on when he was taking a bath and I was trying once again to cook. He'd brought some cold fried chicken from the Jansan's, more eggs and some milk and butter home from the Duvall's. I was cooking butterbeans and more rice. I was trying not to get the stove too hot so it wouldn't burn. I was watching everything real careful and Jesse was scrubbing hisself in the big washtub he'd brought inside. He'd piled his dirty clothes up on the floor by the washtub. I got our dishes to eat off of from the cabinet, put them on the table and said, "Our dirty clothes are piling up, Jesse. We got dirty clothes in the bedroom, dirty clothes in here—I gotta them washed somehow."

Jesse nodded, "Tell you what, honey girl. After we get supper dishes cleaned, we'll put the clothes in the sink to soak overnight."

"What if I burn the food again? We been letting the pots soak overnight."

Jesse used a cup to pour water over his head, "Well then, we'll just put the clothes in to soak in the morning before we head over to the Jansan's to work."

I still didn't want to go to work with him but I didn't say anything. I walked back to the stove, "How did you get along with Leroy today? Wasn't he there?"

Jesse was washing his hair, "Oh he was there. Didn't say the first word to me and I ain't spoke to him either. Everyone else talked to me and asked all about how me and you was doing but old Leroy acted like I weren't even there so I did the same right back to him." He poured water on his head to rinse out the soap.

All of a sudden there was a real hard knocking on the door. We had our board barricade in place and it was moving as someone was trying to get in while they was knocking at the same time. Jesse jumped up and grabbed the towel he had next to the washtub, "MAN! Can't have no peace at all! Didn't realize I'd moved to Grand Central Station!"

"Oh Jesse!" I said, thinking maybe Witch Sue was back for her payment.

The knocking and door rattling kept on. Jesse got out of the tub dripping water on the floor. As he went behind the curtain, he said, "See who it is, 'Cella, before they knock the door down."

Jesse disappeared behind the curtain and I walked to the front door. "Who is it?" I called nervously.

To my relief I heard my Aunt Elmira say, "It's us, Marcella. Let us in."

I moved the board and opened the door. In came my Aunt Elmira and my cousins Fay-Anna, Helena, Crusoe, and Terrance. Fay-Anna was carrying a large package. Aunt Elmira was waving herself with her hat, "Girl what you got this place locked tight for? And hot! Lord Jesus it's hot in this place! No wonder poor old Jesse been running around stark naked! Man couldn't bear to wear clothes in this heat! Girl you trying to cook that baby you got inside you or something? WHEW!" She kept waving her hat and talking. "Fay-Anna, where's your manners child? Give 'Cella the present we brought her. Go on now, give it to her."

Fay-Anna handed me the package and Aunt Elmira said, "I was gonna give you that Saturday but y'all got away before I could." I opened my mouth to say thank you but Aunt Elmira wouldn't let me say a word. "It's just way too hot in here! That's all there is to it. Let's get this window over here open all the way. Helena, prop open that front door there to get some air in this place. 'Cella, where's poor Jesse? You done cooked him or something? Oh, I see you got supper on the table. Been cooking chicken, huh? Where'd you get the chicken? Is that some of chicken Terby cooked for your reception? Terby makes some good chicken. Came up with the recipe all on her own and won't give it to nobody. I fried my own chicken Friday night. Sure did. Done killed that sorry rooster that thought he had to crow his fool head off at one in the morning. One in the morning! Night just as dark as can be and that crazy rooster out there crowing his lungs out right outside my bedroom window. Had all I could take of it the other night. Woke up Calvin—you know Calvin could sleep through the atomic bomb—and told him get out there and kill that fool rooster before I do it. He went right on out there and shot that rooster cause Calvin's learned I mean business." She paused to catch her breath and saw at the same time I did, my little cousins Crusoe and Terrence standing in Jesse's bath water. Aunt Elmira yelled, "Get outta there! Get outta there before I go get me a switch! Lord, you boys are gonna be the death of me. Come on, get outta that water." They did and Aunt Elmira kept talking, "'Cella, you been taking a bath? What you got the bath water left in the middle of the floor for? Don't you know you're supposed to dump out the water once you finish? Just like Madge ain't you? Leave stuff around until you absolutely have to do something with it. I ain't like that one bit. Madge, Callie, and Terby are all like that. Me, Eliza and Zona Mae ain't. We all take after Mama, but the rest of them take after Daddy. Don't do nothing unless they're forced into it."

I wished Jesse would come in here. I really needed him now. My cousins Helena and Fay-Anna had already helped themselves to some chicken. Terrence and Crusoe saw them and got drumsticks for themselves. "Me and Jesse ain't ate yet," I said but no one listened to me.

Aunt Elmira walked to the stove. "What you got cooking over here, 'Cella? Let me look in these pots. Lord child, you gotta turn up the heat on this stove some or this food ain't ever gonna cook. That's why you got it so hot in here? Trying to cook with just air? Is that why you keeping it so hot?" She laughed hard. "Let me show you how to cook this food proper. Come on over here child; can't show you how to do nothing with you clean on the other side of the room."

I looked toward the curtain, thinking by now Jesse had probably climbed out the back window again. I put the package in the armchair and went to Aunt Elmira at the stove. She grabbed my hand. "See you put the rice in the pot and cover it with water until the water comes up to here on your fingers. Now don't stick your fingers all the way to the bottom of the pot. Just to the top of the rice. And when you cook it, you start it off with a high flame to get the water boiling good. Then you turn it down, cover the pot with a lid and leave it be. You can check it every now and then but don't be stirring it or no mess like that. There are two basic steps in cooking and they are—start out high, and then turn down when the food starts boiling. Then you just keep an eye on it until it gets done. You do that and you can cook most anything. Didn't Madge ever tell you nothing?"

Right then I heard, "Move." I turned to see Jesse—fully dressed in jeans and a blue shirt—standing by the washtub. He was talking to Crusoe and Terrence who were standing in the water again. They listened to Jesse and got out, making little wet footprints on the floor.

"Oh, hey there, Jesse!" Aunt Elmira said. "See you got some clothes on now. Shane and Margaret came back by Sammy and Madge's yesterday. Told us all about how you was running around here nothing on." She laughed hard.

Jesse looked mad as he drug the washtub to the door. I followed him outside and watched as he dumped the water over the edge of the porch. "Jesse....honey...." I said.

He shook his head, "Later, 'Cella." He went back inside and I went inside with him. Fay-Anna and Helena were in the rocking chairs each one chewing away on a drumstick. Crusoe and Terrence were sitting by the fireplace each one with a chicken wing and Aunt Elmira was stirring the butterbeans on the stove. Jesse looked at the plate the chicken had been on. There was only one chicken wing left. He reached over and held it up, "Which one of you pigs wants this?"

Aunt Elmira held her spoon in midair. "What did you say there, Jesse? Did you call my children pigs? Pigs? Did you?"

"Yes ma'am I sure did," Jesse said, his eyes blazing.

"Well who in the world do you think you are calling my children pigs? Let me tell you something, boy...."

"No, you wait a minute..." Jesse said in a very controlled voice, "You let me tell you something. I been working hard all day long. Vicky Jansan gave me that chicken for me and 'Cella to eat. I come home tired and hungry. Try to take a bath and get interrupted by you rude pigs...."

I tried to interrupt by saying, "Jesse..."

He just looked at me and kept on, looking right at Aunt Elmira, "You asked who I think I am. I'll tell you who I am. I'm Jesse Jenkins and this is my home. And 'Cella is my wife now. That food on the table was our food—for me and my wife—not for all of 'Cella's relatives who just take the notion to drop in and eat everything we got!"

Aunt Elmira laid the spoon on the stove. "This is the thanks we get Jesse? After all Calvin did to help you get gas hooked up to this place so this stove would work. Your own Daddy wouldn't lift his hand to help you so all of us have been doing our best for you. And now, this is the way you're gonna treat us?"

"I am grateful for all you've done. So's 'Cella. I already thanked Calvin for helping me with the stove. I know he helped a lot and I really appreciated it. But that don't mean y'all can come in here and eat my supper right off my table before I even have a chance to taste it!" Jesse was clearly angry.

And so was Aunt Elmira. She shook her head, "Alright. I can see we ain't welcome. I see that plain as day. Fay-Anna, Helena, Crusoe, Terrence, all y'all come on. We going home. Ain't coming back either!" She began walking to the door and the children followed. At the last second though, Aunt Elmira came to me, "Honey, I'll be praying for you." She hugged me hard.

"Thank you for the present," I whispered.

"Aw, it ain't much. Just an apron and some dish towels and diapers for the little one coming." She looked at Jesse who was still holding the chicken wing. Then she kissed me, "I'll do my best to see you when I can.

"You can come back," I said.

"I don't think so, child. You might want me, but your stuck up husband here sure don't. He made that plain as day. Calling my sweet children pigs. Just cause they ate a few little pieces of chicken! The nerve of him! Especially after all we've done! I reckon I see now why Leroy refused to lift a finger to help him. He knew how ungrateful he was. Knew he'd be wasting his time to do anything!" She called her children again and they followed her out the door.

I stepped out on the porch and watched them walk down the path in the full light of the moon. Then I went back inside the house. Jesse was sitting at the table, still holding that chicken wing. I didn't say anything. I just walked to the stove and checked the butterbeans and rice. They were done and the pots weren't even burned. I took the pots off the stove and sit them on the table on top of a towel so they wouldn't burn the table. Then I got our forks from the cabinet and sat down to eat.

Jesse didn't say anything either. He just got up, closed the front door and barricaded it again. He sat back down and began putting rice and butterbeans on his plate. He got up and got a container of milk from the icebox and poured some into two glasses. He gave me a glass and sat back down. Then he put the chicken wing on my plate and began to eat.

Crying I looked at the chicken wing and pushed it aside. Jesse didn't look at me as he said, "Eat it, 'Cella. And go on and get you some more food. You need to eat good for the baby."

I got some rice and was starting to get some butterbeans when I began to cry so hard I was shaking. Jesse put down his fork, "Come here."

I didn't go. I just dropped the spoon I'd been holding and kept right on crying. Jesse got up; came to me and pulled me up from my chair. Then he sat back down with me on his lap. He held me close. Just held me, kissing my head and face for a long time. After a long while he said, "I love you 'Cella. I really do. But this thing of your relatives coming here right when we're getting ready to eat and then them eating up our food has got to stop."

I wiped my eyes, "They did knock."

He looked at me, "Only because we had the board across the door, honey girl. If that board hadn't been there, they'd came right on in here with me in the tub. That bunch ain't got no manners to speak of."

"I'm sorry. I didn't tell them to come here."

"I know you didn't. I don't mind your people coming to visit...but..." He stopped and started kissing me. He kissed me for a long time and then said, "Let's eat our supper, honey girl and get to bed. I got another long hard day of work tomorrow and you're gonna have your first day of watching Grandma Cal."

Chapter Sixteen

Well, here I am, sitting on this fancy couch in these white people's fancy house. And I do mean fancy. They got the place painted all shiny white outside with green shutters. They got a great big covered front porch—not just steps but a place big enough for a whole bunch of children to run and play. They got a swing, benches, and chairs on that porch like an outside living room. Inside they got plants in the corners and flowers on the tables. Everything looks scrubbed to death and you can smell furniture polish. I bet they go through a bottle a day the way you can smell it so strong.

When me and Jesse first got here this morning, they all started falling all over Jesse, saying hi, good to see you, like they ain't laid eyes on him in forever and he was just here yesterday. They were like that with me too, but I didn't take it in like Jesse did. He was all happy, acting like they're family. He kept grinning all over the place and all happy. Then—Jesse, along with the bald man called Simpson, his wife Alice (who liked to have worn herself out giving me instructions on how to do this and that) and that Bob—all left me with this sleeping old woman so they could go work. As they left they was all talking and laughing away about something Preacher Carl called and told them about. I ain't sure what it was cause I was trying to get all of them instructions that woman gave me straight in my head, but it musta been awful funny the way they was carrying on. Jesse waved good-bye to me all happy and chuckling as they went out the door. But I don't think he stayed all Mr. Happy Happy because not long after they went out, I saw Mr. Leroy's car driving by real slow so he could drive up into the Jansan's yard. Mr. Leroy probably knocked that happy happy outta Jesse right fast.

Once they was all gone, I just sat on the couch, looking around. The old woman I'm supposed to be watching was sleeping away in the rocking chair. I hope she sleeps all day so I ain't gotta do nothing with her at all. I got up and went to the kitchen and looked inside their refrigerator. It was packed full of food. Hungry I helped myself to a slice of ham. I stood at the refrigerator eating it. I ate two slices and was reaching for another when I heard that old woman, "Girly, what you doing?"

I turned to see her standing in the door with her cane. "Mrs. Alice said I could eat some of this food in here if I got hungry."

"Ain't got no problem with you eating," she said, moving slowly into the room. "Problem's with you standing there with that icebox door wide open. Letting all that cold air out into the room. Them things cost money to run."

I closed the door, thinking these people had plenty of money to spare. I didn't say anything, but that old woman looked at me and said, "What's your name?"

"Marcella. Everyone calls me 'Cella though."

She nodded, "Well, let's go on in here and talk. I gotta get to know anyone who's gonna be sitting with me. Although I don't need no one sitting with me. But gotta please Alice. Half what goes on around here is done just to please Alice." She turned and began moving slowly back towards the living room. Once she got past the door she turned around, "Come on, I want to talk with you. If you gonna stay with me, you gotta mind."

I sighed and followed her. We got to the living room and she settled herself into the rocking chair again and I sat on that couch. She stared at me, "So, you married our Jesse." She said that just like he was theirs.

I fought the urge to tell her he weren't theirs and simply said, "Yes ma'am."

She rocked her chair. "I got me an interest in anyone marrying one of my boys." I just stared at her. She rocked her chair some more. "So, tell me about yourself."

I shrugged, "Ain't much to tell...."

"I hear you belong to Sammy and Madge Lewis. Part of that Lewis and Ballard clan."

"Yes ma'am."

She stopped rocking, "Hear that bunch goes through husbands and wives like flies. Hear there's been a lot of divorcing and remarrying in the crew you come from."

"Not all of them," I said, trying to control my temper.

"What about that Bonelle—he's had a whole pile of wives. I've heard he's had so many they gonna start filling his marriage certificates out in pencil so they can erase it when he wants a new wife. And I hear that the rest of your bunch ain't much better. Just about all of them marrying and divorcing like they got a sale on it."

I sighed hard, "Uncle Bonelle's been married a lot. And so has my Aunt Zona Mae. But the rest of them ain't."

"What about that one y'all call Rayson? What about him? See I hear things cause my friend Bertha Hughes—she goes to church with me—her son Frank works at the register of deeds office in the courthouse. He says Rayson comes in quiet frequently to get marriage licenses or divorce papers. Says he comes in more often than anyone else around."

I wrung my hands together, "That's only because him and his wife Vera keep having fights. They get divorced and remarried all the time. But it's always to each other."

She gave me a strange look, "You mean to tell me that they get in a little fight, get divorced and then get remarried?"

"Yes."

"To each other?"

"Yes."

She rocked some more, "Well I reckon that explains what Bertha said Frank told her. He said the judge told Rayson he was gonna ban him from the courtroom. Said that he and Vera had to make up their minds to either stay married or divorced. That there weren't no rotating door on the courthouse."

She was quiet for a while and I just sat, doing my best not to explode.

At last she started to talk again. "So, tell me, do you plan on staying married to our Jesse or divorcing him all the time like your people seem to do weekly?"

I'd had all I could take. "First of all, he ain't your Jesse! He's my Jesse!"

"Hold up there, girly!" She held her hand up in the air. "I ain't trying to make you mad. Just telling you the facts. I know he ain't no blood kin, but that boy is mine in my heart. You might not understand that, but he is. Hallie and Leroy's been bringing him here since he was a tiny baby. Used to bring him in here and lay him on the floor with Bob and Todd. All three of them boys babies at the same time. Used to lay right there on that floor together on a little blue blanket. All of them sleeping all snuggled together. Grew up almost like brothers. I've held all three, burped them and changed their diapers—Jesse included. I watched them all grow up into young men. Bob's my very own grandson, true. But I love

Todd and Jesse just like they was mine. Both of them call me Grandma and I wouldn't have it any other way. So, you see, I got me an interest in you, little girly, because you've married my Jesse. I gotta learn all about you."

"Seems like you already know all about my family."

She nodded, "I know what I hear and I hear a lot. When Hallie and Leroy told us Jesse had gotten himself tied up with you, I started praying. I don't want any of my boys in no revolving door marriage."

I didn't say anything. I couldn't. If I opened my mouth, all kinds of bad things were gonna come out and I was trying not to let that happen. She grunted a little and said, "I hear you're having a baby. Is that so?" I nodded in reply and she said, "Have you asked for forgiveness?"

"Forgiveness?" I repeated. "What do you mean?"

She shook her head, "You're thick, ain't you girl. Ain't you asked for forgiveness for the sin you committed? Having relations without being married—that's a sin, you know." I kept quiet and she finally said, "Well, have you done any praying?"

"I prayed for there not to be a baby, and I prayed for God not to punish me too much for going to Witch Sue and...."

She cut me off, "You went to a witch? Ain't nobody told me that part. Mercy, child, you've really got problems. You said Witch Sue? That woman ain't one bit like Miz Essie used to be. Miz Essie was strange but she was on the Lord's side. This Sue—now I don't know from my own personal experience—I hear she's a voodoo woman if there's ever been one around here. What did she do to you, child?"

"She chanted over me and gave me some leaves to chew. She said they'd get rid of the thing growing inside me. I tried to chew them but they made me sick. So I told Jesse and we wound up married."

"Oh Lordy! Lordy!" she moaned, moving in her rocker, "You need to start praying child. You need to get yourself right with the Lord. That old witch probably cursed that baby you're carrying. You and Jesse need to get in church and go every chance you get. You ever been baptized?"

"No ma'am. We don't go to church much."

"You need to start. You need to get yourself saved. You gotta get Christ in your heart. He's the only one who can make sure your little baby is safe. Need to be baptized and turn away from all that sinful mess you been doing. Now what you and Jesse did is wrong, mind you. It's sin, no doubt, but there can be forgiveness. I had my talk like this yesterday with Jesse and he promised me you and him would be in church come Sunday morning. Now I want you to promise me the same thing. You got to for your sake and that little unborn baby. It ain't ever safe to go around a witch; but it's especially dangerous to go around one when you gonna have a baby. Witches are dangerous. When I was a little girl, there was this old witch woman around who went by the name of Silvana. And there was this young girl by the name of Carrie who was gonna have a baby. Carrie went to Silvana because just like you, Carrie weren't married. And just like you, she decided to do the right thing and get married. Only trouble was, Carrie never got herself right with the Lord and that poor baby was born with no arms or legs. Didn't live but a month or two. Drove Carrie so outta her mind she hung herself in the barn. I know you don't want that happening to you, so...."

I'd had all I was gonna take. Jesse had to take me home now or I was gonna walk. I got up and took off outta that fancy house. Then I started walking hard to the Jansan place. I'd knew where it was because Jesse had showed it to me. I walked with my head down, the anger building and building in me. I turned into their driveway, passed their house and barns, all in a hurry because I just wanted to go home. I finally reached the field where they were working. I saw Jesse and hollered, "I want to go home!"

He stopped what he was doing, looked at me, and hollered back, "Marcella, we can't go home now."

"Well I ain't staying here!" I stomped my foot hard.

Everyone stopped what they were doing and watched us. Jesse shook his head and started coming out of the field to me. "What's wrong with you?" he asked, "You know I've got work to do. And you're supposed to be watching Grandma Cal."

"I ain't staying with that old woman another second!" I yelled. "I don't care how much money I'm supposed to be paid!"

That Alice was approaching me too, "Oh, honey," she was saying, "is she being difficult. I told her not to be difficult."

From across the field, Bob called, "Grandma Cal can't help but be difficult. It's the only way she knows how to be."

Jesse was at me now. He had a look on his face that let me know he didn't like what I was doing one bit. I crossed my arms, "I want to go home."

Jesse shook his head, "We ain't going home. Now you go on back up there to the house and we'll go home when I finish working."

"I want to go home now!"

"Marcella, don't do this here!" He spoke through clenched teeth.

I glared at him, "Fine! I'll just walk home then!"

I turned and started walking but Jesse soon turned me back around. "You're not walking home, Marcella. Don't cause problems." He looked hard at me, and then looked around at everyone else who was staring away at us. Alice was standing right outside the field now, wringing her hands together and biting her lip like her mouth was itching to talk. But she said nothing. Jesse held my arms tight so I couldn't move. "Come here," he said, and pulled me behind the old blue truck they had parked by the field. "Now you tell me what's going on."

I told him as fast as I could what that crazy old woman was saying and he just sighed, "'Cella, she's an old lady. You gotta overlook things like that with her. Just go on back up there and do your best not to pay any mind to what she says. But we're not going home now."

I stared back at him, "I don't like being there with her."

"You're embarrassing me, 'Cella. Please go on back up there. I'll get you when I'm finished and we'll go home."

Before I could protest, we both heard a soft voice, "Jesse, Jesse," and looked to see a young girl about my age standing off from us. She had thick curly hair pulled back into a ponytail. "Daddy says I can go back to Grandma Cal with 'Cella. I'll stay there with her today so she can get used to being around Grandma."

"Alright, Lilly Jean," Jesse seemed relieved. Like this girl going back with me was gonna make everything right. He put his hand on my shoulder, "'Cella, honey girl, this is Lilly Jean. She's only a month younger than you. You two can be friends."

The girl smiled at me, "Sure, I'd really like to be friends with you. And I know how Grandma Cal can be. She can really get on your nerves."

I looked at Jesse and then started walking with that Lilly Jean. She kept talking about Grandma Cal, telling me all about how that crazy old woman used to carry a gun around everywhere she went, how she went crazy shooting at shadows and such. I listened and asked, "Does she still do that?" I was scared now she might decide to shoot me.

"No, she hasn't carried it around in years. You don't have to be afraid of her, she just seems scary but she's not really. I guess we're just used to her."

We got back to the house and old Grandma Cal was waiting on the porch. She poked her cane at me, "What did you take off running for?"

Lilly Jean spoke up, "Grandma, you scared her. You shouldn't have scared her."

"Scared her?" Grandma Cal exclaimed. "I ain't done nothing but tell her the pure truth and she took off outta here. Girl don't want to hear the pure truth I don't know what to think of her. Lilly Jean, what are you doing here? You're supposed to be working. James ain't gonna like you taking off and coming up here in the middle of work."

"He knows I'm here," Lilly Jean said. "He told me to come be with 'Cella for a while until she gets to know you better."

Grandma Cal grunted, "You can stay, Lilly Jean, but it ain't her that needs to get to know me better. It's me that needs to know her better."

Lilly Jean shook her head and opened the front door. "It's almost time for dinner. 'Cella, come on, let's get some dinner for the three of us. Grandma, since it's such a pretty day do you want to eat on the porch?"

"And have to hold my food in my lap? No thank you. I put an end to my eating outside when I put an end to my tobacco and other farm work. We'll eat inside at the table like decent folk."

"Yes ma'am," Lilly Jean said all nice and polite. She went inside and I followed her, doing my best to keep away from that crazy old woman.

I went with Lilly Jean to the kitchen and just watched as she got plates and glasses from the cabinet. "I still say she's a crazy old thing."

Lilly Jean was getting some food outta the refrigerator, "She can seem like that at times, but she's really a very sweet person. You just have to figure out how to handle her."

"I don't think I can ever handle her," I said, thinking of all she'd said about my family. "But Jesse wants me to watch her."

She put the food on the table, "Yeah, we do need someone to do it. I wished Daddy would let me because I can't stand working in that tobacco. I only do it because they make me. But I'd much rather stay here with Grandma Cal."

"Good, you can have the job."

She laughed, "I wish it was that easy, 'Cella." She smiled at me, "Tell me about your baby. My sister Libby's going to have a baby in January. If she has a little girl they're going to name her Rachel Victoria and if it's a boy he's going to be Randall Carl and they're gonna call him Randy."

I shrugged "Ain't much to tell. I reckon I'm gonna have one. I ain't as sick as I used to be and still ain't had my time, so I guess I'm having one."

"Haven't you been to a doctor?"

"No." I didn't tell her about Witch Sue. So far, this Lilly Jean was being nice to me and I wanted to keep it that way.

"Oh. Libby's been going to some doctor up where they live in Harris. That's close to Virginia. I miss her a lot. I wished they'd move back close to here. So, what are you going to name your baby?"

I shrugged again, "Ain't really thought of no names. Ain't had much time. First I started thinking I might be having a baby and seems like the next thing I knew, me and Jesse was standing in front of the judge saying I do. I haven't had time to think at all."

She was putting slices of ham, tomatoes and cucumbers onto three plates. "Maybe Jesse should take you to a doctor. Just to make sure everything is okay. When my Aunt Wanda had my little cousins, Betsy and Sharon, my Uncle Clyde took her to the doctor almost every month."

"Every month! Ain't no way I'm going to a doctor every month!"

She smiled some more, "Yeah, I know what you mean. I can't stand doctors. I had to go to the hospital when I was five and they ran all kinds of tests on me. Sticking needles in me all the time." She stopped and physically shuddered. "It was awful. I don't blame you for not wanting to go to a doctor that much."

I was starting to ask her what she went to the hospital for when that crazy old woman came to the door, "You girls plan on feeding me today or tomorrow? I could go out and grow the food faster than you're putting it on the plates."

"Food's all ready," Lilly Jean said sweetly. "Come on and sit down, Grandma Cal. All I gotta do is pour us some tea and we can eat."

She came in the room and sat in a chair at the table. Then she poked me again with that cane. "And just what are you doing? Looks to me like Lilly Jean is doing all the work."

"She's helping, Grandma," Lilly Jean said. "Don't be so hard on her."

"Hard on her? I ain't being hard on her. What's gonna be hard on her is her own life that she's sit up for herself."

Chapter Seventeen

I didn't say the first word all the way home and Jesse was quiet too. That was fine with me. I was mad with him and didn't care one bit if he was mad with me. I didn't care what he said; there was no way I was going back to sit with that crazy old woman again. Lilly Jean had taken care of her for the rest of the day and from what I saw she did a good job of it and got along with her fine too. She was the one who needed that job—not me.

We got home and Jesse stopped the truck and got out. He headed straight past the house towards the outhouse and I didn't say anything. I just let him go and I went inside the house. We hadn't put the board barricade down cause we were both gone all day long and weren't here for no one to visit. I went inside carrying a bag of ham and biscuits Alice gave me and sit them on the table. I didn't like having them feed me, but they sure were some good ham and biscuits. We had a bucket of cucumbers and tomatoes in the back of the truck Vicky gave Jesse. She'd asked if we wanted to stay for supper but I told Jesse no, I really wanted to go home. Jesse really didn't try to force me into eating with them. I think it's because he didn't want to eat with Leroy.

I sat down in Gran's old rocker and closed my eyes. I hated fighting with Jesse but he just had to understand how I felt. I opened my eyes, and that's when I saw the blank spot on the wall. I rubbed my eyes to make sure I was seeing straight and sure enough the whole wall was blank. I ran outside, hollering, "Jesse! Jesse! We been robbed! We been robbed!"

Jesse came outta the outhouse, "What do you mean, we been robbed."

"Just what I said. The clock Shane and Margaret gave us is gone."

"It probably ain't gone, 'Cella. It probably just fell off the wall. Let's go find it."

I followed him in the house and watched as he looked all over like that clock had legs and just went to hide in a corner or something all by itself. At last he shook his head, "You're right. It's gone. Why would someone come in here and....I bet it was that old witch woman. Had to be her. 'Cella, just what did you promise her when you went to her?"

"I didn't promise her anything. I wasn't even thinking about having to pay her nothing when I went to her. She asked me what I was gonna pay her and I told her I didn't have no money. She said she didn't need money and for the next time I came to bring two valuable somethings with me as payment."

"Well then, she's the one who got it. Came right in here and took it off the wall."

"I want it back. It's mine. Not hers. Shane and Margaret gave it to us."

Jesse nodded, "Well then, let's go talk with her. And the only way I can think of is we'll have to tell her that we'll pay her some real money when you get paid at the end of this week."

"Jesse, I ain't working no more this week. Not watching that crazy woman I ain't."

"Marcella, do you want that clock back?"

"Yes. I like that clock."

"Then that's the only way. James won't pay me until he gets his money from the tobacco when he takes it to market. So you gotta go watch Grandma Cal."

"Why don't you get another job?"

"And when am I gonna have time to do this other job?"

"You could quit doing that tobacco and get another job that pays you more often."

He shook his head, "No, I'm not doing that. I promised James I'd do this and that's all there is to it. Right now we got a lot of work to do—from now until James takes it to market. Then I'll get another job. But now helping in those fields and in the barn is my job. So you need to learn how to get along with Grandma Cal."

"Why don't I go ask my Mama and Papa for some money to pay her? I'm sure they will."

He stared at me hard just like he'd done when I came down to that field, "I'm gonna pretend I didn't hear that, Marcella. When I was working on fixing up this place for me and you I had plenty of time to think. And I made up my mind that I was gonna take care of you and our baby. We ain't going back to your people for money. Ain't no way."

I shook my head and followed him to the truck. We got inside and were quiet once again as we drove to Witch Sue's place. Jesse parked in the yard and got out of the truck. I got out and walked behind him, thinking of everything that crazy woman told me. I was scared it might be true. I didn't want to have no monster baby. I stayed behind Jesse as he knocked on the door. Witch Sue finally came, "My working hours are over," she said.

"Excuse me," Jesse said. "I'm Jesse Jenkins. You saw my wife Marcella a while back...."

She looked around Jesse and saw me then. "Ah, yes, little Marcella Lewis. I saw her once."

"Well, I understand you came out to our house yesterday to collect payment," Jesse said.

"I most certainly did. Have you come this evening to make that payment?"

"Uh....no..." Jesse stumbled over his words, cleared his throat and said more clearly, "We came by to get our clock back and to tell you that we'll be able to pay you at the end of the week."

"I will definitely be looking forward to the payment at the end of the week but I do not know anything about a clock."

I poked my head from around Jesse, "It's a real pretty clock that hangs on the wall. Someone stole it from us."

She gave a strange look "Are you accusing me of stealing? Sue Jones does not steal. Heal people, cast spells, cleanse possessed homes—I do a lot but I do not steal."

Jesse stepped back in front of me. "Would you have taken it for payment?"

"I would. But I did not steal it. I expect your payment by this Friday evening."

I was sure she had my clock. "If we pay you then, will you give us our clock back?" I asked from behind Jesse.

"I know nothing of your clock. And if I ever took possession of it for payment, it would be my clock, not yours." She closed the door hard.

Jesse shook his head, "Oh, 'Cella, why did you ever go to her? Why didn't you just talk with me in the first place?"

"I was scared. I wanted....I thought you'd be mad. I..."

"I wished you'd come to me first." He sighed deeply and we went back to Papa's truck.

We got in and I asked, "Do you think she has our clock?"

"Yeah, but we'll never see it again. And now we gotta pay her money too."

Chapter Eighteen

I don't think I'm ever gonna have any say so in nothing. No matter what I say or want, it don't matter one bit. There's always someone to force me into doing what they want me to and how I feel don't count at all. I thought things might be different with Jesse but they ain't. They ain't one bit different; cause here I sit with that crazy old lady again. I didn't speak to Jesse all morning long cause he said I had to come here again. Didn't cook breakfast either. Just poured me a glass of milk and let Jesse fend for hisself while I hung our clothes out to dry on the line he'd strung for us.

When we got here this morning, he weren't all happy happy and I know that's because of me, but I ain't happy happy either, so I don't care if he's upset or not.

They all left for work not long after we got here and Jesse didn't even so much as wave goodbye to me. I saw that crazy old woman nodding her head and mumbling something to herself as Jesse walked out the door without waving or saying goodbye to me. She was rocking away and I sat in the chair that was closest to the door so I could run out fast if I needed to. Also this chair was right by the electric fan they had running and it felt good to sit in the cool air. Grandma Cal rocked and rocked without saying a word and I sat there with cool air blowing on me. If we could just do this all day it wouldn't be so bad.

But then old Grandma Cal got up and fixed that fan so it wasn't blowing so hard. I stared at her and she said, "Sorry thing makes so much racket I can't hear myself think. Whole world's gone soft. Everyone thinks they gotta have air blowing on them all the time." She sat back in the rocking chair, "I turned that thing down so's we can talk. I noticed you and Jesse seem to be in a little tiff this morning."

"We're fine."

"I don't think so," she said. "I think you're ready for that revolving door of marriage your people love to go through. Yep, think it's already happening and y'all ain't been married a week yet." I didn't say anything. I had to think of a way to get outta watching this crazy woman every day. She kept talking, "What y'all fighting about?"

"Nothing."

"Sure seemed like something to me. I know Jesse. Like I told you yesterday he's been coming here since he was a tiny baby. He was sure upset about something." I still said nothing. She said, "Well, then, let's talk about you running out on me yesterday. You can't watch nobody if you run out on them. Why did you do it?"

I didn't answer. I was happy to hear the knock on the door. Even though it ain't my house I jumped up and answered the door. Lilly Jean was there. She smiled at me, "I talked Daddy into letting me come stay here with you and Grandma Cal again."

I felt so relieved. "Come in," I said.

"Lilly Jean, James letting you get out of work again? What's the matter with him?" Grandma Cal wanted to know.

"Nothing, Grandma," Lilly Jean said. She was carrying a big basket full of butterbeans, "I'm not exactly free from work. I've got to shell all these butterbeans. I was hoping 'Cella would help me."

Before I could say anything, Grandma Cal said, "Them butterbeans got dirt all over them. You ought to do those out on the porch."

"We will," Lilly Jean said. "Will you help me, 'Cella?"

"Sure." I hoped crazy old Grandma Cal would stay inside.

Lilly Jean smiled, "Let me get some bowls for us to shell them in. Grandma, do you want to help?"

My heart sank. Grandma Cal shook her head, "No. I ain't feeling like shelling no butterbeans. Think I'll go make a few phone calls. Feel like talking to Bertha or Louise—someone got some sense." She stood up from the chair and started toward the kitchen and I remembered seeing the telephone on the wall. Lilly Jean went to the kitchen too and I stayed where I was. Then she came back with two bowls and we went out on the porch together. We sit on the bench right by the living room window. "We can sit here and still look inside to check on Grandma Cal," Lilly Jean said, dividing the basket of butterbeans into our two bowls. We started shelling them, throwing the hulls into the basket and softly she asked, "Is Jesse feeling alright today? He doesn't seem like himself."

"He's probably mad at me," I said.

"Oh." She replied, not prying one bit.

I watched her for awhile. She was quiet as we worked. Then she said, "Bob's girlfriend is mad at him. She came by the house last night when we were eating supper. She was all dressed up and came in yelling about how he'd better learn to keep his promises to her. Bob got up and went outside with her but they were so loud we could still hear what they were saying. She claims Bob told her he would take her out to a movie and for dinner last night. Bob said she had to be mixed up about it because last night was Monday and they never go out on Monday. She says he promised but he never showed up. So she was going to the movies with Dale Horton. Bob said fine. Then they stopped yelling and Bob came in all red in the face. He didn't even finish eating his supper."

"Who's his girlfriend?" I asked, happy to get off the subject of me and Jesse.

"Nancy Smith. She thinks she's better than anyone else. She wouldn't even come when my Aunt Wanda's mama and daddy got married again because she wasn't in the wedding party. And she did the same thing when Libby and Carl got married. She says she should have been a bridesmaid and she'd already bought the dress. Just the other day she told Bob that we owe her money for that dress because she's never had a chance to wear it. But none of my people asked her to be a bridesmaid either time." She was quiet for a while and then said, "I like you a lot better. I can talk with you. I tried talking to Nancy once and she got up and left when I was right in the middle of a sentence. Like I wasn't even talking."

"She don't sound too nice." I said and shelled more butterbeans. At last I said, "Me and Jesse got robbed yesterday."

"WHAT?" Lilly Jean exclaimed, nearly dropping her bowl.

"Yeah someone came in and stole the clock my cousin gave us right off the wall. That was a pretty clock."

"Who do you think stole it?"

"Old witch woman."

She gave me a curious look, "A witch stole your clock?"

I nodded, throwing a bug bit butterbean away, "Uh huh. Old Witch Sue. I'm positive it's her."

"Why did she do that?"

I was quiet for a moment and then began telling Lilly Jean all about me going to see Witch Sue. She just listened, not saying I shouldn't have gone or anything. When I finally finished, she said, "Wow. I've never been to a witch. My Mama and Daddy wouldn't let me do anything like that."

"Mine didn't know I did it. I went on my own."

She nodded, tossing away a butterbean that had a big fat worm in it. "What are y'all gonna do about her stealing your clock?"

I shrugged. "Jesse says we'll never get it back and he wants to pay her some money on top of everything. I say he's wrong. She's got my clock she ain't getting none of my money. Old witch woman got all she's gonna get outta me. And besides, those leaves she gave me were so nasty there's no way anyone could get them down the way she wanted me too. Going to her didn't do what I wanted it to, so I shouldn't have to pay her anything."

"You went to her to make sure you weren't going to have a baby, right?"

"Yep, and I'm still having one so..."

"Do you want your baby?" she asked softly.

"I didn't at first, but I do now. I even been thinking about names. I was so mad at Jesse last night over him wanting to pay that sorry witch I couldn't sleep. I got to thinking about you saying your sister and her preacher husband already had names picked out for their baby. So I laid in bed and thought of names. I like Sabrina Suzanna for a little girl. I ain't thought up anything for a boy yet."

"Sabrina Suzanna Jenkins," Lilly Jean said, "That is pretty."

The front door opened and Grandma Cal stuck her head out, "You girls sure are awful slow with those butterbeans. I think you're talking more than you're working."

"We're working," Lilly Jean said. "That basket was packed full of butterbeans."

Grandma Cal stepped out onto the porch. She peered into our bowls and said, "Looks to me like neither of you are putting much effort into your work. Lilly Jean, I think I'll tell James all you're doing is coming here and talking to this Cellar girl all day long."

Lilly Jean spoke right up, "Her name is 'Cella, Grandma. And there's nothing wrong if we talk while we work. Everyone else does it. I promise you that if you go down in that field right now, they're talking with each other."

I was surprised at how bold Lilly Jean was with this crazy woman. Grandma Cal looked sternly at her though and said, "I do believe I'm gonna have to speak to James about you being so mouthy. Being around this Cellar girl has not been a good influence on you, Lilly Jean."

"Oh, Grandma," was all Lilly Jean said in return.

Grandma Cal grunted, "You can Oh Grandma me all you want, but I can tell James what you been doing up here and I know he'll take care of you."

Lilly Jean didn't say anything this time but I saw her roll her eyes as she shelled another butterbean.

Grandma Cal lifted her cane and tapped it on the porch, "Guess what I just learned, Cellar."

"My name is not Cellar," I said. "It's 'Cella. Short for Marcella."

"Don't get all huffy with me, child. I don't care what you call yourself. Cellar or Marcellar—don't make no difference to me. But I got something to tell you. You know that Aunt Hannah you got. Ain't she married to Wallace Imes?"

"Yes."

"Well they just filed for them a divorce. She claims he's been running out on her. So mark up another one for your crew."

I was silent. My whole family had known that Aunt Hannah and Uncle Wallace had been having trouble. Grandma Cal kept on, "Wonder how long they'll stay divorced. Wonder if they gonna do like Rayson and Vera and get married again, or if they gonna be like Bonelle and Zona Mae and get someone else. Tell you what, Cellar, your people keep the courthouse busy don't they?" I refused to answer and she said, "Know what I wonder? I wonder just how long it's gonna be before you and Jesse are up there standing in line behind the rest of your people filing for your divorce." I still said nothing and she turned to go back inside. "You girls better hurry up with those butterbeans. I want my dinner soon. If y'all don't soon get in here and do what you supposed to do, I'm calling Clyde over to the store and have him go fetch James so he can put you in your place, Lilly Jean. You supposed to be shelling them butterbeans and Cellar is supposed to be watching me. Both of you just running your mouth out here. Y'all don't know it, but I been watching you through the window. I been seeing what y'all ain't doing. So you'd both better straighten up or else."

Grandma Cal went back inside and I whispered to Lilly Jean, "Or else what?"

Lilly Jean looked into the window before she answered softly, "Don't worry about her. She's just like that. The other day when Libby and Carl were here she threatened to switch Carl because she'd asked him to go get her piece of pie and he didn't get up quick enough to suit her. She's always threatening people. Nothing ever happens."

"She threatened to switch a preacher? I didn't think you could switch a preacher."

Lilly Jean laughed, "Grandma Cal believes she can."

We finished shelling the butterbeans; still talking in spite of Grandma Cal and went inside to get dinner ready. I looked at the clock when we went inside and it was only 11:30 so I don't know what that old woman was complaining about.

All during dinner, Grandma Cal talked about my people marrying and remarrying and me going to Witch Sue. Lilly Jean kept trying to change the subject but Grandma Cal would start it all over again every chance she got.

After dinner, I helped Lilly Jean with the dishes and Grandma Cal went to sit in her rocking chair. While we were working, I asked Lilly Jean why she'd been in the hospital when she was five. She put the glass she was washing into the sink with the rinse water and said, "It's a long story. I got put in a well."

"A well? You mean like a well you get water out of?"

"Yes."

"I don't understand. How did you get put in a well?"

She started telling me. I just listened, finding it hard to believe that anyone would be that mean to a little child. We finished the dishes, wiped the counters down and swept the floor, with Lilly Jean talking the whole time. She still wasn't through by the time we cleaned the whole kitchen so we peeked into the living room and saw Grandma Cal asleep in her chair. "Let's go back out on the porch." Lilly Jean suggested.

I nodded and we went back outside and sat on the bench again. Lilly Jean kept talking and I kept listening. And the whole time I was listening to her I was thinking that Lilly Jean was the first white person I'd ever talked to so much. All the other white people I'd had anything to do with had been so hateful I couldn't stand them. But Lilly Jean wasn't like that so far.

Chapter Nineteen

Me and Lilly Jean talked until Grandma Cal woke up and came back out on the porch to see what we was doing. She complained up a storm about us talking so much, threatened again to call that man over at the store so he could get Lilly Jean's daddy, but she didn't. Instead she said, "No, think I'll punish you myself. Come inside."

I looked at Lilly Jean, scared and wondering what this crazy old woman had in store for us. We followed her into the house and into the kitchen. She told us to sit at the table and then went through a door that had been closed ever since I'd been coming here. I looked and saw a large shiny dark wood table with chairs that looked like it belonged in a mansion. Before long she called, "Lilly Jean, come here."

Lilly Jean just looked over at me before she left. I stayed at the table and waited, thinking I weren't gonna let that crazy old woman do anything to me.

Lilly Jean came back carrying a box. She sat it on the table. Grandma Cal was behind her with a small bottle of something and two rags, "You girls don't do nothing but talk and no work."

"Grandma, we shelled the butterbeans, got dinner ready and cleaned the kitchen...." Lilly Jean said.

"Yes and took forever doing it. Now, I want y'all to polish up every bit of this silver. And I'm gonna be sitting right in that living room listening. I been hearing y'all giggling and goofing off. And Lilly Jean I'm telling you if you don't start listening to me I'm calling Clyde so he can get James for me. Cellar, you may not know how to listen but you gotta learn." She sat the bottle of polish on the table and walked out.

Lilly Jean shook her head and opened the box. Inside were the prettiest forks, spoons and knives I'd ever seen; all nestled into their own special little sections, surrounded by red velvet. I stared at them thinking these people must have tons of money. Lilly Jean picked one up and said softly, "They don't even need polishing."

Grandma Cal called, "I heard that, Lilly Jean. You just begging for me to call Clyde ain't you."

"She got good ears for such an old woman," I said softly.

"She's got the fan off and I think she's right outside the door," Lilly Jean whispered.

We got to work polishing that silver that didn't need polishing at all. After just a moment or two we heard movement and Lilly Jean whispered, "She's finally gone to sit down."

We'd only polished a few pieces when there was a knock at the door. I had my back to it so I couldn't see who it was. But Lilly Jean smiled and called, "Wanda! Hi!"

I turned around to see the lady who'd carried the baby in that wedding. She was standing there holding a bigger baby, who I was pretty sure was the same baby, Beside her stood the little girl who'd been the flower girl at the wedding. That little girl was carrying a box.

Lilly Jean went to the door, "I'm so happy you came," Lilly Jean said, as she opened the door for them to come inside. "Grandma is having one of her very grouchy days. She keeps threatening to call Clyde to get Daddy because me and 'Cella are talking."

The lady laughed, "You know how she is, Lilly Jean."

The big baby she was holding was doing her best to get down. She even kept saying, "I down, I down, I down."

The lady just held tight to her and said to the other little girl, "Betsy, you can put the cookies on the table." Then she looked at the child she was struggling to hold, "Sharon, if I put you down, you have to be a good girl."

"I dood," the little girl insisted.

She put her down and Lilly Jean moved the polish back on the table out of her reach. The other little girl simply stood there not saying anything. Lilly Jean hugged her, "Hey, Betsy." Then she looked at me, "'Cella, this is my Aunt Wanda and my cousins, Betsy and Sharon."

"Hi," I said.

Wanda smiled at me, "I remember you from the weddings. I understand you and Jesse are married now."

"Yeah, we are. Thank you for the presents you gave us."

"Oh, you're welcome," she paused. "I came over to give Grandma Cal some of my coconut cookies. I just made them and I know how much she likes them. Where is she?"

"In the living room," Lilly Jean said. "I'll get her." She walked to the door but came right back, "She's sleeping again."

"Just let her sleep," Wanda said.

I watched as the smallest little girl toddled to the cabinets. Lilly Jean was saying, "Did y'all go to see Joyce and Harold Sunday?"

"Yes," Wanda said, looking at the smallest girl who was now sitting on the floor right at very bottom drawer of the cabinet. "No, no, Sharon," she said and then, "Yes, we went. Carson got baptized Sunday morning. We got up early so we could go watch him. Church was good but dinner was awful. Joyce tried to cook a pork roast."

"They're not hard to cook," Lilly Jean said. "Mama cooks them."

"Joyce had never cooked one before. Someone at their church told her how to do it. They told her to cook it in a 450 degree oven until it reached a temperature of 150 degrees. Well, Joyce bought a meat thermometer, but she got the instructions confused and thought she had to cook it until it got to 450 degrees inside. She had it cooking in the oven the whole time we were in church. When we got to the house after the services were over it smelled terrible. Harold started yelling at her and I asked what was she trying to cook. She told me about the pork roast then. I went to the kitchen with her and stood back as she took it out of the oven. It was burnt through. Totally black. But she stuck her meat thermometer in it and started to cry that it still wasn't done. By that time Harold was in the kitchen doorway and he was yelling that it was way beyond done. I didn't say anything to Joyce but for once, Harold was right. I asked her why didn't she think it was done and that's when she told me it hadn't reached 450 degrees yet. I looked at her thermometer and told her it didn't even reach 450 degrees and that I'd never heard of cooking something until it reached 450 degrees. Harold was calling her stupid and she was crying. Carson ran off to his room and Leo was saying some kind of silly mess about burnt offerings. Clyde finally got Harold and Leo to walk down to the lake with him and Betsy and Sharon to see the ducks. They tried to get Carson to go with them but he wouldn't come out of his room. I helped Joyce fix some other food. But the day was ruined. I felt so sorry for poor Carson. It was supposed to be his baptism celebration dinner and....."

Betsy interrupted her by pulling on her dress, "Mommy, look at Sharon."

Sharon had opened the drawer and was pulling out napkins and pieces of lace. Wanda shook her head, "Sharon Rose." She went to the little girl and picked her up, taking a long piece of lace out of her hand, causing the little girl to cry, "Mine! Mine!"

"No, baby, this is not yours," Wanda said.

"Mine!" the baby insisted. "Shar's." She kept reaching for the lace.

"No," Wanda told her again. The baby was struggling harder than she had been. "Stop it, Sharon. Don't make me spank you."

Lilly Jean went to them, "Hey, Sharon, can I hold you?"

Little Sharon reached for Lilly Jean, "Want Wilajean."

Wanda handed her over, "Good luck, Lilly Jean." She bent down and began putting the napkins and lace back into the drawer.

"Want mine! Want mine!" Sharon kept saying.

Wanda closed the drawer and stood straight, "I'm sorry. She is into everything. We have to pop Sharon's little hands all the time. She climbs on everything, pulls stuff out of drawers. We pop her but she still does it. Betsy hardly ever got into stuff like Sharon does. Pop her once and that's all it took, but Sharon will just hold her hand for a moment and try it again and again. Clyde says she looks like me but acts like he did when he was little. He had her and Betsy at the store earlier so I could bake cookies. But he called me to come get them...."

Betsy said, "Sharon was bad in the store. She was pulling stuff down and Daddy spanked her. Sharon screamed and screamed so Daddy called Mommy. I had to go too but I was being good."

I watched Lilly Jean holding Sharon who was struggling to get down and thought of my baby. I wondered if what old Grandma Cal said was true. Could that old Witch woman have messed my baby up somehow?

Wanda interrupted my thoughts by saying, "Would you like a cookie, 'Cella?"

I was surprised she offered me one, "I thought they were for Grandma Cal."

"You can have some too," Wanda said. She opened the box and handed me a cookie. I looked at it and then bit into it. It was pretty good. "How is it?" Wanda asked.

"Good."

Lilly Jean put Sharon down, but held tight to her hand. "I tried."

"It's okay," Wanda said. "We're going to have to go home. I've got to get supper cooked. Clyde's really busy at the store so he's probably going to be late but I've still got to get it done." She picked up Sharon again, "It was nice seeing you 'Cella. I hope we see each other again soon. Betsy, honey, come on." They walked to the door, and stopped. Wanda looked back, "Oh, Lilly Jean, do you know a first grade teacher named Mrs. Gates?"

Lilly Jean nodded, "Yes, why?"

"We got a letter yesterday saying she's going to be Betsy's first grade teacher. I was wondering how she is. I'm so worried about Betsy starting school this year."

"She's nice," Lilly Jean said.

"Good," Wanda ran her hand through Betsy's hair. "We're supposed to go out to the school next Monday night and meet her. Betsy's so shy…."

"I'm not going to school," Betsy said.

"Yes, you are, sweetheart," Wanda said. "You have to."

"I think it's good that you get to go meet her teacher," Lilly Jean said. "Are you taking Betsy with you?"

"Yes."

"That's really good. When I started school, I had no idea who my teacher would be. Todd took me to my room that morning; left me there and I cried all day."

"That's what I'm worried about. Hopefully she'll like her teacher and we won't have that problem. Well, we've got to go. Bye. 'Cella, it was nice meeting you."

I nodded and watched them go out the door.

Lilly Jean helped herself to a cookie, handed me one and put the top back on the bottle of polish. Then she closed the lid on all those fancy forks and spoons. "What are you doing?" I asked.

Before Lilly Jean could answer, Grandma Cal came into the room, "Don't close that lid before I inspect that silver, Lilly Jean." She came slowly to the table and looked into the box, "Good job. Looks like you worked hard. Now maybe that will teach you not to run your mouth so much when you're supposed to be working. Y'all got all this done in no time. I'm proud of you." She seemed happy. Me and Lilly Jean didn't bother to tell her that we'd only polished a few pieces. Grandma Cal noticed the box of cookies, "Where did these come from?"

"Wanda brought them over," Lilly Jean said. "She said you like them. You were asleep so we didn't wake you up."

Grandma Cal smiled, "Wanda is a sweet girl. Always doing nice things for everyone. Lilly Jean, hand me one of those cookies." As she ate the cookie she said, "See, you girls can get a lot accomplished if you really want. Wanda even came over and you still got all that silver polished." I looked at Lilly Jean and she just smiled at me.

The door opened and Simpson, Alice and Bob came inside. I was wondering where Jesse was when he finally came in. He looked tired. "You ready 'Cella?"

"Yes." It was the first thing I'd said to him all day. I walked to him and listened as he told everyone goodbye, promising to be back in the morning. Then I followed him out to Papa's truck. We got in and Jesse began to drive, just as silent as he was this morning. We drove through Cedar Cove like this without talking. At last, when we got into the colored section, Jesse spoke. He said, "We've got to quit being like this 'Cella."

"Being like what?"

He sighed, "All this being mad and not talking. It ain't good."

"I know," I said softly.

"Do you love me?" he asked.

"Yes."

"I wasn't sure lately....." He stopped talking. We were almost home. "How was your day with Grandma Cal?"

"She is a crazy old woman, but Lilly Jean is nice. I like talking with her."

"James was saying he doesn't know how long he's going to let Lilly Jean get out of work like she's been doing."

"I like her being with me," I said. "It's the only way I want to be with old Grandma Cal."

"'Cella, please."

"Jesse, that woman is...she's...well, she's just crazy is all. I need Lilly Jean there."

We drove down the path to our house. Now I thought of it as mine instead of Miz Essie's. Jesse stopped the truck in our little cleared yard area; leaned over and kissed me. And I let him even though he was all sweaty and smelly again. I let him because I do love him and I'd missed him all day.

We got out of the truck and walked up to our house. When we were climbing the steps to our porch, we saw a note stuck on the tack Witch Sue had stuck in the door. Jesse said, "What's this?"

I was scared it was another note from Witch Sue. But then, Jesse read it and said, "Aw, man, I'd forgot all about us having to take care of that icebox. Guess I'm just too used to having electricity." He paused, "This is a note from Hank Galloway, the iceman. He says he's come here the past two days and emptied our drain pan and put new ice in. Says he tried to come Monday but couldn't get it. We owe him for the ice and the work he's done. Why didn't you let him in Monday, 'Cella? You were here then."

I shrugged, "I had the board down and I was asleep some."

"He musta came when you were sleeping.

"Do we have any money?"

"A little. I guess I need to go talk with him. I can pay him some now...." Jesse went inside and I went in after him.

Jesse sat in the rocking chair that used to be Miz Essie's. "I'd really forgot all about that ice....Hey, 'Cella, maybe he's the one who took our clock and not Witch Sue. He has been in here."

I was looking in our icebox. We still had some eggs and milk in there. "I don't think he would do it," I said. "He's one of Papa's friends. He's a nice man. I don't think he's a thief. It was that Witch Woman."

"We can't be sure, 'Cella."

"It was her. And I want my clock back."

Jesse just sighed and stood, "Think I'll wash up some and go talk with Hank about this ice business. Why don't you get supper done while I'm gone, honey girl?"

"All by myself?"

"Sure, why not?"

I looked at that stove, not really wanting to cook anything. "I'll try."

Jesse came and kissed me, "Good."

Chapter Twenty

I tried to cook some more rice, butterbeans and corn. I burnt all of it. I thought of that woman who wanted her pork roast to get to 450 degrees and wished I had some kinda thermometer to tell me when the food was done. I burnt everything before Jesse got home and then all the food got cold with me waiting on him to get here. I was scared he'd be mad, but when he got home, he ate everything like it wasn't burnt at all. I ate very little because I didn't think anything tasted good. He told me I needed to eat more. I just ate some cucumbers and tomatoes and had milk. I guess Jesse worked out everything with Hank about the ice. He came in all happy but never said a word about what they talked about.

For the rest of the week, I went with Jesse to the Duvall's. Lilly Jean came over every day and every day Grandma Cal complained constantly. Lilly Jean ignored her and I was learning to. On Friday evening, Simpson paid me and I put the money in my pocket. When me and Jesse got in Papa's truck to go home I kept thinking that I didn't want to give Witch Sue any of my money. But Jesse didn't mention Witch Sue or paying her. We simply went home, ate cold chicken Vicky Jansan gave us and went to bed early.

I didn't think we'd go anywhere the next day because it was Saturday. Papa never worked at the Bait and Tackle Shop on Saturday. But early in the morning, Jesse was shaking me and saying, "Come on, 'Cella, wake up, we gotta go to work."

I barely opened my eyes, "It's the weekend, Jesse."

"Farms don't take a weekend off. We'll be off tomorrow, but until this work is done, we work Monday through Saturday."

I rolled over, "I done been paid for the week and I ain't going back today."

He shook me again, "Part of that money was for today, 'Cella, now come on."

I tried to ignore him. But he kept on. So I got up. I didn't cook breakfast though. If he was gonna be such a pain and not let me sleep when it was Saturday, then I wasn't gonna cook anything for him. It meant I didn't eat either, but I didn't care.

When we got to the Duvalls though I was about to starve and for the first time when Alice offered us breakfast, I agreed and sat down at the table and ate. It was the first hot decent meal I'd had since me and Jesse got married.

Lilly Jean didn't come and to avoid Grandma Cal, I kept looking through a magazine that they had on their coffee table. It was a boring magazine, full of pictures of fancy rooms, but I looked at it a lot to try to keep away from that crazy woman. As for Grandma Cal, she complained about me looking at the magazine. She complained about the way I put the food on the plates for dinner and she complained about the way I didn't answer her fast enough. I just did as little as possible and thought to myself if this was how it was gonna be from now on, I really had to get outta doing this.

I got so tired of her that by the time the day was over, I was waiting on the porch for Jesse. I saw him walking up in the yard and I ran to him. He asked if I was alright and I said, "No, I can't do this job by myself."

He sighed, "It won't last much longer, 'Cella. Just a couple more weeks and we'll be done. Then I gotta find another job and you won't have to work."

We got in Papa's truck and started to drive. Jesse was quiet and I thought maybe he was mad at me. I thought it was over me not wanting to get up and not cooking breakfast but I didn't ask him anything. I was thinking about some of the pictures I'd looked at over and over again in that magazine when suddenly he pulled up into a driveway. "What are we doing?" I asked, sitting up straight, realizing we were stopping at old man Felt Norris's place. "Why are we stopping here?"

Jesse pointed to an old faded red pickup truck, "You see that truck there, 'Cella?"

"Of course I do, I ain't blind."

"Well, it's had a for sale sign on it for a long time now. I'm gonna talk with Mr. Felt and see what kinda deal he'll let me work out." He got outta the truck and I watched him go up to the front door of old man Felt's house. Jesse knocked and knocked and knocked.

He finally gave up and was coming back down the steps when the door opened and old man Felt came outside. "Gotta give me time to get to the door, son. I'm old and slow," he called loudly to Jesse.

I watched Jesse turn back to him. Jesse pointed to the truck, asking what the deal was, did it run and would old man Felt mind working out something so he could buy it. Jesse told him we was using my Papa's truck and said he really wanted to give it back to Papa.

They walked to that old red truck and got inside it. Then, they had the nerve to drive off and leave me sitting there all by myself. I watched old man Felt's dogs fight each other. I watched the crows land in the yard and I watched a big old hornet flying around the eves of old man Felt's porch. Finally, after long last, Jesse and old man Felt came back. They got outta the truck and I watched as Jesse shook the old man's hand. Then Jesse came and got back into Papa's truck. Grinning he said, "We got us our own truck, 'Cella."

"You bought that old red truck?"

"We're buying it. I told him I ain't got much money now but I'm gonna pay him some when James pays me and when we finish up that tobacco, I'm gonna come here and do work for Mr. Felt. I told him I need to get a real paying job and he said fine, so long as I show up sometime everyday to do stuff around here for him."

"What kinda stuff?" I asked.

"Oh, like cleaning the yard, cleaning out the ditches. Helping him fix the porch—just stuff like that. We need our own truck, 'Cella." He backed out onto the road and said, "How would you like to go see your Mama and Papa?"

"I'd love that!" I said.

He grinned some more, "I thought so. I'm gonna take this truck back to your Daddy. You can stay there and visit with them while I come back and get our truck."

Chapter Twenty-One

Jesse was in such a hurry to get that old red truck, he just pulled up in Mama and Papa's yard, stopped the truck, jumped out and headed back down the driveway. I watched him walking away and shouted, "Hey, ain't you even gonna tell me bye?"

He turned around, looked at me a second, then came back, kissed me so quick I barely felt it and said, "I gotta get back there before dark, 'Cella."

I shook my head and watched him take off again. Then I went inside the house. I could smell collards cooking. "MAMA! MAMA!" I called.

Gran answered, "I'm in the kitchen, child. Your Mama ain't here."

I went to the kitchen. Gran was slicing sweet potatoes and putting them in a pot. "Where's Mama," I asked.

"Her and your Papa's gone down to Hannah. Poor girl threatening to kill herself over that sorry Wallace. They been down there just about all day. Gert came over around ten this morning saying that Hannah was having conniptions; pulling out her hair and tearing her clothes. Gert had left her girls, Sal, Fran and Mollie Mae with her but said they was scared to death of her so's she came here to get Sammy and Madge. Hoping to get some sense knocked into her."

"Oh," I felt so awful. I didn't realize until right now how much I missed Mama and Papa. "You know when they gonna be back?"

Gran sliced some more of the sweet potato into the pot, "Can't tell you that, child. All I know is Gert came and they hauled off with her. I'm over here cooking cause your Gramp's got my stove occupied boiling out carburetors on it. Got his truck carburetor, lawn mower carburetor, and got some more people's carburetors cooking up there too. I asked him how is gonna keep track of them all and he says he knows. I asked how come they can't boil them out on their own stoves, but he says he does them special and they paying him to do it. I asked if they gonna pay me for letting them use my stove and of course you know the answer to that one—a big fat no." She washed her knife off, wiped her hands on a towel that was on the counter and opened a bottle of corn syrup. As she poured the syrup all over the sweet potatoes in the pot she said, "What brings you here, 'Cella? And where's Jesse? Don't tell me you and him are having trouble."

"We ain't having trouble," I said, feeling like I did having to deal with Grandma Cal all day. "He's just gone back up to old man Felt's place. He bought that old truck."

"That old red truck?"

"Yeah."

She nodded and put the pot on the stove. I watched her and said, "I sure wished I could cook like you do. I burn everything."

Gran laughed, "I did too when me and Gil first got married. You'll get it, child."

"Could you teach me? You and Mama all the time did all the cooking…."

"Sure, come on over here, let me show you a few things."

I walked closer and listened as she told me about the stove, how to turn on the gas, how to adjust the flame—stuff I'd already figured out on my own but I kept quiet. She was talking away about cooking when she stopped and said, "How'd you like that clock Shane and Margaret gave you?"

"I liked it a lot but old Witch Sue stole it from us."

Gran stirred the collards, "How come old witch woman stole your clock?" She looked at me curiously.

I was looking at the ham she had frying, "She says she didn't but I know it was her."

"Marcella, what you trying to tell me?"

I picked up a slice of raw sweet potato Gran had dropped on the counter and as I bit into it, said, "Nothing, Gran, just that Witch Sue stole that clock. Jesse says it mighta been Hank when he came with the ice and we was gone but I know it was Witch Sue. She says I owe her and I say…."

"Hold up, child. Hold up. Why would you owe her?"

Suddenly I realized what I was doing. I hadn't told none of my family about me seeing Witch Sue. Just Jesse. When Mama and Papa learned about me and Jesse, I never ever, not even once said I'd been to Witch Sue to try to undo the baby I thought I was gonna have. Mama, Papa, and especially Gran and Gramp are scared to death of witches. So I hadn't told them nothing. I put my hand over my mouth and backed up from Gran who was holding her stirring spoon in the air like she was ready to whack me with it.

"Tell me Marcella!" she demanded. "Why would Sue Jones think you owed her anything? Our family don't have nothing to do with no witches!"

I kept my hand over my mouth. Gran raised her spoon higher, "Child, you may be married. You may be carrying your own young'un, but that ain't gonna stop me from getting the truth outta you. Now tell me!"

I started backing up as Gran was coming after me with the spoon, "I thought she could help me undo....I didn't want to have no...I wasn't sure if I was gonna have a....but I thought she...."

"YOU WENT TO HER TO GET RID OF YOUR BABY! DIDN'T YOU, MARCELLA ANTOINETTE! DIDN'T YOU!" She held her spoon higher.

"Yes'um." I backed up some more, terrified at the look in Gran's eyes.

"WHAT DID SHE DO TO YOU, CHILD?"

I stammered but couldn't answer. Gran had me backed all the way to the front door. I slipped and fell in front of it.

"YOU'D BETTER ANSWER ME, MARCELLA! WHAT DID SHE DO TO YOU?"

Cowering and crying, I said, "She blew some smoke over me and said some kinda spell, and she gave me some leaves to chew up and swallow but....."

Gran lowered her spoon and backed away from me like she was scared now. "She said a spell over you?"

"Yes. It was just to undo everything if there was a baby. But it didn't work...I'm still...."

Gran backed up some more, "I'm gonna have to ask you to leave, Marcella. Go out that door and never come back."

I couldn't believe what I was hearing, "WHAT?"

"You heard me child. You been cursed. You can't be in here.....OHHHH....OHHH!" She started to wail and cry. "My own little grandchild, and unborn great grandbaby cursed by a witch! OHHH, sweet Lord Jesus, what am I gonna do! What am I gonna do?"

"Gran, her spell didn't work. I still have my baby. I'm getting bigger and I even think it moved some today...."

"Don't make no difference. She cursed you. Get out. Get out, now, Marcella. You ain't welcome here!"

"I gotta be welcome here. This is my home. My Mama and Papa's home. I...."

"You been witch touched! You are cursed! Now leave!"

I just stared up at her with tears running down my face. "Gran, please! Please!"

"YOU'D BETTER LEAVE MARCELLA BEFORE I GET THE BROOM AND PUSH YOU OUT!"

"NO GRAN! NO! YOU CAN'T MAKE ME LEAVE!"

She stomped off and I lay on the floor crying, wanting Mama and Papa to come home. They wouldn't feel this way. They wouldn't make me leave.

"I TOLD YOU TO GO AND YOU'D BETTER GO!" I heard Gran yell and looked up to see her coming at me with the broom.

"DON'T GRAN! DON'T!" I shouted as I saw her bringing the broom down on me. I covered myself the best I could with my arms, feeling the sharp sting of the broom as she hit me with it again and again, pushing it into my body. "GRAN PLEASE STOP THIS! I BELONG HERE! I...."

"YOU MIGHT HAVE USED TO BELONG HERE BUT YOU DON'T NO MORE!" She kept hitting me. "I AIN'T BEING AROUND NO WITCH CURSED PERSON. AIN'T NO WAY! AND TO THINK I LET YOU USE MY WEDDNG CAKE TOPPER!" she hit me some more, "GET! GET! GET!"

I didn't want to get. This was my home. This was more home than Miz Essie's place was. I'd been born here. This was part of me. I couldn't get. I kept begging, trying to make Gran see that I belonged here no matter what and that old witch woman hadn't done nothing to me. But Gran wouldn't hear it. She just kept hitting me all over, whacking that broom into my body, hitting my head, my back, and my legs—just hitting and hitting and hitting. Finally, she leaned over me and turned the knob on the door and then pushed me out with the broom, breaking the handle of it in the process. I heard it snap right before she closed the door, catching the bottom of my dress in it.

I beat and beat on the door, calling out to Gran, begging for forgiveness. I told her I'd go to church. I told her I'd do whatever it took, but please let me back inside. Please don't do this to me.

Please love me. Oh Gran. Oh please. I beat and yelled until my throat was sore and my hands were bloody. Then I lay on the porch and cried.

It was getting darker and I heard it thunder but I didn't care. Suddenly Gran stuck her head out the front window by the door, "You'd better leave Marcella. I mean it. Don't make me do worse to you. Go now!"

"Gran! Please. Don't you love me? You can't run me off." I was sobbing so hard I could barely talk.

"I gotta run you off. Can't be helped. You cursed. You gotta go. Don't make me do what I don't want to do. And I will if you don't get off that porch and go right this very second!"

"Alright! Fine!" I yelled back and tried to stand but I couldn't because my dress was caught in the door. I managed to rip it and then I stumbled down the driveway to the mailbox. My body sore and painful and my heart heavy, I collapsed on the ground and lay there on the dirt crying my eyes out.

Chapter Twenty-two

I barely saw the headlights and just did hear the engine of the truck when Jesse finally got back. He stopped right in the road. "'Cella! Honey girl! What in the world?" He called as he jumped outta the truck and came to me. Kneeling beside me, he said, "What happened? Why are you laying out here? I woulda run over you if I hadn't been looking so careful."

I couldn't say a word; I just sat up and fell into his arms, not caring one bit that he was sweaty and smelly. I cried and cried hard into his shoulder as he held me.

"You gotta tell me what happened. Who did this to you? Who, 'Cella?"

"Just take me home. Please just take me home. Please." I cried hard.

"Come on; let's get you outta the road. This ain't safe." He gently pulled me up but it hurt like crazy and I cried in pain. Holding me close, Jesse said, "You got to tell me what happened." I shook with my crying and he said, "Let's get you inside to your Mama and Papa...."

"NO! NO JESSE! DON'T TAKE ME IN THERE! DON'T!"

He pulled back and in the light from the truck I saw the worry in his eyes. "Don't take you in there? Why....'Cella, you're bleeding! Oh no! Honey girl, please talk to me."

I felt awful. Like I was gonna pass out. "Jesse, I gotta..."

He helped me into the truck and got in himself. Then he took off his shirt and started wiping the blood off my face, head and arms. "Honey girl, I want you to tell me who did this to you."

"Gran," I whispered.

""Your Gran did this to you? Why?"

"She found out about Witch Sue."

"Oh no," Jesse shook his head, still blotting a spot on my forehead that was bleeding bad. "Ain't nobody beating on my wife like this and getting away with it. Witch or no witch. You wait right here, 'Cella. I'm taking care of this here and now."

"Please don't Jesse. Let's just go."

"I ain't putting up with this, 'Cella. Ain't no sense in beating you like this. None at all." He put his shirt in my lap and got outta the truck closing the door behind him.

Trying to control my sobbing, I watched him go to the front door and try to go in. Gran must have barricaded it somehow because apparently Jesse couldn't open it. He beat on the door demanding that she open it, shouting that she had no right to beat me like she did. I watched him, feeling worse and worse. At last, I called out the window, "Jesse, I'm sick! Please come!"

He came back to the truck and got in, "Where do you hurt, honey girl?"

"Everywhere."

He started to drive. He kept looking at me, kept touching me with one hand while he drove with the other. "I have to ask—how's the baby?"

"I don't know. Alright I guess. She didn't hit me in my stomach, I don't think. She was hitting me so many places…." I started to cry hard again.

Jesse gently rubbed my arm, "Let's just get you home."

When we got home, Jesse carried me into the house and took me to our bedroom. He laid me on the bed and got a match from the little drawer in the table by the bed. Then he lit the oil lamp and sat on the bed next to me. He looked me over careful, even took my dress off and looked at how it was torn. He got one of my gowns from the box under the bed and dressed me like I was a baby. Then he kissed me, "Honey girl, I want you to stay right here. I'm gonna get some help for you."

"You can't leave me, Jesse."

"I gotta get someone. You're beat bad, 'Cella. I'm scared." He kissed me again and got a clean shirt from the box under the bed. He put it on, "Just stay right here. Don't try to get up. I'll be back soon as I can."

Feeling awful I closed my eyes. I heard Jesse walking. Then I said, "Jesse, who you gonna get?"

"I don't know. But I'm gonna get someone. Don't worry about me."

He walked past the curtain and I closed my eyes. I'd never hurt so much in my life. I started to dream and there was Gran, hitting me and hitting me again. I screamed and woke myself up. I was in my own bed, drenched in sweat, staring at the blue flowered oil lamp on the bedside table. I tried to sit up but it hurt too bad. I closed my eyes again. I thought I heard Witch Sue chanting over me. I thought I heard Gran yelling at me again. I screamed and I screamed but there was no one to hear me. I cried because I hurt and I cried because Gran didn't want me no more. I'd sleep, dream, scream and cry. At last, I heard Jesse saying softly, "Honey girl, I got Alice. Her and Simpson are both here. Alice is gonna look at you. Make sure you're ok."

I opened my eyes. Alice was there. I don't think I was dreaming this time. She came to me, touched my shoulder and said, "We need more light in here, Jesse."

"Sure," he said and left the room. He came back with another oil lamp and sat it on the table with the blue flowered one.

Alice looked at the lamps and I heard her sigh. Then she looked at me and said, "Oh, you poor child." She carefully sat on the bed and looked me over, paying a lot of attention to my head and arms, her fingers cool as she touched me. She asked if I minded if she looked at me more and I shook my head. I felt so bad I didn't care about anything. She pulled the blanket back and pulled up my gown, looking me over as best she could in the light we barely had. Then she covered me back up and said, "Jesse, this child needs a doctor. She has been beaten terribly."

Jesse just sighed and sat on the edge of the bed, his head in his hands. I heard Simpson call, "Jesse, come here a minute."

Jesse left and before long Alice was wiping my face with a wet cloth. I ain't sure where she got it but it felt good. Jesse came back and this time, Simpson came right inside the curtain. He cleared his throat before he spoke, "Alice, I told him to bring her to the house and we'll get Dr. Moore."

"That's a good idea," Alice said, gently touching the place on my head that had been bleeding so bad. "They can use Carl's old room. Jesse, why don't you get you and 'Cella some clothes for tomorrow at least? Then we'll go." Alice wiped my face some more then stood up. "We're gonna take good care of you, 'Cella."

Alice and Simpson left and Jesse knelt by the bed to get the clothes out like Alice told him to. I tried to protest but I felt worse than ever. Jesse shook his head at me, "I'm gonna take care of you, 'Cella. That's all there is to it. Let me take these clothes to Alice and I'll come get you."

"I think I can walk," I said and tried to sit up and everything went totally black.

I heard Jesse yell for Alice and then next thing I knew he was carrying me. He put me in our truck, got in and started to drive. I was aware of this but it felt like it was far far off—not like dreaming exactly but like I was watching it all from far away. I lay down with my feet in the floor and held onto a rip in the seat. I tried to keep my eyes open because every time I closed them I saw Gran and her broom. But then Mama was there. We were in a strange room. A pretty room with a golden bed and a yellow bedspread. There were roses on the walls and Mama was feeding me peach ice cream with an ice cold silver spoon. She was smiling at me, "You always did love peach ice cream, 'Cella girl. Always was your favorite."

Then Jesse was carrying me again. I opened my eyes just a little and saw the Duvall's living room as we went through. I started to say I didn't feel like watching Grandma Cal right now, but my head was throbbing too bad to talk. Jesse carried me down the hall and turned into a room. Alice unmade a bed covered in a red plaid blanket. I looked around some, seeing a dark wooden floor, a red braided rug and a dresser with an oval mirror over it. "There," Alice said, "let's get her in bed. Hopefully it won't take Simpson long to get Dr. Moore."

Jesse laid me down in the bed. It was soft and I closed my eyes. Alice covered me, then sat next to me and held my hands, "Honey, what in the world? Your hands look awful."

"I wanted Gran to let me back in. I wanted her to want me."

Alice shook her head and gently placed my hands under the covers. Then she just sat there, not saying anything. I heard a knock on the door and Alice said, "Yes."

Bob opened it slightly, "Is she alright?"

"We don't know yet," Alice said.

"Are you ok, Jesse?" Bob asked.

"No, I ain't," Jesse said. "I'm scared outta my mind. My wife's been beat and I ain't sure how my baby is. I ain't ok at all, Bob."

"Wanta talk?" Bob asked.

"Maybe later. Right now I just want to sit in here with 'Cella."

Bob left and the room was quiet. It was so quiet I could hear Jesse's stomach rumbling. Alice musta heard it too because she turned to him, "Are you hungry Jesse?"

"Yes, ma'am. When me and 'Cella left here, we stopped by old man Felt Norris so I could talk to him about that truck of his. We worked out a deal where I can buy it so I wouldn't have to be driving 'Cella's daddy's truck all the time. He told me he didn't mind for me to go ahead and take it. I wanted to get 'Cella's daddy's truck back to him. I figured it would be good for 'Cella to see them, so I took her there and walked back to old man Felt's place. When I got there, he insisted on me and him washing the truck together. He's so slow. I don't think he'd washed that truck since he first bought it. He had to go over every little part of it. But we washed the truck and I didn't really think nothing of it cause I thought 'Cella was having a nice visit with her Mama and Papa. I had no idea she was being beat nearly to death."

"So you haven't eaten yet?" Alice asked.

"No, neither has 'Cella. At least I don't think she has. Maybe they fed her before they let her Gran beat her up."

I'd been listening with my eyes closed. I opened them. That was getting harder to do. Gran had beat my eyes too. I'd tried to close them to keep the broom out, but still she'd hit me there with it every time I'd tried to look up at her. "Mama and Papa weren't home," I said, my mouth dry. "They were with Aunt Hannah. Gran was the only one there."

Alice adjusted my covers, "And she just beat you like this?"

"She found out about me going to Witch Sue."

Alice shook her head, "Superstitions," she mumbled and stood up. "Jesse, there's some food left over from supper in the kitchen. You're welcome to any of it. And as soon as Dr. Moore says it's alright for 'Cella to eat she can have some too. I just want to make sure it's ok first, because of the baby and her being beat like she was."

"I understand," Jesse said. "I think I'll wait and hear what he says first too before I eat. I just gotta make sure she's alright."

"I think I'll go warm up some food for you so it'll be ready..."

There was another knock on the door. "Come in," Alice said.

This time when the door opened, Simpson and Dr. Moore stepped inside. Dr. Moore looked a lot older than I remembered him looking. He came to the bed, "Simpson tells me you were beaten."

"Yes."

He sat on the bed and opened his doctor bag. Looking me over he said, "What were you beat with?"

"A broom."

"A broom?" he repeated.

"Yes."

"Tell me all about it."

I did the best I could. I kept feeling so sleepy. Dr. Moore listened to me; then he listened to my heart and felt my hands and wrists. To Jesse he said, "I understand you believe she's expecting."

"We think so."

"I'd like permission to examine her further. I need to in order to make absolute certain the baby is alright."

"Sure," Jesse said. "Go ahead."

Alice excused herself from the room and Dr. Moore said, "I'm going to have to ask you to completely undress, 'Cella."

I just stared at him. Jesse came to the bed, "I'll help you. I know you're having a hard time moving."

Jesse undressed me and I kept my eyes closed the whole time Dr. Moore examined me. He did embarrassing things to me and I cried more. "It's alright," he said. "I'm only doing this to check on your baby."

After what seemed forever he said I could get dressed again. As Jesse was helping me he said, "Well, how is she?"

Dr. Moore was packing his bag, "She really needs to be in a hospital. But the closest one that will take her is Wilmington....I despise situations like this. I should be able to just take her to Brookville, but no...." he sighed deeply.

"Is our baby...." Jesse started.

"So far the baby is alive. There is a very strong heartbeat which is good, but with the beating she's received, I'm deeply worried."

"So we definitely have a baby," Jesse said.

"Oh, yes, there's a baby in there." Dr. Moore took a needle from his doctor bag, "I'm going to give you a shot for the pain. You've got to be in a lot of pain."

"I am," I said.

Dr. Moore gave me the shot but after the beating I'd got from Gran it didn't hurt at all. He put the needle back into his bag and stood. "We've got to make a decision, Jesse. She has to be on complete bed rest for a while. At least until her body heals from the beating. And I mean full bed rest—no getting up and moving about for any reason. Someone's gonna have to take care of her completely or there is the chance this baby won't make it."

Jesse stared at me and I realized he was crying. "I don't know what to do," he said. "I ain't got the money for a hospital. I..."

The door opened and Alice came inside, "Sorry to interrupt but I was coming to see how everything was going. I overheard the last part of that conversation. 'Cella needs to be on bed rest?"

"Yes," Dr. Moore said. "The way she's been beaten I'd be afraid to let her up to even use the bathroom."

Jesse sank into the chair, his head in his hands again. Alice said, "Y'all can stay here, Jesse. I'll take care of her. I don't mind."

"You sure, Alice?" Jesse asked.

"I'm sure. I love you and 'Cella. I don't want anything to happen to her or the baby."

Jesse looked at me. "How about it, honey girl?"

"I really want to go home, but I'd rather be here than in the hospital."

"Ok, it's settled then," Jesse said. "Dr. Moore, will that be alright?"

"Certainly. I'll come by daily to check on you, 'Cella. In the meantime, I want you to just stay in this bed, no matter what. You need anything, you get Jesse or Alice to help you. Don't worry about being embarrassed. Just think about that baby and that'll keep you going." He turned to Alice, "Do you have a bed pan? You're going to need one."

"No, I don't have one, but..."

"I've got one in the car I'll get for you," Dr. Moore said. "I want you to call or come get me if she shows any signs of getting worse or if you think for any reason she's going into labor. I sleep right by the phone so I'll hear it ring."

Chapter Twenty-three

There was a great big phone that I was sleeping next to. It was so big that I could crawl up into one of the finger holes for dialing and go to sleep. But I was scared to do that. I was afraid someone would try to dial the phone and squish me. So I stayed lying next to it. While I was sleeping there, Gran kept coming with her broom. I cried and begged her to go away. Mama and Papa were there too. Mama was crying and Papa was yelling at Jesse and Jesse was yelling back at him. Hallie cried over me too; cried so hard her tears fell on my face and she wiped them off with a lace handkerchief. Papa came and told me it was time to pull the carrots from the garden and I'd better get my lazy self up and get to work. Mama took me to that fancy room again and fed me chicken and dumplings and more peach ice cream. Papa kept yelling at me that the carrots had to be four foot long by now and I had to get them outta the ground for him. I told him I didn't even like carrots and he could just get them hisself. He said I was completely useless since going to Witch Sue. Gran kept showing up with her broom threatening to finish beating the life outta me. Alice was there, wiping me down with a cold sponge and making me sip chicken soup. Grandma Cal looked down into my face and said, "Cellar girl, you watched me, now I'm gonna watch you." Lilly Jean was there too. She held my hand and said she wanted me to get better. And Jesse. He would be there next to me, holding me, and then he'd be gone. I'd look up and see him pacing around the room, see him worrying so and he'd disappear. Old man Felt's dogs came and had fights by my bed. I tried to tell Alice that I didn't like those dogs fighting so close to my bed and she smiled and said she'd take care of them. She said that but every time I looked at the floor those dogs were there, growling and snarling at each other. The big brown one would look at me growling and showing his teeth. I screamed wanting that mad dog away from me. Hornets kept flying around near the ceiling and Dr. Moore kept coming in and sticking needles in me. I asked him how come there was so many hornets and he said he was using them to make needles to give me shots with.

I opened my eyes and looked up at the ceiling. The hornets were gone. I looked at the floor. Old man Felt's dogs were gone too. I turned my head and saw Jesse was standing by the bed, getting dressed. "Jesse," I said.

He leaned down and kissed me. He smelled like soap. I was all confused. My mind was a jumble. I was remembering so many things. Which memories were real and which ones were dreams? But one thing I knew—it couldn't be true that Gran beat me with that broom. Gran loved me. She made me do chores too much and she moved too slow but she loved me. She'd held me on her lap and told me stories. She braided my hair and made me pretty dresses. She cooked cinnamon bread with pecans just for me. That part had to have been a dream. But then why was I here in this strange room.

Jesse sat beside me, rubbing my head, "Oh, good," he said, "Your fever's broken. Maybe you're finally getting better."

"Better?" I asked, confused. "Jesse, why are we....Where are we? I don't...." I found myself crying again and not knowing why.

"Your Gran beat you up, honey girl. Don't you remember."

"No, Jesse, that can't be true," I cried.

"I wished it wasn't but it is. Don't you remember?"

"I....I want that not to be real. I want that to be a dream."

"It's not a dream, 'Cella. I know you've probably been dreaming a lot lately. You've really been outta it, but Dr. Moore told us not to worry about you sleeping so much. He said the shots he was giving you would make you sleep."

"Yeah," I mumbled, "He keeps sticking needles in me made from all them hornets he has flying around in here and he gave me a big meat thermometer so I can tell when my fever gets too high."

Jesse gave me a strange look. "Honey girl, he's been here twice a day for the last three days. You've had two shots a day, but they ain't been from any hornets and he ain't ever gave you a meat thermometer so you can check your fever. You've had a fever but he ain't used a meat thermometer on you."

"Three days?" My head was so clogged. "Jesse, did you get that truck? Who got old man Felt's dogs outta here? They kept fighting on the floor and now they're gone. And the hornets. So many hornets...."

Jesse kissed me again, "You've really been outta it, 'Cella. We've been here at the Duvall's since your Gran beat you Saturday evening. It's Wednesday morning now. Your Mama and

Papa have been by and they wanted to take you to their house but I ain't having that. Me and your Papa got in our very first argument. I told him Dr. Moore said it ain't safe for you to be moving around and you were staying right here in Carl's old bedroom. He said you're his daughter and he wanted you at his house. But I reminded him you're my wife now and I get to say what goes with you. Besides, I don't want you nowhere near your Gran. Not ever again. Your Mama says she won't come to the house if you are there but I ain't taking any chances."

"Why am I here? Why didn't you take me to one of my aunts, or to your Mama even? Why here, Jesse?"

He sighed, "Honey girl, the night you got beat, I was scared so bad I didn't know what to do. You were bleeding all over the place; your face was all bruised and swollen. My sweet pretty 'Cella, so beat up..." his voice caught, but then he continued, "I was so put out with your Gran. I wasn't gonna go to any of your family. They mighta felt the same way about you. I thought about going to get my Mama, but then I thought about my Daddy. We ain't exactly been getting along in the fields while we're working every day. On the day you got beat up, I'd taken your Daddy's truck down to the field with us. I drove Bob and Todd down there just cause I felt like it. But at the end of the day when it came time to go back, your Daddy's truck wouldn't' start and old Leroy started in on me. I knew it had everything to do with those sorry battery cables because your Daddy told me about them. I was trying to fix it the way your Daddy told me and old Leroy was right there, telling me what he just knew I had to do. I told him leave me alone. He wouldn't let up and I just lost it. I told him I knew what I was doing and if he'd just get outta the way I could fix the truck. He said fine, don't ever ask for his help again. I said I didn't recall asking for it in the first place. He said he never wanted me to come to him with anything. I said I didn't plan on it. He kept on and we nearly came to blows. I think we would have if James hadn't stepped in and told him to just see if I could get the truck going on my own. He stepped back but he didn't keep quiet. Stood over there mumbling about me using your Daddy's truck just like it was mine and tearing it up. I got so sick of him. That's the main reason we stopped at old man Felt's. Got my own truck now so Leroy can just shut his mouth. I thought about going to my Mama that night but I guess I got too much pride and there was no way I was gonna go in there begging for help with old Leroy. So, I drove right by the house and came here. 'Cella, all my life the Duvalls have been here for me. I knew they'd take care of us."

I was quiet, thinking about what he'd said. "We been here that long?"

"Yes. You've been in and out of it. Out mostly. Alice has been feeding you soup and taking real good care of you. Dr. Moore's been in two times a day and…."

"Who's been watching old Grandma Cal?"

Jesse grinned, "Grandma Cal's been watching you, honey girl. She's spent most of the days sitting in that chair over there while Alice has been taking care of you. Can't get her to stop calling you Cellar but she's been right in here with you. And so has my Mama. She's come every day but she ain't gone down to the field. She's stayed here and helped Alice with you. Lilly Jean keeps coming by too. Everyone is really worried about you."

"And my Mama and Papa?"

"They came once, honey girl. On Sunday after you got beat. I stayed here with you while the Duvalls went to church. Then after dinner, I went back to our house and got the rest of our clothes cause I knew we was gonna be here a while. I went by your Mama and Papa's house but no one was home. I left them a note saying your Gran nearly killed you and we were here at the Duvalls. I said your Mama and Papa were welcome to come but your Gran better stay away. Then I came back here and talked with Clyde about putting locks on our front door and the windows so no one can get in while we're gone. He gave me some locks and went to the house with me to help put them on. When we got back here, your Mama and Daddy were in the driveway. I brought them in here to see you and that's when me and your Daddy got in our argument. I've gone back to our house every day right after dinner cause that's when Hank brings the ice so he won't be going in there by himself…."

"When can we go home?"

"When the doctor tells us. He's been listening to the baby's heartbeat and checking you over really good every day. I ain't moving you until he says it's safe to do so."

Chapter Twenty-four

I fell back to sleep right after Jesse left to go work in that tobacco again. Grandma Cal woke me up, pulling on my blanket and calling "Cellar, Cellar, come on, you need to eat more."

I opened my eyes. She was standing by my bed. "I don't feel like eating," I said.

"You got a baby. You need to eat. All Alice has gotten into you is some chicken soup and very little of that. Old Doc Moore is just concerned with giving you knock out shots. But I know you need more food. Now you tell me what you'd like and I'll see to it that you get it."

I moved a little. It still hurt in spite of all those shots. "I want some peach ice cream."

"Peach ice cream, huh? Alright. We ain't got none here but I'll see that you get some. Now what about some real food—like beans, corn, ham—stuff like that. What would you like? If we got it, I'll get it for you."

I couldn't believe she was so concerned about me. I hadn't really thought about eating anything except peach ice cream. And the chicken soup wasn't bad, it was just I felt awful and eating just wasn't working for me. I looked at the old woman standing by my bed, leaning on her cane. "If I ask you for something how you gonna get it for me? Can you cook?"

"Can I cook? Child, I been cooking ever since I was eight years old. That's been over seventy years now. So, what do you want?"

"But I always have to fix your dinner for you…I have to watch you and make sure you don't fall."

She waved her hand, "Oh, that Alice. She's the one thinks I'm gonna fall all the time. Just cause I slipped on the porch where Bob spilled that glass of milk. Anyone woulda fell in the mess that boy made."

"Where is Alice?

"She walked down to Vicky to get some eggs and give them some milk and butter. You tell me everything you want and I'll take care of it for you, Cellar. A girl with a baby has got to eat. And you ain't eating nothing. Old Doc Moore worried about you getting up and loosing that baby. But I'm worried about you not eating enough and loosing that baby."

"You're worried about me?

She shook her head, "That's what I said."

Maybe I was dreaming again. That had to be it. Grandma Cal wasn't nice to me. She complained about my family all the time. So I looked at her and said, "I would like some stewed pork chops and rice cooked together and some really sweet corn and biscuits and lemonade."

She smiled, "That's better." She turned and walked slowly to the door. I was sure I was dreaming. She stopped at the door, "You need anything else? Glass of water? Something to read? Bedpan?"

I shook my head. Actually, I did need the bedpan, but I'd try to wait on that. I closed my eyes and rolled over on my side. I heard Grandma Cal leave the room and I opened my eyes and looked on the floor for old man Felt's dogs. They weren't there. Just that red braided rug and the dark hardwood floor. Then it struck me. I was in the preacher's bedroom. Sleeping in his bed. Sleeping in a preacher's bed should take care of any spell old Witch Sue mighta put on me. Maybe Gran would.....

There was a knock on the door and it opened slightly. Lilly Jean stuck her head in. "Hey, you're awake," she said, smiling at me.

"I think so, but I ain't sure."

She walked to the bed, "Why ain't you sure?"

"Grandma Cal is being nice to me. I gotta be dreaming."

She laughed, "Grandma can be nice. Mama and Alice are in there helping her cook for you now."

"I thought everyone was working in the tobacco."

"All the men are. I had to help Mama pick butterbeans this morning and do laundry. I'd rather pick butterbeans any day than work tobacco." She sat on the edge of the bed. "Are you feeling any better?"

"Yeah."

"Good. You've been very sick. I've come over every day and you didn't even know I was here."

"I remember you being here. But then there were hornets here and old man Felt's dogs too."

Lilly Jean smiled, "Ok." She paused, "Jesse really seems to like that truck he bought. And Bob is still having trouble with Nancy. I heard him talking with Todd about it this morning."

I nodded. I thought I felt my baby move. I put my hand on my stomach under the covers and silently told my baby please keep moving. Please live. Lilly Jean pushed her hair back, "We've got church tonight. I don't want to go but I have to."

"I thought Jesse said it was Wednesday."

"It is, but we have church on Wednesday nights. I used to like church a lot, but not anymore."

"We never went to church much. Just mostly at Christmas and Easter and when someone in the family was sick and Gran said we had to get in church and pray for them. I was always bored with it, even though there was lots of singing and people all excited. I'd always wish I was someplace else."

Lilly Jean nodded, "I know what you mean about wishing you were someplace else. We go to church all the time. My Daddy is a deacon and we help to clean up the church too. If we're not working, we're going to church."

"Why don't you like it anymore?"

She played with the fringe on my blanket, "Because of Monica Powers. She used to go to the Methodist church but they've started coming to our church and ever since she's been coming, my friend Rhonda barely speaks to me anymore. She just talks to Monica and Monica looks at me like I smell bad or something. Monica is Nancy's cousin and they act just alike."

"Ain't you got anymore friends?"

"Not who go to church. I'm friends with Janey Everette and Maryanne Dowes. But I only see them when we're in school. And I'm scared about starting school this year too. I have to go to high school and I don't think I want to."

"We only have one school," I said. "My teacher this year is going to be Miss Knox. She's the best teacher in the whole school. She takes everyone out for walks in the woods to talk about plants and lets you put on plays and make things. I been looking forward to going to the ninth grade for a long time. Miss Knox lives right next to the bait and tackle shop where my Papa works and sometimes I go there and she gives me bubblegum and we talk about different kinds of flowers that grow wild and bugs and all sorts of stuff. I sure hope I'm well enough so that when school starts I can go."

"She sounds like a good teacher," Lilly Jean said. "I wish she could be my teacher. I don't think they're any good ninth grade teachers at Cedar Cove High. Libby and Todd both didn't have good teachers in the ninth grade. They both had lots of homework every night and Libby's teacher even took points off for erasing too much on the paper. She would hold the paper up to the light to look at it real careful to see if there was a lot of erase marks in it. I don't want her for a teacher and I don't want the one Todd had either. His teacher made them copy the dictionary. She wanted them to copy the whole dictionary but they only got to the middle of the C's. Then she took off points on everyone's grade because they didn't copy the entire dictionary. Todd couldn't stand her. He got sick that year with the flu real bad and was home sick in bed for a week. While he was home sick, that crazy teacher, Mrs. Abbott, called Clyde at the store to tell him to get Daddy because Todd was acting up in class and she couldn't control him. Daddy tried to call her on Clyde's phone in the store, but she said she wanted him to come to the school and get Todd. He went out to the school and told her that Todd was home in bed with a 102 fever and couldn't be acting up in her class. She didn't even apologize. She just said, 'Well, all I know is some boy in here with dark hair has been acting up all day and I want it to stop.' Daddy told her he couldn't do anything about that." She sighed, "I really don't want to go to the ninth grade."

Alice opened my door. "We've got your food cooking, 'Cella and Simpson's going to go get your peach ice cream as soon as he can. Do you need anything now?"

As much as it embarrassed me to say so, I said, "I gotta go real bad."

Alice nodded, "I'll get the bedpan, honey."

"Can't I go on my own?"

She shook her head, "Sorry honey, not yet. Dr. Moore doesn't want you getting up."

"The baby moved just a few minutes ago."

"That's great," Alice said. "Lilly Jean, honey, Vicky wants you. You have to go home with her and help shell those butterbeans y'all picked this morning."

Lilly Jean stood, "Alright. 'Cella, I'll be back when I can. I'll bring you some books. I have some Patty Sue, girl detective books that you might like. Have you ever read Patty Sue books?"

"No," I said, but I was thinking I might actually read them if she brought them because I was already getting bored outta my mind in here.

"I like them," she said. "Patty Sue is a girl our age who solves all kinds of mysteries. I have four of them. Daddy lets me get one every now and then when we go to Davis's in Brookville. I'll bring them over."

"Ok," I said.

Later, after Lilly Jean was gone and Alice had helped me with the bedpan, I was just laying there, looking around that preacher's bedroom. I felt so out of place. I wanted to go home. I looked at the dresser and started to cry. I could smell the food cooking. I wanted to be back in my own bed. Not mine and Jesse's bed, but my bed at Mama and Papa's. The bed I'd slept in since I was four. The bed Gramp and Papa made for me. That's where I wanted to be. I didn't want Gran hating me. I didn't want any of this. I loved Jesse. I even loved this baby inside me now but I still wanted to change things.

I guess Alice musta heard me crying because she came to the room, "Honey, are you ok? Are you hurting anywhere?"

I shook my head. I was hurting, but didn't know how to tell her that it was my heart hurting. She came and sat on the bed. She pushed back my hair. "Is there anything I can do for you?"

"I want my Mama," I whispered.

"Oh, honey, I understand. I'll tell Hallie to tell her you want to see her, alright."

I nodded. "Is Hallie here?"

"No. Her sister Sybil fell off the porch at Leroy and Hallie's last night. She sprained her ankle. Hallie stayed home today to take care of her. Leroy is down in the field. Do you want me to tell him when he gets back this evening?"

I shook my head. "No, don't tell Mr. Leroy anything about me. That man don't like me."

She sighed, "Honey, it's not that he don't like you. It's just he's ashamed of what you and Jesse did. Now I ain't judging you, but as parents you raise your children to do right and when they don't it hurts. Leroy is just hurt. The best thing you can do is keep praying for everything to work out for your entire family." She moved a little, "Your food will be ready in just a little bit. Would you like a magazine or something to look at? I know Lilly Jean mentioned those books but I'm sure Vicky's going to have her busy at home for the rest of the day."

"I'd like anything to do right now."

I never got a chance to look at that magazine because Dr. Moore came. He checked me over, embarrassing me again and I cried because I didn't want him touching me or looking at me and Jesse wasn't there. He listened to my baby and said, "Doing good so far." Then he gave me two shots which did hurt this time, told me to stay in bed and get Alice to help me with whatever I needed and left. I fell asleep shortly after he left and dreamed of climbing the tree in Aunt Callie's back yard with my cousins Fay-Anna and Lucas. I hadn't seen Lucas in years. He'd been sent off to a special reform school for the colored up in Raleigh because he really truly tried to set fire to the school and got caught doing it. Lucas was always mean and hateful to everyone but in my dream he was helping me climb up the tree, saying, "Don't let Gran worry you none about Witch Sue. Gran don't understand having problems and having to figure out how to handle them on your own."

Jesse woke me up, saying, "Honey girl, I got our supper. Sure looks good."

I opened my eyes to see him standing by the bed. He looked scrubbed clean and water was glistening on his hair where he'd washed it. He was holding a tray that had two plates of food and two glasses of lemonade. He grinned, "I'm gonna eat in here with you tonight, honey girl. You sure gave Alice a good menu to cook up for you." He sat the tray on the little table by the bed. "Here, I'll help you sit up so you can eat."

I sit up slowly with Jesse's help and he fluffed my pillows up behind me. Then he put the tray over my lap; pulled that chair up to the bed and moved his own plate and glass to the little table by the bed. He sat in the chair and said, "I think we should say grace, 'Cella. I been thinking about it ever since you got beat so bad. We need to start thanking God for what he's done for us."

"I still got beat with that broom," I said. "God didn't stop that."

"Yeah, but you're still alive and so is our baby."

"Ok," I said, "but you do it."

Jesse just closed his eyes and said, "Thank you, God." Then he opened his eyes and began to eat.

I looked at my plate of food. It was everything I'd asked for. I started to eat slowly. It tasted so good. I didn't even realize I was hungry. Jesse was talking away about the tobacco and how soon they thought everything would be done. I listened not saying anything at first. I kept thinking about school starting and being able to finally be in Miss Knox's room. Papa had told me my school days were over but I saw no reason why I couldn't go to school in the day time while Jesse worked. School started at nine in the morning and got over at three. I could walk to school and walk back home in plenty of time to get supper ready for us. I really wanted to go to ninth grade and be with Miss Knox. I wanted to go on walks in the woods, put on plays and learn about animals. Jesse was talking away, telling about something Bob said when I interrupted him saying, "I sure hope I'm better by the time school starts. I can't wait to be in Miss Knox's room this year."

Jesse put down his biscuit, "'Cella, honey girl, you ain't going to school…."

"That's what Papa told me too, but I could. I could go while you're working….

Jesse shook his head, "Honey girl, they don't let married people go to school…."

"WHY NOT!" I cried out.

"Shhh!" Jesse whispered loudly. "Don't cause a scene, 'Cella. Not here. It's the rules. No married people in school. Especially married girls who are having a baby."

"I don't believe it," I said.

"Well that's how it is," Jesse said. "Think about it. Do you know any married people in school?"

"Most of the teachers are married."

"That's teachers. Not students. You can't go back to school, 'Cella."

I laid back on my pillows and cried. I didn't feel like anything anymore.

Jesse rubbed my arm, "Come on, honey girl, sit up and eat. You ain't been eating nothing lately. I been real worried about you and the baby."

I looked at him, "I just don't understand."

He shrugged, "I guess they don't want the younger children seeing a pregnant woman..."

"They gonna see me in the stores and all around everywhere else. If we went to church, they'd see me there. But they can't see me at school! That don't make sense, Jesse!"

"I know, but I don't make the rules. Sorry, honey girl. Now come on and eat."

I looked at my partially eaten food, sit up and began to eat again. I was so mad. I wanted to hit someone. But there was no one to hit. There was nothing to do. I couldn't stand it. I was thinking about throwing my fork across the room when there was a knock on the door. "Come in," Jesse called.

The door opened and Alice stuck her head inside, "Simpson got your peach ice cream from Preacher Joe's store."

"Thank you," I said.

She came inside, carrying two bowls of ice cream. "I had to kick the door to knock," she smiled. "Jesse, I fixed you a bowl too."

"Oh, great. I love peach ice cream," he said, taking one of the bowls from her. He put it on my tray and then took the other bowl from Alice too.

I looked at the ice cream in the bowl. Alice said, "So, how are you feeling, 'Cella? How's the food?"

"It's good. Did Grandma Cal cook it?"

"No, honey. I did. She told me what you wanted and I did. I don't really trust her with the stove. She thinks she knows what she's doing but...Anyhow, I wanted to tell you that Dr. Moore told me he's going out to check on your Aunt Sybil, Jesse. So I told him to pass on the message that you want to see your Mama, 'Cellla."

"Her Mama's coming here?" Jesse asked.

"I don't know yet," Alice said. "But 'Cella told me she wanted to see her."

"They can come," Jesse said, "but they ain't taking her nowhere."

Chapter Twenty-five

As it turned out, Jesse was worrying about nothing. We stayed here two more weeks and not once did any of my people show up to see me. Hallie came by a lot, but not my Mama or Papa or any of the rest of my family.

Lilly Jean brought over those Patty Sue books and I read two of them out of boredom. They were all about this white girl surrounded by a bunch of ignorant white people who couldn't see what was staring them right in the face. The whole time I was reading I kept thinking this bunch was lucky to have Patty Sue around. She was the only smart one in the book.

After the first week, Dr. Moore said I could start getting up and going to the bathroom on my own, but he still wanted me in bed mostly. He cut the shots down to one a day and I didn't sleep as much. The first time I saw my face in the bathroom mirror, I cried. I looked horrible. There were scabs all over me. After I finished crying about how bad I looked, I cried all over again because Gran had beat me.

During the second week, Alice surprised me by bringing me three new dresses she'd made for me plus some blouses and skirts. I was so shocked I didn't know what to say. She asked did I like them and I said, yes, but why did she make them. She smiled and said she had extra material around and knew I was gonna need clothes to get me through having this baby.

I think this baby likes me laying in bed all the time. I look like I'm gonna have a baby now. My stomach is poking out and I can feel it moving around a lot. Dr. Moore says that's good.

After the third week of us being here, Dr. Moore said I was well enough to go home, but don't overdo it. He told Jesse to keep a close watch on me and don't hesitate to come get him if we needed him.

I'd come here on August 9th and finally went home on September 2nd. Jesse had gotten his money from helping James Jansan with his tobacco and he said he'd gone by Witch Sue and paid her. I told him he shouldn't have done that and asked if he'd seen our clock, but he said he didn't go inside. He ignored me saying he shouldn't have paid her.

I was so happy to be going home. We told everyone goodbye, got in old man Felt's truck that was our truck now and drove outta the driveway. We waved to everyone and then Jesse asked, "You feeling alright, honey girl?"

I nodded.

He looked at me, "So, how did you like staying with the Duvalls?"

"For white people they are really nice," I said. "And I like Lilly Jean too."

Jesse rubbed my hand and drove on home.

When we got home, Jesse walked with me up to the front door. Then he unlocked our door and we went inside. Everything looked familiar but strange. I looked around the room, happy to be here. I remembered the day me and Jesse got married and how I didn't want to be here but I did now.

I sat in the old green armchair that used to be Miz Essie's and tried not to look at Gran's old rocker. It made me sad to look at it. Jesse didn't seem to think nothing of me not sitting in Gran's rocker. He just said, "I'm gonna go get our clothes outta the truck," and walked out.

While he was gone, I got up and went to our bedroom. I stared at myself in the mirror. I was wearing a pale yellow dress that had little white dots all over it. I liked this dress the best of the ones Alice made for me. My face looked a little better. Some of the scabs were gone. Dr. Moore had given me a big jar of salve to put all over them two times a day. He said I wouldn't need any more shots and told Jesse to buy some aspirin for me. Jesse bought the aspirin and got us another clock at Preacher Joe's store. This new clock was nowhere near as pretty as the one Witch Sue stole from us but Jesse said at least it kept time.

I went back into the main room and looked in the icebox. Jesse had been coming each day when Hank came with the ice. We had eggs milk and butter in here. I was surprised. I didn't think we had any food at all. I closed the door and looked into our cabinet. I was staring at everything when Jesse came in with two bags that held our clothes. He smiled at me and carried them to the bedroom. He came right back and I said, "You ain't had time to put up those clothes."

"We'll get them later." He came to me, grinning. "So, how do you like being home?"

I closed the cabinet door, "I like it." And this time, I really did.

Chapter Twenty-six

I got big fast. It seemed like each day I got bigger and bigger. The baby moved all the time, keeping me awake and even kicking so hard it woke Jesse up too.

Jesse started working every evening for old man Felt to pay off that truck and every morning, he headed for the log woods. I fussed and fussed. I said he'd cut his leg off or a tree would fall on him. But he said we had to have money to take care of ourselves and it was the only work he could get. I didn't like it because I was scared for him and he had to work almost every Saturday and when he didn't have to work in the woods, he had to work with old man Felt.

I stayed home and took care of our little house. Alice had taught me enough about cooking so that I didn't burn everything as bad as before.

September turned into October and I watched the leaves on the trees change into orange and red. We had warm days but at night, Jesse had to build us a fire in the fireplace to keep the cold air away.

Lilly Jean's Daddy brought her over a few Saturdays. Let her stay all day with me while Jesse was cutting trees in the woods. We talked and talked. She told me all about school and her new teacher, Mrs. Skipper. This Mrs. Skipper was new to the school and Lilly Jean said she was really nice. Lilly Jean was happy she came to the school because all the other ninth grade teachers were awful.

November arrived and Lilly Jean came over the very first Saturday of the month. She brought over more Patty Sue books. I'd read all of the four she'd had and so far those people weren't getting any smarter and Patty Sue kept solving mysteries that wouldn't be mysteries if everyone around her had any sense. I thanked Lilly Jean for bringing the books. They did pass the time when Jesse was gone and I was all alone.

She also brought over two patterns for baby clothes and a bag of scrap material. I looked at the patterns and said, "What's this for?"

She smiled, "I've noticed the only thing you have for the baby is a few diapers."

"I can't sew nothing."

"You don't have too. Mama and Alice and Wanda are going to do the sewing. We're just gonna cut out the patterns."

I looked at the patterns more closely. There was one with a baby gown, sleeper and hat and another one with a baby coat, pants and little top.

Lilly Jean kept talking, "Libby's used these same patterns to make clothes for her and Carl's baby. A lot of this scrap material can be used for a little girl or a little boy. And I brought over pins and scissors so we can cut them out."

"Ok," I said, "let's do it."

We talked the whole time we worked. It was strange how I got along so good with Lilly Jean. Half the time I forgot all about her being white and she never mentioned at all about me being colored. I was happy she came over. None of my people ever did and now that I wasn't at the Duvalls, Hallie didn't visit us either. I guess my people were convinced I was witch touched and Mr. Leroy probably refused to let Hallie come by because he was still mad with us for starting up this baby in the first place.

By the time her Daddy came back to get her, we'd cut out a whole pile of stuff for the baby. Lilly Jean smiled as she left, promising to bring back the sewed up baby clothes the next time she came.

And she did too. She came over the Saturday before Thanksgiving, bringing not only all those baby clothes but several little blankets and bibs too. "They were Betsy's and Sharon's," she said.

"Thank you," I said and took them to our room. Lilly Jean came with me.

Jesse had built us a crib and we had it sitting just where he wanted it. He had made a box for the baby's clothes too that sat under the crib. I pulled out the box and put the clothes inside. Lilly Jean helped me. Then we went back into the main room and sat at the table and talked. She said Bob and his girlfriend Nancy were still arguing all the time and Bob had gotten a job at the service station in Brookville. She said Todd didn't have a girlfriend yet and was busy helping Clyde a lot in his store. Then she shocked me by asking what me and Jesse was gonna do for Thanksgiving. I said probably not much. I was sure my people didn't want me around and neither did Leroy and Hallie.

"Mama says you can come eat with us,"

I stared at her, "Are you sure?"

She smiled, "Of course. We're going to have lots of food. We always do."

I was quiet. I hadn't thought much of Thanksgiving because I missed my family so much. I wanted them back in my life but Witch Sue had taken care of that.

"Come on," Lilly Jean said. "We really want you to be with us."

"Ok," I agreed. "I'll talk with Jesse about it."

Chapter Twenty-seven

Jesse said we would go to Thanksgiving dinner with the Jansans and Duvalls. Hallie and Leroy had been invited too. I wasn't sure I wanted to go. Not that I didn't like the Jansans and Duvalls but I wanted to have Thanksgiving with my family. I missed Mama and Papa so much. I cried all the time for them but they never came by and I was afraid of going to the house because Gran might kill me this time. Jesse had gone by and Mama told him she'd been deeply hurt by us. By me going to Witch Sue and getting cursed and then Jesse taking me to the Duvalls. She said she didn't know what to think of me and had to stay away. Papa wouldn't have nothing to do with Jesse because they'd gotten into that argument over me staying at the Duvalls. I didn't know how to make things better. I tried not to think about holidays and my family, but I thought of them all the time.

I was so sad by Thanksgiving morning, I could barely get dressed. But Jesse was all happy, whistling and humming as he dressed in clothes like he was going to church. And although we'd promised Grandma Cal, we still didn't go to church. I stared at him, "What you getting all dressed up for?"

"It's Thanksgiving, honey girl."

I shook my head. "You look like you ready for church."

He grinned, "Just getting ready for a day of good eating."

I sighed and put on my navy blue dress with the white trim. I'd planned on wearing my simple brown plaid dress but if Jesse was gonna go so fancy I guess I had to look better too.

I was so big I didn't even need the belt on the dress so I just let the sashes hang at my sides. Jesse came and helped me hook it in the back. I felt so sad I didn't care about anything. He turned me around and kissed me but it didn't help any.

There were so many people at the Jansan's, I could barely breathe for them. They had two big tables sit up right inside their side door with food laid out on both of them when we came inside. Grandma Cal was sitting in a chair right by the door. She grinned at me, "Hey there, Cellar, how you doing? Give me a hug."

I hugged the old woman as she stayed in the chair, "I'm ok." I said.

She rubbed my stomach, "See your little one is growing just fine. Gonna have a big baby seems."

I nodded and stepped back as Jesse hugged her too. Lilly Jean came in the room and said, "Come to my room, 'Cella." I followed her as Jesse started talking with Todd and Bob and Alice and Vicky were trying to get them to move so they could put more stuff on the tables.

Lilly Jean led me through a room where lots of people were sitting around talking. Clyde was there holding his little girl Sharon and those people who'd lost each other for so long then got married again even though they were already married were there too. That little girl Betsy was sitting between them. I saw Simpson and Preacher Carl and his wife Libby too. As we walked through, Libby got up and followed us. She didn't look as big as me even though she was having a baby too. We followed Lilly Jean through a door and Libby closed it behind us. "You look so pretty, 'Cella," Libby remarked

I didn't feel pretty at all. I felt frumpy dumpy; even in this fancy dress. "Thank you," I said, thinking she just said that to be polite.

We went to Lilly Jean's room. "I got a new Patty Sue book," she said. "See."

I looked at the book she held out to me. There was a picture of Patty Sue and her best friend Wendy holding a flashlight as they walked in the woods. "Have you read it yet?" I asked.

"No, I haven't had a chance. I got it yesterday but when I finish it, I'll let you read it."

"Ok."

Libby spoke up, "When are you supposed to have your baby?"

I shrugged, "Ain't sure."

"Have you been to a doctor?"

"No. Dr. Moore saw me when Gran beat me up with the broom but he ain't seen me since September."

"Did he ever tell you when you might have it?"

"Not really. He just said based on what I told him and on him looking at me, he thought it would come sometime in early March. But he weren't sure."

Libby just stared at me. It was obvious I was bigger than her and her baby was coming in January. Just two months from now.

Finally she smiled and patted my shoulder. "Let's go see if we can help them get dinner on the table."

We met Betsy in the hall, "We have to eat now," she said, grabbing Lilly Jean's hand.

Lilly Jean smiled, "Ok, Betsy."

Libby rubbed Betsy's hair, "I haven't had a chance to talk with you, Betsy. How do you like school?"

"I didn't at first but I like it now. I cried and cried at first and so did Mommy."

I still hadn't seen Leroy or Hallie but when we walked into the kitchen, Hallie was there. She took one look at me and said, "Child, you're as big as a house. You sure are having a big baby."

I shrugged, "I guess so."

She shook her head, "I pity you having it. Especially as small as you are."

Before long, we were all seated at those two tables. Leroy and Hallie didn't sit at the same table as me and Jesse. Leroy still had his mad dog look every time he looked at me or Jesse; but mostly he ignored us. Lilly Jean, Libby and Preacher Carl were at our table along with Grandma Cal and Alice. The food was good and everyone talked constantly. I just sit back; ate and listened.

After we finished eating, I went in the kitchen with the women to help clean. I felt like I was in the way but I kept trying to help. I watched them all laughing and talking with each other and wondered what my family was doing today. Everyone probably ate at Gran's and I'm sure Gran cooked her special sweet potato pie and cornbread dressing. I'm sure all my Aunts and Uncles were there, eating and talking and all my cousins were playing games and having a great time. I wanted to be with them. Not here moving outta someone's way constantly.

We didn't go home until late that evening. We stayed longer than anyone else. Those people we'd seen get married—Andy and Abigail left first. Then Clyde and Wanda left with Betsy and Sharon because Sharon was fussy and whiny. Leroy and Hallie were next. Hallie hugged us by but all Leroy did was look at me and say, "Jesse, you done fixed this girl up with a elephant baby. You better be making a lot of money in those log woods to afford to feed that whopper baby y'all gonna have." Jesse ignored him and I tried to. The Duvalls went home next, but Bob stayed, talking with Jesse and Todd. I looked at Jesse, trying to get him to see that I was ready to go too, but he acted like I weren't in the room. He kept talking and talking to Bob, Todd and Preacher Carl. I gave up on trying to get him to notice me and went out on the porch with Vicky, Lilly Jean and Libby. It was after dark when Jesse finally came outside and said, "Honey girl, we need to go home."

I stood, thinking reality had just hit his head. "Alright."

After Thanksgiving, the weather really turned colder and we had to keep the fire going in the fireplace all the time. Jesse went every day to the log woods and I stayed home. I was afraid I was gonna have this baby all alone. Jesse started coming home earlier because I think he was worried about the same thing. He still helped old man Felt, just didn't stay at his place as long every day.

I was still sad and knew there was nothing I could do about it. Christmas was coming and I didn't even want to think about it. We didn't have no decorations or presents and I flat out didn't care. On Friday before Christmas, Jesse came home with a tree. He was grinning as he came inside, holding that pine tree. "What is that?" I asked.

He leaned it against the wall and kissed me, "You know what it is, 'Cella. It's a Christmas tree." I stared at it. It wasn't very big. Jesse seemed so happy. "Our very first Christmas tree. It ain't really a whole tree. Just the top outta a big pine we cut today. But I think it makes a great Christmas tree."

I smiled because I wanted him to be happy. "I like it. How are we gonna make it stand up?"

"I'm gonna take care of that right now," he said and turned to go back outside. "We're gonna put it in a bucket with some dirt and water it every day so it won't dry out." He went outside.

I stood in the doorway and called after him as he walked off the porch, "We ain't got no decorations or presents."

He turned back to me, "We're gonna get presents tomorrow and we can make our own decorations. I know you've got some of that scrap material left over from where you and Lilly Jean made the baby clothes and we can make a star outta tin foil. It's gonna be pretty, 'Cella."

I nodded. "How we gonna get presents?"

"We're going to Brookville and go shopping. I'm off work until Monday and old man Felt said I could have tomorrow off from working with him too. I been getting paid 'Cella. We're gonna have Christmas and I know just what I want to buy for you."

"What?"

He grinned, "Can't tell you that, 'Cella. You'll find out Christmas morning. Now, let me go get that bucket of dirt so we can get our Christmas tree sit up right."

Chapter Twenty-eight

We'd got the tree sit up and it did look pretty. We made a chain outta left over lace and cut star shapes in the scrap cloth I had. Jesse made the tin foil star and hung it at the top. Then he went outside and came back in with some pine cones. We tied string to the pine cones and hung them on the tree too. As we did this I laughed, "This is silly," I said.

"Why's it silly?"

"Cause these pine cones went to all the trouble to fall off the tree and now we're putting them back on."

Jesse laughed and smiled at me. He thought my saying that meant I was in a good mood. I wasn't. I just wanted to act like I was happy because he was trying so hard to make me happy.

The next day we drove into Brookville and went straight to Davis department store. Jesse actually gave me some money so I could buy him a Christmas present. Then he kissed me and said he'd meet me in front of the store in an hour. I'd walked around looking at nearly everything in the store before deciding to buy Jesse a new wallet and a little case that had fingernail clippers, a razor and little tiny scissors in it. We'd wrapped up our presents in the paper bags we'd gotten at Davis's when we bought the stuff.

It was now Monday and Jesse had gone back to the log woods and I was home all by myself again. I cleaned the house, looking at our little tree and the four presents underneath it. I poured some water into the tree bucket and decided to start reading Lilly Jean's new Patty Sue book. She'd brought it over last Saturday but I hadn't read it yet. I fixed myself a glass of water and sit it beside Gran's old rocker. Then I sat down with the book. It took me a while to get comfortable but I did at last. This big baby was getting bigger and getting comfortable was a huge job for me. I finally got settled in the chair, and began to read. Patty Sue was totally normal, still surrounded by all those dumb people. I was reading away, trying to figure out what the mystery in this book was gonna be when all of a sudden there was a hard knocking on my front door. Startled, I dropped the book. I got up slowly and walked to the door, wondering who it was. Jesse would come on inside of course. Lilly Jean always knocked very softly and all my people were evidently scared to death of me because of Witch Sue.

The knocking continued as I walked to the door. "Who is it?" I called, not able now to bend down and look under the crack of the door.

"It's me!" I heard Aunt Hannah say. "Let me in!"

I opened the door and Aunt Hannah came inside, looking wild as everything. She was carrying a large something I didn't recognize in one hand and had a stuffed pillowcase in the other. Her hair was sticking out in all directions and her eyes were darting all over the place like a mad person. "Have you seen Wallace Imes running around here?"

"No, ma'am," I said, thinking Aunt Hannah sure wasn't afraid of me because of Witch Sue. But then with the way Aunt Hannah looked, Witch Sue would probably need to be scared of her.

"You sure about that?" she asked, her eyes getting wilder by the minute.

"Yes ma'am, I'm sure."

She came further in the house, "How 'bout my young'uns Devona and Howie?"

"I ain't seen them either."

"Well they gotta be around somewhere! I'm sick of that man doing as he pleases! Yes sirree, I am sick and tired of it. Leaves me for another woman and then nearly every day he's coming back taking this away and that away. Then this morning, bright and early shows up this morning and takes off with my babies. My little Howie and Devona! Just took them right away! Well, let me tell you, I'm gonna fix him! I ain't gonna be in that house no more for him to come take things from me and aggravate me. So I'm gonna stay here."

"Here?" I repeated. "Aunt Hannah, we ain't got no room here."

She held up the something I didn't recognize. "Brought my own cot. I'll sleep wherever I can sit it up. Won't be no problem. And from the looks of you; you could do with someone staying here." She leaned her cot against the wall and sat the pillowcase down.

She started unfolding the cot right in front of the door. "Aunt Hannah," I said, "you can't put that there."

She looked back at me with her wild eyes, "How come! Don't tell me you've gotten all bossy too! I been living with enough bossing me around! Fed up with it! Yes sir, I am!"

I swallowed hard. "But you're right in front of the door," I said. "Jesse won't be able to get in when he gets home."

"Jesse!" she shouted, "He's a man, ain't he?"

"Yes."

"Then we oughta keep him out. Men ain't worth nothing. Nothing but trouble. Pretend to love you, then run out on you and take everything they can get from you. 'Cella, we both better off without a man in here."

"But Aunt Hannah, Jesse ain't like that. And if he can't get in the door, he'll climb through the window. This is his home."

She shook her wild looking head, "Alright then, I'll move my cot." She pulled it over to the side wall; then finished unfolding it. She had it sit up so that when Jesse did come home and opened the door, she'd be hid behind it.

I watched as she sat on the cot and pushed the pillowcase up under it. At last I said, "Aunt Hannah, ain't you scared to come around me because of Witch Sue?"

"Nope. I don't believe in none of that Witch nonsense. Ask me the ones you gotta be scared of is men. Can't trust a man for nothing in the world. Nope, I ain't scared of you, Marcella. But I know everyone else is so maybe they'll all leave me be. If it ain't Wallace trying to come by and take stuff that's perfectly mine away, it's Ma, or Sammy and Madge, Callie, Elmira, Nesta,—the whole crew of them coming and trying to get me to do all sorts of stuff I got no heart in me to do."

I nodded. I fully understood that part. "I miss everyone. I want to see Mama and Papa."

"Oh, you'll see them, 'Cella. They all just waiting to see this baby you gonna have. Ma's got everyone convinced that if Witch Sue truly did curse you it's gonna show up in the baby. She talks about it all the time. Says you must not have been totally cursed because you lived through her broom beating and they all gotta wait on the baby now. You give birth to a nice healthy child and they'll be back quick as a wink."

"But if they just waiting on the baby, why don't Mama or Papa come by now? They came once when I was at the Duvalls."

Aunt Hannah waved her hand, "Yeah, that's because Madge was stubborn and wouldn't listen to Mama. But Mama's been telling her how your eyes turned bright red when you mentioned Witch Sue and said you had smoke coming from your ears when she was beating you with the broom. She claims you had to be cursed some for that to happen but she don't understand you living through the broom beating. And Madgy is so confused right now. She wants to see you but she thinks Mama just might be telling the truth. And as Sammy, well he's a man and men don't think like they should. But he's all torn up over Jesse refusing to take you outta those white people's house. Said he thought Jesse respected him and he's learned different......So, 'Cella, what you got to eat around here. I'm powerful hungry."

"Right now I ain't got nothing cooked."

"Alrighty, you just sit wherever you please and I'll cook. You don't look to me like you fit too good at a stove now." She got up and walked to our icebox. As she looked inside it, she said, "Yep, you sure are gonna have one more big baby. Gonna have to feed that baby grits and eggs to start with. Won't be wanting no milk big as it's gonna be. Yes sir, gonna need some good solid food for that baby." She pulled out our bowl of eggs and the plate of butter. She sit them on the table, "And you'd better be glad I showed up. Jesse just like a man—go off and leave you here all day long big as the house, about ready to pop open with that young'un of his. Ain't right 'Cella, child. Ain't right at all. You need someone here with you and I'm gonna be that someone. Yes sir, I am."

Chapter Twenty-nine

I sat back in the arm chair and watched as Aunt Hannah began cooking. Normally, Aunt Hannah could cook really good, but her wildness seemed to be taking over everything with her. Before long, she had the table covered with flour and cornmeal as she worked at making biscuits and cornbread at the same time. She would mix a little here and a little there. Then with flour all over her hands, she went to the cabinet and pulled out jars of corn, butterbeans and potatoes. She poured them into pots, singing bits and pieces of songs as she worked. She got back to her biscuit and cornbread, slinging flour all over the place and I cringed when thinking about having to clean it all up, but I didn't say a word. With the way she was I was scared to death to even try.

I thought Aunt Hannah would stop cooking once she got everything done, but I was wrong. She just turned the biscuits and cornbread out onto the table and got to work making more. I did try then to stop her but I don't think she heard me at all.

I think Aunt Hannah would have kept right on making biscuits and cornbread until she ran out of flour and cornmeal but Jesse came home.

He came in all happy, calling out, "Hey, honey girl!" just like he always does. Then he stopped, leaving the door wide open, as he stared at Aunt Hannah who was on her fifth batch of biscuits, "What are…." He spoke in shock.

Aunt Hannah didn't let him finish, "I'm taking care of things around here. Ain't got no husband that wants me, and this morning he done made away with my babies, so I'm gonna be here with you and 'Cella. Gonna take care of y'all. Have a seat, I think I'll soon have enough food cooked for us to be able to eat."

Jesse stared at the table with the biscuits and cakes of cornbread all over it. Then he looked at the stove with the potatoes, butterbeans and corn waiting in pots. "And just when will you have enough food cooked? You've got food all over the place."

Aunt Hannah stopped then and looked at the biscuits and cornbread all over the table like she'd just seen them and said, "Oh, didn't realize I'd made so much. Guess I'll just throw this dough out."

"No, no, don't throw it out," Jesse said. "Go ahead and make what you got going. Just don't get any more started." Jesse closed the door and walked to the table, gathering the containers of lard, flour cornmeal and baking powder himself. He put them in the cabinet and looked at me. Then he noticed Aunt Hannah's cot. "What is that?" he pointed.

"That is my bed," Aunt Hannah said, making biscuits with her hands.

"Your bed?" Jesse repeated.

"Yep. My bed."

"What's it doing here?" Jesse asked.

"Right now it ain't doing nothing. Later, it's gonna be holding me as I sleep."

"You got your own house to sleep in," Jesse said.

"Don't want to sleep in my own house. Gonna be sleeping here from now on."

"Oh no. Oh no, you're not!" Jesse exclaimed.

"Yes I am!" Aunt Hannah yelled back.

Jesse looked at me. I was just sitting back watching them go at it. "Marcella, come outside with me a minute."

I got up and followed him out the door. It wasn't that cold, but I wrapped my arms around myself anyway. "Whatever gave her the idea that she's gonna stay here?" Jesse asked.

I shrugged, "I don't know. She just showed up with that cot acting all crazy."

He shook his head. "She can't stay here. We ain't got no room. We won't have no privacy at all with her here. And the way she's cooking we ain't gonna have no food left either."

The baby seemed to be doing flip flops inside me. I put my hand on my stomach and said softly, "I think I might need her here, Jesse. I'm scared about having this baby. I could start having it all by myself while you're gone to the log woods or out at old man Felts."

Jesse stared at me as though he'd just noticed how pregnant I was. Of course he saw me all the time, but his eyes looked like he'd just realized how close we were to having this baby come. Very softly I said, "I don't want to have this baby all alone."

He ran his hand over his face, "You need your Mama is what. All this you being witch touched mess has to stop." He sighed loudly. "Go get your coat, honey girl. We're going to have us a long talk with your Mama and Daddy."

"What about Aunt Hannah?"

"I don't know," Jesse shook his head. I don't want to leave her here, but we've got to take care of this mess. You're liable to have that baby any time now. And your Aunt Hannah…." He sighed again, "Maybe she won't burn the place down. Might cook up all the food we got but…."

"What about Gran? What if she's at Mama and Papa's? She might….."

"Your Gran ain't getting nowhere near you as long as you're with me. Ok, 'Cella. So let's go."

Chapter Thirty

I was scared to death all the way to Mama and Papa's. I kept seeing Gran with that broom, remembering all over again her hitting me and hitting me. When Jesse pulled our truck up into the driveway, I just stared at the old dogwood trees between Mama and Papa's and Gran and Gramp's. Jesse stopped the truck and got out. I stayed right where I was. He called me but I didn't even look at him. Then he came to my door, opened it and said softly, "Trust me, honey girl. I ain't gonna let no one hurt you."

I looked at him and finally slid outta the truck. Jesse held my hand and closed the door behind me. Together we walked up to the front door and I had to close my eyes to try to block out the memory of me laying there in pain, crying out for Gran to please love me. Jesse held tight to my hand and knocked on the door with his other hand. We waited a little bit and Jesse knocked some more. At last the door opened slightly and Papa stuck his head out. His eyes fell on my big stomach first but he didn't say anything to me. He looked right at Jesse, "What do you want?"

Jesse cleared his throat, "Mr. Sammy, me and 'Cella are here to say we're deeply sorry about everything and we want us to be family like we should be."

Papa stepped out onto the porch, leaving the door open, "So you want to apologize. Marcella, child, you look ready to bust. I suppose that's the main reason you're here."

"Well, yeah," Jesse said. "She needs her Mama. She could have this baby anytime...."

We heard Mama call from inside, "Sammy, who is it?"

Papa looked back, "It's 'Cella and Jesse, Madgy."

"'CELLA!" Mama exclaimed. "Oh, my Marcella! My baby!" We could hear her coming through the house and it sounded like she was running. Soon she was in the doorway, her eyes full of tears but she was smiling. Her smile fell away as she looked at me. "OH NO! DEAR SWEET JESUS NO!" Mama put her hand to her mouth and began to scream loudly. I backed up behind Jesse, still clinging to his hand.

"Mrs. Madge, why are you screaming?" Jesse asked, sounding confused.

"Oh, I didn't want to believe it. I kept telling myself it couldn't be true. But now...Oh Lord, why did you let this happen to my baby? To our little sweet Marcella? Dear Lord, why?"

"What are you talking about?" Jesse asked.

Mama shook as she answered, "Just look at her. How big she is. Ain't no normal baby in there. She's way too big for a normal baby. That baby's been cursed by Witch Sue just like Mama said she was. I didn't want to believe her. I didn't but now....OH LORD NO! NO!" Mama was crying hysterically.

Papa put his arm around Mama and said, "Go on back in the house, Madgy. I'll take care of things out here."

Mama ran back inside, slamming the door behind her. I called to her but it didn't do one bit of good. Papa shook his head, "I suggest y'all go on home."

"Papa, please," I begged softly.

"No, there ain't no more Papa please," he said. "When you went to that witch, you cooked everything. And when you cook something it can't be uncooked, Marcella. I just think y'all need to go on now."

"What about the baby?" Jesse asked. "I work every day. She needs someone."

Papa shook his head, "Jesse, if that was a normal baby, we'd be more than happy to help. But we all know now that she went to Witch Sue and we know the power a witch has. And there is definitely something strange about her being so big. That day we went to try to get her from those Duvall's, old Doc Moore was there. He said he estimated this baby was coming in March. She's way too big to be waiting till March to have a baby. There is something definitely wrong. We can't help with no witch touched baby. Sorry." And he went back inside, closing the door behind him.

When Jesse turned to look at me, I had tears streaming down my face. "I knew we shouldn't a come here," I said.

He kissed me gently, "Let's go home."

We walked to the truck and as I got in I said, "At least Aunt Hannah ain't scared of me being witch touched."

"I guess we have to let her stay. She didn't act like she had a whole lot of sense. But she's the best we got now."

Chapter Thirty-one

It is now Christmas Eve morning and I'm sitting in Miz Essie's old rocking chair watching Aunt Hannah sleep with lemons on her big toes. As it turns out, Aunt Hannah likes to sleep late every day and every night she sticks her big toes in lemons before she goes to sleep. When me and Jesse got home from Mama and Papa's that night, we found Aunt Hannah sleeping in her cot, her feet sticking out from the blanket and lemons on each big toe. Jesse took one look at her and said, "I think I got it figured out why Wallace Imes left her. Woman is crazy as a bat. I do believe she's one person that the space people got a hold of and did something to her brain."

I told Jesse to hush, Aunt Hannah might wake up and hear him. But Aunt Hannah slept on. The next day, after Jesse left for the log woods, and I'd cleaned up Aunt Hannah's cooking mess, she woke up and took the lemons off her toes; then put the lemons under the bed. I looked at her and said, "Why do you sleep with lemons on your big toes?"

"Keeps corns and calluses off. I used to have the worst corns and calluses in the world. One day I was up at old Joe Black's getting some peanuts and I had little Howie with me. Howie was about two and a half and faster than the wind. He got away from me and I could hardly go cause them corns and calluses hurt me so bad. Old Joe took off after Howie, caught him and I asked how did an old man like him move so good. I asked didn't he get corns and calluses on his feet. He said no. He said he slept with lemons on his big toes at night and it kept them away. Said they'd get rid of them too for me. Then he let me and Howie go in his house. Man has his very own lemon tree growing in there. Pretty as you please. I go buy lemons off him all the time now. Wallace thought I was clean outta my mind, but let me tell you I ain't. Got fed up with my feet a-hurting all the time. Lemons help me, so I sleep with lemons."

I'd just nodded and said, "Oh," thinking that it must be awful uncomfortable to sleep with lemons stuck on your big toes every night.

And speaking of uncomfortable, I am so uncomfortable I can't stand myself. No matter what, I don't feel good. My legs hurt like crazy and so does my back. I wiggle and wiggle in the chair, trying to feel better as I sit and watch Aunt Hannah and her lemons.

Jesse went to work in the log woods again today. I begged him not to because it's Christmas Eve and he said he had to go because he was gonna to make extra money today and he thinks we really need it. He says tomorrow we'll spend Christmas just me and him. He's got it in his head that Aunt Hannah will go to Gran's for Christmas because she's been talking about it. I tell him don't count on it.

I get tired of watching Aunt Hannah sleep. My eyes wander to the Christmas tree and our four little presents under it. I looked back at Aunt Hannah and suddenly realized that we didn't have anything for her. That just wasn't right. I wasn't convinced she was going to Gran's so she might not even get a present there either. The more I stared at the tree and the presents, the more I knew I had to do something for Aunt Hannah. It would just be awful for her not to get anything on Christmas. At last, I got up, went to the bedroom and got some money from the drawer in the bedside table where Jesse kept it. I didn't get it all and I was sure he'd understand. Then I got my coat and headed out of the house.

I'd decided to walk to Brookville and buy Aunt Hannah a present. I was gonna do this because if I waited for Jesse to get home, all the stores would be closed. I'd walked to Brookville a year or so ago with my cousins, Zenobia and Fran. We'd started out early in the morning and got home late that evening. I figured I'd walk to Davis's, get Aunt Hannah a fancy handkerchief, pretty pin—something—and be home by the time Jesse got in from the log woods. And maybe, the walking will help my legs and back feel better cause sitting down sure ain't working.

It ain't too cold and at first, the walking does help. It helps a lot. I'm feeling much better as I walk along, thinking of the different things I can get Aunt Hannah for Christmas.

I walked and walked, thinking that Brookville seemed a lot closer when me, Zenobia and Fran walked there. Maybe it was because I was so big, but I was starting to get miserable again. And then something started happening that scared and embarrassed me. I had water running down my legs. Something was bad wrong with me. I'd wet myself without even realizing I had to go. I stopped walking and tried squeezing my legs together to make the water stop. It wouldn't. I started to cry and tried walking faster. Nothing helped and to make matters worse, I was so sick now my stomach was hurting like mad. I kept trying to go, hoping my coat would cover up the wetness that kept coming and coming.

I tried to keep going. I really did. But I couldn't. I had to stop. I had to sit down right on the side of the road in the dirt. I cried and cried. I wanted Jesse. I wanted the pain to stop. I had to get back home. I would try to make Aunt Hannah a handkerchief myself from that left over material. That's what I should have done in the first place. I tried to stand, but the pain was so bad, I had to sit right back down. Crying hard, I prayed. I was scared to death.

Then I looked up and saw a familiar car coming down the road. I backed off the road some more, because the familiar car I saw was Mr. Leroy's. I didn't want him to see me like this. I wanted to hide. To disappear. But that weren't gonna happen.

Soon he was stopping right next to me. He leaned over and opened the passenger door. "What are you doing on the side of the road, Marcella?"

"I was on my way to Brookville to buy Aunt Hannah a Christmas present." I tried to sound happy and normal, so maybe he'd think I'd just decided to stop and rest a while on my way.

He gave me a hard look. "You don't sound too good."

Right then, one of them sharp stomach pains hit me hard and I cried out in spite of myself. Mr. Leroy got outta his car and came to me. "You're having your baby, ain't you, girl?"

That hadn't even occurred to me and I felt awful stupid. I'd had no idea what to expect when the baby started coming. I'd heard I was gonna have a hard time because I was so big and I knew I was gonna hurt, but I didn't have no idea how I was gonna hurt. Lamely, I said, "But it ain't March. Dr. Moore said March."

He shook his head. "I've seen plenty of women when they start having babies and believe me, you're having this one now, not March." He put his arms under mine and began pulling me up.

"Hey, what are you doing?" I cried, resisting him.

"I'm gonna get you to Hallie," he said. "I can't leave you on the side of the road like this. Now come on. Marcella, stop fighting me. You don't want to have your baby right out in the open."

Realizing he was right, I let him pull me up. I hurt like crazy as he led me to the car. He opened the back door and helped me inside. "Goodness, girl, your water's broke too. Ain't you realized you were having this baby?"

"No. No one's told me nothing about what to expect."

He shook his head, "Didn't you know that when your water breaks like that it means the baby's coming?"

"No."

"With all the women you got in your family and all the babies that's been born in that bunch, you didn't know nothing about water breaking before you have the baby?" He seemed so angry with me.

I wiped tears away, "No. When everyone in my family's had babies, they've always just said the baby's coming. They whispered about stuff around the children. My own Mama never had none but me and when she'd go to help my Aunts, she never talked about water or anything else breaking! And all anyone's told me is that I was gonna have a hard time cause I'm so big!"

He shook his head, "Lay down," He closed the door. I lay there and listened as he got back in the front seat behind the steering wheel again. As he started to drive, turning in the road, back in the direction of his house, he asked, "Where's Jesse? What in the world is he doing letting you walk down the road in your condition?"

"Jesse's in the log woods. He's making extra money today. He don't know I'm walking.

"Ok. Well, I'm taking you to Hallie and then I'm gonna go find him. Tell him this baby is gonna be here for Christmas."

Chapter Thirty-two

I think Mr. Leroy thought he was flying a plane he drove so fast back to his house. I was sure we'd take off up into the sky at any moment. It was no time before we were stopping at his house. Mr. Leroy opened his door and I heard Hallie, "Leroy, what you doing back? You ain't had time to go to Brookville and pick up that spring form pan I need for that cake I'm gonna bake."

"Hallie, we got other problems besides your cake," Mr. Leroy said.

"What are you talking about? I promised Sybil I'd make that orange sponge cake and my spring form pan is broke. I need a new one. You said you was gonna get it."

"Hallie, please. Marcella needs you...."

"Marcella! How do you know she needs me? You won't even let me go see them! All your mad taking over us all the time! And now you tell me she needs me! Leroy, I declare..."

"Hallie, would you please hush!" Mr. Leroy yelled and opened the back door so Hallie could see me laying there, still holding on tight to the seat.

"Oh my goodness!" she exclaimed. "What is going on? Why is she in the back of the car?"

"If you'd just hush, I'd tell you," Mr. Leroy said. "I found her on the side of the road. She's having that baby right now. Let's get her inside and then I'm gonna go find Jesse. That orange sponge cake will just have to wait."

Hallie came to me, "Marcella, child....Oh my, you are soaked through. Come on, honey, let's get you in bed. You gonna be giving birth to this baby before long." She helped me outta the car. I leaned heavily on her as we walked to the house. Mr. Leroy even came and held onto my other side as we went up the steps. I kept crying and crying. I couldn't stop. Hallie led me to Jesse's room and I couldn't help but remember the times me and him had been together in here when Leroy and Hallie were both gone. Mr. Leroy turned the covers back on the bed and Hallie said, "Leroy, go in our room and get one of my nightgowns. I'm gonna change her. Get a bunch of towels too."

"Sure." He left the room.

Hallie held me tight, "Child, what were you doing walking down the road? Were you trying to get Jesse?"

"No, ma'am. I was trying to walk to Brookville to buy Aunt Hannah a Christmas present. We ain't got nothing for her. She's staying with us, you know."

"No, I didn't know."

Mr. Leroy came back with a blue gown and an armful of towels. Hallie told him to lay the towels out on the bed. She kept holding me as he did this. When she was satisfied with the way the towels were, she said, "That's good. Now, go find Jesse."

"That's what I intend to do," Leroy said.

He started to leave and Hallie said, "Go by and tell Madge what's going on. Tell her we've got her here."

"Alright. I'll do all that too."

He left and Hallie had me sit on the towels. She undressed me completely, put the blue gown over my head and told me to lie down. I did. "I hurt so bad."

"You're gonna be hurting a lot more before it's all over. Having a baby ain't no fun at all." She left the room and came back with a sheet. I watched as she tied one end of it to the left post on the foot of the bed. Then she lay the other end up close to me. "Here. You're gonna need to pull on this. It'll help with the pain you gonna be in later on. You might even need to bite down on it. But that's ok. Now let me see how much you've opened up."

She checked me just like Dr. Moore had done when Gran beat me. "You're getting there," she said. "Gonna be a while but you're getting there."

She started to leave but I called her back, "Where are you going?"

"I'm gonna get some ice water to wash your face with. You're gonna need that too. Don't worry, I ain't leaving altogether. I'll be right back."

She left and I stared around the room. I thought of Aunt Hannah sleeping with her lemons and wondered if she'd ever woke up yet. Hallie came back with a big bowl of ice water, a pair of scissors and more sheets. "What you gonna do with them scissors?"

"That's for cutting the cord," she said gently, sitting beside me.

I looked at her, "Ain't you scared of me?"

"Scared of you? Why should I be scared of you?" she moved my hair back.

"Cause I went to Witch Sue. My Mama's terrified of me because of that."

Hallie shook her head. "No, child I ain't scared of you. I don't believe Sue Jones is a bit more witch than I am. She just found a way to get money outta gullible people."

"Mama says I must be cursed by her cause I'm so big."

"That's ridiculous. You just having a big baby is all. You shoulda seen my sister Sybil when she had her Anthony. She was big just like you and she hadn't been near Sue Jones or any other witch for that matter." Hallie sighed, and combed her fingers through my hair some more. We were both quiet for a long time. Then she said, "Maybe now we can all get around to being a family."

Chapter Thirty-three

I ain't never been in so much pain in my life. Even Gran beating me with the broom is better than this. I believe if someone threw me in a pot of boiling water and put a lid on me it couldn't be no worse. I keep screaming and crying in spite of myself. Hallie is constantly here, telling me to relax, just breathe and go with it. I can't relax. There ain't no way.

I don't think I'm ever getting out of this. I'm gonna hurt forever. I just want to die. I keep asking Hallie what time it is and she'll tell me. It's always only a minute or two later than the last time I asked. I think time is stopping so I can be hurt more. I'm sure I'm being punished for going to Witch Sue. I even tell Hallie this, but she shakes her head, "You're just going through labor, 'Cella. All women go through this to get their babies."

"I just want this baby to hurry up so I can stop hurting!"

"It's gonna take some time, just be patient."

And the pain goes on and on and on. I writhe and squirm in the bed. I cry out and scream. Nothing helps. Nothing at all. After forever passes, I hear Jesse at the door. "Can I come in."

Hallie goes and opens the door. "You can stay for a minute. Then you gotta go. Ain't no place for a man."

Jesse has a stack of diapers in his hands. He sits them on the dresser, then comes and sits on the bed, "Hey honey girl, how you doing?"

I look at him like he's crazy. "I'm flat out dying is how I'm doing!" I shout at him. He looks like I slapped his face and I feel bad for him. But not too long, cause the pains are back and I can't stand my own self anymore. Jesse holds my hands and watches me as I struggle with the pains. An idea comes to me. I don't want to do this no more. "Jesse, take me home."

"Honey girl, I can't take you home now."

"Yes you can. Please. We can go home in our truck. You have it with you, don't you?"

"Sure I do, but you ain't going nowhere now."

"Yeah, I am. I decided I don't want to do this now. I'll do it later."

Jesse laughed a little, "You can't do it later, honey girl. You gotta do it now."

Hallie is soon there, "Jesse, you have to go now. I need to check her and see how far along she is."

"Ok." He stands. "I'm gonna be right out here, 'Cella. I ain't leaving you." He leans close to me, kisses my forehead and then he's gone.

Hallie pulls the blanket back and starts checking me again, "Oh, yes. Good, good 'Cella. You're coming along just fine. Coming along fine at that."

I don't think the pain can get any worse but it does. And it never stops. I beg Hallie to make it stop, but she only washes my face with ice water and tells me to keep patient. I hold that sheet she gave me earlier; wring my hands tight in it. She brushes my hair and sings to me, I guess trying to make me feel better. It ain't working at all. I'll never ever feel better. I'm gonna tell Jesse we ain't having no more babies. This is it. He'd better be happy with this one cause there ain't gonna be no more coming outta me.

The day wears on and my pain grows worse and worse. I look at the window and see it's getting darker. "Did Mr. Leroy tell my Mama?" I finally ask Hallie.

"He told her honey. She just said she couldn't have nothing to do with no witch touched monster baby."

"What about Aunt Hannah?"

"Jesse went by there to get the baby's stuff after Leroy found him in the log woods. She said she'll take care of the house for you until you get back."

I ask Hallie what time it is and she tells me almost five in the evening. I say it has to be later than that and she says well it ain't. She stays right with me as I go through one horrible pain after the other. She keeps checking me and at last she says, "Ok, 'Cella. You're ready for the next part."

"Next part! What do you mean next part!"

"You're ready to push this baby outta you. Just bear down hard like you going to the bathroom. Come on, you can do it."

"Will that finally get this big baby outta me?"

"Sure will. Come on, push. Push hard."

I do. Ain't no baby or nothing comes out. "It didn't work! It didn't work!"

"You gotta do it more than once," Hallie says. "Now, push, push!"

I push and I push and I push. I get so tired from pushing and hurting I just want to lay back, close my eyes and go to sleep but I can't. The pain won't stop.

At long last, Hallie says, "I see the head. Come on, 'Cella, push hard. HARDER! This baby is coming now."

I push and push as hard as I can. I feel something plop outta me. I look and there is a wiggly wet messy baby girl laying on the bed between my legs. Hallie grabs her up and looks at the clock, "It's Eleven fifty,'Cella. Remember that so we can write down the time she came. Then she started wiping the baby's tiny face with a wash cloth. The baby starts to cry and the bedroom door pops open. "Is the baby…" I hear Jesse.

"You've got a little girl," Hallie says. "Go on back in there, now. I'll bring her out when we get her ready."

Hallie wraps my baby up in a blanket and lays her on top of me. Then she gets those scissors. I watch her cut the cord, scared it's gonna hurt, but it don't. Then she takes my baby away. "Pretty little baby girl we got here, 'Cella. Does she have a name?"

"I want to name her Sabrina Suzanna but Jesse wants Sabrina Marcella."

Hallie kisses my baby, "Well, y'all gonna have to get together on that middle name." She hands little Sabrina to me. I hold her close and Hallie is telling me to push again.

"I thought it was over," I said.

"Afterbirth, child. Afterbirth. Just push."

I do, feeling more stuff come outta me. I look at Sabrina, thinking she's a whole lot smaller than I thought she was gonna be. She ain't no big baby at all. Hallie calls for Leroy to bring a scale so we can weigh her. Suddenly, I'm hurting all over again. Hallie is gathering stuff up, but I'm feeling worse than ever. I hurt so so bad. "HALLIE! HELP ME!" I cry out and she turns right to me.

"What is it, 'Cella?"

"The pain! It's back! It's back!"

Hallie checks me again. "Oh my goodness. We've got another one coming! 'Cella, give me Sabrina. I'm gonna let her Daddy take care of her while you have this next one.

"Next one? All I'm having is Sabrina. No more. She's it."

"No, honey, she ain't. This is the reason you were so big. You're having twins."

Twins. Two babies at once. I'd never even thought about having two at once. Hallie takes Sabrina and leaves the room with her. I feel this other baby pushing out of me even though I ain't pushing. Hallie comes back and looks at the stack of diapers Jesse brought with him. "I forgot to tell Jesse she ain't even got a diaper on. Oh well, let's see how you're doing with this one."

She makes me push and push and push some more again. Then something else plops outta me. "Well looky here!" she exclaims, "We got us a little boy this time."

I look. Sure enough there is now a tiny wet messy baby boy on the bed between my legs. He's tiny but bigger than Sabrina. Hallie picks him up and starts wiping him down just like she did Sabrina. "Well ain't this something. Got us a little girl and a little boy. Little Miss Sabrina born on Christmas Eve and this one here, born two minutes into Christmas day. Has he got a name, 'Cella?"

"We ain't thought of no boy names," I say, listening to my baby boy cry in Hallie's arms.

"Well you'd better think of one. This little boy needs a name."

Jesse is soon at the door. He don't knock this time. He just comes right on in, carrying Sabrina. "We've got another one."

"Yep, sure do," Hallie grins widely, "Merry Christmas, Jesse, meet your son."

Jesse grins big as everything as he stares at the baby boy Hallie's holding. Then he comes to me, "Merry Christmas, 'Cella. I love you." He kisses me and I pass out cold.

Chapter Thirty-four

I stayed passed out for a long time. Then I'd wake up and hear Hallie, Jesse and Leroy talking. I'd hear the babies crying and I'd go right back to sleep. It was late Christmas evening when Jesse finally got me fully awake. "Come on, honey girl, you got me worried."

I opened my eyes. He was sitting on the edge of the bed. "Where's the babies?" I asked, filling empty without them inside me.

"Daddy went up to the attic and got my old cradle down. They're sleeping in it. Mama got some bottles from Aunt Sybil and fixed them some milk."

"I thought I was gonna feed them," I said.

"You are, but you was sleeping so much we couldn't get you to stay awake. Mama says it's cause you had such a hard time. It's ok, 'Cella. You'll be feeding them soon. They're both so tiny. That little Sabrina looks just like you honey girl and Mama says the little boy looks like me. And speaking of our little boy, how about we name him Stephen Jesse after my Grandpa. He died when Mama was pregnant with me. That's where they got the Jesse for my name."

"Sabrina and Stephen," I said. "Ok, but I want him to be Stephen and not Steve. I don't like Steve."

"Whatever you say, honey girl. I went by your Mama and Daddy's house earlier today when you were asleep. I told them we have the prettiest little girl and boy ever and there's no way either one of them are monster babies. Mama went with me and said there was no way monster babies could be born on Christmas Eve and Christmas day. Your Gran was there and kept saying they had to wait for the evil to show up in our children. I wanted to slap her. My children are not evil. I told them all that. I told them I was sick and tired of this witch Sue business. Your Papa told me not to make a scene and then your Mama said she'd think about coming to see you."

I nodded. "How is Mr. Leroy?"

"A lot better than he was. I think him having to help you actually helped our relationship."

"How much did our babies weigh?"

"Little Sabrina is four pounds and Stephen is five pounds six ounces. Sabrina is seventeen inches long and Stephen eighteen and a half inches long. There ain't nothing wrong with either one of them, honey girl. And oh, I got something else for you too."

"What?"

"Your Christmas present. It is Christmas, remember."

"I don't have your presents here. It's..."

"I brought all the presents, 'Cella. And your Aunt Hannah went to stay with your Aunt Callie. Callie said Hannah could turn her panty into a small bedroom. Hannah went for it because she claims she saw Wallace looking through the windows last night."

"Was he?"

Jesse shrugged, "Probably not. That woman ain't right in the head, 'Cella. When I went back there yesterday before the babies came, she'd cooked just about every bit of the food we had left and was killing invisible spiders on the walls. We're better off with her gone. Now, let's me and you have our Christmas." He reached onto the floor and handed me the biggest package that was under the tree. "Open this one first."

I did. It was a pretty picture frame, all gold and silver trimmed. "Oh Jesse, it's beautiful, but we ain't got no pictures. We didn't even have a picture made of us when we got married."

"I know and I regret that. But now that Sabrina and Stephen are here, we are gonna have us a family picture made as soon as possible and put it in this frame. Ok, I get to open my presents now."

He reached on the floor again and came up with both of his packages. He opened the wallet first and then the little razor case. He kissed me after each one and said, "Now for the most important present of all. What I've been working and working for and am still working for." He paused and reached onto the floor one more time. He handed me the smallest package, "Here, 'Cella. I love you with all my heart."

I opened it. Inside was a red velvet box. I opened that. Inside that box was a diamond engagement ring and a plain wedding band in silver. "OH JESSE JESSE JESSE! I love it! THANK YOU!"

He kissed me, "I couldn't afford the gold ones, honey girl. I hope you don't mind."

"I don't mind at all. They're beautiful." I took them out of the box and started to put them on, but Jesse stopped me.

"I think that's my job, honey girl." He slipped the rings on my finger. They were a little loose but not bad. I looked at them on my hand. "Now I really feel married."

"Well, we are married, honey girl. Married with two sweet little babies."

Oh, Jesse, our babies. They ain't got no Christmas presents."

"We'll get them something soon, 'Cella. They're both too little to care right now. Being born and being taken care of is their present. That and us being here with my Mama and Daddy and everyone getting along fine is present enough."

"I just wish my Mama and Papa would love me."

"So do I honey girl."

Chapter Thirty-five

Gramp used to have a girl dog named Sheba. She had puppies on top of puppies and I used to watch her feed them on the front porch. I remember her looking miserable. I know now just how she felt. Hallie helped me learn how to nurse my babies—one on each side. So here I lay with Sabrina on my left and Stephen on my right. They are nursing away and I'm stuck, laying here like some animal trapped with these babies. They are pretty and sweet babies, sure, but all they want to do is eat eat eat. I feed them constantly. And when I ain't feeding them, I'm hungry myself. I am so glad Hallie likes to cook because I could eat everything in the house now.

We are staying with Hallie and Leroy. I'm sleeping in Jesse's old room and the babies are in his old cradle right next to my bed. Jesse is sleeping in the spare room. I asked why and he said that way I'd be more comfortable for a while until I healed up more. I'm kinda glad in a way because every time I move or the bed moves I hurt like mad all over again.

It was Saturday after New Years before Mama and Papa came to see Sabrina and Stephen. I was laying in bed feeding them. Hallie was running her sewing machine; Jesse was in the log woods and Mr. Leroy was I don't know where. I heard the knocking on the door over the hum of Hallie's sewing machine. Thinking it was probably someone else I didn't pay it much mind. The Duvalls and Jansans had been by, all of them bringing something for the babies, admiring them; telling me and Jesse how pretty they were. The only one of my people who'd been by so far was Aunt Hannah. She'd came two days after Christmas and sit for a long time with me. She stayed until she declared she could hear Wallace Imes in the floorboards and just had to leave before he came up outta the floor to bother her.

I laid there in bed, because I couldn't get up and listened as Hallie answered the door. I was shocked when she said, "Hey, there, Sammy, Madge. Good to see you! It sure is! Come on in. "Cella and the babies are back in Jesse's bedroom. And just wait till you see those precious little darlings."

Then I heard Mama, "Are you sure there's nothing wrong with them?"

Hallie laughed, "There ain't the first thing in this world wrong with them, Madge. They are as perfect as perfect can be. Even old hard headed Leroy has fell in love with them."

"Well, we'd like to see them for ourselves," Papa said. "Lana was convinced Marcella was cursed by that witch woman. You just don't know how it's been around our place."

Hallie made a little sound; then said, "No, Sammy, I don't. But I do know that poor Marcella is broken hearted over how y'all've treated her. She needs to know her Mama and Daddy love her."

"We love her," Mama said. "But we was scared of her. You just don't go messing around with witches and such like that from the devil. It can cause all kinds of problems."

It was quiet for a moment and then Hallie said, "Let me see how Marcella and the babies are. She was feeding them just a little bit ago. I'll tell her you're here."

I looked down at my babies. Little Sabrina had stopped nursing and was sleeping against my breast. But little Stephen was still eating away like he was half starved. I covered my left side where Sabrina was the best I could and waited for Hallie. She was soon coming in the room. "Your Mama and..."

"I know, I heard them," I said.

She came closer. "I see little Stephen's still eating. Hungry little boy, ain't he."

"All the time," I said, moving him so I could cover myself, causing him to cry out in protest. I kissed his little head, telling him to hush. He didn't hush. He just cried more.

Mama and Papa were at the door. "Can we come in?" Mama asked.

"Sure," Hallie said, moving aside so they could come to the bed and see me and the babies.

They came to the bed and stood there, staring down on me, Sabrina and Stephen. I didn't know what to say to them so I said nothing. I tried to hush little Stephen but he was hungry and wouldn't hush. His crying woke up Sabrina and she started crying too. I tried to hush her and had no luck at that either. Then Mama said, "They look like fine babies."

"They are." I said softly. "Not cursed at all."

Papa sighed, "Marcella, honey, you have to understand. Witches can have powers. We just couldn't take no chances."

I nodded, cuddling both Sabrina and Stephen in an attempt to quiet them. "Do you want to hold them?" I asked.

They looked at each other first, making me nervous. Then Papa said, "How 'bout it, Madgy? Want to hold our grandchildren?"

Mama stared at me some more. "You sure it's safe, Sammy?"

Hallie who was still in the room cried out, "Oh for goodness sakes, Madge! They're sweet little babies. Of course it's safe. We all been holding them—Leroy included and ain't nothing happened to none of us! Marcella wasn't cursed by Sue Jones a bit more than I've been cursed by her."

Mama sighed. She leaned close to me and picked up little Sabrina. Papa got Stephen and as they held them both, they looked at them closely. Mama asked me what their names were and I told her, "Sabrina Marcella and Stephen Jesse." I'd given in to Jesse about Sabrina's middle name.

Mama moved Sabrina to her shoulder, "Didn't you know you were having twins? Didn't Dr. Moore tell you?"

I shook my head, "I didn't know nothing, Mama. He never told me there was two babies in me."

Papa spoke up, "Twins can surprise you, Madge. Don't you remember Olivia Johnson back when we were younger. She had twins and only thought she was having one. I remember that good cause her husband Ron was working at the bait and tackle shop with me when they came and told him. Poor man was so shocked when they told him he had two babies, he nearly fell to the floor."

Mama nodded, still looking Sabrina over. "Let me look at the other one, Sammy."

They traded babies and Mama was now looking over Stephen. At last she said, "Well, they do seem fine right now. But I still think they bear watching. If there is something wrong with them it might not show up until later."

"Oh Mama!" I couldn't help but say.

Mama laid Stephen back beside me, "I'm sorry, Marcella. I want to be able to love these babies without reservation. But the fact is you went to that Witch woman and she spoke over you. I can't get over that. Sammy, let's go home."

"Wait," I said as Papa gave me Sabrina, "Will you be back?"

"Maybe," Mama said as they turned and left the room.

Chapter Thirty-six

Every day for the next two weeks, I waited for Mama and Papa to come back. Each time there was a knock on the door, I hoped it was them. I strained my ears and begged silently for them to come to me. I wanted them to love me and my babies. But they didn't come back. And neither did any of my family. I guess they'd all decided I was witch cursed and they couldn't have nothing to do with me.

I tried not to think about Mama and Papa. Tried not to let it bother me that they wouldn't come. But it did bother me. It bothered me a lot. At night I would wake up crying about it. Jesse was sleeping with me now and he'd hold me, always asking if I was crying over them and always the answer was yes. I wished I could go back and not go to Witch Sue. I wished I could undo that day, but I couldn't. I loved my babies now that they were here and was glad she didn't get rid of them for me. But what she had done was get rid of the rest of my family and I didn't know how to get them back.

My babies were growing and Hallie was always there to help me. I was getting up more now, although even moving was torture. Hallie kept telling me I'd feel like myself soon but I didn't really believe her. Jesse had started trying to hug and kiss me a lot and I told him forget it. I didn't even feel like being looked at much less what I thought he had in mind.

Jesse didn't mention us leaving here yet and I was glad. I needed Hallie to be helping me. There is no way I could have taken care of cooking, cleaning, washing the babies' dirty diapers, tending to them and taking care of myself. I was just too sick to do it.

But Hallie seemed to love it. She sang as she worked, all bright and sunshiny like. I grew to like hearing her sing although it bothered me at first. But then I started liking it. She could actually sing very good and I told her so. She just smiled and said, "Thank you 'Cella." And my babies loved her too. I could tell by the way they quieted right down when she picked them up.

Jesse was still working in the log woods and every day when he came home, he would kiss me first and then hold our babies; one in each arm. They were content with him and I liked sitting back watching the three of them together. So far he hadn't mentioned us going home and neither had I.

We settled in here with Hallie and Mr. Leroy. Even Mr. Leroy was being easy to get along with. He never mentioned the way he'd been when he found out about me and Jesse. He just acted like it never happened. At first, I didn't like that, but Jesse told me to leave well enough alone. "He's being nice to us," Jesse said. "Let's just keep it that way."

I think Mr. Leroy was being nice because he'd fallen in love with Sabrina and Stephen. They were so tiny and sweet, but they had a lot of power. Just holding them made you fall in love with them. I was sure if Mama and Papa broke down and let themselves they'd love them too. But Mama and Papa wouldn't even come to see them.

On the last Saturday in January, Mr. Leroy came home from helping James Jansan plow his tobacco fields and said that the night before Libby gave birth to her baby. She had a boy, Randall Carl Duvall. They were calling him Randy and all of the Jansan's and Duvalls were going up to Harris to see Preacher Carl, Libby and little Randy. I thought about Libby and her new baby. I wondered if she'd hurt like I did when she had him. Was he a good baby? Did he cry a lot? Did she have any help way up there in Harris away from her family? I mentioned all this to Jesse and he said Libby had her baby in a hospital with lots of nurses and doctors to help. I said that must be nice but it was not right for her to have all that help and I had to give birth in awful terrible pain.

I looked around at all the Jansans had given us for our babies and I mentioned it to Hallie that I wished I had something to give Libby for her little Randy. Hallie smiled, "Let's make him a little blanket. I can help you do one real simple."

I told her I had no idea how to sew and she said it was high time I learned. We wound up making a small baby quilt together by sewing together different pieces of scrap cloth. We used some of the scrap material I had and some Hallie had. It took us about two weeks to finish with Hallie doing most of the work. The Jansans and Duvalls had already gone to see the baby and came back home by the time we finished. But Jesse took the quilt to the Duvalls and Alice said they would mail it to Libby right away. She said it was very pretty and she was sure Libby would appreciate it and be able to use it for Randy because it was freezing cold up in Harris.

In addition to teaching me how to sew, Hallie started teaching me how to cook. She even started letting me help cook meals. I was learning how not to burn food and how to cook it all evenly.

I was so content being here that it shocked me when during the first week of March; Jesse came home from the log woods and casually mentioned that we needed to start thinking about going home. We were sitting on the couch together with Jesse holding Sabrina and me holding Stephen. Hallie was in the kitchen and Mr. Leroy was over tending to the Mr. Esau museum. A bunch of people had stopped by wanting to see it and Mr. Leroy was giving them the grand tour as he called it.

I just stared at Jesse and he said, "I know we're all getting along fine here, 'Cella, but we do need to get home."

Chapter Thirty-seven

We went home on the second Saturday in March. Hallie cried the whole time we were loading the truck to go. She made us promise to come see them and said she'd be over every day to hold the babies. I told her I wanted her to do that and even said I wished she was coming with us. She told Jesse we could stay but he said no, we needed to go home. I didn't really know why. He and Mr. Leroy seemed to be getting along fine with each other. I liked Hallie a lot and the babies were happy too. But Jesse wanted to go home so we went.

We rode with me holding Sabrina in one arm and Stephen in the other. They slept all the way and when we got home, everything looked closed up and strange. Jesse helped me carry the babies inside and we put them in the crib he'd made earlier for them. They looked so tiny in that crib. I was used to seeing them side by side in the cradle. We covered them with a blanket and Jesse kissed me for a long time. I let him but told him I still wasn't ready to do what he wanted yet.

He went back out to the truck and brought the cradle inside. We sit it by our chairs and I looked in the cabinet at the food we did have. Hallie had sent food with us and I was happy I wouldn't have to cook at least for today.

The weekend wasn't bad because Jesse was there to help with Sabrina and Stephen. He held them, changed them and even helped me give them baths. But on Monday morning, he went back to the log woods and before long, I was losing my mind. Both babies were crying and I was trying to wash their stinky diapers. I left the diapers in the sink to soak and lay in bed, feeding my children. I soon learned that doing anything but holding them was out of the question. I was thrilled when Hallie showed up and helped me. She stayed nearly all day but I didn't complain. I needed her with me.

Hallie kept her promise about coming over and I don't know what I would have done if she didn't. Lilly Jean came by and brought pictures of Libby's baby. He looked red and wrinkly, but I told Lilly Jean he was pretty. She said Libby really liked the quilt because it was thick and warm. Lilly Jean brought a new Patty Sue book and I let her leave it with me only because I didn't want to hurt her feelings by saying I didn't have time to read no book right now. But she was so nice it was hard not to say, "Sure, leave it and I'll read it soon."

March turned into April and the days were warmer now. We had wild flowers growing around the house and I liked picking them and bringing them inside in bunches. I started putting Sabrina and Stephen in little baskets that the Duvalls had given us and taking them outside with me while I picked the flowers. Jesse told me some of them were weeds but I didn't care. They were pretty and that's all that mattered to me. I even made me and Sabrina little wreaths of flowers for our hair and because Stephen actually looked jealous, I pinned a tiny bunch of flowers to his diaper. He liked looking at it and would coo and make little baby sounds, smiling and being all happy. When Jesse saw it, he made me take it off. He said Stephen was a boy and didn't need to go around with flowers pinned to his diaper. I told Jesse he sounded like Mr. Leroy and he told me he just don't want his son to be a sissy boy. I still pin flowers to Stephen's diaper when Jesse is gone, but I remember to take them off before he comes home. Stephen is too little to know about being sissy. He just likes looking at the flowers.

Clyde and Wanda came to see us one evening with their little girls, Betsy and Sharon. They brought a playpen for us. Wanda said they didn't have one with Betsy but it had been wonderful with Sharon. I watched Sharon getting into everything and asked didn't Wanda still need this playpen for Sharon and she said no. Sharon had learned how to climb out and Wanda was afraid she'd get hurt. I asked didn't Libby need it and Wanda told me someone at their church had given her one already. We had a nice visit in spite of Sharon wanting to rearrange everything in my cabinet and throwing a fit when Clyde and Wanda wouldn't let her. After they left, Jesse sit the playpen up where we used to have the cradle. They were too big for the cradle now and Jesse had taken it back to Hallie and Leroy's attic. Hallie said we could keep it up there for the next baby and I said there weren't gonna be no more babies. She just laughed and patted my back.

On Easter Sunday, we dressed the babies up and went to church with Hallie and Leroy. We'd gone some with them when we were staying with them, but we hadn't been since we'd been home. Hallie was all happy to see us and she told us we needed to come more often. All during the service, I kept looking for Mama and Papa to show up but they never did.

After Easter my birthday came the next Saturday. Jesse took me to Davis Department store, let me pick out a new dress and then he bought it for me. We'd dressed up the babies in their Easter clothes and Jesse was wearing his brown suit that he wore when we got married. Wearing my new dress, we went to have that family picture made. The man taking the picture said he would mail it to Hallie and Leroy's house since we didn't have a mailbox of our own. Afterwards, we walked around Brookville, carrying the babies and looking in store windows. As we were walking along, I saw Mama. She was with Aunt Zona Mae. They were coming out of the drug store. "MAMA!" I called. She turned in my direction and went right into a store that was marked for whites only. I started to go after her, but Jesse held me back. Aunt Zona Mae did go in after her and it weren't long before they were coming back out, being scolded by a big white man. Mama was apologizing, saying she didn't see the sign. He told her she'd better keep her eyes open.

I called to her and hurried to her carrying Sabrina. Mama acted like she didn't hear me, but Aunt Zona Mae stopped and waited on me. "Hey, how y'all doing?" I said.

Aunt Zona Mae turned to me, "We're good. How about you? Are you going to church?"

"We went last Sunday," I said, moving Sabrina a little. "We didn't see any of you."

"Well I'm going to church here in town now," Aunt Zona Mae said. "Dating me one of the deacons."

"That's nice," I said, looking at Mama who was standing a few feet from us watching. I looked back and saw Jesse coming with Stephen.

Aunt Zona Mae looked at Sabrina, "So, this is one of the twins."

"Yes," I smiled. "They're both wonderful babies...."

"Are you sure about that, Marcella?" Aunt Zona Mae asked.

"Of course we're sure," Jesse said, putting Stephen up to his shoulder.

"Mama, do you want to see them again?" I called to her.

"Yeah," Jesse called, "they won't hurt you none. I hold them all the time and ain't been cursed yet. Ain't seen no horns growing on them or nothing evil at all."

Mama approached us cautiously, like we had some kind of catching sickness. "I don't need none of your mouth, Jesse. Did you know that none of my flowers bloomed this year? Not a blossom on my dogwoods, roses, daffodils or any of it. Mama says it's all because of Marcella going to that witch woman. That curse might not a showed up in these children yet, but you just wait. I'm sure it will."

"But Mama, how can you be sure?" I asked. "My babies are fine. Both of them."

"Marcella, I don't want to stand here arguing with you on the street. I'm just not gonna do it. Zona, come on. We've got other shopping to do." And she started walking away.

I called after her, but she didn't turn back. Aunt Zona Mae surprised me by kissing me and saying, "I'll be praying for you, 'Cella. Be praying for this whole family."

"Thank you." I whispered.

Chapter Thirty-eight

April ended and May came. Me and Jesse were getting along good. I felt like myself again and was even letting Jesse do all of his loving to me again. The babies were bigger, happier and Hallie still came by all the time. Jesse started talking about working for James Jansan in the summer and I said if I was gonna help again with Grandma Cal, the babies would have to come. He said they understood that. Everything was fine; everything except the fact that my Mama and Papa still wouldn't have nothing to do with me.

We were going to church with Hallie and Leroy just about every Sunday and every Sunday Mama and Papa weren't there. I told Jesse maybe they were going with Aunt Zona Mae in Brookville. He said he didn't think they were going anywhere. I tried not to think of them. Tried to just think of me, Jesse and our babies. Tried to be happy with Hallie and Leroy accepting and loving us at last but it still hurt that my own Mama and Papa would have nothing to do with us.

Somewhere along the middle of May I started noticing a nervousness in Jesse. I would ask him what was wrong and he'd say nothing. I figured it was because it had been raining a lot and he'd been home instead of working in the log woods or in the fields with James Jansan. I'd been telling him we needed to add onto this place soon because Sabrina and Stephen were getting bigger not smaller and we needed more room. He just nodded and said sure, he knew that. Then he'd go out and take long walks in the woods, even though it was raining. I thought he was worried about money and I even tried telling him we didn't need to worry about adding on now, just we'd need to do it later. He just nodded and looked like he was thinking far far off. I thought maybe the babies were bothering him and I tried to keep them quiet. I was better at cooking now and I tried cooking all his favorite foods, but he still seemed nervous and not at all like himself.

On Saturday, May 16th, it was raining steadily and Jesse was home again. I'd just gotten dinner fixed and was sitting it on the table when we heard knocking on the door.

Jesse was sitting in the armchair and Stephen and Sabrina were in the playpen. Jesse got up and went to the door. He opened it, "Bob! Hey there, come on in."

Bob Duvall stepped into our little house, dripping water. "Sorry I'm so wet. It wasn't raining bad when I left the house."

"It's ok," Jesse said. "Honey girl, get Bob a towel."

I did and as Bob dried off, Jesse invited him to eat dinner with us. I had stew and biscuits cooking. Bob agreed and soon we were all sitting down to eat. As we ate, Bob made small talk about the rain and farming. I listened to him and Jesse talking, thinking Bob had something else on his mind. At last, when the meal was just about over, Bob said, "I don't hear the rain as loud now."

Jesse looked toward the window, "Don't seem to be coming down as hard."

"Jesse, do you think me and you could go talk out on the porch? Me and Nancy are having problems and I just gotta talk with someone."

"Sure," Jesse said, standing. "Honey girl, do you mind?"

"No, but it's getting awful stuffy in here. Could you leave the door open for air? I won't bother you."

Jesse nodded and they went out onto the porch. They had to sit right down on it because we still didn't have any porch chairs. I hoped the porch weren't wet and got to work cleaning the table and dishes. As I worked, I could occasionally hear Bob talking about him and Nancy, but I didn't pay it much mind. Stephen and Sabrina grew restless, so I carried them one by one to the bedroom and then lay on our bed nursing them. They ate for a long time before falling to sleep. I put them in the crib and went back to finish with the dishes. I got them cleaned and started sweeping the floor and that's when I heard Jesse say, "Man, I don't know what to tell you. I got problems of my own."

"What kind of problems do you have?" Bob asked. "You and 'Cella seem happy. She's even cooking good now. That was some good stew."

"Yeah, I know. Everything's fine with me, her and the babies. But there's something going on that's about to change all that. And I can't do nothing about it."

I stopped my sweeping, scared stiff. What was he talking about? Bob must have been thinking the same thing because he said, "What are you talking about Jesse?"

"I've been drafted."

I dropped the broom to the floor and ran out onto the porch. "You've been what, Jesse Jenkins?" I shouted.

"Oh, 'Cella, honey girl, please!"

"You can't be drafted! Ain't no way!" I cried.

"Well I am," Jesse said. "They mailed the notice to Mama and Daddy's a week or so ago. I have to go Monday morning for my physical."

"Well you just tell them you can't go. Tell them you got a wife and two babies…."

"It don't work that way 'Cella."

I was fuming, "Well, when was you planning on telling me? When you left for Lord knows where?"

"I was gonna tell you, honey girl. Honest. I was just trying to figure how."

It was quiet for a while and then Bob said, "Drafted. We all signed up together but you're the only one called so far, Jesse. Maybe I could go and beg to get drafted and that would help me outta these problems with Nancy."

"Maybe you could go in Jesse's place," I suggested. "Tell them you wanta go and he can't."

"That won't work either, Marcella," Jesse said. "Look, maybe it won't be so bad. I can go someplace for my basic training and then maybe they'll station me someplace where we can all be together."

I wasn't ready to hear him explain things away. "Did Hallie know about this?" I asked, thinking of how she'd been over visiting me and the babies never mentioning at all about Jesse getting drafted.

"She don't know either. Daddy got the draft notice outta the mail and brought it to me in the log woods. I told him I'd think of a way to tell you and Mama both. And he said he was gonna let me handle it."

I was crying. Jesse stood and held me. "I was gonna tell you, honey girl. I really was. I was just trying to think of a way that wouldn't hurt you."

"There ain't no way to tell me something like this that won't hurt, Jesse," I said. "I don't want you going."

Chapter Thirty-nine

I was so upset with Jesse I wanted to be mad at him all night long but he wouldn't let me. He kept talking with me, telling me how he couldn't help this but the government was saying he had to do this to serve his country. I didn't want to hear any of it. In the end though I decided to hold Jesse and love him instead of being mad at him. But I still cried because I was scared he'd get killed in sorry Korean War. I'd never paid it any mind. Never really worried about it even when Jesse signed up for this draft but I was worried now. I cried myself to sleep in spite of Jesse holding me.

The next morning, I felt numb. Like the world had ended and I was just moving around but not really alive. I took care of the babies and we got ready to go to church with Leroy and Hallie. As we were getting into the truck, I said, "When are you gonna tell your Mama, Jesse?"

"I'll tell her today after church when we're eating dinner with them."

"It's gonna be a real fun meal." I said, as he handed Sabrina to me. I was already holding Stephen. Jesse got in the truck and started to drive. I looked at Sabrina and Stephen. They were almost five months old now and getting bigger all the time. It was getting harder and harder to hold them both at once. When we pulled up into the church yard and Jesse stopped the truck, he reached over and took Stephen as he usually did. I looked at him tearfully, "Jesse what am I gonna do without you? You can't leave me."

"Honey girl, I ain't leaving you. I would never leave you."

"Then you gotta tell them Army people you can't go. I need you. Me, Sabrina and Stephen need you. I can't do this without you, Jesse. I can't."

He sighed and kissed me softly. "It'll be okay, honey girl. I promise you."

He got out of the truck then with Stephen; came to my door and opened it so me and Sabrina could get out too. When we went into church, Hallie saw us and waved happily. She and Leroy moved down so me, Jesse and the babies could sit with them. Hallie was talking about how pretty Sabrina and Stephen looked when she stopped, looked at me and said, "What's the matter, 'Cella? You look so sad."

I couldn't help myself. I know Jesse said he was gonna tell her at dinner but I couldn't help it. I blurted out, "Jesse's been drafted."

"DRAFTED!" Hallie shouted, causing everyone in church to look at us and Jesse looked like he wanted to disappear into the floor. "JESSE LEROY JENKINS YOU ARE NOT DRAFTED!"

"Mama please!" Jesse said.

Hallie kept on, "They can't have my baby! Oh no! They ain't doing that. This ain't gonna happen!"

"Hallie, stop!" Mr. Leroy said. "You're making a scene."

"Well maybe if more Mama's made a scene then we wouldn't be having all these senseless wars! I ain't putting up with no government making my baby go get shot at!"

"Hallie, please!" Mr. Leroy said. "This ain't the time or place."

But Hallie wouldn't stop. She kept at it until Sabrina started to cry and that hushed her at last. Rev. Wheeler got up to do his sermon but I didn't hear anything he said. I was too busy worried about Jesse, and trying to keep Sabrina happy.

Later as we were on the way to Hallie and Leroy's I said, "Jesse, I'm sorry about telling. I just couldn't help it."

He sighed, "It's ok 'Cella. At least it's out in the open now."

When we got there, we got out of the truck and Jesse gave Stephen to Leroy so he could hug Hallie. "Mama, I can't help this," he said softly.

"You'd better find a way to help it," Hallie said.

"He can't." Leroy spoke up.

Hallie wiped her eyes, "Well, when do you have to go?"

"I do my physical tomorrow morning," Jesse said, still hugging her.

"Tomorrow?" Hallie brightened. "Well, then there's still hope. Maybe they won't want you for some reason. Maybe they'll turn you down."

"What are they gonna turn him down for?" Leroy asked. "There ain't nothing wrong with him."

"They turned down my cousin Luke because he couldn't hear right in one ear. And they turned down Lon Sands because his heart skips a beat and they turned down Skip Johnson because of kidney stones. Who knows what they might find that they don't like in Jesse. Who knows what kinda physical problem he might have that will actually be a blessing to us." She smiled big and hugged Jesse tight, "Honey, you just go in there tomorrow and make sure they learn everything wrong with you, alright."

"Ok, Mama," Jesse said.

Mr. Leroy was shaking his head, "Hallie, you are crazy."

"I ain't crazy. I just don't want my baby getting killed. Now let's go in the house and have dinner. I got fried chicken, fresh turnip greens, and a big blackberry cobbler baked."

Chapter Forty

On Monday morning, Jesse took me and the babies to Hallie and Leroy's before he went for his Army physical. He said that way we wouldn't be alone. I clung to him before he left. I didn't want to let him go, but he said I had to. "It's alright, 'Cella," he whispered in my ear. "I'm just doing the physical today. They ain't sending me nowhere yet."

And then he kissed me, Sabrina, Stephen and Hallie. He hugged Mr. Leroy, kissed me again and was gone. I sat on the couch crying. Hallie was holding Sabrina; crying too. Mr. Leroy had little Stephen. After a few minutes, he stood up, brought Stephen to me and said, "Here, take him, 'Cella. I got work to do."

"How can you go do any work when our baby is about to go line up to be killed?" Hallie asked, wiping her eyes.

Mr. Leroy sighed, "My working ain't gonna change nothing Hallie. It'll give me something to do while we wait."

I took Stephen and Mr. Leroy went out the front door. Not long after, Hallie decided me and her needed to do something to keep us occupied too. "'Cella, why don't me and you start us up a batch of pecan bread? I'd like to have some good pecan bread."

"Ok," I said, not really feeling like doing anything at all. Soon, me and Hallie were in the kitchen with Sabrina and Stephen propped up in little baskets on the floor. They were almost as big as the baskets now and Hallie made the comment that we would soon have to get something bigger to keep them in. The whole time we were working, Hallie talked about Alice and Vicky. She said they were worried about Todd and Bob being drafted too. She said everyone knew it was coming; just wanted to put it off as long as possible. I kept looking at the clock on the wall. Time was dragging just like it did when I had Sabrina and Stephen.

We got the bread dough mixed, covered it to rise and took Sabrina and Stephen to the living room. There we laid them on a blanket on the floor with some rattles and baby squeaky toys. Sabrina was real fussy today. Hallie said she was probably teething but I think she realized something was going on with her Daddy. At first, Stephen was calm but then Sabrina's fussiness got him going and soon me and Hallie were having to hold them both. Hallie had little Stephen and she gently put her finger in his mouth. Kissing him, she said, "Yep, this little boy is getting teeth too. Let's get some ice on those sore little gums of yours precious." Hallie stood, "Come on, 'Cella, we gonna fix up little Sabrina too. Ain't gonna let our babies hurt."

We took them to the kitchen and I sat in a chair holding them both while Hallie wrapped two ice cubes up in two clean kitchen rags. She then took Sabrina from me and said, "Just let them suck on this ice real careful like. Hold it so it don't slip down his little mouth. The ice will numb his gums and he'll feel better." She was already letting Sabrina suck on the ice. I watched her and did the same with Stephen. We took them back to the living room and sit rubbing the ice on their swollen gums. I think Stephen was trying to cut all his little teeth at once. They grew sleepy, and the ice was working some but they were still restless. Hallie suggested that I go lay in Jesse's old bed where I'd given birth to them and feed them. I agreed and was soon doing just that. Hallie stayed and talked with me a while, then she got up and went to check on the bread.

I was sleepy but I couldn't sleep. I looked around Jesse's old room. I thought of me and him together in here. I thought of having Sabrina and Stephen in here and of sleeping in here so much after they were born. I just wanted Jesse to come home and tell me the Army didn't want him after all. I didn't want nothing wrong with him. I just didn't want the Army having him. He was mine. My husband. My Jesse. He belonged to me, Sabrina and Stephen. We needed him more than anyone. I didn't mind sharing him some with Hallie and Leroy but that was it. No one else.

Sabrina and Stephen finished nursing and lay sleeping in my arms. I managed to get up, button my dress and put pillows around the babies so they wouldn't fall off the bed. I found Hallie in the kitchen punching the bread dough down so hard it looked like she was fighting it. "That looks like fun," I remarked and she turned to see me.

"Oh, hey there, honey. It sure takes out frustrations. Want to give it a try?"

I walked to her and started punching down that bread dough too. I thought of Jesse going away from me and I punched it harder and harder. I started to cry and my tears fell in the dough. "Don't worry about that," Hallie said, "I've cried into it too."

I looked up at the clock, "What is taking so long? He's been gone hours. He left right after breakfast and it's nearly dinnertime."

"True," Hallie nodded. "I just hope they find some reason to turn him down. Him being married and having two babies should count for something." She paused, "Let's get dinner ready, 'Cella. Are the babies asleep?"

"Yeah," I remarked, still punching that bread dough.

I helped Hallie make several ham sandwiches and fried potatoes for dinner. We added some leftover blackberry cobbler and Mr. Leroy came inside right before we sit down to eat. He just grabbed a sandwich off the plate and stood at the counter with it. "No word from Jesse yet?" He asked, looking inside the sandwich.

"No," Hallie said. "Why don't you join me and 'Cella; Leroy. Sit down and eat."

"Nah, I'm all dirty. I'll just stand."

"What are you all dirty from?" Hallie asked.

"Been cleaning out that ditch on the other side of Mr, Esau's old place. Got some kinda slime all in it. I washed my hands at the outside spigot but I got that mess all over me. I'll just eat right here." Then he asked the blessing fast and began to eat.

Mr. Leroy ate fast; Hallie ate slow and I just nibbled at my sandwich, all the while waiting for Jesse to come back.

We finished eating and still no Jesse. Mr. Leroy went back to his ditch cleaning, and I helped Hallie in the kitchen until I heard Stephen crying. I went and got him so he wouldn't wake up Sabrina and sit in the chair in the room nursing him, all the while listening for Jesse. I had a terrible thought. What if they wouldn't let him come home like he thought they were going to do? What if they went ahead and sent him someplace far away without letting me see him again or even tell him goodbye. I was thinking on all this and getting more afraid by the second when I heard the front door open and Jesse say, "Hey, Mama, where's 'Cella?"

I jumped up and took my breast from Stephen's little mouth. He started to cry but I kissed him and pulled my dress up to cover myself, "I'll feed you later baby. Right now I gotta go see your Daddy."

While I was doing this with Stephen I could hear Hallie, "Well, honey, what did they tell you?"

"Just let me see 'Cella first," Jesse said.

I hurried to the living room carrying Stephen after glancing at Sabrina making sure she was still asleep. Mr. Leroy came in the front door just about the same time I came into the living room from the hallway. I looked anxiously at Jesse hoping to see him all happy, but the look in his eyes told me nothing was right at all.

"OH JESSE NO!" I screamed.

He held me and Stephen together, "I'm so sorry, honey girl. I....."

Hallie joined in, "You did try to get them to turn you down, didn't you?"

Jesse kept holding me, "They ain't turning me down, Mama. I can't help it. I leave for Fort Raynor in two weeks."

I was crying and couldn't stop. Hallie said, "COULDN'T THEY FIND ANYTHING WRONG WITH YOU?"

Jesse sighed and Mr. Leroy said, "Leave him alone, Hallie. Jesse, just where is Fort Raynor? I don't think I've ever heard of it."

"It's in Texas, Daddy..."

I found my voice, "TEXAS! OH JESSE NO, NOT TEXAS!"

"Honey girl, that's where they're sending me. I ain't got no control over it...."

"But Jesse they can't send you to Texas. You know what they say about Texas."

"No, I don't. Only thing I know about Texas is cowboys and stuff like that...."

"I ain't talking about no cowboys!" I cried out. "I'm talking about people saying the only certain thing in life is death in Texas."

Jesse pulled back and looked at me curiously, "'Cella, honey girl what are you talking about?"

I moved Stephen because he was wiggling so. Hallie took Stephen from me and I wiped my eyes, sniffling, "You know what I mean Jesse. You hear it all the time. I've heard it lots. The only thing in life you can be sure of is death in Texas. That ain't a good place Jesse. I don't want you going and I really don't want you going there!"

Jesse looked confused, "I've never heard that, 'Cella. Lots of people live there...."

Mr. Leroy cut in, "Marcella, I believe the saying you might be thinking of is death and taxes. Not death in Texas."

Jesse started to laugh and suddenly I was so mad I couldn't stand it. I ran out of the house, and was almost at the main road when Jesse finally caught up with me. I heard him calling me before he reached me but I kept going. But he caught up with me and pulled me to him, "Honey girl, please...."

"YOU LAUGHED AT ME! I BEEN CRYING FOR YOU AND MISSING YOU MORE THAN ANYTHING IN THIS WORLD AND YOU LAUGHED AT ME!"

He kissed me hard and I tried to pull away but he wouldn't let me. "I had to laugh, Marcella," he finally whispered, still holding me tight. "I had to. Do you think I want to leave you and the babies? I don't want to go. I don't. But I ain't got no control at all over this. I told them I was married and had two children but when they learned about my mama and daddy and your mama and daddy, they signed me up anyway. I did everything I could think of to get out of it and they won't let me. When you said what you did about death in Texas, it was just funny, honey girl. It was cute. That's all." He pulled me back so he could look into my eyes. "I love you Marcella Jenkins. I always will."

"I love you too, Jesse. I just don't want you to go."

"I don't either but it can't be helped. Come on, let's go back inside. I want to talk some things over with Mama and Daddy."

When we went back inside, Mr. Leroy had changed his clothes and was holding Stephen while Hallie had Sabrina. I could tell Sabrina was looking for food the way she was moving her little head. I needed to go nurse her, but Jesse pulled me down on the couch beside him. Mr. Leroy looked at us and said, "Well, are y'all ok now?"

Jesse nodded, holding my hand. Then he said, "Like I said, I have to leave for Fort Raynor Monday morning, two weeks from now. That'll be June first. Then I'll be gone for nine weeks. After that they should let me come back home for a couple of weeks before they send me off someplace else. And 'Cella, I've already talked with them about them stationing me someplace where you and the babies can be with me. The man I talked with said there are plenty of places where you can be with me. You just can't be with me while I'm doing my training."

"What about that war they got going on?" Hallie asked, letting Sabrina suck on her finger.

"They ain't said nothing about that, Mama. Just told a bunch of us to show up early Monday June first to be sent out to Fort Raynor for basic training. That's all I know right now. I just want to ask something very special. Please, can Marcella and the children stay here while I'm gone? I'd feel so much better knowing they were here."

Mr. Leroy and Hallie spoke at once. Hallie said, "Of course they can stay, Jesse."

And Mr. Leroy said, "I wouldn't have it any other way. We'll take care of her and the babies for you, Jesse. You won't have to worry about them at all."

Chapter Forty-one

Jesse talked with James Jansan and with Thurman Reece, his log woods boss. They both agreed that since he'd been drafted he could spend the next two weeks with me and the babies.

On Tuesday evening after Jesse had his physical, we went to visit Clyde and Wanda. Jesse wanted to talk with Clyde since he'd been in the Army too. Wanda was cooking supper when we arrived and her parents, Andy and Abigail Rose were there too. I tried to tell Jesse we'd come at the wrong time but he thought it worked out perfect since Andy Rose had been a major in the Army. I wound up helping Wanda and Abigail and Betsy and Sharon played with the babies while Jesse talked with Andy and Clyde about the Army.

We ate supper with them and the whole time Jesse, Clyde and Andy kept talking and talking about the Army. I listened some but mostly I was busy trying to keep Sabrina from pulling my plate off the table. Jesse was holding Stephen and more interested in talking than in paying attention to Stephen's little hands. Several times I had to move Jesse's plate outta Stephen's way but Jesse didn't take no notice at all.

On the way home I asked Jesse did all that talking help him any and he said, "I think so. The hardest part's gonna be being away from you, honey girl. I can't call you at all and I can't even write for the first two weeks. You can write me, but I can't write to you."

"OH JESSE!"

He reached over and rubbed my arm, "I'll write you a letter first chance I get."

The next day, me and Jesse were out in our little yard area. He was clearing out some weeds. I didn't know why. He was gonna be leaving soon and I'd be with Hallie and Leroy, But there he was, swinging Mr. Leroy's bush axe while I watched Sabrina and Stephen up close to the house. I was making Sabrina a flower necklace when I heard Uncle Rayson holler, "Hey, Jesse, heard you're going to the Army!"

I looked up from my flowers to see him stumbling up our little path. Jesse stopped swinging his axe and glanced back at me,

Sabrina and Stephen, "'Cella, I think your uncle is drunk. Get the babies inside."

I stood and picked up Sabrina first because she was closest to me. While I carried her into the house, I heard Uncle Rayson, "Yep, that's what I heard. Man, you gonna have some fun in the Army. Gonna have more women than you know what to do with."

I put Sabrina in the playpen and hurried out to Stephen. Uncle Rayson was standing not too far from Jesse now. Jesse was saying, "Yeah, I'm going in the Army. But I don't want any woman besides Marcella."

I picked up Stephen and Uncle Rayson said, "You'll soon change your mind about that. You sure will. When I was in the Army, I had me a different woman every time I was on leave. You gonna be just like that Jesse. Marcella gonna be here and you gonna be....Where you gonna be, Jesse?"

I took Stephen to the playpen as Jesse was telling him he was going to Fort Raynor in Texas. I got little Stephen settled and hurried back outside. I ran out to Jesse. "He ain't gonna be with no other women!" I shouted at Uncle Rayson.

Uncle Rayson laughed "You ain't gonna be there,'Cella. Won't be able to do nothing about it. He gonna be all the way in Texas. Texas! Man, I'd love to go to Texas. I did my training right down there in South Carolina. How'd you get them to send you to Texas?"

Jesse shrugged, "That's just where they're sending me."

Uncle Rayson laughed some more, "You gonna have you some fun in Texas. Gonna be down there with all them Texas women!"

I'd had all I could take of Uncle Rayson. "Ain't you scared to be here with us because of Witch Sue?"

He faked looking scared, "AHHH Witch Sue! Oh no, don't cast a spell on me, Marcella! Please keep away!!!" He laughed so hard he doubled over.

"Go in the house with Sabrina and Stephen," Jesse said softly to me.

"No, I'm gonna stay right here!" I said. "Uncle Rayson, you're drunk. You need to leave right now!"

"I ain't drunk, 'Cella. Happy, but not drunk. I just wanted to come by and see Jesse before he took off for the Army. And don't think that witch business is gonna scare me off any. Poor ole Lana scared to death of witches. But me—well, right now I'm too happy to care about any power Sue Jones or any other witch may have" He reached out and patted Jesse's shoulder, "You have all the fun you can in the Army, Jesse. They gonna work you like a dog, sure, but when fun time comes, it's gonna be great."

"WHY DON'T YOU JUST GO ON!" I yelled.

Uncle Rayson laughed some more, "I'm going, Marcella. Jesse, you take care now and remember what I told you about having fun." He turned and started stumbling back down the path.

I watched him and looked at Jesse, "I don't want you with no other women."

"Honey girl, you ain't got to worry about that. You know I only love you."

I looked at my rings. I twisted them on my finger and said, "You ain't even got a ring so other people can tell you're married."

He kissed me, "That don't matter, honey girl. I know I'm married."

"Yeah, but I'd still like you to have a ring."

He held me close, "Alright. Tomorrow, we'll go to Brookville and see if we can find one we can afford. But 'Cella, you don't ever have to worry about me with someone else. I got who I want and it's you."

We went to Brookville early the next morning. We looked in Davis department store and wound up buying a cheap silver colored ring that matched mine for Jesse. I don't think it was real silver even, but Jesse said that was ok. I should have been happy about him having a ring but I was still just sad. We walked around Brookville until the babies grew too fussy then we went back to our truck and started home.

On the way, I looked out the window, thinking of Jesse being gone, thinking of me without him. We were almost home when I said, "What about this truck, Jesse? What are you gonna do with it?"

"This is our truck, 'Cella. I can't take it with me this time, but maybe I can soon. I'll just leave it at Mama and Daddy's. It'll be fine."

The truck might be fine but I knew I wasn't gonna be fine. He wasn't even gone and I was so sad I couldn't see straight.

Sabrina and Stephen were asleep when we got home. Jesse carried Stephen inside and I took Sabrina. We put them in the crib as we'd done so many times before. As Jesse was laying Stephen down, I couldn't help but look at the ring he was now wearing. I burst into tears and Jesse held me for a long time by the crib. Then he took me to Gran's old rocker and we sit there together with him holding me. I wanted time to stop. I wanted to sit here with him forever and ever and him never go anywhere at all.

The next few days went by in a blur. Jesse kept talking about us still having another week, like that week was gonna last forever but I knew it wouldn't. We spent a lot of time with each other, so much so that I told him I was afraid we were gonna get another baby started. He just kissed me and said don't worry about it because we were married now. I told him I didn't want to ever have to go through the pain and torture of having another baby. He held me close and told me that since he was in the Army now, that if I did have another baby, I could have it in the hospital with doctors and nurses and they would take care of any pain I was in. I asked him was he really truly telling me the truth and he said sure. That was one good thing about the Army.

On Saturday we were cleaning up our dinner dishes and Sabrina and Stephen were rolling into each other in the playpen when we heard a truck stopping out front. Jesse looked out the window, "It's Bob and Todd." He put the drying rag on the table and went to the door. I watched as he opened it and called, "Hey there! Good to see y'all. Come on in."

Soon they were in the house. Jesse asked did they want anything to eat or drink and they said no. I was glad because we didn't have that much. They sat down in our chairs and I kept cleaning. Jesse said, "So, how y'all doing?"

"Alright," Bob said. "I'm getting my wish. I been drafted too. So's Todd here. We both go for our physicals the same day they're sending you off to Texas."

"Looks like we're all going someplace," Jesse said. "What do y'all think about being drafted."

Bob shrugged, "I don't really think I mind. Like I was telling you the other day, me and Nancy are having so many problems. Now Todd here, he ain't got a girl to have problems with…I keep telling him he should date Linda…."

"She would just cause me problems," Todd spoke up.

Jesse nodded, "Do you want to be drafted Todd?"

"I don't know. Not really. Mama doesn't want me too. She's so upset. But I've talked a lot with Clyde and he says I'll be fine."

Jesse sighed and I saw him look over at me. At that moment, Sabrina grabbed Stephen's teething ring from him causing him to cry. I picked him up and carried him to our bedroom. It wasn't long before Sabrina was crying too, so I left Stephen in the crib and got Sabrina too. The only way I could get them quiet was to lay on the bed and nurse them. As they were eating, I could still hear Jesse, Bob and Todd talking. Jesse was saying, "I really don't want to go. I can't tell you how many times I've thought of putting 'Cella and the babies in the truck with me and just taking off to anyplace. Just driving and driving. But that wouldn't work. I know it wouldn't. But I've thought about it. The other night I stayed awake a long time thinking of what we should pack and how much money I had, how far we could get and then I realized they'd just come after me for desertion and that would be worse than me being in the Army. At least this way there is hope for us being together. They'll probably send us all over the place but I do hope we can be together."

Chapter Forty-two

If time drug by when I was having Sabrina and Stephen, the next week flew by so fast I barely realized we'd had it. All too soon it was time for Jesse to leave. On Saturday before he left, we took most of my clothes and the babies' clothes to Hallie and Leroy's. Then on Monday morning, we got up extra early, loaded the play pen into the truck; got the babies up and while I was laying on the bed nursing them, Jesse took the crib apart and put it in the back of the truck too. I wanted it to take a long time but it didn't. In no time at all, we had all of our clothes packed. Mine, Sabrina's and Stephens. Jesse was packed for the Army in a cheap suitcase he'd bought just for going to Texas. He sat on the bed, "Honey girl, it's time."

"It can't be time yet."

"I'm sorry, it is."

Sabrina and Stephen were no longer eating but were just laying beside me. Jesse picked up Sabrina, kissed her and said, "I'm gonna miss you so much little girl. I love you, baby. You be a good girl for Mommy." He gave her back to me and picked up Stephen. He kissed him too, saying, "I don't want to leave, little Stephen. I love you so much. Be a good boy and don't pull your sister's hair."

I sat up and leaned against him. I could only cry. Jesse held me close and somehow we all wound up in the truck together. I cried all the way to Hallie and Leroy's. The sun was shining but I felt like it was the darkest day ever.

Hallie and Leroy met us in the yard. Mr. Leroy told Jesse not to worry about the babies's crib and play pen. "I'll get it all set up for you. We'll take really good care of Marcella, Sabrina and Stephen for you."

"Thanks," Jesse said softly.

We left our truck in Hallie and Leroy's yard. Jesse got his suitcase from the back of the truck and put it in the trunk of Mr. Leroy's car. Soon me, Jesse, Sabrina and Stephen were in the back seat of Mr. Leroy's car while Mr. Leroy and Hallie were up front. Mr. Leroy was driving us to the bus station so we could tell Jesse goodbye.

I held Stephen and sat close to Jesse who was holding Sabrina. I was crying and looked up to see that Jesse had tears in his eyes too. I touched his face and he looked at me. He put his arm around me and I leaned against him.

There were lots of young men at the bus station; several of them colored; all of them lining up to go to Texas for the Army. Jesse had to sign in with an Army man in uniform. They took his suitcase, marked his name off of a list and told him he could tell us goodbye. He came back to us, looking empty. I don't know how I kept moving, but I went to him and he held me like he didn't want to let me go. I cried harder than I've ever cried. Jesse kissed me, kissed Sabrina who I was still holding. He let me go and I felt lost. He went to hug Mr. Leroy for a long time; then he hugged and kissed Hallie who was holding Stephen. He kissed Stephen and took him from Hallie. He came back to me and held me, Sabrina and Stephen all together. All the other men were telling their people goodbye too. Another man wearing a fancy Army uniform started calling for the men to get on the bus. Jesse kissed me again, kissed our babies again. I held onto him as tight as I could. The man called again. Jesse whispered, "I have to go, honey girl."

"No."

"I don't want to...."

"Oh, Jesse, please..."

"'Cella..." He kissed me, "Write to me." He kissed me once more, stepped back from me and said, "I'll write the first chance I get. Promise. I love you, Marcella. I love you, Sabrina. I love you, Stephen. Mama, I love you too."

Hallie stepped closer to us and took Stephen, "You be careful, baby. Don't let no one hurt you."

"I'll be fine," Jesse said. He looked at Mr. Leroy, "Daddy, we've had our problems, me and you, but I do love you."

Mr. Leroy came and hugged Jesse close, "Love you too, son. Don't you ever forget that."

The man called again. Jesse kissed me one more time, turned and got on the bus. I wanted him back. I wanted to get on that bus and get him off of it. I watched as he made his way to the back. He waved to us from the window. I waved back to him. I felt so so bad. Sabrina reached out her hand as the bus started to move slowly. She said her first word, "Da! Da!"

And following her like he always did, little Stephen reached out his hand and called after the bus, "Da! Da!" I should have been happy at them saying their first word. But it broke my heart because Jesse was gone.

Chapter Forty-three

Hallie led me back to the car and we all got inside. She held both babies and I was thankful. I was so sad I didn't have the energy to hold anyone. When we got back to the house, I just went inside and laid on the couch. Mr. Leroy got the playpen sit up first. He put it in the living room so that me and Hallie could see it when we were in the kitchen too. Hallie put the babies in the playpen and asked did I want to help her with dinner. I said no, not really. She said she understood and went to the kitchen alone. Mr. Leroy sit up the crib in Jesse's old room. I would be sleeping there until Jesse came home.

I cried all the time. I wrote Jesse two letters a day and each letter was tear stained. I don't know what I would have done without Hallie and Leroy helping me with the babies. I didn't want to eat or do anything, but they made me. Hallie kept telling me I had to take care of myself for my children and for when Jesse came back. "He wouldn't want you doing this to yourself," she kept saying. I knew she was right. So I ate. But I couldn't taste anything at all.

On Saturday after Jesse left, Lilly Jean came by with her Daddy. She came in the living room where I was sitting with my babies and sat on the couch next to me. She asked how I was and I told her not good at all. I asked where were they sending Todd and Bob and she said nowhere. That shocked me. "How can they be in the Army and not get sent somewhere? They sent my Jesse all the way to Texas!"

"They didn't get in," she said softly.

Hallie came in with a basketful of laundry, "They didn't get in?" she asked. "How did they manage that?"

Lilly Jean handed Sabrina a squeaky toy lamb, "Well, they won't let Todd in because of the time Reuben hit him in the head and he had that crack in his skull and concussion. Todd said they told him there's a chance of him having hidden brain problems. They say he could just pass out for no reason even years after and they can't take the chance on him. And Bob has flat feet. So they won't let him in either. Todd's happy he don't have to go but Bob's all upset."

I don't think Hallie heard much about Bob because while Lilly Jean was talking, she sat the basket down and went to the door. Mr. Leroy was outside with James Jansan. Hallie called out the door, "Leroy, did you know that they turned Todd down for the Army because Reuben Hammond hit him in the head all those years ago."

I heard Mr. Leroy, "That's what James was just telling me."

Hallie was shaking her head, "You shoulda hit Jesse in the head sometime Leroy. You'd always threaten to knock him upside the head. Why didn't you do it?"

It was quiet for a moment; then Mr. Leroy said, "Hallie, all these years you've found reasons to call me crazy. But let me tell you, I ain't the crazy one now. You are. If I hadda hit Jesse upside the head hard enough to cause him to have a concussion like Reuben did with Todd, you would have killed me. And you know it."

Hallie sighed, "I guess you're right. I just want my baby back." She shook her head, closed the door and went back to her basket. She disappeared into the hallway and I looked at Lilly Jean, "Why is Bob all upset?"

"I think he wanted to go because of the problems he's having with Nancy."

"If he's having so much trouble with her why don't he just break up with her? It ain't like they're married."

Lilly Jean nodded. "Sometimes I don't think Bob has much sense." She laughed softly, "I've never said that to anyone."

I shrugged, "Well, it sounds like the truth to me."

That night I wrote Jesse a long letter telling him all about Todd and Bob not getting in the Army and how crazy I thought Bob was. I still cried but not as much.

On Sunday Hallie helped me dress up the babies and we all went to church together. Several people hugged me saying they were praying for Jesse to be safe. I thanked them and looked the church over for Mama and Papa but of course they were not there.

The next week I helped Hallie more. We walked to her sister Sybil's house and helped Sybil can early tomatoes while Sybil's husband Jarvis cleaned a mess of trout he'd caught. The fish reminded me of Papa and I missed him. I felt like I was losing everyone. And that feeling made me want to hold Sabrina and Stephen even more. I was even afraid of Hallie somehow not liking me anymore so I tried to do everything she wanted. I told her how I felt one morning and she hugged me and said, "Marcella, as far as I'm concerned, you're the daughter I never had. I love you honey. Ain't no way I could not like you." Then we got to work in Hallie's own little garden patch.

On Tuesday after Jesse had been gone a little over two weeks I went to the mailbox for Hallie and pulled out a letter. It was addressed to me and the return address was where Jesse was stationed in Texas. I ripped it open right there at the box and begin to read:

My Dear Darling Marcella,

Hello honey girl. I hope you are doing good. I pray for you and Stephen and Sabrina every day. I am really enjoying your letters. Please keep writing them. There are ones in here who don't get letters at all and it's been harder on them.

They are working me hard and at first I couldn't stand it but I'm doing a lot better than some of the rest here. I guess I can thank Daddy and James for working me so hard all these years. I miss you so so so much. Just remember I love you and will be back to you as soon as they let me. I have to go now, 'Cella, honey girl. Kiss the babies for me. Tell Mama and Daddy I love them too.

All my love,

Jesse

I took the letter in the house and let Hallie read it. She hugged me and said "At least he sounds good."

"Yeah, but it's a really short letter."

"Probably all he had time for."

I kept writing my letters to Jesse. I told him all about Sabrina and Stephen calling out Da Da all the time. They were also saying Ma Ma and I told him that too. I told him about Hallie's little garden, about Sybil's tomatoes, how just about every day people were stopping by to see the Mr. Esau museum and anything I could think of. Writing helped me. I just wished he'd write to me more. Mr. Leroy said they were probably working him so hard he didn't feel like writing. I went to the mailbox for Hallie every day. At the end of that week I got another letter from him. I ripped it open just like the other one.

My Dear Darling Marcella,

Hello again honey girl. Sorry I haven't wrote every day but I've been so busy running and climbing and learning how to use all these weapons that I barely have time to think. It's great about our little Sabrina and Stephen talking. Are they sitting up on their own yet? I miss them just as much as I miss you. I've made a new friend here. His name is Johnny Harper. He's colored too. Fort Raynor is what they call integrated which means they got colored and white together. It don't bother me because of the Jansans and Duvalls and it don't seem to bother Johnny but there's one more colored man in here and he don't like it one bit. His name is Lawrence Tripp. He keeps trying to get them to transfer him out of here to an all colored unit and there's a lot of the white men who are complaining too. But not everyone is like that. Most of them are nice. There's one white man from New York named Keith. He keeps complaining that it's too hot here. I have a hard time understanding a word he says but we've all figured out he don't like nothing.

Please keep writing. Kiss the babies for me. I love you more than anything.

All my love,
Jesse

I took the letter inside to Hallie and let her read it too. She said she thought everyone should be together. "It's senseless dividing people up just cause of what color they are. Make just as much sense to say skinny people and fat people couldn't be together."

I nodded. Hallie could make a lot of sense. I told her I just didn't want them sending Jesse off to war. She patted my shoulder and said, "Honey, I pray about that constantly."

Chapter Forty-four

I kept writing to Jesse and he kept writing to me. He told me all about Sergeant Bowers who was over him and the others in Jesse's group. Jesse said Sergeant Bowers thought he was tough but had nothing on Leroy Jenkins. I laughed when I read that part and when Mr. Leroy read it he just grinned and handed the letter back to me.

Life for me was settling into a routine of just getting by without Jesse. Leroy had been to help James Jansan top and sucker his tobacco. Hallie stayed home with me because both babies were teething so bad and we knew their crying and fussiness would only bother Grandma Cal.

On the last day of June, I went to the mailbox again and this time there was another short letter from Jesse plus a package in a stiff envelope addressed to Mr. Jesse Jenkins, Rt. 4 Box 45 Cedar Cove, N.C. I opened Jesse's letter and read it quickly. He was telling me more about the all the running and hiking he was doing and how Keith the New York man passed out from the Texas heat. He ended like he always did by saying he loved me, the babies and Hallie and Leroy. I put the letter back in the envelope and opened the stiff envelope then. I pulled out our family picture. There we were—me and Jesse sitting side by side. Jesse holding Sabrina and me holding Stephen. Suddenly I started crying. I hadn't been crying as much, but this picture brought it all on. I looked at Jesse in the picture. I wanted him back so bad. I was staring at the picture when I heard, "How you doing, Marcella?"

I turned to see Gramp and his old dog Goldy. I was surprised to see them both. Gramp usually never walked anywhere and I'd never seen poor old Goldy take more than three steps at once before laying back down. I stared at him and said, "Ok, I guess. How are you?"

"Oh, bout normal. Bout normal that is except Lana's after me to paint the house. Ain't feeling like painting nothing. So me and Goldy here went for a walk. I'm hoping that by the time we get back Lana will have forgotten all about painting anything."

I nodded. I didn't know what to say to him. He came closer and I stepped back some, afraid. He shook his head, "You ain't gotta be scared of me child. I ain't gonna hurt you none."

Just then I heard Mr. Leroy, "Morning Gil, what brings you by here?"

I looked behind me and saw Mr. Leroy coming from the back yard. Gramp scratched his head, "Just out for a walk, Leroy. Me and Goldy here. Saw 'Cella at the mailbox and figured I ask how she is."

"She's alright," Mr. Leroy said, coming to stand beside me. "She's staying here with us while Jesse's off at boot camp."

"I heard the Army had him," Gramp said.

"Yeah, he got drafted," Mr. Leroy replied.

I watched Goldy lay down at the edge of the driveway and put her head on her paws. It didn't surprise me any. Gramp scratched his neck, "How's the babies?"

"Good," I said.

He sighed, "Marcella, listen, I know what happened was bad. I told your Gran she shouldn't have beat you like that and she made me sleep on the couch for three nights straight. Woman is terrified of a witch. See when she was a little girl; right around nine or ten, she had a friend named Hilda Barnes. Has anyone ever told you about Hilda?"

"No," I shook my head.

"Well, your Gran and Hilda got bored one summer day and went to see a Witch around here by the name of Lucinda. Lucinda Jones. She was Sue Jones great grandma. They wanted their fortune told. She did Hilda first. She had one of those glass balls and everything. Lana says that when she looked into that glass ball, Lucinda Jones got a strange look on her face and refused to tell Hilda what her fortune was. Hilda begged her but Lucinda wouldn't do it. She finally agreed to write the fortune down on a piece of paper but she wouldn't give it to Hilda. She gave it to Lana and told her not to open it until after midnight. Well, by this point, Lana was scared to have her fortune read so she refused when Lucinda offered to look in her glass ball for her. Both girls were scared silly by the time they left. Later on that evening, Hilda was up in the loft of her Daddy's barn. She fell and broke her neck. Died instantly. When they told Lana, she ran in her room and read the fortune. It said Hilda would die before sunup the next morning. Ever since then, honey, your Gran ain't wanted nothing to do with a witch. She's studied how to avoid them and what you need to do if confronted with one. That's why she went crazy with you that day. I know you didn't mean any harm."

"But Witch Sue didn't do nothing to me," I said, holding my picture and Jesse's letter in my hand. "I'm fine and my babies are good too."

Gramp nodded, "I'd like to see them babies if you don't mind. They are my great grandbabies after all."

I looked at Mr. Leroy and he nodded, "Come on in the house, Gil. They're right inside."

When we went in, Hallie was holding Sabrina who was crying away with her hurting gums. Little Stephen was in the playpen, gnawing on a little blue squeaky puppy. Hallie tried to hush Sabrina but she wouldn't hush. "She's teething," I said, not even looking at Gramp while I took Sabrina from Hallie. I was sure her crying would convince Gramp she was cursed by Witch Sue.

Hallie took the letter and picture from me and said, "So, you've come to see these little darlings, Gil?"

"Yeah. I figured it was time."

Mr. Leroy got Stephen from the playpen and handed him to Gramp. I watched Gramp with Stephen and wondered what Gramp was thinking. He held Stephen for a while, looking down into his little face. Then he gave Stephen back to Leroy. He took Sabrina from me but she pitched such a fit he soon gave her back. "Guess she ain't feeling none too happy today." I said and cuddled her close, nodding to Gramp.

He sighed, "Well, guess I'll be going. Marcella, do you plan on moving off with Jesse whenever he gets finished with his training?"

"If they'll let us," I said, trying to hush Sabrina.

Gramp nodded, "I'd tell you to come see us sometime honey, but your Gran is convinced you're Witch cursed. We planted some tomatoes and cucumbers and they ain't done nothing. Everything that goes wrong she blames it on you going to Witch Sue. I told her sometimes you just have a bad year. We didn't have any rain at first and then it rained so much nearly everything drowned, but you can't tell her nothing." He stepped close to me and hugged me, surprising me. He stepped back, "I'll do my best to tell your Gran you are normal as can be. I'll try, honey, but you know as well as I do how hardheaded she can get."

Chapter Forty-five

I put our family picture in the frame Jesse gave me for Christmas and sit it on the dresser in Jesse's old room. Every day I looked at his picture and every day I showed it to Sabrina and Stephen so they wouldn't forget their Daddy.

Gramp's coming by made me think that at least he still loved me. I wrote to Jesse, telling him about Gramp hugging me and saying I was normal. I was hoping that somehow Mama and Papa would start loving me again too. I missed them. Jesse wrote me back telling me he didn't want me doing anything crazy like trying to go to my Mama and Papa's alone. He said he still didn't trust Gran. I wrote him telling him don't worry; I was still afraid of Gran.

The middle of July arrived and with it came scalding temperatures and work at the Jansan farm. Sabrina had cut three teeth and Stephen two, but they were still cutting more. Mr. Leroy went constantly to help James Jansan with his tobacco but there were a lot of days when me and Hallie stayed home because the babies were just too fussy.

On July 27, Mr. Leroy had gone to help James again and me and Hallie were home because both my babies felt warm. We let them suck on ice cubes, I nursed them and they finally went back to sleep. They were sleeping in the crib and I was cutting up cucumbers for mine and Hallie's dinner when Hallie went in the living room and turned the radio on. "Let's listen to a little music, 'Cella."

"Will it bother Sabrina and Stephen?"

"I don't think so. I didn't turn it on loud."

At first there was singing on the radio. Hallie was draining the grease from the frying pan into a can and I was peeling another cucumber when a man on the radio interrupted the song by saying, "We have an important announcement to make. An armistice has just been signed by the Koreans to start a ceasefire."

He said more but I didn't hear because Hallie hollered, "Thank the Lord that mess is over. Won't be sending our Jesse there! Thank you Jesus!"

"You mean it's over?" I asked Hallie.

"Sure sounded like it to me, 'Cella."

I stared at the kitchen door. The singing was back on the radio. I hoped Hallie was right. I didn't want Jesse going to war. I wanted him home with me.

I was hoping Jesse would be home for our first anniversary. I'd looked at the calendar Hallie had on the wall and figured out he should be coming home sometime the week before our anniversary. I was all excited about him coming home. I wrote to him asking if he knew what day he'd be coming back and he wrote to me and said:

'Cella,

Honey girl, I hate to disappoint you but I won't be back with you in time for our anniversary. I love you and I want to be with you but it's impossible. I will finish up this boot camp that week and then they are sending me to special infantry school for a week. They haven't told me yet where I'm gonna be stationed but I'm hoping and praying it'll be someplace I can bring you and the babies. As soon as I learn something, honey girl, I'll let you know. It's great that the war in Korea is coming to an end. I don't think I'll have to go there.

Kiss the babies for me and remember I love you more than anything.

All my love,
Jesse

I read the letter and cried. I wanted him back for our anniversary. He had to do that. Hallie found me crying and she held me, telling me Jesse couldn't help it. I knew she was right but it didn't make me feel any better.

Our first anniversary fell on a Sunday morning and as Hallie and Leroy got ready for church, I just lay in bed, watching Sabrina and Stephen coo in the crib. I didn't feel like moving. Hallie came to the doorway, "Honey, ain't you coming with us?"

I shook my head, "I don't feel like going nowhere."

She came to me, "Are you sick, honey?" she felt my forehead.

"I ain't sick. It's just I wanted Jesse home by today and he ain't."

Hallie glanced back at Leroy who was now standing in the doorway, "Oh, yes," she said. "It's your anniversary today. Honey, I'm sure Jesse wants to be here...."

"I know he does but I just don't feel like going to church or anywhere else." I rolled over away from her.

She rubbed my back. "Leroy, I'm gonna stay here with her."

I heard him sigh. Hallie kept rubbing my back. Little Stephen started to fuss in the crib. I looked towards him. Leroy walked to the crib and picked up Stephen, "You know what little boy? Me and you have a job to do today. We gotta stay here and watch after our women."

"You ain't gotta watch us," Hallie said.

Mr. Leroy turned to us, "I think we do. Me and Stephen have you, 'Cella and Sabrina to look after. We got our work cut out for us today."

"You could go to church," Hallie said.

Mr. Leroy shook his head, "Well, I'm not. Y'all staying home and I am too. Gonna help Stephen take care of y'all." He carried Stephen from the room.

Hallie sighed, "Well, I reckon we're all staying home."

I nodded. I didn't care what they did. I just wanted Jesse. It felt like forever since I'd seen him. I was sick of writing and reading letters. I wanted him for real.

Chapter Forty-six

Two more weeks went by and still no letter from Jesse. I was worried sick over him. Every day I went to the mailbox and every day there was nothing. I went back to crying all the time. Hallie tried to comfort me but I wasn't accepting any comfort. I only wanted Jesse.

I went to church the next two Sundays with Hallie and Leroy. I went to try to get my mind off worrying and to please Hallie. She seemed happier when I agreed to go. The first Sunday was normal, but the next Sunday I wound up walking outside with Stephen for nearly the whole service because he'd decided it was his turn to be fussing with new teeth coming.

On August 19, the following Wednesday afternoon, I was sitting in the living room holding Sabrina and watching Stephen play with his rattle on the floor. It had been raining hard this morning so Mr. Leroy stayed home instead of going to help James. It stopped raining after dinner and now Mr. Leroy was over at Mr. Esau's old place giving his grand tour to some tourists. Hallie was in the kitchen scrubbing the floor. I should have been helping her but I didn't have any energy at all. I'd already been to the mailbox three times—even going in the rain and every time I went there was nothing.

I was so worried about Jesse I didn't know what to do. And I'd started to think that no matter what I'd never have a relationship with Mama and Papa again. So much time had gone by since Gramp's visit it was obvious he hadn't been able to convince them I was normal.

I was thinking about putting Sabrina and Stephen in the playpen and trying to help Hallie when the front door opened and Jesse came inside. I thought I'd gone to sleep and was dreaming. But there he was, grinning at me. He was wearing his Army uniform and didn't have hardly any hair. I couldn't believe he was here. Before I could get up, he came to the couch and pulled me up, kissing me and holding me and Sabrina both so tight she started to cry.

Jesse pulled back and looked at me. "Are you really here?" I asked.

"I'm here, honey girl." He ignored Sabrina's crying, rubbed her little head and kissed me again.

Hallie came in the room, "Oh dear Lord. You're home! You're home!"

"I'm home, Mama," Jesse let me and Sabrina go and went to hug Hallie.

I watched him hugging Hallie. He let her go and Hallie said, "Why didn't you tell us you were coming home?" She hit him with her cleaning rag.

"I wrote y'all. I told you all about it in my last letter..."

"What letter?" I said. "We ain't got no letter telling us you were coming home."

"We sure ain't," Hallie said, touching Jesse's head. "Got you nearly bald, don't they?"

Jesse rubbed his own head, "Oh, it's coming back, Mama." He picked up Stephen and kissed him. Stephen just stared at him like he was trying to figure who Jesse was. Jesse came back to me and Sabrina who was still crying. Jesse put his hand on her back, "Hey, little girl, what's wrong?"

"She's been teething a lot and I don't think she knows you without your hair."

"Well we're gonna fix that," Jesse said. "Here, honey girl, you take Stephen and let me have our Sabrina."

We traded babies and at first Sabrina cried so hard when Jesse held her it scared me. I watched them together. Jesse held her close, whispering in her ear. She must have remembered his voice because she settled down and started sniffling instead of screaming her head off. Jesse kissed her, "That's better, my little Breeny. I'm still Daddy, no matter how much hair I ain't got." He pulled me to him and kissed me again. Then he said, "Let's sit down, I'm tired."

We settled down, me and Jesse and the babies on the couch and Hallie in the chair by the playpen. I leaned against him and was starting to say again that we'd never got a letter from him telling us he was coming, but Mr. Leroy came inside, "Well look who's home!" He grinned widely. Jesse took his arm from around me, put Sabrina on my lap along with Stephen and stood to hug Leroy.

Mr. Leroy patted Jesse's back, "Sure is good to have you back, Jesse. We expected some kinda notice. How'd you get here?"

Jesse sat back beside me and took Sabrina once more. He put his arm around me and said, "I wrote. I promise I did. The letter must have got lost in the mail. I left the base Monday morning and started back here. I got to the bus station in Brookville this morning and waited for over two hours for y'all to come. When you didn't come, I decided to walk. It was still raining a little but I wanted to get home. I hadn't walked far when Jake Anders drove up beside me and asked did I want a ride. I said sure. He drove me back to his place and I walked from there. My Army bag and suitcase are on the front porch."

"I'm just happy you're here." I said, the reality of his presence finally sinking in

He smiled at me, "Me too, honey girl."

Mr. Leroy was sitting across from us in the old wooden rocker. "So, do you know what your next move is?"

Jesse nodded, "We got a little time here. I have to be at Fort Compton in Vester, Louisiana September eighth no later than seven in the morning. I plan on being there the day before."

"You mean you're leaving again!" I cried.

Jesse hugged me, "You're coming with me, honey girl. You and the babies. We have base housing. I've already seen it and I've got the keys to the house. The infantry school was at Fort Compton and while we were there I got housing and so did Johnny Harper. He's gone home to Florida to get his wife, Trisha and their little boy Scott. It's a nice little house. We have electricity, running water, a full bathroom with a tub, a nice little kitchen with a new stove and refrigerator, two bedrooms—everything. We're moving, 'Cella."

Chapter Forty-seven

"MOVING!" Hallie shouted. "YOU CAN'T BE MOVING!"

"Hallie please!" Mr. Leroy said loudly.

At the same time, Jesse said, "Mama, we have to move. I can't help it. The Army has stationed me at Fort Compton and I'd better be there September eighth just like they want."

"Well, couldn't they put you someplace closer home? Louisiana! Might as well send you to the moon!"

Jesse shook his head, "Mama, me and 'Cella are lucky to be going to Fort Compton. They're running an experiment there—letting colored soldiers families live on base. They got a whole street just for us. The only way me and Johnny got in was we scored high enough on our final infantry test. There's eight houses on that street—four on each side of the road. We're in number 503. They have two colored families living there already. I met one of the men when I was there. His name is Bull Robinson..."

"Bull?" I interrupted, "You mean someone actually named a little baby Bull?"

Jesse laughed, "No, honey girl, it's his nickname. But his real name ain't no better. It's Bardolph."

"I believe I'd prefer Bull too," Mr. Leroy said.

Jesse nodded, "Me too. He's got a wife, Sandra and two little girls—Candace and Harmony. There's another colored man and his family there too—Richard Tucker. Bull didn't tell me what his wife's name was. But he did say they have a three year old son. They'd gone home to Missouri on leave so I didn't meet them."

Hallie was crying, "I just don't know what I'm gonna do. You living all the way in Louisiana! All of you!"

"Hallie, he's gotta do this," Mr. Leroy said. "It ain't something he can help."

Hallie wiped her eyes, "Well we gotta figure out something. I ain't gonna survive without my babies."

I watched Hallie cry and felt sad myself. I'd been praying and praying for Jesse to come back to me. I'd been praying for us to be together. But I honestly hadn't thought of really leaving Cedar Cove. Sure, Jesse had written in his letters that he wanted me and the babies with him, but actually leaving Cedar Cove hadn't been in my mind. I leaned against Jesse, thinking about not living in Cedar Cove anymore; thinking of that house he seemed so happy about. "Jesse, what about Miz Essie's old house where we are now?"

Jesse looked at me and Mr. Leroy said, "That's your place, Jesse. I signed it all over to you."

"We're gonna keep it, 'Cella. We can stay there when we get to come home and I'd like to someday add on to it. Get electricity hooked up and make us a nice place to live for when I'm through with the Army."

"How are we gonna get there?" I asked.

"We're driving our truck. We're gonna take apart our bed, load up our chairs, dishes—everything but the kitchen table. There's a table and chair set in the house already. It'll take us a few days. Mama, do you think if we could get up with Aunt Tansy and asked her real nice she'd let us stay at least one night when we get to Georgia? We're going right through Sawville."

"Tansy?" Hallie looked strange. "Honey, you know we ain't seen Tansy in years. Last time she was up here you were only four years old."

"Who is Tansy?" I asked, feeling that my world was spinning and there was no stopping it.

"She's my baby sister," Hallie said. "I'm the oldest, then there's Sybil and Tansy. She moved to Sawville, Georgia right after she got married. We write to each other some.....see, 'Cella, Tansy thinks she's better than me and Sybil. Her husband, Paul works in a law office—like a lawyer's helper. Whenever Tansy does write me it's to brag about herself and Paul.....Things ain't been right with me and Tansy for a long time."

"Well, maybe me and 'Cella staying there could make things a little better," Jesse said. "I just thought of her because it's gonna be hard finding places that will let us stay for the night and I'm thinking of money too. But I don't know of any other way than to drive down there."

"Makes sense to me," Mr. Leroy said. "Hallie, didn't Tansy write you a while back saying they had a telephone now?"

"Oh yes. Bragged up a storm on it. Didn't even ask how we were. Even sent me a picture of that telephone. Can you imagine? She ain't never sent me pictures of her little Grace, but I get pictures of a telephone. That should tell you what kinda woman Tansy is."

"If she's got a phone," Jesse said, "we could go to the Duvalls and call her. I'm just trying to think of how to make this trip a little easier on us."

It seemed Jesse had everything planned out. We stayed until after supper talking and talking about the trip we had to make. Jesse brought in his suitcase and new Army bag. He had several road maps in that bag and him and Mr. Leroy spread them out on the kitchen table after we ate. They sit there discussing the best roads to take. While they did that, I helped Hallie with the dishes and Sabrina and Stephen babbled with each other in the playpen.

We left for home around eight o'clock that night. We put the playpen in the back of the truck but not the crib. Jesse said he didn't see why Sabrina and Stephen couldn't sleep in the play pen and we could just take apart the crib for our trip to Vester.

When we got home they were both sound asleep and didn't mind being in the playpen at all. I was worried because we didn't sit it up in our bedroom, but right outside the curtain. "It's just a curtain, honey girl," Jesse said, pulling me on the bed with him. "We'll hear them if they cry."

It was so good to be home and even better to be back with Jesse. I loved him more than anything and did my best to show him just that.

The next morning, Jesse surprised me by wanting to go out to the Jansan farm. I asked was he gonna work in the tobacco and he said, "If James wants me to. We only have a little over a week left here, honey girl. In order for us to get to the base on time, we have to leave early Friday morning on the fourth."

All the way to the Jansan farm, I thought of leaving here. I looked out the window as we drove, thinking of how this was home, how familiar it all was and soon we'd be gone. I started to cry, but wiped my tears away before Jesse could notice.

When we got to the Duvall's, Jesse stopped there because Preacher Carl's car was in the driveway. "I didn't know Carl was here," Jesse said. "This is perfect."

We got out of the truck. I carried Sabrina and Jesse carried Stephen. I told him that if the babies gave me too much trouble I wanted him to take me home. But Jesse seemed to think that they'd be just perfect. I think he'd been away from them too long.

We walked up to the Duvall's front door and Jesse knocked. Bob soon opened it. "Hey there!" he exclaimed. "We didn't know you were home! Come on in!"

"We're here for a little bit," Jesse said as we stepped inside. "Then we're heading to Louisiana."

"Louisiana!" Bob let out, "Wow!"

I heard Grandma Cal call, "Boy, what are you shouting so much about...." She came into the room with her cane. She stopped and smiled when she saw us, "Well if it ain't Jesse and Cellar! Good to see you two. Come give me a hug."

We did and she said, "That Army been good to you?"

"Yes ma'am," Jesse said, moving Stephen a little.

"They better be," Grandma Cal said.

Jesse grinned, "I'll tell them you said so."

Alice and Simpson came into the room followed by Preacher Carl. They all had to hug us and say how good it was to see Jesse again. Carl asked how long Jesse was gonna be here and Jesse told him a little over a week. I stood back, listening. Libby came into the room carrying her baby. He was a little bigger than Stephen and Sabrina but he was completely bald. She smiled at me, "Hello, 'Cella. I'd like you to meet Randy."

I walked towards her, carrying Sabrina, "This is Sabrina," I said, "and Jesse has Stephen."

"They're beautiful," she said. "Are they scooting around yet?"

I nodded, "Yeah, they're moving all over the place. They can sit alone pretty good and they both try to talk all the time."

"That's good," Libby said. "Have they been sick much?"

"No, not really. They've had a bad time teething but that's been it."

"Teething is awful, isn't it. We've sit up all night long with Randy because of his bad little teeth." She kissed her baby's bald head.

"Yeah," I said, "it must really hurt them because they sure fuss a lot. Hallie showed me how to let them suck on an ice cube....that helps a little."

"We've done that too," she said. "But the other night, he nearly scared me to death. He was sleeping in the crib right next to our bed. I woke up and realized he was having trouble breathing. I got Carl up and we took him straight to the emergency room. They kept him overnight. I stayed right with him."

"What was wrong?" I asked, thinking I would die if Sabrina or Stephen couldn't breathe.

"He had bronchitis. It's colder up there than it is here. I think if we could somehow move back down here, he'd be better. Poor baby, he's had trouble with colds since he was born."

"Are y'all gonna be able to move back? I thought your husband was..."

Libby nodded, "Yeah, Carl's still preaching. And it's a good church. The people are so sweet. I just miss being home."

I didn't know what to say. I was soon gonna be leaving home myself. Libby looked at me, "Oh, 'Cella, I'm so sorry. You're leaving too, ain't you?"

"Real soon. I don't want to go, but I'd rather go than be without Jesse. It was awful when he was gone for that training."

She moved her baby some, "I understand. I wouldn't want to be away from Carl either. I knew when we got married we'd be moving. But you know, you get all wrapped up in loving someone and being with them. You talk about moving, you plan on moving, but you don't really stop to think of what it really means. Then when you do it, it hits you hard. At least it did me."

"I think I'm gonna be the same way," I said softly.

Chapter Forty-eight

Jesse got up with his Aunt Tansy later that day. She said sure we could stop and spend the night with her any time. When we went home that evening, Jesse was quiet. I asked what was wrong and he said he thought we needed to leave here early. He said it was gonna take us a long time to drive down there on our own and there was no way he wanted to miss his deadline. Jesse talked things over with Mr. Leroy and we all agreed that leaving on Tuesday would be better. We would pack up most everything into the truck Monday night, stay with Hallie and Leroy that last night and then load up the babies' crib first thing Tuesday morning and head on.

The days leading up to the time we had to leave were full of planning, visiting the Jansan's, Duvalls, Abigail and Andy Rose, and of course Hallie and Leroy. I thought about Mama and Papa. I thought about them all the time. I mentioned it to Jesse and he said we'd go by to see them before we left.

We did too. We tried but every time we went, they weren't home and I was afraid to even knock on Gran's door.

The Duvalls had a going away party for us on Saturday before we left. Vicky gave us extra food she'd canned, Clyde and Wanda gave us two more suitcases for our clothes and Hallie and Leroy gave us a camera and some film so we could take pictures and send them back here. Preacher Carl, Libby, Todd, Lilly Jean and Bob all went in together and got us a double stroller for the babies. I was shocked but happy. Libby smiled at me, "We've watched you and Jesse carrying them all over the place."

Clyde agreed, "That stroller will come in handy for you. It's good you're able to live on base, but I know Jesse's gonna be busy with the Army and you're gonna be on your own a lot, 'Cella"

I agreed, looking it over. It was a pretty stroller done in pale blue plaid material. There were two metal baskets on the back—a little one up close to the handle and a bigger one at the bottom. In front of each baby seat there were little beads strung for the babies to play with.

Andy and Abigail gave us two folding metal high chairs for Sabrina and Stephen. I was really happy with this too because it would make feeding them a lot easier and they were eating more and more real food now.

Preacher Joe came in late. I didn't know he was coming, but he hugged Jesse and said, "When are you leaving?"

"Early Tuesday morning,"

He patted Jesse's shoulder, "I sure am gonna miss you. You've been coming into the store since you were a little baby. It just ain't gonna be the same around here without you, Jesse. I've thought and thought on what to give you and I think I've come up with the perfect gift. Stop by the store Tuesday morning and I'll have a whole cooler full of Pepsi's and orange and grape drinks for your trip. I'll pack it all in ice so they'll stay cold for at least a while. I'll give you a couple loaves of bread, some peanut butter, cookies, potato chips and nabs too. I know it's gonna be hard on y'all getting food."

I watched as Jesse hugged him and felt like hugging him too. Everyone was being so nice. But I was still sad. I didn't want to go and I was sad because even though Mama and Papa, my aunts and uncles and all my cousins had been invited to this going away party none of them showed up.

All too soon it was Monday. Hallie and Leroy came over to help us pack the truck. Hallie helped me pack up our clothes, dishes and food. We didn't have anything in the ice box because I'd cooked all the eggs and we'd drank all the milk. While me and Hallie worked, we were mostly quiet which was strange for us. When we did talk, it was just about what we were doing and what we had to do. We both knew that if we started talking about what was really on our hearts we'd fall apart.

Mr. Leroy helped Jesse take apart our bed and they loaded it piece by piece into the truck. They put the mattress in with our pillows and blankets. They loaded up the playpen, Gran's old rocker and the three chairs that used to be Miz Essie's. They got everything in and then rearranged it several times before they were satisfied with the way it was packed. Me and Hallie sit on the steps of the porch with the babies and watched. I told Jesse we couldn't even see out the window and he said, "Don't worry about it, honey girl. It's what we have mirrors for."

When they got everything like they wanted it, we looked through the house one last time. It looked empty. I couldn't help but cry. We were leaving our stove, table and chairs that went with it, the icebox, kitchen cabinet, washtub, and the curtain Jesse had hung to give us some privacy. I stood looking at all of it, feeling so empty I couldn't stand it. Hallie had walked back onto the porch. Jesse came inside. He came up behind me and held me close not saying anything. I turned and cried against him and at last he whispered, "At least we're gonna be together, honey girl."

We spent the night with Hallie and Leroy as planned. I didn't get much sleep at all. I kept thinking about leaving Cedar Cove, not seeing Hallie and Leroy, not seeing my cousins or aunts and uncles, and not being able to convince Mama and Papa I wasn't witch cursed at all. Sabrina was restless and I wound up trying to keep her quiet nearly all night long so that Jesse could sleep.

Morning came all too soon. I'd finally gotten to sleep and was dreaming that me and Zenobia were planting trees on the roof of Gramp and Gran's house so they could have plenty of shade. Zenobia wanted to plant pine trees and I was telling her no, oak trees were prettier and gave better shade when I felt Jesse shaking me. I opened my eyes to see him sitting up in bed, the sunlight coming in the window.

"It's time to get up, honey girl."

"It can't be."

"It is," he lay back down and kissed me. Then he kissed Sabrina who was in bed with us. He sat up, stretched and yawned. I watched him get dressed and I got up too. I got dressed and looked at Jesse. "Could we please go by and at least try to tell Mama and Papa goodbye?"

He was buttoning his shirt, "We'll try, 'Cella. We will, but I'm afraid it's only gonna make you cry."

Breakfast was sad with Hallie crying and me wanting too. I could barely eat I felt so bad. As soon as breakfast was over, Mr. Leroy and Jesse loaded the crib into the back of the truck. Hallie helped me pack a bag with extra clothes for the babies and lots of diapers. She hugged me tight when we finished, "'Cella, honey, I want you to know I love you just like you was my very own born to me daughter. Please send me pictures. Please write."

"I love you too, Hallie," I said. "You are like a Mama to me. I'll never forget how nice you've been to me and I promise to send you plenty of pictures so you can see Sabrina and Stephen."

Before we left, Hallie and Leroy had to hug us again and again. They held Sabrina and Stephen, kissing them and telling them goodbye. Poor Hallie looked ready to pass out. She grabbed Jesse and said, "I ain't gonna let you go. I've decided the Army can't have you. It can't have you or 'Cella or my babies. You have to stay here."

Jesse kissed her, "I wish we could, Mama. I really do. Believe me, I'd rather stay here and live in Miz Essie's old place, work for James every summer and in the log woods every winter but I can't. I have to do this."

We got in the truck and sit Sabrina and Stephen between us. They liked sitting up like this and even waved to Hallie and Leroy as we left, causing me to cry and Hallie to cry so hard, Mr. Leroy had to hold her up so she wouldn't fall. Jesse stopped the truck, got out and ran to her. I watched him holding her for a while and when he got back in the truck he had tears in his eyes too.

We were both quiet as we drove towards my Mama and Papa's house. When we got there, Jesse stopped the truck in the driveway and said, "Stay here, 'Cella. I'll see if they're home and willing to talk with you."

"Ok." I nodded. I kept Sabrina and Stephen in the truck with me and watched Jesse go up to the house. He knocked on the door several times but no one answered. Papa's truck wasn't anywhere around so I figured he was at work. Jesse came back to the truck, "Ain't no one home, honey girl."

"We could go by the bait and tackle shop."

Jesse sighed, "I guess we could."

He started to get in and I asked, "Do we have a pencil and some paper? I could leave them a note."

"Yeah, there's a pencil and some paper in the glove box."

I opened the little box and took out a stubby pencil that barely had an eraser and one sheet of paper folded in half. I thought a minute and then wrote:

Dear Mama and Papa,

I am so sorry that I went to Witch Sue. If I could go back and not go I would. Jesse got drafted into the Army and we have to go live in Louisiana. Our new address will be Unit 503, Fort Compton, Vester, Louisiana. I will send you pictures of the babies. I still love you and want to be your daughter.

Love,

'Cella

I gave the note to Jesse and watched as he went and slid it under the door. I hoped they would see it and read it. I hoped they'd want to get in touch with me somehow.

We stopped by the bait and tackle shop but old man Stew who ran the place said Papa was out gathering more bait and he didn't know what time he'd be back. I wrote another note to Papa on a scrap of paper old man Stew gave me. I just told Papa we were moving and I was going to miss him and Mama. We left the note with old man Stew and headed on to Preacher Joe's store. Jesse and Preacher Joe talked forever it seemed before they loaded the cooler full of soft drinks into the back of the truck. Jesse put the bag of food up front by the diaper bag. I put my feet on the diaper bag to be comfortable.

At the last minute, Jesse decided to stop at Clyde's store to tell him goodbye. They talked for a while, then we went to tell Wanda, Betsy and Sharon goodbye too. Afterwards, we went to the Jansan farm to tell them goodbye. I hugged Lilly Jean and thanked her for being so nice to me and letting me read all those Patty Sue books. After we left there, we stopped off at the Duvalls to see all them. We talked with everyone, hugged them all except Preacher Carl, Libby and little Randy because they'd gone home to Harris the night of our going away party. We hugged Grandma Cal last of all and she said, "Cellar, I gotta take something back. I thought you and Jesse was headed for one of them revolving door marriages, but I do believe you two are gonna make it."

I smiled at her, feeling totally different by her now. "Thank you."

At last we got in the truck and Jesse said, "Well, honey girl, we're finally ready to start for Louisiana."

Chapter Forty-nine

We've been driving for a while now. The sun is bearing down and the trees have been flying past us as we go along. Not long after we crossed the South Carolina state line, Jesse pulled off onto the side of the road and said he was hungry. He got out of the truck to get us some Pepsi's from the cooler and said, "Honey girl, I got a bunch of road maps in the glove box. Look in there and find the South Carolina one. We're gonna be needing it."

I found it and laid it up on the dash. Jesse got back in the truck with the Pepsi's and I got us some nabs from the food bag. While we were eating, Jesse unfolded that map and started trying to look at it. Stephen thought that map was a great thing and wanted it for himself. He kept hitting it with his little hand and I had to pick him up and hold him so Jesse could read that map. Once Stephen was out of the way, Sabrina decided she would go for that map and I wound up having to hold her too. I was glad when Jesse finished looking at it so I could eat. After I ate, Jesse started driving again. Sabrina and Stephen were hungry too so I fed them each a jar of baby food that we'd packed in the diaper bag. It was hard feeding them in this moving truck but I did it. Then I cleaned them up the best I could and then nursed them, covering myself with a baby blanket to keep hid. I had to nurse them one at a time to keep hid. I nursed Stephen first just because he was closest to me. This made Sabrina jealous and she kept peaking under the blanket, fussing. Jesse glanced at me, "Ain't there anyway you can feed them both at once?"

"Not and keep myself covered. I don't want no one riding by looking at me."

"I don't think anyone is paying you any mind."

"I ain't taking no chances." I finished with Stephen and since he was asleep I laid him on the seat. Then I held Sabrina and nursed her.

She fell asleep too and I was just holding her, watching the trees go by when Jesse said, "'Cella, look at that map and tell me where we are."

I put Sabrina on the seat next to Stephen and hoped they wouldn't roll off. Then I got the map and unfolded it like I'd seen

Jesse do. I couldn't make any sense of it at all. Jesse looked at me, "Well..."

"Jesse, how can I tell where we are just by looking at all these squiggly lines on this big old piece of paper?"

"It's a map, 'Cella. Its job is to tell us where we are."

I stared at it. "Well, it ain't doing a good job at all cause I can't tell you anything just by looking at this map."

He shook his head. "Me and Daddy marked the route. You'll see it if you really look at it."

"Are you saying I ain't looking at this map?"

"No, I ain't saying that. Just look on there for the route we marked. Daddy marked it with a red pen."

I looked. I saw the red line, but still had no idea where we were. I looked out the window. Nothing but trees on each side of us and cars and trucks headed back towards North Carolina on the other side of the road. "Jesse, the only thing I can tell you is we're in this truck."

He sighed and pulled off the road, "Hand me the map."

"Are you mad at me?"

"No, just give me the map, please. I have to make sure I'm on the right road."

I handed it to him, "Here, maybe it will tell you more than it does me."

He shook his head and began to study the map. It must have taken him a long time to get that crazy map to tell him where we were because we just sit there and sit there while Jesse looked at that map. At last he said, "Ok, I got it now. We can go."

We started driving again. Jesse started telling me more about Johnny Harper. I listened, commenting every now and then. I thought about meeting all these people he kept talking about and hoped they'd like me. But more than anything, I hoped Mama and Papa would read the note and want me back.

We kept driving and driving. We stopped so me and Jesse could use the bathroom in the woods and I could change Sabrina and Stephen. I put their stinky diapers in a bucket in the back so we wouldn't have to keep them up front and we got back to driving.

We made several stops like this. I thought South Carolina would never end. It began to get late. I was getting a terrible headache when I saw a sign welcoming us to Georgia. "Oh good!" I said, feeling some relief. "We're finally in Georgia. How long will it take to get to your Aunt Tansy's?"

"We ain't gonna get there until tomorrow night," Jesse said, pulling the truck onto the side of the road.

"Tomorrow night?" I said in disbelief.

"Yeah, tomorrow night. Georgia is a big state. Let's have supper."

"Ok." I made us some peanut butter sandwiches and we had grape drinks and potato chips. Jesse looked at that map some more and I fed Sabrina and Stephen and changed them before we started driving again.

It got darker and Jesse had to turn the lights on. We kept driving and I said, "Are we gonna stop someplace for the night?"

"We'll try, honey girl. But you know how places are. We're getting ready to go into the town of Martinboro. Keep a look out for motels that don't say white only. If they got a sign out, ain't no need for us to stop."

We had to slow way down when we got in town. I started looking. We passed by two motels but each one of them said whites only. We kept driving. We passed a diner, grocery store and two shoe shops but no more motels in Martinboro. "They ain't got nothing," I said.

He nodded, "I see, honey girl. We'll keep looking. If we have to, we'll just sleep here in the truck."

"Jesse, we can't sleep in this truck."

"We might have to 'Cella."

I sighed. I was holding Stephen who was wide awake. "When you went to Texas where did you stay at night?"

"Didn't take me that long to get to Texas."

"Then how come it's taking so long to get to Louisiana? All the maps I've seen have Louisiana coming before Texas."

"It does, 'Cella. It just didn't take us that long to get to Texas."

"Jesse, I don't understand you. Quit playing with me."

"I ain't playing with you, honey girl. I'm serious. We were in Texas that night."

"How did you get to Texas that night Jesse? It ain't possible."

"It is if you fly."

"Fly? You mean like on an airplane?"

"That's exactly what I mean."

"You didn't get on an airplane. You got on a bus."

"I know I did. That bus took us to Fort Nelson in Jardin, South Carolina. We got on a plane there and flew to Texas."

"You were actually on a airplane? Up in the sky?'

"I sure was, honey girl."

We'd stopped at a red light. "You never told me that," I said.

"I know."

"You never told Hallie either. She sure wouldn't like you flying around up in the sky."

"I know that too. That's why I didn't tell. If she found out I'd been in an airplane she might have a heart attack and I wouldn't have a Mama left. It weren't no big deal really, 'Cella."

"No big deal. It has to be a big deal."

"Well it weren't for me. I didn't even get to look out the window because I was sitting in the middle. It just felt like we were going really fast and then you couldn't feel it moving at all. There was nothing to it. Look, honey girl, we've been so busy being with each other, all our special loving and getting ready to move to Louisiana, I just hadn't gotten around to telling you yet, but I was going to."

"Did you know you was gonna be in an airplane before you left?"

"No. I was just told when I had to report and that's what I did. I had no idea we'd be flying. I guess if I'd thought about it, I might have figured that we would, but I honestly didn't realize that's what we were gonna do until they told us." He laughed, "Some poor boy was so scared when they took us to get on that plane he took off running. They had to go after him. Carried him on that plane kicking and screaming. He hollered half the way to Texas. I was glad he wasn't near me. Still aggravated me out of my mind."

"Are you gonna tell Hallie?"

"Sometime. With me being in the Army there's a good chance I might be on another plane someday."

"Why would they put you on a plane just to fly around this crazy fort place we're gonna be living?"

"Honey girl, there's no telling how long we're gonna be here. A while at least because they gave us housing. But when the time is up, they might send us off someplace else. Our life isn't gonna be in one spot. It's just how it is in the Army. And if I have to go someplace where you and the children can't be with me, then I'm taking you back to Mama and Daddy."

"But Jesse, I've got to be with you! They can't do that to us."

"I hope they won't, but they can. Let's don't worry about that now, 'Cella. We're gonna be together at Fort Compton and that's all that matters right now."

"How long are we gonna be there? I don't want to only be with you a few months and then have to be gone from you again."

"It should be a couple of years at least. Hopefully longer and hopefully when we do move, we'll be together. Everything depends on what the Army wants to do with me."

We drove on. I was getting sleepier and sleepier. At last, Jesse pulled the truck off into a clearing on the road. "What are you doing?" I asked.

"I gotta get some sleep, 'Cella. We're fine. Lock your door."

"We're sleeping here?"

"Looks like we have to tonight, honey girl. Tomorrow night, hopefully we'll be at Aunt Tansy's."

I was still holding Stephen. He'd gone to sleep. I looked out into the darkness, "Are you sure this is safe?"

Jesse leaned carefully over Sabrina who was sprawled out on the seat between us. He kissed me slowly, "Don't worry about anything honey girl. I'm here to take care of you and our babies."

I put my hand on his shoulder. He kissed me again, then moved, turned the truck off and adjusted himself in the seat so he was lying partially down. I did my best to get comfortable. Finally I managed to lean my head against the door and stretch my legs out on top of the diaper bag and our food bag. I fell asleep only because I was so tired I couldn't hold my eyes open any longer.

Chapter Fifty

Sabrina woke us up early the next morning. Somehow she'd gotten off the seat and was on the floorboard. She wasn't crying, but her babbling as she hit the food bag woke us up. I was all cramped and could barely move to get her back on the seat. Jesse woke up too. "Little girl, what are you doing?" he asked, and picked her up, taking a pack of nabs from her little hand.

I stretched, "Maybe she's hungry."

"Probably is," Jesse said. "She's wet and stinky too."

"I'll get her changed." I moved Stephen who'd slept on top of me all night long. "He needs changing too."

Jesse nodded, "Let's get the babies changed; eat breakfast and head on."

We did just that. Me and Jesse ate honey buns and had orange drinks for our breakfast. All the ice had melted in Preacher Joe's cooler. Jesse started to dump it out but I told him no, please don't. I could use that water to wet wash cloths to clean Sabrina and Stephen with. He agreed and left the water in the cooler with the drinks we still had.

I fed the babies some baby food pears and we got to going again. My head hurt so I took some aspirin. Jesse looked at me, "You ok, honey girl?"

"Yeah. It's just all that cramped up sleeping ain't good."

"No, but it's the best we could do. We'll be at Aunt Tansy's tonight."

I nodded. "Do you think maybe she'll let me wash the babies' diapers when we get there?"

"You can ask her," Jesse said, looking at the road.

We stopped to get gas and the man owning the station was nice enough to let us use his restrooms. He and Jesse talked about driving and Jesse bought us some ham sandwiches and pears. "I need some real food," he said.

We got back in the car and started driving again. We ate the sandwiches and pears for our dinner as we drove. They tasted wonderful after having to live off nabs.

We drove on and on. Stephen was now beside me and I was holding Sabrina. I started braiding Sabrina's hair, putting little white bows on the end of each little pigtail. She put her little hand on the partially rolled down window. "Out."

"You want to go out?" I asked.

She nodded, "Bay out, Ma Ma out."

"I like that idea," I said. "Let's all get out of here."

Jesse sighed, "It won't be much longer. We should be at Aunt Tansy's in a few hours."

I finished Sabrina's hair. "How do you think she looks?"

Jesse turned to us, "Very pretty." He reached over and rubbed her little head, "My sweet little girl." Then he rubbed Stephen's head. Stephen was sitting between us playing with his little blue squeaky puppy. "Your sister looks good, Stephen," Jesse said. "Maybe Mama will see what she can do with your hair."

I put Sabrina on the seat and picked up Stephen. I started brushing his hair trying to make it lay down. Jesse looked over at us, "I think when we get on base; I'll take him up to the barber and get him a G.I. cut."

"You mean like they did you?"

"Yeah."

"Oh no you ain't either," I said, brushing Stephen's hair. "You ain't shaving my baby bald. You do and I'll snatch your hair out so it never grows back, Jesse."

He laughed, "You know what, 'Cella, you're violent."

"I ain't violent. I just ain't having nobody make my baby bald."

Jesse shook his head and put his hand on Stephen's head, "I won't make him bald honey girl, promise you. But you gotta admit he needs something done. He looks like a wild man."

I kissed Stephen, "He's my precious little wild man. And ain't nobody gonna mess him up."

We were quiet for a while and I started playing with Stephen's wild hair, "I could braid it like I do Sabrina's. He'd be cute."

"Marcella, you are not braiding my son's hair. No way. I ain't having it. " Jesse shook his head as he talked.

"Now who sounds violent?"

"I ain't violent, but I'm not having my son's hair braided. Sabrina is pretty like that but braids are for a little girl, not a little boy."

"I was only playing."

He reached over and patted my leg, "I know honey girl."

We drove on with Jesse telling me more about his Army training. I liked him talking with me like this even though I didn't understand a lot of what he was talking about. It started getting dark and I was happy when he said, "We're getting close to Sawville. Look for a road called Accent Lane. That's where she lives. In house number 755."

Soon, we were slowing way down again because we were in town. I was holding Sabrina again and Stephen had climbed on Jesse's lap. I told Sabrina to help me look for that Accent Lane even though I knew she didn't have a clue what I was talking about.

As it turned out, Jesse found his Aunt Tansy's house instead of me and Sabrina. We pulled up into the side driveway and stopped. It was a big, two-story house with a big front porch and brick columns. I stared at the house as we got out. "Are you sure this is the right place?"

Jesse nodded, "She told me Accent Lane, house number 755 and that's what this is." He was holding Stephen and closed the door behind him.

I followed him towards the house carrying Sabrina. I felt nervous and shaky. Soon a colored woman wearing a blue dress edged in lace like she was ready for church came out onto the porch. "JESSE!" she shouted, "Is it you?"

"Yes ma'am," he said walking closer to her as she came closer to us.

"It's been so long!" she exclaimed. "You're such a fine looking young man. Yes you are! My goodness, you're gonna be a good catch for someone!" Then she looked at me and put her hand to her mouth, "What am I saying? You've already been caught, haven't you?"

"Yes ma'am," Jesse nodded. "Aunt Tansy, this is my wife, 'Cella and our babies, Stephen and Sabrina."

"Well they're just as precious as precious can be. Come on inside, you must be give out. Paul is at work. He won't be home until later tonight. They've got a case going on and he has a lot of research to do. Grace is right inside. She's starting third grade this year. She's so smart. Makes me proud."

We followed her up the steps into the house. The floor was highly polished and slippery looking. She led the way into a big room with red velvet furniture. The couch reminded me of the one I sit on when I went to Witch Sue. On the couch sit a little girl in a white frilly dress. Aunt Tansy said, "Grace, darling, this is your cousin Jesse. You've never met him honey."

Grace smiled, "Hello," she spoke politely.

Jesse smiled back, "Hey there, Grace."

Aunt Tansy said, "Have a seat. I'm sure you're tired."

"Actually, it feels good to stand up," Jesse said.

"Well, at least put the babies down. I'm sure they'd like to move about some. Are they crawling yet?"

"They're scooting," I said.

She nodded, "Grace was walking by the time she was eight months. I guess with twins it's a little slower. So, Jesse, tell me all about Hallie and Sybil too. I hardly ever hear from them. I wrote to both of them when we got our phone but you're the first one from up there to call. I thought once I told them about our phone they'd be calling me, but no."

Jesse sat in an oversized armchair and put Stephen on the floor at his feet. "Well, Mama and Daddy don't have a phone and neither does Aunt Sybil. And it's a long distance phone call down here, so...."

Aunt Tansy nodded, "Yes it is a long way from Cedar Cove." She looked at me, "Don't you want to sit down? There's plenty of room."

I sit carefully into a very uncomfortable chair. The velvet felt just like Witch Sue's couch. I held Sabrina who clung to me, not sure of where we were. Stephen on the other hand was scooting across Aunt Tansy's floor, heading for her fancy fringed rug. I wanted Jesse to get him but didn't say anything because Jesse and his Aunt Tansy were talking about Hallie and Sybil.

After awhile, Aunt Tansy stood, "I've got to check on supper. I've got a roast in the oven. I thought you'd enjoy a good meal."

" We sure would," Jesse said, getting up and taking that fringe out of Stephen's hand.

"Oh, let that baby be, Jesse," Aunt Tansy said. "He's fine."

"I don't want him tearing your rug up," Jesse answered, putting Stephen up to his shoulder.

"He can't tear that rug up. It's the finest made. Imported all the way from China. I've got Oriental rugs all over the house. Only the highest quality you can buy. We've had them for years and no one's ever pulled the fringe out yet."

Jesse sit back down with Stephen, "Just the same, I'd rather not take any chances."

Chapter Fifty-one

Aunt Tansy's roast was delicious. I felt like it had been forever since I had good food. Jesse's Uncle Paul came home right as we were getting ready to eat. He sat right down and talked the entire time, not giving anyone else a chance to get a word in. He wanted to know all about the route we were taking and every time Jesse tried to tell him, he'd just interrupt, telling Jesse better roads to take. "You got maps with you?" Uncle Paul asked.

"Sure do," Jesse said.

"Let's take a look at them when we finish eating," Uncle Paul said. "I can show you a way that'll cut hours out of your trip. Leroy's got you going way out of your way."

We finished the meal and Grace played with the babies while I helped Tansy clean the kitchen. Shyly, I asked her about washing clothes, worried that I'd waited too late. "Oh, sure!" she exclaimed. "I've got a brand new gas powered clothes dryer so we can have everything washed and dried in no time. Go get everything you've got to wash, 'Cella. We'll take care of it."

While Jesse and his Uncle Paul studied the maps, I took a bath so I could get clean and change my clothes. It felt so good to lie back in the hot water. I washed my hair twice and scrubbed all over. Afterwards, I gave the babies a bath and then went downstairs to check on Jesse. He was still map looking with Uncle Paul. I looked at the map. They had so many routes marked I knew I'd never make any sense out of it now.

Aunt Tansy had put the babies diapers in to wash while I was taking my bath and washing the babies. She told me she was bleaching them to get them good and clean. I thanked her and softy told Jesse he needed to take a bath or shower so we could get his clothes in to wash. He just nodded absently at me while listening to his Uncle Paul who was showing him yet another way to get from here to Louisiana. I stood beside them and watched Paul marking more routes. It looked to me like we could take any road we wanted and wind up in Louisiana with the way Paul had marked the map up so much.

Jesse finally went to get clean, leaving Paul to mark up our maps some more. I went upstairs with him to the room where we'd be sleeping. We had our suitcases in there. As I helped him get some clothes I said, "You ain't gonna be able to make heads or tails outta that map once old Paul gets through with it."

"I know," Jesse said. "He's even drawing new roads in. I ain't saying nothing cause he thinks he's helping and I don't want to offend him."

"We follow all his ways and we're liable to end up in Mexico," I said.

Jesse laughed, "We just might."

Jesse went to take a shower and Aunt Tansy helped me get all our clothes cleaned. I was surprised at that gas powered dryer. The clothes came out hot and dry. "This is better than putting them on the line," I said.

"Sure saves time," she said. "And it's really nice when it rains."

"I wished I could have one," I said.

"Tell Jesse."

"They probably cost too much," I said.

Aunt Tansy didn't answer. She just started telling me about all the women's clubs she belonged too. Listening to her I knew why she had to buy this dryer. She wouldn't have time to put clothes on a line to dry. She had too many meetings to attend. I asked did she have any meetings tonight and she said, "I called and told them I couldn't come to anything tonight because I'm having some very special company." She smiled at me and I smiled back.

We got the clothes folded and packed again, all except for what we were going to wear riding tomorrow. Aunt Tansy suggested that we all sit down and play Monopoly. I was tired and wanted to go to sleep, but I watched her sit up the game on the dining room table. Grace was playing with the babies on the floor, having a great time with them and they were laughing at her. Aunt Tansy got everything just like she wanted and went into the kitchen to get Paul, "You've marked up their map enough, Paul, let's play Monopoly."

He put down his marker, "Monopoly! I get to be the car."

Before long we were all sitting around the Monopoly board. I had the iron and Jesse had the ship. I was so tired I didn't care who won or if I owned anything or not. Paul acted like it was real life and was so serious about it I couldn't see how he could have any real fun at it. I was glad in a way when Sabrina and Stephen grew so fussy Grace couldn't control them. "They're sleepy," I said, standing up from my chair. "I need to take them to bed and nurse them."

"You're nursing?" Aunt Tansy asked.

"Yes."

"I bottle fed Grace."

"Well, I've been nursing these two since they first came." I walked over and picked up Stephen who clung to my leg.

Grace stood and picked up Sabrina, "Can I carry her upstairs for you?"

I looked at her, not sure at all about letting her do this, but I said, "Just be careful."

"I will," she said. "I'm always careful."

"Ok," I said, looking back at the table. Jesse looked like he was sleeping in his chair. "Jesse, I'm going to bed."

He didn't reply.

"Jesse," I said louder, "I'm going to bed."

Still no answer. Paul shook him and Jesse sat up straight, "Huh?"

"Your wife is talking to you," Paul said.

Jesse looked at me and I repeated, "I'm going to bed."

He nodded sleepily and I left the room with Grace following me. We went upstairs and I had her put Sabrina on the bed. She did, saying how sweet Sabrina was. "I wished you and Jesse could stay forever," she said, kissing Sabrina who kissed her back.

"That would be nice," I said.

We heard Aunt Tansy calling for Grace. "I have to go to bed too," she said.

"Ok, goodnight Grace."

"Goodnight, 'Cella," she smiled and left the room.

Once she was gone, I put on my nightgown and dressed the babies for bed. Then I lay down with them letting them eat. It felt so good to be in a real bed. I hadn't been feeding them long when there was a slight knock at the door. "Yes," I called.

Jesse came in the room, "It's me, honey girl. I've got to give up Monopoly and get some sleep. I told Paul he can own the whole board."

Chapter Fifty-two

I slept hard all night long and so did Jesse and the babies. We didn't wake up until after nine o'clock the next morning. And me and Jesse might not have woke up then if it hadn't been for little Stephen trying to crawl over the top of Jesse. I heard Jesse saying, "Where do you think you're going, wild man?" and opened my eyes to see Stephen on top of Jesse. Sabrina was still sleeping next to me. I stared at the clock on the dresser, "Jesse, it's almost nine thirty."

He stretched, yawned and said, "I wonder if Aunt Tansy and Uncle Paul are up yet?"

"I don't know. Your Uncle should be going to work."

But later when we went downstairs, there sit Aunt Tansy, Uncle Paul and Grace all at the table. And the table was loaded with food. Aunt Tansy smiled, "Good to see you up. Did you sleep well? That's a new mattress on that bed. How'd it do for you?"

"It was good," Jesse said, sitting down and trying to smooth Stephen's hair.

I sit down holding Sabrina. Soon we were eating. And again the food was wonderful. Maybe it was because we'd eaten peanut butter, nabs, potato chips and cookies so much, but everything tasted fantastic. Uncle Paul and Jesse were talking about the Army. He was telling Jesse about when he was in the war. How he'd fought in the Pacific. I listened only halfway as they talked. At the same time they were talking, Aunt Tansy was asking me more about Hallie and Sybil. I was telling her about Sybil's tomatoes when I heard Uncle Paul, "Tell you what, Jesse—I know a man in Alabama who owns a boarding house. His name is Homer Adams. I grew up with him. Good God fearing man. His place is in a town called Dog Run. They don't have street names there—just numbers. It's on thirty-third street. You go there and tell him you're my nephew. His wife Sally may be the one you talk to, but you tell her Paul Fisher is your Uncle and I'm sure he'll let you stay for free."

"Are you sure?" Jesse asked.

Uncle Paul nodded, "Yep. He'll do that for you. He's a good man, like I said. Now if you needed a place for more than a night, he'd probably charge you, but I'm sure you won't be staying for more than one night."

"We'll only stay one night," Jesse said. "We need to get on. I'd like to get on base before I absolutely have to be there."

After we ate, Uncle Paul took Jesse to get some fresh ice for our cooler and I braided my hair while Grace watched and played with Sabrina and Stephen. Aunt Tansy came and sat on the bed. We had the suitcase open and she saw the camera inside. She picked it up, "Nice camera."

"Thank you. Hallie and Leroy gave it to us so we can take pictures and mail them back to them."

"We should take pictures before you leave, 'Cella. Make some of Grace and the babies."

When Jesse came back, we did just that. Then we got everything packed back into the truck and hugged them goodbye. As Aunt Tansy hugged Jesse she said, "Send Hallie some of those pictures and tell her don't be such a stranger. Please."

Jesse hugged her again, "I sure will. Thanks for letting us stay."

Uncle Paul spoke up, "Jesse, you just consider this your place to stop and stay any time. They give you leave and you want to go home—just stop by here. There will always be a place for you."

Grace had to hug and kiss the babies again and again. She wanted to give them something and even though I told her she didn't have to, she took off running into the house. She soon came back with a doll and a teddy bear. "Here," she said, handing me a little colored doll wearing a red dress and a little bear in blue overalls. "This is Karie and the bear is named Sunny. I want Sabrina and Stephen to have them."

I hugged her, "Thank you, Grace. That is very sweet of you."

We got in the truck and waved goodbye. "They're nice," I said to Jesse.

"They are. And that's good because we're gonna need a good place to stay whenever I do get leave and can go home. I'm gonna have to tell Mama how good Aunt Tansy was to us."

Soon we were settled back into the routine of driving and eating out of our food bag. We talked with each other, talked to the babies and kept going. I'm not sure what route Jesse followed but whenever he wanted to look at the map; he pulled onto the side of the road and looked at it himself. We made stops for gas and for going to the bathroom whether it was at a station that would allow us or in the woods. It was after dark when we finally reached the town of Dog Run. It took us a while but at last we found thirty-third street. It just looked like an old house. Jesse stopped the truck out front and I said, "You go in and see if it's really alright for us to be here."

"Alright," he said, sounding like he weren't too sure himself.

I waited in the truck for him. Sabrina and Stephen were both sound asleep. I waited and waited, getting worried about him. At last he came, "It's ok, 'Cella. He does know Uncle Paul. And they're gonna let us stay for free. But I gotta tell you, this place ain't nowhere near as nice as Aunt Tansy's."

He got Sabrina off my lap and I carried Stephen inside. We walked into a room crowded with furniture and filled with smoke. I could barely breathe. Jesse led the way upstairs and opened a door on the right. There was a bed, dresser and lamp. The floor was bare and I watched a bug run across it. "Look," I said.

He did, "We're only gonna be here one night, honey girl." He lay Sabrina on the bed, "I'm gonna get our suitcases. I'll be right back."

I lay on the bed and waited for him. There were spider webs near the ceiling and the window sill was dust caked. I saw more bugs and decided that our old Miz Essie house was better than this.

Jesse came back and locked the door behind him. We went to sleep but I didn't sleep good. All night long I kept getting woke up by people talking and going up and down the hall. And I was constantly thinking bugs were running across me. I was glad when morning came.

When we went downstairs, the smoke was still thick. Some woman invited us to breakfast but Jesse said no, we needed to get on the road. We got in the truck and ate more nabs and cookies for breakfast with some Pepsi to drink. "I hope you didn't mind me saying no," Jesse said after awhile, grabbing another cookie from the box.

"I didn't mind," I said. "I really didn't like that place. I guess it was better than sleeping cramped up in this truck but it wasn't that good."

"I agree, but we're probably gonna wind up sleeping in the truck again tonight. Then tomorrow night, hopefully, we'll be home."

"Jesse, we left home."

"I'm talking about Fort Compton, honey girl. It's our new home."

Chapter Fifty-three

Jesse was right about us having to sleep in the truck that night. We tried to find a place to stay but we couldn't. Then to make things worse after we'd stopped and gone to sleep, a policeman came and told us we couldn't sleep on the side of the road in his town. Jesse apologized, saying we were on our way to Fort Compton and were tired. The policeman shone his flashlight into the truck, waking up Sabrina and Stephen, causing them to cry. "I'm sorry you're tired," he said, sounding disgusted at their crying, "but you gotta find someplace else to sleep."

Jesse told him we would, rolled the window up and started driving again. I cried too as I did my best to hush and comfort my babies. "He was awful," I finally said, letting Sabrina and Stephen nurse at the same time.

Jesse was quiet. "We gotta find someplace, 'Cella. I'm so tired."

"I wished your Uncle Paul knew someone in Mississippi with a boarding house. I'd be glad to have that stinky room now."

"I know what you mean," Jesse said.

We finally found a place by driving down a dirt road and then off into a little clearing in the woods. Jesse turned off the truck, "Hopefully no one will run us off from here," he said.

Then he leaned back and pulled Stephen, who was still crying, on top of him, "Come here, little wild man," Jesse said softly, "you can sleep with me." And with Jesse holding him, Stephen went to sleep.

We woke up early the next morning. Jesse wanted us just to use the bathroom, get the babies changed and go. He only took time to look at the map a little before we started to drive. As I made us peanut butter sandwiches and Jesse opened two grape drinks for us, I said, "I am so sick of peanut butter."

"I am too. There's a store on the base. It stays open until nine at night. Hopefully we'll get there before it closes tonight and we can buy some food."

"We've got the food Vicky gave us—what we brought from home."

"I was thinking about getting some bacon, sausage, eggs. We've got grits. But I'd love a good meal of meal of grits, bacon, eggs and biscuits. I'd like some pork chops, rice, butterbeans..."

I stared at my peanut butter sandwich, "Please don't talk about real food, Jesse."

He reached over and put his hand on mine, "We're gonna get us some real food as soon as we can, 'Cella."

We drove for the rest of the day. Sabrina and Stephen were both fussy constantly and I was so sick of being in this truck I didn't know what to do. I was beginning to think Louisiana didn't even exist when we passed a sign welcoming us there. "Oh good!" I said, pulling Sabrina back onto the seat.

"We've got an hour or so more, honey girl. Then we'll be at our own house. We'll have to get everything unloaded, but we'll be there."

"I don't care if we have to sleep on the floor. I just want out of this truck."

We stopped for gas. Jesse took care of the babies for me while I went to the restroom. When I came back, he had his Army uniform on his lap. "What you doing with that?" I asked, getting back into the truck.

"Got to put it on before we get to the base. I have to be wearing it when we get there."

I waited with the babies while Jesse went to the restroom to change clothes. It didn't take him long and soon we were driving again. It grew darker. I was sleepy and wanted to stay awake but I just had to close my eyes. Sabrina was on top of me and Stephen leaning right against me. I held them both as I drifted off to sleep.

Bright lights shining into the truck woke me up. I jumped thinking there was another policeman telling us we had to move. Then I saw Jesse talking to a man in uniform who was standing right outside the truck. I realized we must finally be at Fort Compton. I listened as the man said, "Alright, Private Jenkins, you may enter."

"Yes sir," Jesse said and saluted the man.

He handed a small card to Jesse, then looked over at me and the babies, "Welcome to Fort Compton, ma'am."

"Thank you," I said, rubbing Sabrina's back.

He stepped back and we drove slowly onto the base. I looked at the buildings wondering where our house was. There were lights everywhere and I wondered how anyone got any sleep. We turned down a few roads and came to a street with little houses on it. We passed that street, then two more before we finally stopped in front of a little white house. There was a small front porch and a set of steps on the side. I looked at the numbers on the front door. 503. Jesse leaned over and kissed me, "Well, this is it, honey girl. Home."

"It looks pretty from the outside," I said.

"It's nice inside too. Come on, I'll show you."

We got out, me with Sabrina and Jesse with Stephen. He put Stephen to his shoulder so he could unlock the house and I followed Jesse inside.

He turned on the light and I looked around our living room. There was a hardwood floor with a round gold colored rug in the middle of the room. A covered light shone from the ceiling. There were also two lamps on the wall. "You can turn those on by themselves," Jesse said.

"Ok," I answered.

"The hallway's over here," he said, opening a door and turning on another light. On one side was a small bedroom next to a small bathroom. I looked at the tub, sink and toilet and said, "Thank goodness we don't have to go to an outhouse anymore."

Jesse laughed, "And over here is our room, honey girl." He opened the door on the other side of the hall. This room was bigger. I saw the closet, "Did the other room have a closet too?"

"Yes and there's a closet in the living room too."

"I didn't see it."

"Come on, I'll show it to you."

I followed him, still carrying Sabrina. The closet was right by the door. "I just didn't notice it when we first came in," I said.

"It's ok, honey girl. Let me show you the kitchen." We went through a door not far from the closet. The kitchen floor was gold specked linoleum. There was a round gold speckled red table with silver metal legs and four chairs padded in matching red and gold speckled slick shiny material. I rubbed the chairs, "They feel like plastic."

"It's vinyl. Bull says they clean up real easy," Jesse said, moving Stephen a little.

I looked around the room some more. There was a double sink with a window over it. The window was covered with red and white checked curtains. We had a stove and a real refrigerator, not an ice box. There was a side door with a window that had red and white curtains hanging on it too. "Where's that door lead?"

"That goes out to our little side steps."

"Oh." I paused, adjusting Sabrina who was getting heavier by the second. "Jesse, we need to find someplace to lay these babies down."

"Yeah, I....

Right then we heard a knock at the front door. I followed Jesse back to the living room. He opened it and grinned, "Bull! Hey!"

"Good to see you back, Jesse!" A very tall man stepped into the house. He was followed by a thin tall woman. He kept talking, "We were listening to the radio and Sandra told me she thought she heard something. I looked out the window and saw that truck in front of your house here. Figured you might need some help moving everything in."

"It sure would help," Jesse said. He turned to me, "Bull, this is my wife, 'Cella."

He nodded, "Pleased to meet you, Mrs. Jenkins."

""Cella," I said.

"Ok, 'Cella it is. And this is my wife Sandra. We left our girls, Candace and Harmony at the house."

Sandra nodded, "And they'd better still be in bed. 'Cella, you look give out. Why don't you bring those babies over to my house and rest while these men get your house livable."

I looked at Jesse and he said, "That sounds like a great idea."

Sandra smiled, "I can take this little one," she moved to Jesse and he gave her Stephen who stayed sound asleep.

I followed Sandra to the house right next to ours. We went inside and I saw that she had the exact same lay out, same gold rug on the floor, same lamps on the wall. But she had furniture. A brown plaid couch, two brown chairs, and a little short table in the middle of it all with a radio on it. She led me down a hallway just like mine and Jesse's and we went into a room just like the one we had in our house. Only in here was a bed with a white chenille spread and matching maple dresser and chest. "Do you think your babies will roll off the bed?"

"When I put them on the bed like this, I like to put something around them like pillows."

"Ok, we can do that." She lay Stephen down and I put Sabrina beside him. Sandra left the room and I stood there waiting. She came back with four small pillows. We put them around the babies and she said, "Would you like some coconut pie and a glass of milk?"

"That sounds good," I said.

"I made a coconut pie fresh today."

We went to the kitchen and it was just like mine except in this one everything was blue. "Have a seat," Sandra pointed at the table.

I pulled the chair out and sit down, "These houses are alike."

"Yes they are. It's the only way the Army knows how to be. I'm surprised we all have different colored kitchens." She opened the refrigerator and took out a pie that had some slices missing and a bottle of milk. I watched her get plates and two glasses from the cabinet and felt like I was in a dream. She sat the pie in front of me and poured some milk into a glass. Then she fixed herself some and sat at the table with me. She asked me how long we'd been traveling and I said, "Forever."

She laughed, "No, seriously."

I had to stop and think, "Ever since Tuesday."

"And it's Saturday now. That's five days. That would seem like forever to me too. Where did y'all come from?"

"Cedar Cove, North Carolina."

"That is far away. We come from Hannah, Mississippi."

"I have an Aunt named Hannah. She sleeps with lemons on her toes."

"What?"

I nodded, eating some pie. "She says it keeps corns away. This is good pie."

"Thank you. I've never heard of anyone doing that."

"Aunt Hannah is a little strange," I said. "How long does it take y'all to get back to where you come from?"

"About six hours."

"I wished we were that close."

We talked and talked. We finished the pie and I helped her clean the plates and glasses. Then we went to the living room where we sit down and talked some more. I liked Sandra but I wanted Jesse to hurry up and come get me.

At last the door opened and Bull, the giant man came in with Jesse behind him. "We got it all in the house for you," Bull said.

Jesse stepped up in front of him, "Yeah, we even got the crib sit up too, honey girl. Got blankets in it and everything. It's all ready for them."

"Did you put it in their little room or our room?" I asked.

Jesse grinned, "Don't worry honey girl. It's in our room. I knew you'd want them close by. I put the playpen in their room. Now lets' get the babies and go home."

Chapter Fifty-four

The first thing I noticed the next morning when I opened my eyes was the gold colored curtains hanging at the window. The sun was shining but I had no idea what time it was. There was no clock in the room and Jesse had his arm tucked under his head so I couldn't look at his watch without waking him up. I didn't want to disturb him; I knew he was completely give out from all the driving. I got up and as I was walking to the door, I watched little Sabrina actually pull herself up; holding onto the crib rail. She stood there smiling at me, "Ma Ma."

"OHH Breeny! Look at you!" I whispered loudly, going to her. "Such a big girl!" I picked her up and kissed her. She was soaked. I carried her to the other bedroom, got a clean diaper for her and changed her on the floor. She babbled away and I talked to her like I always did. I picked her up, picked up the wet diaper and carried it to the bathroom. Last night after we came back here, I'd found a pull out hamper in the bathroom. I threw the diaper in and let the hamper close.

We went to the living room where I sit in Gran's old rocker and nursed her. It was peaceful in the room with the curtains on the windows closed filtering out the sunlight.

Sabrina finished nursing. I carried her to the kitchen and sit her in one of the high chairs Andy and Abigail gave us. I was so glad Bull came over last night to help Jesse get everything ready. I looked in the cabinet and got out our last box of cookies. I gave Sabrina one and began to look around the kitchen more carefully. Jesse had put our dishes and food in the cabinets. I turned the water on and off at the sink and looked the stove over good. There was a separate light over the stove and an exhaust fan too. There was a door on the other side of the refrigerator that I hadn't noticed last night. Curious, I opened it to find a small laundry room. There was a washing machine, a shelf with an iron on it and an ironing board that folded out from the wall. There was also a large counter that could be used to put stuff on. "Wow, this is nice," I said out loud to no one.

I went back into the kitchen and noticed our clock that Jesse bought from Preacher Joe's store hanging near the side door. I wasn't sure I wanted it there. According to that clock it was already after ten. "We really slept late this morning, Breeny," I said. "And your Daddy and brother are still sleeping."

I opened the refrigerator to look at it better. I was expecting it to be completely empty but there were two bottles of milk, a box with the word margarine written on it, eggs in the egg compartment and a bottle of orange juice. Confused, I opened the freezer area and saw several packages wrapped in white paper. I took them out one by one, reading the labels: ground beef, chicken, pork chops, ham, hotdogs and sausage. I put them all back and closed the freezer compartment door. I noticed a white package in the refrigerator part and took it out to look at it. Bacon. I was holding it when Jesse came into the room, "Morning, honey girl." He came to me and kissed me. "How do you like our new house?"

"I like it. It grows food for you." I put the bacon back into the refrigerator and closed the door.

He laughed, "It wasn't quite nine o'clock last night when you went over to Bull's house. I gave him some money and told him what I thought we needed. While he was doing that, I moved in a lot of things on my own. Then Bull came back with the food and helped me with everything else. I wanted to go ahead and get us some food because nothing's open today with it being Sunday and tomorrow is Labor Day and the store here on base won't be open. Bull said the stores in town will be open but I wanted us to have some food today."

"I'm glad you did. What would you like for breakfast?"

He smiled, "Everything." He pulled me to him, "I love you, 'Cella," he said. "I know neither of us wanted to leave Cedar Cove but I think this move is going to be good for us. We have a much better house and so far I don't really mind what the Army is having me do."

"You ain't been in it that long, Jesse," I said.

"No, but so far it's not as bad as I thought it would be." He kissed me again.

I got Stephen up because I didn't want him sleeping all day. Then I cooked some bacon, eggs, grits and made biscuits. Jesse got a coffee pot and some coffee from the cabinet and made himself some coffee. I watched him getting it ready and said,

"This place grows appliances too. We didn't bring an iron or coffee pot with us and here they are."

He grinned, "They come with the house, honey girl. We've got a little tool shed attached to the back and in it is a rake, shovel and a push lawn mower. I'll have to keep the blades sharp but it works pretty good. I tried it out when I was here for that special training. And everyone has a picnic table in the back yard. All that stuff comes with the house and stays with the house. When we leave, someone will come inspect it and it all better be here or we have to pay for it"

"What if something breaks or something? When you were in Texas for your training Hallie had to get a new iron because hers stopped heating up."

"If that happens, I just go turn it in and we'll be issued a new one. No problem. We just can't take it with us when we leave."

After we ate, Jesse took Sabrina and Stephen into their room to let them scoot around on the floor in there and get used to our new house and I washed our dishes in the new sink. It was so nice being able to just drain the water out by pulling a plug instead of having to get Jesse to dump the sink. I thought about all that and decided that if we ever did move back to Miz Essie's old house we really needed to make some changes in it.

I was cleaning the sinks out when Jesse came to stand in the kitchen doorway, "I think I'm gonna go buy a newspaper. See what's going on in the world."

"Where can we buy a newspaper?"

"There's a rack of them outside the store. You put your money in and it lets you open the rack. I got newspapers from there when I was here earlier." He came into the kitchen and kissed me quickly, "Stephen and Sabrina are scooting in their room with their toys. I'll be back soon, honey girl."

He turned to go and I said, "Wait, Jesse. Could we all go? We could put the babies in that fancy double stroller."

"We could. That sounds like a great idea. That way I can kinda show you around."

Jesse got that double stroller from the living room closet and we took it outside to sit it up. We got Sabrina and Stephen from their room and put them in the stroller. They weren't sure what to think of it at first but when we started pushing them along, they liked it. I could tell by the way they were laughing and babbling happily.

I walked beside Jesse as he pushed the stroller. He pointed out the streets to me. Our street was the fifth one. He said that was why all the house numbers on our street started with 5. He showed me different buildings and I listened as he talked. I thought the whole place was huge and I did my best to pay attention to what he was saying.

We got to that store and sure enough there was a stack of newspapers on a rack. Attached to the rack was a little box with a slot in the top. Jesse put a nickel in that slot and took one of the papers. "They just keep these papers out here like this?" I asked.

"Yes."

"What's to keep someone from just coming up here and taking all of them?"

"They know how many they put out and when they count the money it better all add up or we're all in trouble." He put the newspaper in the little basket behind Sabrina and said, "You know what honey girl, me and you need to celebrate our anniversary."

"You missed our anniversary," I said softly.

"Yeah, I wished I didn't. But it couldn't be helped. Anyhow I was just thinking, there's a drive in theater in town. Bull was telling me they let coloreds in. You sit in your car or truck and watch the movie. We'll have to bring our own food, but it would be fun."

"You mean we'd really get to see a movie?"

He smiled, "Sure."

"What about the babies?"

We started walking back towards our house, "Well, we could take them with us....Or, we could see if they could stay with Bull and Sandra while we celebrated."

"Ok," I said. "I'll think on it." I was quiet for a while as we walked. "When could we do this?"

"Maybe next weekend. I'm sure I'm gonna be on duty for a while come Tuesday."

"But we could go to the movie at night."

Jesse stopped walking, "Honey girl, I'm not gonna be able to be home every night. Some yes, but there's gonna be a lot of times when I have to sleep in the barracks...."

"JESSE JENKINS! I THOUGHT WE WERE GOING TO BE

TOGETHER!"

"Marcella, please don't make a scene. You could get me in trouble. It's just how it is. I'll be home a lot, sure, and if anything goes wrong at the house, someone will be able to get me for you. We do rotating duty. I will have days off and on those days I will be home with you and the children. I promise you that."

I felt like crying. I didn't like this at all. He hadn't told me any of this. I was so mad I had trouble seeing straight. I wanted to hit him. I wanted to run off from him, but here I was in the middle of this Army base and I was scared if I got him in trouble they'd make us leave. Instead I did cry and walked along beside Jesse in complete silence. We got home and I went in the house first. I went to our room and threw myself on the bed. I lay there crying, feeling betrayed. Jesse finally came in the room and laid down beside me. He held me, "I'm sorry, 'Cella. I should have told you how it was going to work. Please forgive me."

"I want you with me at night. I don't want to be alone."

He kissed me, "I want to be here too. I do. But you gotta admit this is better than me being down here and you still in Cedar Cove. We wouldn't get any time at all together that way."

Chapter Fifty-five

On Monday morning, right after breakfast I washed all our dirty clothes in the new washing machine and hung them on the line outside to dry. Then me and Jesse wrote a long letter to Leroy and Hallie, telling them we were here safe, all about our trip, Aunt Tansy and Uncle Paul and our new house. We ended the letter by promising to send lots of pictures as soon as we got the film developed, signed our names and Jesse even let Sabrina and Stephen mark on the bottom of the paper then signed their names by the marks they made. We took the letter up to the base post office, dropped it in the outside mailbox and when we were going back to our house, Johnny Harper and his wife Trisha passed us on their way to their house. They were driving an old blue car with a trailer attached and the trailer was loaded down with furniture. We finished walking home and as soon as Jesse helped me get the babies inside, he went to help them move in. While Jesse was gone, I looked out the window and saw another car go by—it was gray and the back was rusted.

Later when Jesse came home, he said that Sandra was having a party to welcome all of us here. They were serving hotdogs cooked on their outside grill, potato salad, coleslaw, coconut pie and chocolate cake. He said he thought we should go and I said yes, thinking I really didn't know these people, but Jesse wanted me to get to know them so I wouldn't be so lonely when he was on duty.

When we walked over to Bull and Sandra's back yard, their little girls—Candace and Harmony ran to us. Candace looked like she was around nine and Harmony seven. "We can take care of the babies for you," Candace said. At first, both Sabrina and Stephen clung to me and Jesse but after a while they let Candace and Harmony take them. I met Johnny and Trisha and their five year old son Scott. Richard Tucker, his wife Carman and their three year old son Ricky came in last. Carman was short and big. She came in acting like she owned the place, telling Sandra she should have laid the food out different and asking me and Trisha what we thought of Fort Compton, then never listening to our answers at all. She talked on and on, so much so that I stopped listening to her. We ate supper in the back yard and me and

Jesse held our children on our laps. After dinner, me, Trisha and Carman helped Sandra clean the dishes while the men talked in the living room and the children—Sabrina and Stephen included all played in Candace and Harmony's room.

When we got the dishes all cleaned and put away we went in the living room. Richard and Carman were on the couch, Bull was in one of the brown chairs and Jesse was in the other chair. Jesse motioned for me to come to him and I sat on his lap while Sandra sat on the couch.

They were talking about space people. Jesse was telling them about the lights he'd seen in Cedar Cove and Richard said, "I ain't never seen nothing myself but my big brother Harry was in the Air Force and he was stationed in France. He says one night he was flying and there was all kinda lights all around him that weren't supposed to be there. That was one reason I just waited for the Army to draft me. Don't want to be flying around with no outer space creatures. Ain't no telling what their true intentions are."

I leaned back against Jesse, listening to all the space talk, wondering about the babies and thinking about him leaving in the morning. The men kept talking about flying saucers, creatures from space and strange lights in the sky. I jumped up when I heard Sabrina cry and ran to the bedroom. Jesse followed me. When we got there, Harmony was holding her, "She was standing at the window and she fell."

I took her from Harmony, "It's ok, little Breeny girl," I kissed her.

Jesse rubbed her little head, "I bet you're sleepy too, little girl."

"She probably is," I agreed. "We need to go home."

He nodded, and walked into the room to get Stephen who was playing peak-a-boo with Ricky; Stephen was laughing his head off and fussed when Jesse picked him up. Jesse kissed him, "You'll have to play some other time, little wild man. It's bedtime for you."

We carried them into the living room, told everyone goodbye and went home. We gave the babies a bath, I nursed them both and we went to bed ourselves. I tried not to think about the fact that I'd be in this bed by myself tomorrow night. I tried to just hold onto Jesse and love him the best I could so that we'd both feel better. I could tell he was sad too, so I didn't say anything about him having to go.

I fell asleep and slept hard. I was dreaming that I was back home, helping Aunt Callie sort out buttons and pieces of lace when Jesse woke me up by jumping up and leaving the room in just his underwear. Confused, I got up and went after him. He was in the kitchen, "Jesse, are you ok?" I asked, squinting my eyes against the brightness of the kitchen light.

Jesse was looking at the clock. "I gotta get ready honey girl. I'm gonna leave you some money. I want you to go up to the store and buy an alarm clock. We need one."

"They sell clocks in that store?"

"They sell a little bit of everything in that store. I'll leave you enough money for that and some extra for food or whatever. Just be real careful with it." He came to me and held me tight. "I'm gonna miss you so much. Just knowing you're close by is what's gonna keep me going." He kissed me for a long time. "Fix me a big breakfast, honey girl. I'm gonna take a shower."

I looked at the clock, "It's only a quarter after five."

He kissed me again, "Yeah, but I've got to be there by seven. I don't plan on getting there just in time to fall in line. I'm gonna be there a little ahead of time." He walked out of the kitchen and I got to work. I got the coffee to going in the coffee pot like I'd seen him do, started the grits, cracked the eggs into a bowl and put some bacon into a pan to fry. I mixed up some dough for biscuits and was putting them into the oven when Jesse came back with just a towel around him. He sat down at the table briefly, then got up and left the room, making me wonder if he was alright. He soon came back, laid three keys, some money and a small white card on the table. "'Cella, honey girl, this is all yours."

I looked at the keys money and that card and said, "Ain't those your keys?"

'No, we've got two sets. Those are yours. Keep the house locked especially at night just to be safe."

I nodded, "How am I supposed to keep up with all that? I ain't got a pocketbook or a key chain and most of my dresses ain't got pockets."

He sighed, "Wear one with pockets today, go to the store and get you a pocketbook, little key chain and an alarm clock. This key here is to the front door, this one the side door and this one is to our box in the post office. If Mama or anyone writes us, they'll put the letter in our box—number 503—and we need this key to open it to get it out. When you go in the store, you're gonna need this card. It says that you're my wife and they'll let you shop there."

I turned the frying bacon, laid my fork on the stove and walked to the table. I picked that card up and read, "Private Jesse Leroy Jenkins; House: 503, Spouse: Marcella Jenkins, children Sabrina Jenkins, Stephen Jenkins.

"They got all of us on here."

He nodded, "That's how it is. I've got a card too. When you go in the store, there'll be a soldier checking. Just show him the card and you shouldn't have no problem."

I nodded then put it all in the top kitchen drawer. Jesse got up and poured himself a cup of coffee. I looked at him with that towel and said, "Is that what you plan on wearing to the Army?"

He laughed, "No. I just don't want to spill anything on my uniform." He sat back down at the table. I took up breakfast, got the biscuits from the oven and soon Jesse was eating. He asked did I want anything and I got a biscuit, some bacon and poured myself some orange juice. Softly I asked him if he had any idea when he could come home and he said, "I don't know.

"What if something happens? Something bad?"

"If you or the children get hurt—if it's an emergency, someone will get you for me. You can just go up to the store or post office and any soldier there will be able to start the process of getting the message to me. Now I know it's gonna be hard, but honey girl please don't send for me unless it's a real emergency. I don't think the Army wants you calling me if it's just something simple. Try to handle things on your own. Ok?"

I nodded, doing my best not to cry. Jesse noticed and told me to come to him. I did, sitting on his lap and crying hard at last. He held me close. "I'll be back home as soon as they let me. Promise you. Just be patient and remember I love you and Sabrina and Stephen." He kissed me for a while, then said softly, "Get up, honey girl, I have to get dressed."

I did; then I followed him to our bedroom and sit on the bed, watching while he put on his Army uniform. He sit on the bed to tie his boots, got his Army bag which he'd packed the day before and motioned for me to follow him. We went to the living room and I said, "I love you."

He pulled me to him, "I love you too. I'm so happy you're my wife. Take care of the babies, kiss them for me and know that I'll be thinking of you all the time." He kissed me some more.

"Are you gonna walk to where you have to go or drive the truck?"

"Walk. I'm leaving the truck here. It's ours, not the Army's." He kissed me again. "Remember everything I told you."

"I will." I followed him outside. It was barely light. He kissed me one more time, "My 'Cella," he whispered; then turned and walked to the road.

"I love you, Jesse!" I called after him.

He waved, "Love you too; honey girl and I will be home." He waved again.

I wanted to run to him, but instead I waved and watched him walk down the road until he turned at the corner. Then I went inside and cried just like I'd done when he left for Texas; only this time was worse because Hallie and Leroy were not there to comfort me at all.

Chapter Fifty-six

Jesse has been gone four days. Johnny went in the same day as Jesse and Bull and Richard left yesterday. Bull and Sandra's daughter's started school on the day Jesse left. Sandra drove them to their school because they would have to walk and she said there was no way her children were walking that distance.

I went up to the store the day Jesse left and bought myself a pocketbook that fit perfectly in the top basket on the stroller, a key ring for my keys, some apple juice for the babies, a wind up alarm clock and a new box of cookies because we were just about out.

I still haven't set that alarm clock. It's just sitting on the table by the bed. I look at it and think that it's going to be waking Jesse up when he does get to come home; telling him he has to go again.

Sandra has come by some; Trisha only once but talking Carman has come by every day---even before Richard had to go. She brings her son Ricky with her and talks and talks. Mostly she talks about the all the diets she's tried to help her lose weight. She's helping me fold clothes now and as she folds a towel she says, "I've got me a new diet started."

"Oh, what is this one?"

"I'm on the green bean diet."

"What is the green bean diet?"

"It's where you eat only green beans—for breakfast, lunch and supper."

"That's all you get to eat?" I asked.

She nodded, "Well I do get to have two small apples a day—for snacks but that's it."

I looked at Stephen who was smearing his cookie on his high chair tray. "Is it working?"

She laughed, "I'm scared to step on the scale to find out. I started it first thing Tuesday morning. Made Richard fix himself sandwiches. Yesterday I went over to Trisha's and she was cooking ribs. Girl, let me tell you the smell alone liked to have drove me crazy. I'm getting so sick of green beans I don't even want to open the can. But then I'm even sicker of seeing my rear getting bigger and bigger every time I look in the mirror so I'm hoping these green beans do the trick."

Ricky interrupted us, "Mrs. 'Cella, can I have another cookie?" Carman answered, "No, you cannot have another cookie. Keep eating like you do and I'm gonna have to put you on the green bean diet."

We kept working and after a while, I said, "I miss Jesse. Do you know how long it is before they usually let them come home?"

She picked up a kitchen rag to fold, "Well, I can't say for everyone but usually Richard works seven days has three days off, then works ten days and has five days off. But if they need him they'll come get him. They keep crazy schedules."

"I keep seeing that white man who lives back behind us on that street over there—he comes home every night. How come he gets to come home every night? I know he does because I've been out in the yard with the babies and I see him walk up to their side door."

"Oh, I know who you're talking about. He's a Lieutenant. When they get higher up in rank they get the privilege to come home every night."

"I wished Jesse could come home every night."

Carman folded one of Sabrina's playsuits, "Well when Richard is home he's as lazy as all get out. Man don't do nothing but sit. I keep telling him if he don't get up and move the buzzards are gonna start circling. But he still sits. Tells me he's tired. Too tired to cut the grass, too tired to figure out why that old car is making those funny sounds, too tired to walk to the store or post office—just tired all the time. I asked him how does he survive all he claims the Army makes him do and he says that's what makes him so tired."

Little Stephen started fussing to get out and I told him, "Hold on honey, I'll be finished in just a minute."

Ricky said, "I get him out."

"No, you might drop him," Carman said. "Besides, Ricky, me and you have to go soon. The mail should have arrived up at the post office now. I'm looking for a letter from Scarlett."

"Who's Scarlett?" I asked putting the kitchen rags in the drawer.

"My sister. She was up in Illinois visiting her husband's family when me and Richard were home. Mama told me she'd have her write. I want to go see if I have a letter from her."

"Oh," I said. I watched her and Ricky go out the side door. "Thanks for helping me with the clothes." I called after her.

She grinned, "You can come help me with mine tomorrow." She closed the door and was gone.

While I was cleaning Sabrina and Stephen with a wet rag, I wondered if there might be a letter for me at the post office. Maybe Mama and Papa had written me and didn't even know about it. I decided to go find out.

I got the stroller from the closet and took it outside. This stroller unfolded and then folded back so easy for Jesse but it was awful to me. On the day he left and I went up to the store to buy my pocketbook, I'd had to beat the latches into place with my shoe. And when I got home I couldn't get it to fold back up so I'd drug it into the house and let it sit in front of the closet door. Sandra saw it when she came over and she tried to fold it. She couldn't get it so she got Bull who hadn't gone to work in the Army yet and he folded it up for me.

Now I opened it and again had to beat the latches down with my shoe to get them to lock into place. I finally got it and went back inside to get Sabrina and Stephen. They were both crying and the only way I could stop them was to take them to my bed and let them nurse. They fell asleep in spite of me begging them not to. I left them laying on the bed and went to the living room. I could wait until tomorrow but the more I thought about it the more I wanted to go see if Mama and Papa had written to me. I know by now they'd read my note. I got Sabrina first, holding her careful so she wouldn't wake up. I put her in the first seat and laid the seat back so she'd be more comfortable, then I got Stephen and did the same thing with him.

I went back inside got my pocketbook, locked the door behind me and pushed my sleeping babies to the post office. When I opened the door to go inside, the white soldier working in there saw I was having trouble holding the door open and pushing that big stroller through so he came and held the door open for me. I thanked him and asked if I could just let them sit where they were while I checked my mailbox.

He nodded, "Sure. Let's just move them out from in front of the door a little."

He went back behind the counter and I walked down the little hall where the mailboxes were. I found number 503 and looked in the little glass window on the door. My heart pounded hard. There were two envelopes inside. I put the key in, turned the lock and took the envelopes out. The one on top was from Hallie and Leroy and when I moved it to look at the other one, my heart fell. It was addressed to Jesse and the return address was Bob Duvall, Rt. 5, Box 43 Cedar Cove, N.C. I closed the mailbox, turned the lock and went back to my babies. I put the letters and my keys in my pocketbook and started to leave. The soldier came and held the door open for me again. I thanked him and he said, "No problem, ma'am. See you when you come back."

I nodded and left. All the way home I thought about Mama and Papa. I wondered if they missed me at all.

When I got home, Sabrina and Stephen were still asleep. I unlocked the door, put my pocketbook in the arm chair which was closest to the door and went back outside. I carried the babies in one by one to the crib and when I got them settled, I went to fight with that stroller. I tried my best but I couldn't get it to fold. I looked for a button or something to push to make it unlatch but there was none that I could find. I tried prying the latches up but they refused to budge. Finally I drug it up the steps and into the living room. I pushed it next to the closet and let it stay there just like I'd done before.

I sit in Miz Essie's rocking chair feeling sad. I was lonely, bored and defeated by a double stroller. I read Hallie and Leroy's letter over and over again. Reading it made me miss them. I wished I had something else to read to get my mind off missing Jesse and now missing Hallie and Leroy too. I thought about the letter Bob sent Jesse but didn't think it be right to read it. I put his letter in the kitchen drawer and thought that I'd be happy to read about Patty Sue and her ignorant neighbors now. I looked at the stroller and made up my mind to go up to that store tomorrow and see if they had any books that I could buy. Maybe that would help me pass the time.

Thinking of Patty Sue reminded me of Lilly Jean so I decided to write a letter to her. I went to the kitchen, got the paper from the drawer and wound up writing a three page letter to her. I told her all about our trip, our new house, how the babies were doing, our new neighbors, Carman and her green bean diet—everything I could think of. I asked her how they were, how was school, if she'd seen Leroy and Hallie and I ended by asking if she'd read any new Patty Sue books lately. I signed it your friend 'Cella, folded it and put it in an envelope. I didn't know Lilly Jean's address so I just wrote Bob's on the envelope, knowing they'd give the letter to her. I put a stamp on it and put it in my pocketbook so I could take it to the post office tomorrow.

Chapter Fifty-seven

I went to the store the next day and bought two used paperback books. One was called The Mysterious Disappearing Woman and the other was Fall Away Quickly. I mailed Lilly Jean's letter and went home. Then I pushed the babies down to Carman's house. I helped her with her laundry and listened to her go on and on about her green bean diet. I didn't tell her but I couldn't see where that diet was doing any good. She told me she was putting sugar and fat back in those beans to make them taste better and I thought that was probably killing her diet but I didn't say a word.

The days went by. On Sunday I went to the little church on base with Trisha. She said they had a separate little chapel for the men to attend while they were on duty; and they could go here with their families on their time off. We were the only colored people in the church and it felt strange. Some of the people looked at us strange when we came in with me carrying Sabrina and her carrying Stephen. We sit in the back and her little boy Scott sat between us. After the service, the preacher introduced himself to us as Reverend Lance Murphy. Trisha asked him if he was in the Army. He smiled and said that everyone on this base was either in the Army, married to someone in the Army or born to someone in the Army. He said he looked forward to seeing us next Sunday and we left.

I spent Monday reading because it was raining and Carman didn't come over. I was reading Fall Away Quickly which was all about a girl named Iris living by herself in a log cabin. I was at the part where she was trapped in the house by howling wolves. It was very good and it helped me not think about missing Jesse and why Mama and Papa wouldn't write.

Wednesday came and Jesse still wasn't home. I started thinking he was probably on the ten days of work. I took the babies up to the post office to check our mail, and of course there was nothing. I was walking home thinking I'd never hear from Mama and Papa again when I looked up and saw Jesse walking from the restricted area. He was carrying his Army bag. I called to him and he came running to us. He dropped the bag; picked me up and kissed me hard. "Oh, honey girl, I've missed you so much!"

"I've missed you too." I said, holding onto him. Sabrina reached out from the stroller and grabbed his pants leg.

Jesse looked at her, "Did you miss me too, Breeny?"

"They both did. They kept looking around calling Da Da. I took pictures of them."

He hugged me. "Good. Now what are you doing?"

"I just came from the post office. I was seeing if Mama and Papa had wrote to me yet."

I saw the look of disapproval on his face. "Honey girl…have you got anything?"

"Not from them. But we got a letter from your Mama and Daddy and you got one from Bob."

"Bob?" Jesse asked and started pushing the stroller for me. "What's he got to say?"

I shrugged, "I don't know, I didn't read it. I read Hallie and Leroy's but not Bob's."

"How's Mama and Daddy?"

"They're ok. They want us to send them the pictures. Hallie said she called Tansy to thank her for being so nice to us."

We were home now. We got the babies and Jesse's Army bag inside. We went back out for the stroller. I told Jesse the trouble I was having with it and he said, "Watch me, honey girl. Just push this down here and it will unlatch." I watched him fold it so easy just like he always did. He smiled, "See, it's simple."

"For you it is."

He grinned and kissed me, "I'm glad I'm home."

"Me too. For how long?"

"Until Monday morning, honey girl." He kissed me again. Then we went inside; Jesse carrying that stroller.

Jesse put the stroller in the closet; picked me up; carried me to Gran's old rocker and we sit there kissing for a long time while the babies played on the floor. I asked him how the Army was and he said, "Nowhere near as good as you, honey girl." We got Sabrina and Stephen and held them too; all of us in the chair together. I was happy like this—my family all loving and nice. We stayed like that for a while; then Jesse said, "I wonder what Bob wanted."

"I'll get the letter for you," I said, moving Sabrina so I could get up.

I brought the letter from the kitchen and handed it to Jesse. We put the babies on the floor so he could read it without them grabbing the paper. I watched him reading and he shook his head. "Poor Bob. Poor dumb boy."

"Why you calling him dumb? What did he do?"

"He's gone and gotten himself engaged to that stuck up Nancy Smith. Poor Bob. He'd been better off in the Army."

Chapter Fifty-eight

It's now near the end of October and I'm a whole lot more used to being here. I've gotten more used to Jesse being gone while he's on duty and keeping everything going until he comes home. He's been working around eight or nine days and so far, he's always had four days here with us in between times. On his first time off, he did take Stephen to get his hair cut and I cried. I begged him please don't mess up my baby. He promised he wouldn't and when he brought him home, Stephen wasn't bald, but he looked more like a little boy than a baby which made me cry. Jesse just kissed me, held Stephen up in the air and said, "You had fun getting your hair cut, didn't you little wild man."

I told Jesse he couldn't call Stephen wild man anymore because he didn't look wild now. Jesse laughed and said Stephen would always be his little wild man.

We're settling into life here in Louisiana. Jesse took the truck to get Louisiana license plates on it and got his driver's license switched from North Carolina to Louisiana. We've been to town to visit the library because I like to read so much and we've been to two movies. Bull and Sandra kept the babies the first time so we could celebrate our wedding anniversary late and the next one we took them with us. I like going to the movies. It's fun. We carry Pepsi's, potato chips and cookies, park the truck next to one of those little sound machines then sit back and watch the movie.

We also went to town and bought a small coffee table to sit on our gold rug. We have our chairs around it and Johnny is talking about helping Jesse cover them with new material so they look new again. We bought a picture album for our pictures and we keep it on the coffee table.

When Jesse is gone, I visit with Carman, Trisha and Sandra. Carman has given up her green bean diet, has tried eating only cabbage and is now trying to lose weight by eating applesauce and cottage cheese. I'm just watching to see which one really works.

I still can't get that stroller to fold up right so I just leave it open until Jesse comes home. He keeps showing me how to fold it but it never works for me unless he's right there helping me. I've stopped letting it bother me and just drag it up and down the steps.

Sabrina and Stephen are both crawling and pulling up on everything. I have to watch them around that stroller because it will roll with them so I don't leave them on the floor in the living room by themselves. They are talking better and I like listening and talking with them. They are both so sweet that I can't even imagine not having them. Every day I thank God that Witch Sue didn't get rid of them. Me and Jesse both love them more than anything. When Jesse is gone they crawl around the house calling for him and when he comes home, they get all happy calling Da Da, holding up their little arms so he can pick them up. They kiss him and I can tell they are happy he's back with us.

Lilly Jean writes to me and I write back to her. I even sent her some pictures of the babies and she wrote me back to tell me how cute they are. We write to Hallie and Leroy, Aunt Tansy and Uncle Paul and Jesse writes to Bob and Todd. Both Jesse and Todd are worried about Bob marrying Nancy Smith. Todd wrote Jesse and told him that Bob didn't even ask Nancy to marry him—her Daddy bought the engagement ring and told Bob it was high time he showed his proper intentions to his daughter. Todd says Nancy is in complete control and poor Bob is just being drug around on an invisible leash. He says they all try to talk with Bob but Bob acts like he's walking around in a fog and won't listen to no one.

Keeping up with Hallie and Leroy, the Jansans and Duvalls, and Aunt Tansy and Uncle Paul has been easy. I still haven't heard anything at all from my Mama and Papa. I even wrote to them, sending them two pictures—one of the outside of our house and another one of Sabrina and Stephen sitting on the ground in the backyard. They are hugging each other and are so adorable in the picture I can't see how anyone could look at it and not want to pick them both up and love them too.

The other day I wrote a letter to my cousin Zenobia hoping maybe she'll write back. I'm thinking about writing to some more of my cousins to see if any of them will write back to me.

It's Monday, October 26. Jesse's asleep because he's been on guard duty at his barracks and he's so tired he can't keep his eyes open. Sabrina and Stephen are squealing back and forth to each other so loud I'm afraid they're gonna wake up Jesse so I drag the stroller down the steps and take them one by one to it. Then we walk to Carman's. When I get there, Carman is sitting on the front steps eating a big sandwich while Ricky pushes a truck around in the yard. She calls hi to me and although I want to ask her if she's on a sandwich only diet now, I don't. I just push the stroller up to her steps and say, "Jesse's home but he's in bed sleeping. I don't want the babies keeping him awake."

Carman nods and takes a big bite of her sandwich, "Yeah, Richard is in bed too. He always sleeps the first day he's home. Then he sits around and does nothing the rest of the time he's home. Come on, let's go in the back yard and let the children play."

Once we get back there, I take Sabrina and Stephen outta the stroller and let them crawl around on the grass. Then I sit at the picnic table with Carman. She takes a bite of her sandwich and says, "This sure is a good sandwich. Want one?"

"No, we had dinner already with Jesse."

She licks mayonnaise off her finger, "Oh, we had dinner too with Richard. Fried chicken and tater salad. I was still hungry so I made me this chicken salad and ham sandwich."

"Chicken salad and ham?" I remarked.

"Yep. I'm sick of diets, 'Cella. I'm just gonna have to be big. The way the good Lord made me." She took the last bite of her sandwich and said, "Would you like a cupcake? I made some chocolate cupcakes last night. My sister Scarlett sent me a recipe. Chocolate with cream inside and fudge icing."

"Sure, sounds good."

"Oh, they better than good. Make anyone give up a diet."

She left me watching the children and soon came back with a tray of cupcakes. I took one off the tray for me and divided one for Sabrina and Stephen. Carman helped me put them in the stroller so they could eat in there. They got cupcake all over themselves. The cream was in their hair, eyebrows and even their ears. The cupcake was good but so sweet it made me feel sick. I forced myself to eat it because I didn't want to hurt Carman. She'd already gone through three of them like they were air. I watched her eating and felt even sicker. I tried to clean Sabrina and Stephen with some napkins but only spread the cream and chocolate more. I gave up and decided the only way to get them clean was take them home and give them a bath. I talked with Carman just a little more; and pushed my messy babies home.

When I got there, Jesse was still asleep so I took the babies in one by one and dragged the now chocolate smeared stroller into the house. I took them to the bathroom, started the water in the tub, made sure it wasn't too hot and put them in.

They like being in the tub when the water is running. I wash their hair and little bodies while they're playing. I sing to them like I always do. I don't think I can sing as good as Hallie but my babies like it.

I turned the water off before it got too deep and that's when I heard, "Ain't nothing prettier in this world than little black babies in a white bathtub." Shane.

I jerked around and screamed when I saw him. He was my cousin, but he terrified me. My screaming scared the babies and they both started to cry.

"How did you get here?" I yelled, throwing the bar of soap at him.

He ducked out of the way before the soap could hit him. "I drove my car."

I grabbed one of the babies little rubber ducks from the water and threw that at him too, "How did you get inside my house!" I yelled.

The duck hit him on the arm even though he tried to get out of the way. "'Cella, this ain't no way to greet someone."

I threw the other duck, "Just tell me how you got inside my house!"

He picked up the ducks and soap from the floor, "Through the front door." He came closer and put the soap on the side of the tub and the ducks back in the water. The babies were still crying.

"Jesse is right!" I cried at him, scooting back on the floor, "You are rude and ain't got no manners. Why didn't you knock?"

Shane sighed, "I did knock. You probably didn't hear it because you were in here running water…."

And then I heard Jesse, "What are you doing here?"

Shane turned to look into the hallway, "Jesse! See the Army has at least got you some pants."

Jesse came to stand behind Shane and I could see that he was wearing jeans and no shirt. "How did you get on base?" he asked Shane.

"I just told the man out there at the main gate that I'm your cousin and what house number y'all are in and he told me have a good visit. No problem at all."

"You just came all the way here for a visit?" I asked, getting Stephen who was crawling out of the bathtub, wet, naked and crying. "Ain't you scared of me being witch cursed?"

Shane laughed, "I ain't scared of you. Never have been. But it sure looks like you're scared of me." He laughed some more and now Sabrina was crawling out to me too. Jesse made his way past Shane and came to help me with the babies. Shane watched us and said, "We're on our way to Galveston. Figured we'd stop by..."

Jesse was wrapping Sabrina up in a towel, "Galveston. What are you going to Galveston for?"

"Looking for work. I lost my job in Wilmington; then we lost our house. We had to move in with Daddy and Varlene in Cedar Cove. That ain't worked at all. I been doing odd jobs here and there, but it's not enough to make a living on and I know Margaret wants our own place again. I'm hoping to get me a job on one of them oil rigs or something."

We had both babies wrapped in towels. Jesse led the way past Shane and said, "Where are Margaret and the boys?"

"Right there in your living room. Moving my whole family to Texas. Starting over fresh. New State. New life."

"Tell Margaret we'll be there as soon as we get these two little ones of ours dressed," Jesse told Shane.

I followed Jesse to the bedroom carrying Stephen. We dressed the babies in more play clothes and I said, "He scared me to death."

Jesse was buttoning Sabrina's play dress, "I know, all the screaming woke me up."

"I'm sorry."

"It's ok honey girl. I don't mind."

We took the babies to the living room. Margaret was sitting in Miz Essie's rocker looking hot and tired. Shane was in the arm chair and the boys, Bill and Will were pushing the stroller back and forth.

"Y'all might get messy on that stroller," I said. "The babies smeared chocolate cupcake all over it."

Bill and Will brightened at the mention of cupcake, "Ohhh, can we have a cupcake?" they asked.

"I don't have any cupcakes. We had them down at my friend's house."

They ran to Shane, "Daddy let's go to her friend's house and get some cupcakes."

"We ain't doing no such thing. You boys behave."

Margaret stood, "'Cella, let me hold one of those precious babies. They are both just adorable."

I handed her Stephen and as she was going on about how cute him and Sabrina are, Shane said, "Oh, we were so tired and happy to get here I almost forgot....Bill, run out to the car and get 'Cella's clock."

I turned to him, "MY CLOCK! HOW DID YOU GET MY CLOCK?"

Bill was running out the door and Shane said, "Witch Sue died. I found her myself. I was walking along, and thought I saw something laying up near the side of her house. It was old Sue. She'd electrocuted herself. Wires going up to her house had so many bare spots. Evidently she grabbed hold of one and it fried her. I knew you thought she had your clock so I went inside the house and sure enough there it was in her back room. Just laying up on a table. She didn't even have it on the wall, it hadn't been wound or nothing. Weren't keeping time at all. Old crazy woman had all sorts of stuff in that room. Jewelry, silver candlesticks, trays, cups, little boxes—all kinds of mess. I got your clock and picked up a pile of magazines she had. Them magazines is where I read about all the work they got in Galveston..." He stopped because Bill was coming back in the house with our clock. Shane told Bill to give it to me and as I held it, I felt the room starting to spin. I looked at the clock and thought of Gran beating me, whacking me over and over again with her broom. I laid it on the coffee table and was starting to sit down when Shane said, "'Cella, now that old Sue is dead, your Mama and Papa want to have a relationship with you again. Your Gran and them believe that when Sue died, all of her spells died with her so now they think it's safe to love you again." He stood and reached into his pocket. He pulled out something and handed it to me.

It was Gran and Gramp's wedding cake topper that she'd put on mine and Jesse's wedding cake. I stared at it in my hand. Safe to love me. I wanted him to say that Gran was sorry she beat me, that Mama and Papa were sorry about shunning me and my babies. I wanted them to say they were wrong for all they'd done to me. Not that it was safe to love me because some old woman who fooled people into thinking she could do magic died. I was starting to say all that to Shane when the room started to spin faster and got darker. I saw the floor coming to me and as I hit it, it didn't hurt at all. Everything just turned pitch black and there was absolutely nothing.

Chapter Fifty-nine

I woke up in a sea of white. White walls, white sheets, white floor. Everything was white. "Hey, honey girl," I heard Jesse and turned my head. He was wearing a blue plaid shirt now and sitting on a chair close to the bed I was in, "Where am I?" I asked; my head hurting.

He kissed me gently, "The infirmary. You fainted, 'Cella."

I remembered then about Shane, the clock, Witch Sue dying. "Jesse, I don't want them to just think it's safe to love me. I want..."

He sighed, holding my hand, "I know what you want, honey girl. I want it too. But we might not ever get that. You remember how things were between me and my Daddy when we told them we thought you were having a baby."

"Yeah, he nearly killed you."

Jesse nodded, "I couldn't stand to be anywhere around him. We did nothing but argue. On Christmas Eve when you were in labor and he came in the log woods to get me the first thought in my head was 'what does he want?' Then later on when Sabrina was born and Mama brought her in the living room, he jumped up grinning like everything and took her right from Mama. He held her before I did. He's the one who handed her to me. Ever since that point in time, we started getting closer. He never apologized for choking me, but I know he's sorry."

"You're saying I should just forgive them and act like nothing ever happened."

"I'm saying it might be best. You've been missing them so much, 'Cella. You know that's true. And now, they're willing to have a relationship so I say let's don't start shunning them just because everything ain't exactly like we want it to be. Let that come as it will."

I looked around the room, "Who's taking care of the babies?"

"Shane and Margaret. I told them they could stay the night. I remember all too well how hard it is to find a place to sleep when you're traveling. I told them they gotta sleep on the floor and Shane said it would sure beat sleeping in the car. Margaret said they had plenty of blankets and pillows so it wouldn't be bad at all."

A white curtain that hung in around my bed pushed back and a nurse came in, "Oh, good, Mrs. Jenkins, you're awake. I'll tell Captain Whitman. He's the one who examined you." She disappeared back around the curtain.

I was starting to ask Jesse to please take me home when a tall colored man walked past that curtain. "Hello, I'm Captain Whitman. I have very good news for you, Mrs. Jenkins. First of all there is absolutely no need to worry over fainting like you did. It's common at this time. I'm going to put you on a good vitamin regimen and...."

"Whoa whoa whoa," Jesse said, "I don't mean to be disrespectful sir, but what do you mean it's common at this time? What time are you talking about?"

"Why the timc of pregnancy, of course. Private Jenkins, your wife is having a baby."

I sit up in bed, "A BABY! I ALREADY GOT TWO BABIES! I AIN"T NEVER EVEN HAD MY TIME OF THE MONTH SINCE THEY BEEN BORN! I CAN'T BE HAVING ANOTHER BABY!"

"Marcella!" Jesse scolded me, "Settle down. Don't make a scene."

"Her reaction is perfectly understandable, Private Jenkins. Now Mrs. Jenkins, may I ask are you currently nursing your babies or bottle feeding."

"I'm breast feeding them. They're twins born last Christmas Eve and Christmas day."

"I see. Well it's normal for a woman not to have her time of month as you put it when she's nursing but you can still get pregnant and believe me, you are."

"How far along is she?" Jesse asked, grinning.

"I estimate her due date to be around May 9th. In the meantime I've sit up a schedule of visits and Mrs. Jenkins, I want you to feel free to come here anytime you feel the need. If I'm not available, someone else will see you." He reached into the pocket of his white coat and took out a bottle, "Take one of these vitamin pills every morning." He gave me the bottle and took some papers from another pocket on his coat, "And read all this. It's a copy of your scheduled visits to me and useful information on pregnancy and giving birth." He handed the papers to me and said, "You can get dressed and go home as soon as you feel ready, Mrs. Jenkins.

I'll be seeing you in two weeks unless you feel the need to come see me sooner. Congratulations."

He left the room and I stared at the wall. Another baby. I turned to Jesse who was grinning so big it looked like his mouth would break. "I'm scared to have another baby," I said softly.

Jesse leaned close, "It won't be like it was with Sabrina and Stephen. You're gonna see the doctor like you're supposed to and give birth here at the infirmary or in the hospital. Not at home. It'll be a lot better, honey girl. Just wait and see.

I was quiet for a while then I said, "Jesse, if we have twins again, I'm gonna kill you."

He laughed hard and kissed me, "You ain't gonna kill me, honey girl. You love me. And you'll love this little baby just like you do Sabrina and Stephen."

"Yeah, I do love you, Jesse. And our babies. Just the same this had better be only one baby."

Jesse laughed and kissed me again. "Just think of it like this, honey girl, we've got a chance to start fresh with your family now. We can tell everyone about this new baby coming and they can all be excited, not mad at us. There won't be any Witch Sue or any other problems this time. Everyone can be happy now."

"Are you really sure about that?"

He grinned at me, "I'm sure about everyone being happy this time. And I'm sure that I love you and all our babies. Let's get you ready to go home so we can tell everyone about our new baby we've got on the way."

The End